THE HUSBAND WHO
REFUSED TO DIE

THE HUSBAND WHO REFUSED TO DIE

ANDREA DARBY

Matador
9 Priory Business Park,
Wistow Road, Kibworth Beauchamp,
Leicestershire. LE8 0RX
Tel: 0116 279 2299
Email: books@troubador.co.uk
Web: www.troubador.co.uk/matador
Twitter: @matadorbooks

ISBN 978 1785899 355

British Library Cataloguing in Publication Data.
A catalogue record for this book is available from the British Library.

Printed and bound by CPI Group (UK) Ltd, Croydon, CR0 4YY
Typeset in 11pt Baskerville by Troubador Publishing Ltd, Leicester, UK

Matador is an imprint of Troubador Publishing Ltd

In memory of Ann

CHAPTER 1

I'll never forget the day Dan told me he wanted to be frozen when he died …

It's a sticky August afternoon and we're unpacking shopping after being stuck in a lengthy road diversion en route from the supermarket.

'It's called cryonics,' he says, catching my eye as I tuck a pack of slightly warm organic chicken thighs into the top drawer of the freezer.

'I hope you have a better shelf life than these birds then. They only get an extra six months in here.' I assume he's pulling my leg – not just because of his comic timing and the fact he's dropped it out so casually; and in the kitchen. I can't believe such a thing really happens, except in those weird sci-fi movies.

'Seriously, bodies can be effectively preserved now – with the right chemicals.'

'You daft bugger. Anyway, you don't like preservatives.' I wait for his dimples to stretch, like they always do when Dan's trying not to smile. Nothing.

He frowns, turning to peer into one of the bags he's lined up neatly along our kitchen island. The dark hair at his neck looks almost black with sweat.

'Have you thought about being stuffed? You'd make

a great draught excluder for the french windows.' I grin. This will surely crack him.

'Come on, Carrie,' he snaps. 'Any chance of telling you something important without the jokes?' He stares and I stop smiling. 'I've been thinking about it for a while. Science has really moved on. I believe there's a good chance of being brought back to life after—'

'You're not ill, are you?' The thought makes me feel sick with dread.

'No – course not.' Dan rips the top off a bottle of a deep red smoothie, taking a huge swig that seems to last forever. 'Well, not that I know of.' I'm reassured by a grin. *Thank God.*

I watch Dan return to his task, unsure what to say next. He looks so strong – and fit in both senses of the word – emptying bags with needlessly urgent movements like it's one of his exercise sessions, triceps tightening as he throws tins into tall cupboards, a patch of moisture spreading on his fitted T-shirt. His physique could so easily belong to a man twenty years younger.

'You gonna join me, or just watch?' Dan smiles and the dimples deepen.

'I'd prefer to watch, but go on then.' I grab a carrier.

It seems he really is serious about this cryonics thing, I think, bundling fruit into the three-tier bowl. He's certainly stepped up his health campaign in recent months. First it was the superfoods, then the revolting concoctions of herbs and the raw regime that led to his fennel fetish. And there was the day I caught him necking a glass of wee behind the frosted shower screen in our en suite. 'It's full of nutrients,' he'd declared. Luckily, that fad was short-lived.

2

But this was something else. I really didn't want to think about my husband dying – or his body being messed with. I refuse to carry a donor card; I'm so squeamish about these things. Feeling uneasy, I grab the bread knife, hacking clumsily into the stiff plastic packaging of a punnet of nectarines.

'Do many people do this … this preservation thing?'

'A few hundred are signed up in the UK apparently, thousands in America.'

'So what happens then?'

'I've got some leaflets, and there's an online video – I could show you later.'

'Is Sunny involved? It sounds like something your sister might—'

'No. She doesn't even know about it. No one does.'

'I'm guessing it costs a bit?'

Dan nods. 'I wondered about selling the Aston Martin to pay for it.'

Silence follows and my head whirrs with unsettling thoughts and images.

'Shall I take the present up to Eleanor?' I'm glad Dan's switched the subject. He pulls a book from a bag with a broad smile; two adorable dogs – fluffy fictional war heroes – pictured on the cover. He'd snuck off to buy it while we were at the cheese counter, desperate to surprise her. 'I can't wait to see her face. I wonder if I'll be allowed to read it with her. Or is she going to play the "I'm too old for that, Daddy" card?'

I force a grin. Dan puts down the book, a concerned look putting thin white creases on his lightly tanned forehead. He walks over, gives me a hug.

'Oh, yes. Hang on.' He heads over to his briefcase. 'It's officially National Surprise Gifts Day. I got this in that new stationery store.' It's a vintage notebook, its ornate cover dazzling in the glare of the sun through the pyramid skylight. 'Thought it would replace the one you drowned in coffee.'

'Thanks. I love the gold foil. Gold.' I repeat the word, belting it out Spandau Ballet-style, in a forced baritone voice. Dan throws his head back to laugh.

'Miss Silly Socks.' He wraps his arms around me from behind, head nestled in my neck. 'Hey, I love you.' He lands several light pecks that tickle my skin.

'I love you too.' I know what's coming. He pulls his lips into an exaggerated pucker, then lands a rasping kiss that vibrates noisily at the top of my spine. I can't suppress a girly giggle.

'Oh double yuk.' We both turn to see Eleanor, head to toe in pastel purple, her new sequinned pumps twinkling beneath wiry legs, squirming with her whole face. Her eyes wander to the table, widening as she skips across.

'Yes! Wow!' She snatches it up. 'You got it.' She looks over, as if to seek reassurance the book's for her. 'They're soo cute.' She kisses the collies on the cover in turn, then chuckles at her own daftness. 'Thanks, Daddy. That's brilliant.'

She bounds over, bashing into Dan's legs, her grip tight, but not as solid as her dad's – the impenetrable, protective barrier around his princess.

Dan beams and I choke. Our perfect family of three…

★★★

4

… Three.

We Three Kings. Three wise men.

Three o'clock service. Three's a magic number. Three Little Pigs.

'We learned about number three today.' I hear Eleanor's high-pitched voice, the younger, four-year-old her. I imagine her in the little skater skirt she loved, strands of hair escaping from her pigtails, smelling of her favourite strawberry soap.

We're in her bedroom, back when it was the pink palace. Dan's just got in from work, still in his suit jacket, and she's trapped him with her excitable talk. He looks exhausted, but he doesn't complain. Never does.

'Can we do the three bears? Us three. The porridge thing. We did it at nursery. I've got some pretend dishes.' She's hurriedly rooting in her toy box, throwing things aside.

Eleanor lays three brightly-coloured plastic bowls in a row on the cream carpet. 'And there's one spoon.' She's almost delirious with excitement. Dan's knees click as he kneels by her side, pretending to stir the contents.

'Not yet, Daddy.' She snatches the spoon. 'I want to be Goldilocks.'

'But there won't be three bears then, darling,' Dan says.

'There has to be three bears, Daddy.' She scowls.

'You could be Baby Bear – AND Goldilocks,' I offer.

'I want to be just Goldilocks.'

'What about Mr Fluff?' Dan says, grabbing the stuffed toy from the foot of her bed. 'He can be Baby Bear.'

'He's not a bear. He's a dog.'

5

'He's a really good actor,' I say. 'He can pretend – like we're going to.'

'I'll get Paka; he's like a bear.' Eleanor fetches a plastic figure from her shelf, a mean-looking panda wearing dark shades. Dan takes it from her, puts it in front of his face.

'Who's been sleeping in my bed?'

Eleanor chortles and hiccups at the same time. 'That doesn't sound like a baby voice, silly Daddy. Perhaps Mummy can do it?'

I oblige.

'Well done, Mummy.' She's so earnest, teacher-like.

'That joint drama degree's paying dividends,' Dan says in an undertone, nudging me playfully.

'That voice was just right,' Eleanor says. We both laugh, proud of her joke; hoping it was intentional.

'Bless you.' Dan pulls her into a cuddle. 'Oh, I love you, Princess.'

She lets him kiss her face several times, then pulls away. 'Goldilocks, not Princess.'

The phone rings. 'Daddy Bear, Mummy Bear needs to answer that. It might be that flooring guy,' I say. 'I'll put the kettle on too – you must be parched. I'll be two minutes, Goldilocks.' Eleanor looks indignant.

Later, I listen at the door. The other two bears have clearly given up waiting. Dan's reading *Cinderella* – again. He still hasn't changed out of his work clothes.

Dan's interrupted mid-flow by Eleanor's enquiries – as always.

'Why does Cinderella's Daddy die?'

'He got very, very ill, I guess.'

'Will I die?'

'Everyone has to die.'

'But I don't want to die. I don't want Mummy to die.

'Or you, Daddy.'

In the months after Dan's announcement, he mentioned cryonics often, bombarding me with information. It was important to plan it well, get all the details right, he said.

'If you enjoy life, why wouldn't you want to take a punt at having a second go at it?' That was Dan's reasoning.

'Fair enough,' I told him. It was his choice. I'd support him, though I'm ashamed to admit that I ignored much of it, keen to focus on the here and now.

'Well, that's a bombshell and a half,' my best friend Imogen said when I told her. 'I've never heard of it. He's a bit young to be thinking about that.'

I only told a few other people, all intrigued, but – like me – a touch bewildered. They asked questions I couldn't really answer. Can people really come back to life? What had led Dan to want to do something so unusual, and radical? What did I think? I thought it was all way above my head, and much too far into the future to dwell on. I was convinced he'd go off the idea anyway.

But it wasn't. And he didn't.

Looking back, the bombshell turned out to be more of a tremor, with tiny aftershocks that rippled through our lives, testing the foundations of our marriage.

Then this – just four years later.

Total destruction.

My head returns to the room. I can smell an ancient aroma, maybe burnt incense or candle wax. I look up at the vicar's serene face, mouth moving gently, eyes doling out comforting blinks. I can feel Eleanor's hand under mine; hot and clammy. All I hear are confused, muted sounds drowned out by a strident internal voice:

'*Dan's dead. You're a widow. Dan's dead. Dead.*' Or is he?

After this, he won't be buried or cremated – no, he *can't* be.

I grip the service sheet with a rigid thumb. Dan stares up from the page, a photo taken next to Edinburgh Castle during our city break just months before. Mum reaches over and I feel her plump hand cupping my knee. I can't look at her, my poor little Eleanor and Imogen next to her, or any of the small gathering squeezed into two neat rows of office chairs on either side of the claustrophobic room.

Four weeks without my husband – each one dark, empty and unnavigable. Every morning the sickening realisation strikes me again, as if for the first time; the stomach-churning shock and self-pity undiminished, the duvet a painful barrier I fear I lack the strength to break through to enter another Danless day.

I can't do this. I'm only forty. I'm on my own, with no one to love me, an eleven-year-old girl who desperately needs her wonderful daddy, an emptiness inside that's consuming me, and a confusion that's torture.

The vicar's head leans as he speaks; his white hair is patchy. My eyes fix on the burgundy curtains hanging either side of the blank wall behind him.

There's no coffin in front of those curtains. But there's always a coffin.

8

I glance back at the photo. The picture of health. And Dan so handsome; his clear, olive skin, jaw still chiselled, grey hairs concealed by the dye he hid in his home filing cabinet.

But the image lied. Dan had a rare cardiac defect. No knowledge, no warning. No genetics to explain it. Collapsed on the bathroom floor. A massive heart attack. He was just forty-eight. *Why didn't any of your special diets or supplements ward off that one, Dan?*

They whisked him to hospital, but the man I visited there wasn't my Dan. I held a cold hand, pleading to the God I'd lost touch with since occasionally praying at bedtime as a kid for my husband's warm smile to break through. But it never came. '*I love you so much, Dancer. You can't go. We need you.*' For five days I uttered those words. On the sixth, there was no one there to hear them. He'd taken a last, laboured breath.

Then everything got blurred, things happened without me; the curious cryonics emergency procedure that involved putting Dan's body in a big plastic bath filled with ice inside a converted ambulance, then pumping it with chemicals, before shipping it out to America, to be stored until … who knows?

Of course, I didn't witness it. I couldn't. Who'd watch someone they love being subjected to that? But I'd seen what happens, in the video Dan had insisted I watch and the distressing flashbacks I'd had since he'd … gone. I saw machines bleeping and heaving on a silicone corpse, syringes piercing fake flesh, drips hanging from sterile metal bars – and lots of water; freezing cold water.

I still couldn't really get my head around it. And whoever said childbirth was the worst pain you'd ever endure was a big fat liar. It doesn't come close to losing your husband. And not knowing if you're supposed to say goodbye adds another dimension to the pain, forcing the hurt into shapes you can't recognise, with sharp angles you can't measure.

'I want you back, Dan, but I hate the thought of you in limbo. Where are you now – if not deceased? And your soul? Everything's so difficult without certainty.'

I realise, with dismay, that I may have just spoken those thoughts. Mum's gently rocking my leg, a consolatory smile on her pained, matronly face; a sort of 'there, there' look.

'Sorry ... I'm so sorry,' I whisper, forcing my eyes along the row of faces. I take in the comfort of Imogen's lingering look and try to smile at Eleanor, her beautiful young face pale, wet and crumpled with grief.

Facing ahead, I see Mark now. Such a great friend to us both. He's stood by the lectern, the face that never failed to bring cheer set with an uncharacteristic solemnity. He's talking, recollecting, praising – at last smiling. His eyes meet mine. I stare. Words break through – 'devoted husband ... father ... businessman ... fellow Beatles fan ...' Several muted chuckles are swallowed by the close walls and thick carpets.

Hours later, wandering like an intruder around the house, there's so much of the service I can't remember. I recall walking out to *Ave Maria*, weeping uncontrollably, face collapsing under the weight of sorrow and scrutiny. I know I can never listen to that music again. Each long, dark, drawn-out note's left a tiny scar inside me. And I recall Sunny appearing beside me several times, offering soothing words. The shock of seeing her in black. No tears. Staying strong for her brother. She'd been devastated not to make it back from her travels before Dan died. Her flight delayed, she'd arrived at the hospital too late.

Dragging myself up the stairs, I know I have to face the spare bedroom – his special space. As I climb, my mind returns to the church steps, the kisses and condolences. Dan's auntie had smothered me in the most extravagant embrace, clinging; and clinging. I'd surrendered, relieved to hide my face in the crook of her neck, relishing the softness of her huge black cardigan. It had been a lovely service, she'd said, finally releasing me. 'Just right. You did Dan proud.'

'Yes, it was,' I'd said. But was it? I wish I'd known what Dan wanted. The cryonics procedure had been planned, down to the last daunting detail – but what next? What about the farewell and finality for those left behind? Not even a few scribbles on one of his Post-its to guide me.

We should have discussed the funeral. It was my fault. I didn't ask; maybe didn't listen. But then, who knew it would all happen so soon? We were both supposed to die in old age, worn out and weary, but much wiser.

I'm grateful to Mum, Imogen and Mark for taking over with arrangements. I was incapable. Without them, there wouldn't have been a memorial. And the vicar was so understanding. It wasn't a circumstance he'd ever encountered, he'd said, suggesting the low-key service in the church's adjoining prayer room.

'But was any of it really right?' I wonder as I sit, at last, on the sofa bed, still in my dark clothes, Dan's brightly-coloured fitness equipment filling the room, yet accentuating the emptiness.

No body, no coffin, no earth, no ashes, no stone carved with the permanence of an epitaph. No drawing of curtains. No laying to rest.

You're not in heaven, and what the hell do I do without you now, Dan?

CHAPTER 2

6 months later

I dally outside the whitewashed building, waiting for a sign; a spur. Perhaps the sun will break through the morning haze and light the way, or a voice inside my head will order me in. An empty juice carton passes in the gutter, dragged by a swirly summer breeze, then stops in the recess of a drain.

A car horn sounds in the distance. Several urgent blasts. 'Go on!' it says. 'Do it!'

I gather the courage to enter, legs impossibly heavy, carrying so much fear – and hope – as I climb the twisted stairs.

Opening the only door, I see a group of around ten people sat in a neat circle on assorted chairs. An awkward hush is broken by a woman with short, feathery hair and kind blue eyes that match her plain blouse.

'Hi, I'm Ingrid – you must be …' she glances at her clipboard, ' … Carrie?'

'Yes.' I head across the patterned carpet to the empty chair, needlessly smoothing down my jersey top and wishing I'd been brave enough to arrive earlier; or not at all.

'You haven't missed anything,' Mrs Clipboard says. 'We were waiting.' She straightens in her chair. 'Before we start, as I always say, coming here's a sign of strength, not weakness. This is a non-judgmental environment, somewhere to explore your emotions ...'

My eyes wander to the pale green walls, the matching curtains and frameless pastel painting above the suited man sat opposite, his shoes gleaming beneath grey socks. To his right sits a woman wearing nautical stripes and loafers. Her hair's like mine; a low maintenance bob, with blonde highlights. She looks over, giving a gentle 'join the club' smile. I hear sniffles next to me, catching a glimpse of a fleshy cheek and frizzy hair and inhaling a floral scent that momentarily masks the damp air in the room.

Mrs Clipboard catches my eye. 'We're all here to share our grief, thoughts and experiences in a supportive way,' she says.

Yes, and I'm here because I don't know what else to do. Mum suspects I'm not coping despite the smiles I coax on to my face. And she's right. I'm here because the advice and support from friends has been great, but it's not enough, the positive morning mantras my sister-in-law Sunny prescribed don't work for me and the medication from the doctor is dulling my senses and I hate functioning in this fog.

'As we have two new people today, I think it would help if everyone introduced themselves and told us who they're grieving for. That's if you're happy to.' Mrs Clipboard sweeps her eyes around the circle, her crow's feet a testament to the persistence of her warm smile. 'Anyone?'

I swallow hard. Mrs Stripes introduces herself. She's lost a husband. Others oblige: a son killed in a car crash, a

14

brother by a genetic heart problem, a mum lost to cancer, the suited man had also lost his wife to the disease. The lady next to me chokes on her words. Her husband went in for a routine operation, but never came round. Tears turn to sobs. 'He should still be here.' Her fractured voice grows angry. 'They took him from me.' Mrs Clipboard offers tissues. The woman apologises.

'Please don't apologise. Emotional outbursts are natural. They're not censored.' Mrs Clipboard utters more soothing words. She has a suitcase full of them, it seems. But her compassion feels genuine; comforting. The drama's distracted my nerves, but it's my turn. My pulse accelerates.

'My husband died six months ago,' I say, gaze darting uncomfortably. 'It was his heart.' Mrs Clipboard urges me to continue with a gentle nod. I hesitate. 'His body's been frozen.' A few shuffles. Mr Suit coughs. I expect surprised looks, frowns, sneers perhaps, but I see mostly blank, distant expressions.

'I see … so …' Mrs Clipboard flashes a kind smile.

'He believes he can be brought back to life.'

She nods supportively. 'And do you share that belief, Carrie?'

'No … I mean, I'm not sure.' My words seem to have pushed the others further away. I'm straining to see them, and not sure they can see me any more. Maybe they think I have some fine fragment of hope that they don't. *But things feel just as hopeless for me,* I want to say.

I drift inwards, filling my lungs to calm the adrenalin. It feels as if we've been playing a game of bereavement snap and I'm the card without a match. I hear scraping chairs.

People are moving and Mrs Clipboard's asking us, in pairs, to consider what we miss most about our loved ones.

A shy young woman sits by me, chin down, twiddling with the tie cords of her hoodie. She misses her mum's lasagne, her singing around the house, their chats. I miss Dan's strong arms folding around me, his earthy, sweet smell that conjures up burnt toffee popcorn, the rasping, comedy kisses he landed on my neck in daft – and difficult – moments. I can't stop. I miss his advice, his knowledge, sharing things with him; thoughts, problems – a slice of carrot and walnut cake with coconut milk icing (Dan had gone off the sugary stuff). At times, I even miss his tidiness and 'to do' lists. Finally, Mrs Clipboard hands out leaflets.

'I hope you've found today helpful. It can be daunting, but I assure you it gets better. Remember, we're all in the same boat.' Her eyes seem to avoid mine.

Relieved it's over, I shove the leaflet in my bag on my way to the door. In the street below, I collide with a man staggering from the betting shop, his beer breath hurling obscenities at me. Rushing past a few more people, I stop to sit on a low stone wall.

Somehow, I feel even more lonely in my sorrow than before I'd entered that room. I'm not in the same boat. They've all lost a travel companion, searching for strength as they make their way back to shore to begin a new life. I'm still floating.

★★★

It's several hours before I can face my sister-in-law. I don't feel like company, particularly hers, but I accepted her invitation to tea several days ago and feel it's too late to cancel.

Sunny greets me at the door in a heavily patterned blouse with fussy purple embroidery around its loose neckline. With my mood so dark, I want to turn down the brightness – not just of Sunny, but all the possessions in her tiny lounge; burners and candles in sparkly containers, odd-shaped crystals and surfaces covered with garish drapes and throws. I often joked that I was scared to stand still for long when I visited, in case she wrapped me in something more colourful and outrageous.

'So, how was the group counselling?' Sunny drifts over to clear clutter from the sofa.

'I'm not sure it's for me.'

'You've got to give it a chance, sweetness.' Sunny gestures for me to take a seat.

'Perhaps.'

Later, we're sat with bowls of lentil casserole perched on two patchwork pouffes by our knees, surrounded by throws and tassels, and I'm relaying how Eleanor's beginning to feel more settled at secondary school when Sunny reaches over, rubbing my leg with her bony fingers. Two earnest eyes stare out from a mass of crazy caramel curls and she does one of her slow-motion blinks.

'Dan told me he was convinced cryonics would give him a chance to live again, but it wouldn't be the same if you didn't … you know, join him, Carrie.'

'I'm grieving. Just let me grieve,' I say firmly, taken aback, but trying not to get angry, to spoil her gesture of goodwill. She pats my leg, as if to say sorry, and we continue eating in silence.

17

My wounds are gaping and raw, and it feels like Sunny's rubbing one of her citrusy oils into them. Not for the first time. Three weeks ago, while looking after Eleanor, she had the audacity to wear the 'cryonics emergency procedure' bracelet Dan kept in his bedside drawer. She'd asked for it as a keepsake, along with a pair of engraved cufflinks. I didn't imagine she'd wear it, but I returned home late after an editorial meeting to find it hanging from her wrist. Eleanor was deeply upset, and, of course, I got it in the neck.

'Why didn't you keep it?' she'd yelled, screwing up her lips and glaring through tearful eyes. 'I hate you.' It's the first time she's said that. Not one I'll ever forget.

I leave Sunny's soon after the meal, taking a detour so I can be alone at the wheel for longer. Swinging the car on to the drive, I miss the thrill I used to get pulling up outside our home. Replaced by a sinking feeling, and an echoing emptiness as I open the front door.

Yet it's gorgeous; one of two double-fronted houses in the ash-tree-lined street, designed by a local builder. It was love at first sight for me – modern, yet elegant, with Georgian-style windows (perfect for my pencil pleat curtains), an arched porch, lawns front and back, a huge garage for Dan's cars and all the mod cons inside to keep a lazy wife happy. Mum was smitten when she first saw it too. 'Haven't you done well for yourself?' As if I'd finally achieved something. But I couldn't take the credit. Dan's business success had paid for it. He had enough drive for both of us. He was shrewd too. I guess I was his slightly ditsy blonde – not dumb, just not as smart as Dan.

Soon after she arrives home, Eleanor asks if Bethany can come round, despite my 'no friends on a school night' rule.

'Please, just for a short while.' She sweeps her fringe melodramatically, pleading with doe-brown eyes that are so much like her dad's. 'She's really upset about something. She needs me.' She looks so earnest, I have to titter.

'And the "teen who can turn it on" Oscar goes to Eleanor Colwell,' I tease. Eleanor curls her lip.

'Has anyone ever told you you're not funny?'

'Yes, many times, but it doesn't stop me.' I know her surly "I've lost my dad so cut me some slack" face is a flick away, to be followed, no doubt, by a strop. I give in; hop on my Conflict Dodgem. Again. 'OK. Only until eight.' Always was one to fall for an actor.

The two girls spend most of their time applying make-up – still a novelty for Bethany who's forbidden to wear it – and Eleanor then spends almost as long taking it off, her face puffy and red as she heads for bed.

After consoling myself with wine, I call Imogen, telling her how difficult I'd found the counselling, and what Sunny had said.

'What a thing to say. What an insensitive …' Imogen stops and I picture her steaming as she stands by the oven in full multi-task mode, a raised shoulder pinning the phone next to the short flicks of her choppy chestnut hair, one sturdy hand stirring something delicious in a pan, the other brushing a perfect glaze on to freshly-made pastries lined up on a baking tray for tomorrow's breakfast.

'Yes, it seems Sunny's on some sort of "Convert Carrie to Cryonics" crusade. She clearly thinks it's her duty to ensure I honour Dan's wish.'

'How dare she! Dan accepted you weren't keen to sign up. She should too.'

'But Dan assumed he had time to persuade me – several decades at least. We both did. And I thought he'd go off the idea, ask for a refund and buy a Maserati instead.' I grimace at my flippancy.

'I bet Sunny's not signing herself up any day soon,' Imogen says. 'She'd surely prefer some higher, spiritual sequel to this life, a space filled with fairy dust and candlelight where she can float around freely and look down on us lesser mortals.'

'Cruel.'

'Seriously, you need to put her right, let her know how much she's hurting you.'

'You know I'm rubbish at confronting people,' I say. 'I hate the drama. Besides, she's family, she was special to Dan – his baby sister – and I think she means well.'

'Really?' Imogen humphs.

After our goodbyes, I find myself looking through all the condolence cards, still in a pile under the coffee table. Some I can't recall. It's reassuring to re-read the sincere sympathies and heartfelt thoughts and prayers, to take in the comforting images of candles and crosses. Everyone seems so sure Dan's gone forever. I guess there aren't special cards for someone who believes they'll come back.

I reach for the card at the bottom of the pile. Belated. A single, fuschia-pink flower curled across the front. I shoo away the inappropriate flutter as I hold it. Inside, his brief message; the familiar thin sloping letters – no curls on the descenders: '*So sorry for your loss. Ashley.*' He had so much more to be sorry for.

At first, I'd been baffled by how he'd got my address, but then I realised it was because Dan's story – our story – had been splashed across so many newspapers. And that same caption: *Businessman Dan: 'I'll be back'*. The one that was full of hope. I take the card upstairs, shutting it away in my bedside drawer.

Pulling on my dotty PJs, the familiar feeling of dread descends. I miss Dan so much more in the dark. I miss the sex too. I used to initiate it more than he did, often with a gentle nibble of his left lobe, though he rarely complained.

I lift Mr Fluff off the pillow, relishing the comfort of his beady eyes on me. He was an engagement gift, a cuddly toy dog with copper-coloured fur. Sadly, he'd become matted and seriously deformed, with limp legs and a fat tum where the stuffing had migrated. Eleanor had insisted on taking him to bed until she was about ten, declaring herself too old for teddy toys one night and flinging him back at me in horror.

Mr Fluff beckons my mind back to the hotel in Suffolk, the one Dan had spent about a fortnight's wages for us to stay in for two nights …

He'd suggested an evening stroll around the grounds and I was following him, carrying my heels up the steps that led to a weather-worn statue of a nymph, coloured gravel replacing water in the pond she emerged from. We'd both dressed up, Dan dapper in suit trousers and a favourite white button-down shirt, me in a floral tea dress bought for the occasion.

I recall looking back at the hotel, topped by a white summer sky, the burnt reds of the original bricks blending with the new additions in near perfect harmony. The grounds had a delightful formality – several lush, lawned areas and rectangular rockeries bordered by box hedges and neatly trimmed topiary. I felt giddy, unused to wine then.

I turned to see Dan retrieving a small green box camouflaged in the crook of the nymph's mossy arm. He dropped to the ground, one knee bent beneath him.

'Will you make me the happiest man alive and be Mrs Carrie Colwell?'

'Ye … yes, I will … do.' The shock almost winded me. I hadn't seen it coming, the set and staging so perfect; a water nymph bearing gifts. In the box was a large, luminous diamond, an oval set high on a gold band with tiny stones sparkling at the sides, as if lighting the way to the main attraction.

Dan smiled, sliding the ring along my shaky finger. 'I hope you like it. Imogen helped me choose it.'

'Sneaky lady – I had no idea.' I stared down, hand trembling. 'It's so beautiful. I love it. And I love you.' I giggled childishly.

'Me too.' Dan kissed me, then held me tight. The excitement of the event was twisting and turning inside me.

'Can I keep my surname?'

'Really?' Dan looked crestfallen.

'No – just joking, you daft devil. I like a bit of alliteration.'

'You like a bit of the other too,' he said, dimples stretched with a zipped-up grin. 'Come on.' He took my hand, his curved to negotiate the diamond for the first time.

In our hotel room, I was greeted by Mr Fluff, brown coat vibrant against the ivory satin pillowcase.

'You said you've always wanted a dog.' Dan grinned.

I picked up the toy, breathing in the word '*Fiancée*' on a tag hanging from a blue collar.

'That was a bit presumptuous,' I said. 'What if I'd said 'no'?'

'I'd have asked someone else – that ring cost a fortune.'

I thumped Dan playfully, pushing him back on to the quilt. We made love for hours, at one point becoming a threesome, Mr Fluff appearing between us as we rolled over on the bed.

Later, after drinking fizzy wine that Dan had smuggled into his holdall wrapped in his university towel, he asked what I fancied doing the next day.

'How about the theatre?' I suggested.

'I wondered about that walking history tour. It's such an interesting town.'

The tour it was. Interesting it wasn't – not that I remember much about it.

In fact, did it happen like that at all? Had I suggested the theatre, or just thought it? Was it a warm evening and did Dan wear the white shirt? Things were starting to blur, facts and feelings that once stood out with clarity, like red jewels on a silver plate, now fading too fast, lost in a mosaic of clashing colours.

I reluctantly return from the journey in my head, laying Mr Fluff on the empty side of the bed. I can see his collar again, and the word fiancée – though it's not there; first frayed, then torn off in a vigorous washing cycle after Eleanor had spewed on him during a bout of tonsilitis.

I lie on the cold sheet, still keeping to 'my' side. The tears come. Slow, helpless tears. I haven't cried for a while – as if I've run dry. In the beginning it happened a lot, often when I least expected it – grief hijacking me, still wearing that mask I couldn't pull off.

I want Dan to visit me in my dreams, though I want him here with me more – before I close my eyes. I don't want the click of the lamp switch to be the last sound.

I miss our little ritual. 'Good night, Dancer,' I'd say, cuddling into his firm chest before we drifted off. 'Goodnight, Miss Silly Socks,' he'd respond. They were pet names from childhood we both loved to hate. Dan's mum called him Dancer because, apparently, he never kept still, always jigging away. My dad called me Miss Silly Socks – I guess because I'd inherited his daftness. Out of habit, I'd actually said 'Good night, Dancer' out loud a few times and the silence and darkness that devoured the words was agonising. I nearly say it again, as my wine-soaked mind messes with me.

But I'm not sure I want to keep saying 'goodnight'.

Maybe I can bid him adieu – like Ashley did to me all those years ago.

CHAPTER 3

16 months later

I'm in my bedroom reading the letter I keep hidden in the ripped lining of my padded jewel box when I hear the familiar knocking noise, the tippy-tap-tap that heralds Sunny's arrival. She refuses to ring doorbells.

I shove the letter in my handbag – a nervous glow of secrecy adding to my anxiety about the evening ahead – then stub my toe on the bedroom door, the sharp pain forcing out a tirade of expletives.

It's too late to cancel the date. Or retract the lie.

'Hi, sweetness.' Sunny's at the door, a joyous grin revealing the Madonna gap between her two front teeth, her petite figure lost in a huge suede jacket and a long, frilly blouse in a riot of clashing colours.

'Hi,' I say, smile unsteady. 'Come in.' I yell up the stairs. 'Eleanor, Auntie's here.'

Sunny leans in for a hug. 'You smell lovely,' she says breezily. It's my usual Dior Dune perfume (or Dior-gasm, as Dan called it). I rarely wear anything else; just up the dose for special occasions.

'And you look exquisite.' She sweeps back to view my drop-waist tunic. My shoulders are rigid with tension, everything below them double knotted.

'Thanks.'

Sunny drifts behind me up the hallway, declines my offer of a herbal tea. Her eyes scan the kitchen, no doubt noting the mess. *Wasn't like this when Dan was around. What would he think?*

I did marvel at my ability to transform a huge, sleek and shiny room with all its space and time-saving gadgets into a total bloody mess. But Sunny's in no position to judge. Clutter fills every inch in her little Victorian semi.

She sits perfectly still, bright façade reflecting in the glass of the kitchen table. The gaudiness makes me queasy. Or it is nerves?

'Is that new?' Sunny's eyeing my outfit again.

'No, I've had it a while,' I say, voice lost to the clatter as I put a sauce-crusted plate into the dishwasher. I'm not sure why I fib; maybe because I don't want to risk exposing the bigger lie by appearing to have made too much effort. Perhaps because I suspect she's lying too – about liking my bland tunic. Our dress sense couldn't be more different; hers all boho, different and daring, mine safer than a primary school playground – tops, leggings and blouses in muted colours, labelled 'suitable for a staid woman of a certain age clinging on to a size twelve thanks to gruelling step classes and occasional 'no carbs' days. Sunny made the statement, while I whispered, occasionally mumbled, in the background. Adventurous for me was brown boots with a black handbag. I played safe with my hair too, occasionally growing it a few inches, and feeling a rare thrill of bravery as it tickled my collarbone.

'Can I help?'

'No, it's fine thanks,' I say, regretting I'd taken so long getting ready, as if that extra sweep of blusher or dab of concealer would make anything better – or easier.

'Help yourself to anything you fancy tonight.' I gesture to some flapjacks and kiwis on the worktop.

'How sweet of you. Have you been cooking something nice?'

'No, it's … just some tea for Eleanor.' I turn my back to clear more clutter, resisting another fib. It's another pre-packed pasta dish plated up for my daughter to microwave. Imagining Sunny's despair over its lack of nutritional value, and the subsequent depletion of vitamins from the nuclear blast, I grab an apple from the fruit bowl, thumping it down next to the meal, hoping for some redemption.

'I've bought some oils – thought I could give Elle a massage, relieve some of the tension in her shoulders from sitting so long at that computer,' Sunny says. 'Oh yes …' she roots in her bag ' … I've handed in my notice. I've got several more reflexology patients, so no more waitressing from next week.'

'Great.' *Did that mean she was staying in Tetford?*

Sunny places two small glass bottles on the table, a train of bangles clanking as they disappear into the cavernous cuff of her blouse. My mobile rings.

'Hi, my lovely.' It's great to hear Imogen's voice. I've missed her terribly since her husband Ben's promotion prompted their move to France.

'Hi … just a moment.' I excuse myself and head to the living room, closing the door. I perch on the corner sofa. 'How's Reims?'

'Oh, fine. Just wanted to wish you luck for the date.'

'Thanks. I need it. I've got a big fat knot in my stomach. I can't believe I'm putting myself through it again.' And I couldn't. I'd loathed the last one, carrying Dan, disbelief and a heavy conscience through the stilted, getting-to-know-you talk.

'Just enjoy it, my lovely,' Imogen urges. 'Least it's not a stranger this time.'

'I guess – if you count seeing him for about five minutes at the office.'

'Is anyone looking after Eleanor?'

I lower my voice. 'Yes … Sunny's here.'

'You mean, you've asked her – after she sabotaged the last one?'

'I don't really have a choice, do I? My other babysitter pissed off to France.' Imogen laughs and I imagine her big gummy smile, which makes her nose wrinkle in the middle.

It took months to pluck up the courage to face a first date and ask Sunny to babysit. She obliged, but it didn't take a supersleuth to spot her disapproval. She called during dessert to say Eleanor was very unwell, so I dashed home early, only to find my daughter queasy after overdosing on granola bars. I didn't get cross. Sunny had done me a favour really. Sales rep Nigel had bored me through two courses, then shown me his hernia scar while I was eating profiteroles.

'Seriously, Eleanor refuses sitters now. Sunny's family, so it doesn't count apparently.' I hesitate. 'Anyway, I fibbed – said I'm going out with Tash.' Silence. 'Well, I am! It just happens Tash's new boyfriend's bringing his divorced friend along too.'

'Won't Eleanor let it out?'

'No – I've fibbed to her too.'

'Tut, tut. The dreaded white lies again.' Imogen adopts her familiar tone of mild rebuke.

'It was easier.'

'Maybe … but … well, better not keep you. Give you time to paint on some 'snog me' lips!'

'Stop it,' I say. We often discussed which bits of each other's bodies we'd trade. Top of Imogen's list was my 'innie' waist and blue eyes (she described her own as pond-weed green), while I coveted her 36DDs and happily confessed to an acute case of lip envy. Imogen's were plump, with a cupid's bow to die for, while mine were pathetically thin.

I crane my neck, peering at my heavily-coated pink lips in the mantel mirror, unsettled by the thought of kissing a near stranger.

After the call, I find Eleanor being subjected to an over-the-top hugging ritual in the kitchen. She's all smiles. She doesn't seem to mind it from her eccentric auntie, just another of her endearing quirks. I get far more scowls than cuddles these days. Sunny's long fingers disappear into her bag.

'Oh, I found this, Elle. I adored it when I was your age.' She holds out a book with a picture of children flying on a dragon on the cover. I stifle a giggle as I watch Eleanor pretend to be pleased. The only thing she reads made out of paper these days is *Heat* magazine. But the drama tuition's paying off; she's becoming quite the actress.

'Thanks.' Eleanor flicks a fake grin, then turns to me. 'Is Tash coming here?'

'No, we're meeting at the pub.' I avoid Sunny's eye, adrenalin bubbling in my chest. I shouldn't have agreed to Tash's stupid double date plan. I pat Eleanor's arm. 'Don't forget to clean the hamster cage, darling, it stinks. I've had to use half a can of air freshener to mask it. And, remember – bed by ten.' Eleanor slams the book on the table, eyes narrowed to slits.

'Jeez. I'm thirteen, not a flippin' baby. You so stress me out.' She flounces out, muttering things under her breath that my ears bleep. I trail her up the stairs, beaming potent glares from behind. Unable to bear further tension, I let her flee to her room while I fetch my handbag.

Downstairs, I find Sunny staring wistfully at our silver-framed wedding photo, next to Dan's 'Midlands Business of the Year' award on the walnut sideboard.

'You two had something so special.' She's holding it close to her chest. 'I'm sure that one day you'll be together again, whether in body or spirit.'

I bite hard on my cheek. Not now. I say my goodbyes.

★★★

'Carrie, over here!' Tash yells, waving a manicured hand.

I'm late and the others are already settled at a table next to a sash window, dressed with plum damask curtains.

For a moment, I'd thought I was in the wrong pub. It had changed so much since Tash and I scraped our work shoes across a threadbare carpet one lunchtime to face several old men with stained trousers and forbidding stares, perched on scuffed stools around the bar. It was full of perfume and excitable chatter that bounced off the flagstone floor, the rickety pine seats replaced with big oak carvers covered in plush fabrics.

I intend to sweep across the room in a confident cloud of Dior-gasm, but with dread dragging in my belly, a swollen toe, four unfamiliar eyes on me – and after Tash's big introduction – each step feels hideously cumbersome and I find myself shuffling like an OAP on a parquet floor.

Tash leaps up, spiky necklace swinging between bronzed boobs squeezed into a silky red top as she lands an energetic kiss on each cheek.

'You look gorgeous. Is that tunic new? You've had more highlights. I love the fringe shorter!' Tash doesn't wait for a response. 'This is Toby.'

'Hi.' He beams through a set of perfect teeth framed by a ring of dark designer stubble.

'And you remember Gaz.' He stands, kisses my cheek. 'Oh yeah, you spilled coffee on his paperwork didn't you, you clumsy cow.' Tash guffaws, running a set of multi-coloured nails through her thick brown hair. Gaz looks startled.

'Says you!' I protest, flushing. Tash is the undisputed queen of klutz, nothing safe in her elegant but unsteady hands. 'I'll keep my drinks well away from you tonight,' I say, addressing Gaz as I grab my glass of wine and sit next to him.

'Phew.' He swipes a hand across his forehead.

I'd met Gaz, the safety inspector, briefly, when he'd visited the office to talk about fire regulations. My colleague Mark had cruelly remarked that he looked like Daniel Craig's uglier twin brother. 'I think he's hot for an oldie,' Tash had whispered. 'Mark's just jealous.' But he's ditched the drab suit – not very James Bond as I recall – for a pale denim shirt and black chinos, making him look more youthful.

As always Tash hijacks the conversation, pretty head tipping from side to side, saucer eyes glowing with all the attention. She could chat for England, which was why I'd let her talk me into the evening's arrangements. Besides, I couldn't refute her allegations that the lonely life I now led wasn't good for me. 'Why don't all four of us meet, yeah, to like, break the ice, then Toby and I can pop off to that party. It'll take the pressure off – pinkie pledge,' Tash had assured, wiggling a polished little finger.

Sedated by the Friday-night buzz and caught in the snare of Tash's easy chat, I've almost forgotten it's a date when she makes their exit excuses, leaving Gaz and I to move to the dining area with a distressed table, wonky white candle and lots of awkwardness between us.

I find myself making inane comments to break painful pauses, hacking into a stuffed mushroom as if I've only just learned to use a knife. Gaz clearly finds it equally daunting, keen grey eyes darting about as he slurps green soup, his spare hand fiddling with the leather placemat. His large gold watch is similar to Dan's and I feel a fall in my chest each time he lifts his wrist.

Fortunately, with the second Merlot bottle drained, Gaz turns quite chatty, telling me about his seventeen years as a policeman.

'Did you solve any terrible crimes?' I ask.

'Yes – nicked a guy stealing begonias from the park. Caught him red-handed!' I chuckle. 'Tetford's not exactly the crime capital, is it?'

'I think you should lie. Pretend you helped convict a serial killer.'

'Good idea.' He smiles with his whole face and I grin back, feeling light and giggly.

He's describing the rock 'n' roll antics of his youngest daughter's drummer boyfriend when a few errant loops of linguini escape the clump I've painstakingly bundled on to my fork. One plops straight down my cleavage. I'm mortified, blushing hot as I hoick it out.

'Oh dear.' He laughs. 'Let me.' He leans in, patting at a sauce trail on my chin with his serviette. Our eyes lock and I get pleasing wafts of a dry, citrusy cologne. I feel a slight thrill – which shocks me. An alien feeling. I suspect he's flirting, and I'm tempted to reciprocate, but I've forgotten how. I continue eating, avoiding his gaze.

It turns out Gary has a string of hobbies – fencing among them – making my weekly fitness class, occasional theatre trips and daily TV-watching sound desperately dull. In my tipsy state, I find myself imagining Eleanor and I heading off on some great adventure, like learning to street luge in the Alps or nursing sick alpacas in Peru. Reality hits. Things have to change. I have to do something about the big fat work rut I'm in – still in the same, dull corporate communications job that, twenty years ago, was supposed to be temporary.

'I'd love to be a writer,' I say, keen to impress, yet surprised by my confession. I seldom said it out loud, and never to strangers. But I'm warming to him.

'Books?'

'God, no. Women's magazines; just light-hearted articles or a column, that sort of thing.'

'What's stopping you?'

'Lack of courage. And skill, I suspect. It's stupidly competitive.'

'You should try, you never know.'

I shrug. 'I quite fancy the idea of working in a theatre, too, behind the scenes, or maybe front of house. I used to do am dram years ago.'

'It's never too late to change careers. Several of my friends have.' Gaz stops eating. 'Your husband worked at Cullimore's too, didn't he?'

'Yes. Left to set up his own business selling health products.'

'It must have been a difficult time for you.'

I nod. Gaz knows I'm a widow and I wonder whether Tash has broken her promise not to elaborate, or if he's used super-police powers and honed observational skills to link me to the news reports after Dan's death. I'd been quite a celeb in Tetford, half expecting people to point and jeer when I was at the cashpoint: 'It's the widow of that frozen guy.' I hated that Dan had been labelled a weirdo. '*He wasn't – you didn't know him!*'

'Yes. Being a widow at forty isn't much fun. And my husband's body is being preserved.'

'Seriously? How?' Gaz's mouth has fallen open slightly, soiled knife held mid-air. I'm cross with myself for overdoing the wine, blurting it out.

'It's called cryonic suspension. The body's basically frozen, so it can be brought back to life one day – well, in theory.'

'Gosh.' Gaz raises his eyebrows, then continues eating – a respectful silence perhaps – though I sense he's desperate to know more, as people invariably are. And I could oblige. Before Dan went, I'd been reluctant to listen when he'd tried to explain the finer details of what would happen to his body after death. I'm not sure why. Fear? Denial? Maybe stubbornness. Suspecting he'd go off the idea, I didn't think I needed to fully comprehend it. I'd once read about a woman with a fear of water who went through hell learning to scuba dive so she could better understand her husband's hobby. Six months later, he'd taken up golf. But after Dan died, I read the literature more thoroughly. I owed him that. I tried to force my squeamishness aside, get my head around the science, though it was several galaxies beyond me.

So I could tell Gaz, as he tears into his sirloin, how a mechanical compressor heaves on the chest to keep oxygen flowing while the corpse is cooled in ice, then – as he sips wine – how various intravenous liquids are pumped in and fluids drained out …

Instead I say: 'Don't worry, I don't understand it either!'

'So, your husband really thought … thinks, he can come back to life?' I see the outline of a sneer on Gaz's wine-stained lips.

'Yes. One day, when science has moved on.'

Gaz's attitude seems to change after that. He appears more distant during dessert, back a little straighter in the chair, eyes wandering again.

We exchange numbers and, as we part company, he kisses my cheek, saying he's enjoyed it, we should do it again some time. I agree. Yet I doubt his words.

I decide that if there are other dates, I'll be just an ordinary widow.

I'm relieved to get out the taxi. Feeling slightly pissed, I'd longed to be left in peace but the driver was extremely chatty and contagiously chirpy. I'd tried to re-read the letter still in my handbag, but the words and sentences jumped and jumbled. Only '*Liar*' stayed still.

That word could apply to me as much as to *him* tonight, I'd thought.

Scrabbling with the key in the lock, I shudder at a gust of biting winter wind, bracing myself to face Sunny. I'll have to try hard not to slur. Or expose the fib.

I feel like a naughty schoolgirl, desperate to assure her mum she's spent the evening watching TV with her best friend, when she's been drinking Bacardi Breezers on a park bench and losing her virginity.

Fortunately, Sunny's keen to leave. She doesn't do late nights.

'I'm so glad you're socialising more. We all need companionship.' She's hovering at the front door. 'Is Tash still doing all that dating?' I nod. 'I can't understand what makes women … like her want to keep meeting strangers. Did she have a date with her tonight?'

'Yes.'

'I didn't think you'd be so late if you were just meeting … I wondered if you …' Sunny stops, eyes snaring mine. 'I see Eleanor's put a new photo of Dan by her bedside. I told her, he'll like that.' She's used the present tense; AGAIN. I'm incensed.

'Dan's dead! It's been nearly two bloody years!' I

bellow. 'And leave Eleanor out of this. Things are hard enough for her without your stupid comments.'

I feel awful as the words pierce our eardrums. I catch Sunny's expression in the full-length venetian mirror as she reaches for the door handle, a flick of alarm in her eyes, mouth pinched. Of course, she keeps her shawl of serenity wrapped tightly around her, doesn't yell back.

'Oh dear, I didn't mean … I think you've had too much … I'm sorry I've upset you,' she utters softly. 'I sense you're carrying a lot of stress.' Sunny clasps her hands, as if in prayer. 'Dan believed he wouldn't expire and I respect that. We all have our own beliefs, and perhaps what we believe can come true.'

I breathe deeply, wait for her to step outside: 'Well, I believe I've got a right to get on with my life.' I close the door firmly.

Two coffees, lots of tears, and a spell of trash TV later, I finally creep upstairs, head still spinning. In the bedroom, I draw the aqua satin curtains across on another difficult day.

I tuck the letter back in its hiding place, then throw some clothes in the laundry basket on the landing.

'Hey, Mum, did you have a good night?' It's Eleanor's voice. I peer round her door.

'Yes, thanks.' She switches on her lamp, giving me a bleary-eyed stare. She looks so much younger tucked up in bed, so naturally pretty. The night's knocked off the hard mask of maturity she chooses to wear by day, exposing the soft little girl I yearn for, and often imagine her still to be.

'Tash says hi.' I perch on the bed, keeping my boozy breath at a safe distance. Dan stares out from the white wooden photo frame on her chest of drawers, his image replacing Eleanor's school 'selfie' with her two besties, Freya and Bethany.

'Cool.' Eleanor sits up. Her mild honey smell, one I love better than any, has been obliterated by a cocktail of essential oils.

'Blimey, what happened to you?'

'Oh, yeah, my hair.' She grabs at the greasy clumps. 'Auntie Sunny did a head massage. Put loads of oil in it. I look a proper state, don't I?'

'It's not your best look.'

'I had a shoulder massage too. That was well nice and the oils smelt beaut.' Eleanor pulls her fleecy pyjama top off one shoulder, urging me to take a sniff. 'But the head thing was so weird. Auntie does it on the cats, says they love it.'

I smile. I have two Eleanors now, the old, adorable version and a new, complex model – with extra wind-up mechanisms and buttons I keep unwittingly pressing. She's like the terrier my gran had; melting your heart as it nuzzled into your chest with its warm breath and soft snout for strokes one minute, then tensing up and tearing off your fingernails the next. But Eleanor's been through a lot; she has good reason to snap and occasionally bite.

'Jeez, Freya's auntie gives her highlights and mine does this.' She pulls her freakishly flexible lips into a comical curl and I laugh heartily, relishing her cute terrier mode and commending her sense of humour.

Yours isn't the only head Sunny's been messing with, I think, leaning over to kiss her goodnight.

CHAPTER 4

Imogen phones the next morning, desperate to hear about the date. I'm stretched out on the bed in my PJs, with my third coffee and a heavy head, relieved to be horizontal again.

'He smelled really nice,' I say.

'Well, that's a big positive for someone with the nose of a bloodhound. *And* …'

'We seemed to get on pretty well, but …' I pause, ' … then I told him about Dan and he changed. I think it put him off.'

'Really? That's daft. It's more likely you putting out those negative vibes again.' Imogen titters, as if to make it clear it's a joke.

'Possibly. Dan's a hard act to follow.'

'Yes, but—'

'I know – I can't compare everyone to him.'

'So, will you be seeing him again?'

'He took my number, said he'd ring – but I doubt it.'

'The negativity again.'

'Sorry, I'm just feeling rough. I still don't think I'm ready for this dating stuff. Maybe Sunny's right, I shouldn't be doing it at all. I should be waiting for—'

'Don't be daft.' Imogen sounds terse. I tell her about

Sunny's comments. 'Wow, she doesn't learn. She's so sodding tactless. And judgmental.' I can hear the hiss of her steam.

'But I lied to her about who I was out with – I think she knew. And I don't think she realises how hurtful—'

'She knows exactly what she's saying.' I can sense Imogen's cogs whirring in a silence. 'Perhaps you should settle for someone you know then, like that dishy dad from Eleanor's old school, the interior designer … or Mark?'

'Stop it! He's Eleanor's friend's dad – a no-no. And Mark was Dan's friend. We're colleagues. Change the record.'

'Just saying! If you won't do internet dating and want to skip the 'getting to know you' bit …' She pauses. 'Or you could get in touch with a certain ex.'

I thought Sunny had the sixth sense. 'Stop right there.' Imogen had become more candid since crossing the Channel, but I'm stunned by her audacity. 'Anyway, I'm probably about the last person Ashley Baird wants to hear from.'

'Maybe not. He's tried to get in touch before.'

'That was years ago – probably pissed at the time.'

'What about that phone message on your birthday you couldn't decipher?'

'I doubt that was from him.'

'Just saying.' Imogen yawns. 'Sorry, I barely slept last night as Laura and her loud cough joined me in bed. Still, it stopped Ben from trying it on. As if I'd be up for it in the middle of the night? Saying that, I'm not up for it in the morning, afternoon or evening either.' She laughs rather loudly.

I chuckle obligingly, though I sense Imogen's lack of libido's no longer a laughing matter. She claims her sex drive slipped out with Katie's afterbirth. That was two years ago. I worry about how much Imogen has on her plate, besides her exquisite home-cooked food and cakes worthy of their own spotlight in a gallery. Both of her girls had sleep issues, yet she still worked full-time as a freelance graphic designer, wrote blogs on baking and always looked immaculate. Although apprehensive about moving – the upheaval, rebuilding the business – she was determined to make it work. I don't know how she did it. She was superwoman.

After hanging up, the phone rings again. I feel a tiny dart of excitement. Maybe it's Gaz.

It's Tash, asking how we'd got on. Her voice turns urgent and whiny. She didn't want to tell me in the pub, spoil the atmosphere. She'd overheard the secretary talking to her husband on the phone at work while she was mopping up a coffee spill in the corridor. She wanted to warn me. At least one of us was going to be made redundant before the next financial year.

'That's if the company doesn't go under before then – or Pete doesn't have a frickin' heart attack from all the stress,' she says.

I click the phone off with a sturdy sigh. I don't need the job as desperately as the others; not financially, at least. I should go. Redundancy could be the kick up the arse I need. But it all seems so overwhelming – everything in a state of flux.

Under the full pelt of the monsoon shower, I reflect on Sunny's words and my parting shot: '*I have a right to get on with my life.*' Trouble was, I wasn't convinced I believed it. I was desperate to feel an overpowering force pulling me forwards. Yet while Dan was in this third state – or 'suspended' as cryonicists called it – it felt as if my life was the same.

Everyone seemed convinced I shouldn't be going it alone. But maybe Sunny was right – I should sign up to join my husband in the freezer in Arizona when I die and share his hope that science will come up with a cure for whatever ailments put us there, so we can be revived – a sort of *Carrie and Dan Part 2*. Did I owe it to Dan? Would it ease my conscience? Yet I was pretty sure I couldn't. Besides, what Sunny seemed to be forgetting was that if I died in my seventies or eighties, I'd be coming back to life as Dan's mum.

Sunny looked shocked when I'd yelled that it was nearly two years since Dan's departure. So was I, saying it out loud. I tot it up: 22 months, 19 days – that was two Valentine's Days and three of his favourite *History of Britain* series.

Some days it seemed that long; others, so much less, grief regaining its tight grip. Sorrow had created huge holes in me, deep craters that I worked so hard to fill. Yet one comment, or bad experience, even a thought or memory, could open them right back up.

I settle on the chaise, trying to inhale a comforting waft of cinnamon from the scented oil diffuser and chastising myself for drinking too much. I consider the morning mantras Sunny coaxed me to recite when the wounds of grief were raw, when I'd try almost anything in the hope of some respite from the negative voices throwing words around my head, the crippling fear for the future that stopped me functioning. Each day, Sunny thought of three things in her life to be grateful for and proclaimed them, over and over – writing them down if she needed a more potent affirmation. I'd be struggling this morning. Did my three cups of strong coffee count?

I grab the bulky beige cushion from Dan's armchair, tucking it behind me. I need all the lumbar support I can get. I still call it Dan's chair. He bought it after complaining computer work was giving him back problems, though I was convinced over-exercising was to blame. It still smelled of Dan. No one ever sat on it. Even visitors seemed to sense something.

Ruling out mantras, I email Sheena instead – always a release. I'd found Sheena, or *She67,* on an online forum for those coping with loss, not long after I'd attended the first – and only – group counselling session. We were soon corresponding regularly, sharing our grief, both of us surprised at how effortless, and cathartic, we found it to open up to each other, revelations and thoughts occasionally spewing across cyberspace that even our nearest and dearest weren't privy to. I no longer had to constantly burden family and friends with my widow woes, hear their pitying tones, force them to keep refilling the sympathy dispenser. We could talk about normal, everyday things again.

What Sheena gave me beat all the other help and advice about coping. There was an unexpected affinity between us. Despite our distance as computer acquaintances, she felt inexplicably close. Her situation was unthinkable – her husband missing for months; presumed dead (by everyone except Sheena, it seemed) – yet similar in some respects. Everyone else I'd chatted to online had loved ones dead and buried, past relationships laid to rest. But '*She67*' lived with relentless uncertainty.

In her last message, she'd shared her fear that the police had all but given up their search. She wondered about taking her girls to the coast for a few days. They all needed a break. But she was torn. What if her husband returned to an empty house? I asked her if she'd been away; how she was feeling. I told her about my date, and the redundancy threat at work.

Later, after dropping Eleanor off at the cinema, I decide to wait around for her. Dragging my hangover across a busy road, desperately seeking the relative solitude of a back-street café and keen to avoid the fine drizzle and madness and mayhem of Saturday shoppers, I notice a woman with a pram stopped in the middle of the pavement ahead. Clearly exhausted, she's gripping her sides. A huge bump bulges beneath an unzipped padded coat that reaches her knees. Then the pram tips, a carrier slipping off the handle, its contents emptying on to the damp ground.

Moving closer, I catch sight of a familiar face. It's Kirsten, Dan's old secretary. Pregnant – again; it must be her fifth. I want to rush to her aid – she can barely bend – but, to my shame, I step aside to plough on, in no mood for a chat, happy that someone else obliges, another young woman stopping to help scoop up the items.

Seeing Kirsten again, so unexpectedly, feels so strange. It's a potent reminder of a past life, like picking up a thread leading back to a different Dan: Daytime Dan – the one I rarely saw – the businessman and boss, perfectly groomed and gorgeous in his dark tailored suits and pastel shirts.

Eleanor's friend Freya is meeting her cousin after the film, but we offer Bethany a lift.

'I'll come and say hi to your mum – I haven't spoken to her in ages. I'm assuming she's in,' I say, climbing out the car.

'OK.' Bethany's cute baby face flushes a little.

'Bye, B.' Eleanor looks up from her phone. She clearly has no intention of moving from the back seat.

As Bethany rings the doorbell, I spot her mum, Ruth, in profile at the window, her short grey hair hooked behind a tiny ear. We wait.

'I think she's upstairs,' I say, though she's no longer in view.

'She might be resting – I've got a key.' Bethany looks a touch flustered as she scrabbles in her denim bag. She pulls out a keyring, a huge, sparkly letter 'B' and chunky silver cross dangling as she turns the key. 'Thanks for the lift.' She steps in without looking back, shutting the door behind her promptly.

Back at home, Eleanor and I meet our regular food delivery driver, a friendly chap with a lazy eye and hands so huge he can hook five full carriers over each one, whistling a high-spirited tune in the porch.

'I thought you'd be on your way, madam,' he says with a playful smile, just the one eye on me as always.

'Sorry – it slipped my mind.'

'Again,' Eleanor mutters, dashing up the stairs in a blur.

In the kitchen, I stare with dismay at the abstract arrangement of green bags. I hate putting shopping away even more these days. I still hear Dan's words in my head often – '*I want to be frozen when I pass*' – chasing away the reassuringly mundane everyday thoughts like 'should I cook or will it be a ready meal again?' and inducing a restlessness that lingers.

He stopped using the word 'die'. For him, it was a pause. Yet I often wish I could press rewind, go back in time and delete that moment. Things seemed to change after; or was it before?

I know it's stupid, but I sometimes wonder if planning his death had somehow made it happen.

I feel a strong grip of guilt as Eleanor's favourite frozen burgers, with a piri-piri glaze, head for the freezer. I imagine Dan frowning at me: '*Tut, tut, junk food*'.

'*But she's thirteen – she loves them*,' my conscience proclaims. *Silly me – Dan's not watching. He's not here. He doesn't know, does he?*

The fridge freezer's still Dan's in my mind. We'd called it Mitsy. He'd been so excited about getting a huge, American-style one. 'I've found her,' he'd declared, shoving a shiny Mitsubishi brochure under my nose, tongue tucked firmly in his dimpled cheek. 'Look, she's got different zones, humidity drawers and an anti-bacterial lining. And she makes ice cubes.' He'd always called his sports cars 'her' and 'she' but never something without a pulse or engine. He was genuinely excited, though he pretended he was exaggerating his pleasure for comic effect. 'An impressive CV,' I'd said, scanning the fridge's extensive features list. 'But can she peel potatoes or zap cellulite?' We'd both chuckled, him with a despairing shake of the head.

I rearrange a few items, desperate to make space, but the drawer won't shut. I give it a gratuitous kick, wincing as I catch my sore toe on some protruding plastic cracked from a previous blow. I'm angry with myself – that everything's still in such disarray without Dan. Dan the foreman. He steered through life the way he drove his beloved sports cars, the route all mapped out, every detail and possible deviation anticipated, mind totally focussed, both hands firmly on the wheel; in complete control. Yet even Dan couldn't negate for the dead end – the no through road that wasn't on his life's map.

★★★

Next day, Eleanor's indulging in one of her weekend lie-ins.

'Get your lazy bum out of bed, you'll be late for school,' I yell from the landing. It's a Sunday, but I never tire of that joke.

The phone rings. More disappointment. It's not Gaz. It's the leader of the school fundraising group; there's a meeting the following week and she wonders if I'd be able to produce a flyer for the next fayre.

'Sure. I can't make tray bakes that will have the mums dribbling into their M&S knickers like Imogen did, but I think I can knock up a hand-out.'

'That's great – you're a star. So we might see you next week then?'

'I'll try,' I say.

I'd been badgered to lend a hand at various events over the years, but this was the first request I'd had since Dan died. I got the impression members of the cash-raising committee weren't the only people who'd decided it was time my mourning veil was lifted. Before, it felt like I was wearing a sign around my neck – *'Warning: Widow – Handle With Care'* – everyone keeping their distance or treating me with extreme delicacy. Nobody wanted to be the one to cause me to shatter and witness the mess, or pick up the pieces.

'Why do you do that? You're so not funny. It's Sunday.' I jump at the sight of a dishevelled Eleanor at my bedroom door. She marches to the mirror. 'Aarrgh! I need my fringe cut. Jeez, I look such a mess. And my skin's so bad.'

'How about a trip to town? We could get you a new school bag, have lunch.' I'm desperate for some comfort food, some proper mashed potato. I've recently resorted to ready mash – my guilty secret; aka *Eazy Spudz for Lazy Cowz*. It's not the same.

'We could do.' Eleanor's breath leaves condensation as she does her usual close-up check for spots.

'Don't sound so enthusiastic.'

'Can we go to the Chinese all-you-can-eat – their spring rolls are amazing?'

'Eleanor, it's a Sunday. Don't be such a heathen.'

'A what?'

'Never mind. Go on then.'

★★★

'Freya's nan is ill, so she's not going to theirs for lunch. Please can she come with us – she proper loves Chinese,' Eleanor pleads as we amble out of the shopping arcade.

'I suppose so.' I'm such a pushover. The idea was

48

to spend quality time with my daughter outside the increasingly hostile home environment.

Of course, it's my fault she can't find the perfect bag. 'You're not helping,' she snaps in the sports store, when, with my patience fully tested, I wander off.

'You don't want my help. I'm too ancient to have an opinion,' I tease.

Back outside, I spot Bethany and her mum walking past in a bustle of pedestrians. Convinced Ruth has caught my eye, I wave – but they hurry on, seemingly oblivious.

'Bethany and her mum just passed,' I tell Eleanor, who's in a teenage trance, gazing at the Barbour-coated models in a shop window. 'I don't think they saw us.' She shrugs.

Later, with Eleanor's mission finally accomplished and her mood temporarily lifted by food – and Freya – I drag the girls into a few of my favourite stores. But then Eleanor announces there's no way she can walk home, her new shoes are agony.

'I'll actually die if I walk another step.' I think she has a taxi in mind, and looks horrified as we climb on the bus with our bulging bags.

Imogen calls again that evening. She's trying out a new cassoulet recipe, waiting for her beans to blanch. She wonders if Gaz has called, if I've called him. I deliver a double no.

'Still – early days.' I detect a thread of desperation in Imogen's voice. I hear one of her girls giggling in the background. 'That's Laura with her new joke book.' The laughter gets louder. 'Not now, Laura ... one minute, Carrie.'

While Imogen has a quiet word with her daughter, I think back to how much I loved my collection of kids' joke books. 'How do you make an apple puff?' I'd ask Mum. 'Chase it round the kitchen!' She'd laugh the first time, next a strained smile, then exasperation. Dad fared better, always giving me an encouraging chuckle or 'boom boom'. I'd often crack a joke after Mum and Dad rowed. 'There's a time and a place,' Mum would chide sternly. Yet it seemed perfect timing. Mum got so tired of the same gags I invented an imaginary friend, Miss Giggles, to tell them to. She always roared – once or twice she'd even wet herself. I read jokes, in secret, on the loo if Mum was in a mood. I'd passed a few books on to Eleanor, but she'd never loved them like I did. And I was distraught when my favourite one got ruined – another victim of her tonsillitis. I'd found it under her duvet, its lime-green cover and a clump of dog-eared pages soaked in sick. Ironically, I used to love the book's mustardy scent. It was no longer in print.

'Sorry about that,' Imogen says. 'Laura's desperate for me to share her news. She's going to be Mary in the Year 1 nativity.'

'Wow. That's brilliant. She's a star.'

Imogen promises a video. She knows I'll be desperate to see it. While most parents of older children thanked God and all that's holy they no longer had to sit in draughty halls and churches watching strung out and stilted manger scenes – however cute the kids – I couldn't get enough of them. All because of Ashley; my Joseph.

'By the way, more news – Ben's decided to get in touch with his real mum.'

'Really?' He'd previously refused, even though Imogen had used a professional service to trace her. She suspected he feared rejection, though Ben vehemently denied it – he was just happy with things the way they were.

'Yes, he feels the time's right – now his adoptive mum's passed. He needs to know the truth, why she gave him away, however painful that may be.'

'That's brave – I hope it works out for him.'

After our farewells, I can't shift Imogen's words from my head. Perhaps now my life's changed, the time's right for me to face a truth I've been evading; however much it might hurt.

I have a strong urge to look out my old school photograph. Ten minutes later – the contents of my white chest scrambled, several items flung to the floor as if by a frenzied burglar – and I've unearthed it: my tatty snakeskin purse buried under old cosmetics and other bits of junk in its disordered depths.

I slide out the photo, careful not to inflict more damage. It's faded now, a tear roughly sellotaped down the middle. I'd ripped the photo in anger but, unable to throw it away, had bodged a repair years later.

I hold the image close. It's hard to believe it was thirty-five years ago. He's there, centre stage; my Joseph – the heavenly Ashley Baird all draped in white.

'Hold hands!' one of the many proud mums brandishing a hefty camera had demanded as we posed for post-performance pictures. We'd been too scared to refuse. One of the wise men, Nick somebody, was stood on my other side, crotch stinking of cottage cheese. I did whatever it took not to sit by him in class. But it didn't matter that day. I was too excited to breathe in properly anyway. Mum had made my Mary costume out of a pale blue sheet from a C&A sale and the belt from her spare dressing gown.

Eleanor startles me. She's holding up her new bag, various adornments already hanging from it; among them a diamante dog and the lucky amber charm from Sunny.

'Nice,' I say, smiling. 'You'll be jangling into school.' About to flounce out, curiosity drags Eleanor's grouchy face to the bed.

'Oh, the Mary photo. Memories,' she says, with a mocking sigh. It's a shame her own school nativity didn't evoke such happy recollections. She'd been an angel, looking all calm, bright and ethereal on stage until one of the shepherds snagged his crook on her sparkly gold wings, pulling them clean off and getting a rapturous round of applause that made both children cry in unison.

'Imogen's just told me Laura's Mary in her school nativity.'

'Aw, sweet.' Eleanor moves closer. 'It's kind of rubbish – blurred and stuff. Who took it?'

'Grandma. Cameras weren't as good back then.'

'Yeah, like, a hundred years ago!'

I can't begin to explain how special the photo was. How the quality didn't matter. How the picture, along with some of the finer details of that day, may be blurred but the feelings had the sharpness of a million pixels in my memory. That nativity had ignited a love of the stage that had never faded.

Yet the event was marred, just like the photo; spoiled by what came after. Ashley had left me with scars that I thought had healed.

I slip the photo back into the purse, my smile streaked with sadness.

CHAPTER 5

'Put that rat back and go and let Grandma and Granddad in,' I instruct Eleanor, dodging scowls as I dart around her room bundling clothes and make-up into drawers and cupboards.

Despite promising a brief visit – on their way to see friends – Mum would surely make time for one of her inspections, so she could wonder all over again at how slovenly her only daughter had become, how her 'neat and orderly' gene had skipped a generation.

'Hamster,' Eleanor corrects, with a frown, landing Pepsi a kiss on his furry head as she eases him through the cage door. I'd insisted she clean the cage in honour of Grandma, who found the very thought of a rodent in a bedroom so abhorrent it triggered one of her flushes. Like me, Eleanor longed for a dog, but Dan was never keen and I had to concede it probably wasn't practical. Pepsi was the compromise.

I kick several shoes under the bed and peer through the window. Dad's new blue Honda shimmers on the drive and I can see Mum's navy handbag poking out of the porch.

I'd definitely inherited Mum's penchant for curtains, I think, gathering them into the tiebacks as I gather my composure. I suspect it's the association with stages for me – the excitement of what unfolds behind and between them. I prefer them in rich fabrics, but plain and unfussy. Mum, on the other hand loved patterns, a pelmet and swag. I'm convinced she judges a woman by her drapes. 'I think she'd sooner be seen with her knickers off than not have her windows properly dressed,' I'd said to Dad one day, out of her earshot as she fussed over a new pair in the dining room. 'Hell will freeze over before either happens,' he'd quipped, wiggling his dense eyebrows.

'I hope we haven't spoiled any plans,' Mum says, greeting me in the living room, dressed like an aunt at a wedding in a blue floral dress with a navy jacket and matching shoes. Her bouffant hair looks newly permed; not a strand has escaped the Elnett assault.

'Not at all. It's great to see you,' I say, giving her a hug.

'Ooh, it still smells of Christmas in here… cinnamon… lovely.' She sniffs the air. Eleanor catches my eye, desperate not to laugh. Mum says that virtually every time she visits.

'Cinnamon's for life, not just for Christmas,' I joke.

Mum ignores me. 'When your dad looked at the route to our friends' new house in Stoke, it seemed a shame not to pop in.' Dad's arm's draped around Eleanor. He nods, with a goofy smile. 'I say "house",' Mum continues, undoing her jacket. 'It's one of those park homes. Goodness knows how they can live in one of those – after having a four-bedroomed place. But each to their own.'

I shrug. 'How you feeling, Dad?'

'Fighting fit.' He releases Eleanor to do a boxer pose, calloused knuckles protruding from fists held tight in front of his contagiously cheery face. And he looks it, still

54

wiry and dapper for a man in his mid seventies, with an impressive head of bouncy, two-tone silver hair.

'Well, I wouldn't say that,' Mum says. Eleanor and I can't suppress smiles as Dad pulls an overly glum face.

It isn't long before Dad comes up with an excuse to hijack Eleanor – he needs a techno teen's help to operate the music system in the new car – and Mum seizes the opportunity to talk about his health.

Dad has 'unstable angina'. I remember when Mum first told me. We were in her gleaming kitchen, choking on Cif fumes. Mum wasn't one for displays of emotion, and I cried when I saw her welling up, assuming the worst. Although my parents bickered a lot, they'd be lost without each other. And the thought of losing either of them was one I couldn't contemplate. But typical Dad – he'd waltzed in, dismissing the 'drama' and declaring that a few blood pressure pills and half an aspirin each day would keep it at bay.

'Your dad insisted I was making a fuss, but I knew the tablets were upsetting his stomach, Carolina,' Mum says, shadowing me as I make drinks. I still wince when she uses my full name, which she insists on doing every so often, as if to remind me. Mum wanted me to have a name with substance. She'd always considered her own, Yvonne, a little inadequate. So I got four syllables. However, I decided Carolina was far too prim for a little tomboy who collected snails in a bucket behind the shed and put bogies under her microscope, and – to Mum's horror – I shortened it.

'Dr Mills eventually agreed to change them – I had to be quite insistent – and he felt better almost immediately,' Mum adds proudly.

'That's good,' I say, finding myself arranging chocolate biscuits on a plate in Mum's honour.

Later, with Dad, as always, keen to tidy the back garden for me, my suggestion that Mum help Eleanor to make a Victoria sponge for school is favourably received.

'Well, I must have made several dozen over the years,' Mum declares. 'Has to be real cream – none of that UHT nonsense.'

While Mum and Eleanor walk to the shop – the jam they unearth at the back of one of Mitsy's shelves has grown an impressive mould – Dad appears at the french windows, secateurs in hand, asking if he can be cheeky and check the sports news. He winks: 'While your mum's not here.' He's still watching TV when I return from the kitchen.

'That guy puts me in mind of Ashley … you know …' Dad falters, shifting his weight in the chair.

I catch a side-on glimpse of a man with shoulder-length fair hair before he disappears from the screen. It's a good job Mum's not there. Ashley's name's a close second to Nigella on her hate list, and only just above bacteria.

'I suppose you heard about his accident?' Dad's eyes avoid mine.

'No.' I sit on the arm of the sofa for support.

'Yes, some stage equipment fell on him. Very badly injured by all accounts.'

'You sure it was him, Dad?' My heart pounds on my ribs. How had I missed that?

'Yes. It was in all our local papers – and the *Standard*.'

I really don't know how I feel, but I bet Mum's so pleased.

'Still up for a shopping trip next weekend?' I ask Tash on the phone. 'I need your help to choose a dress for the ball.'

'Hell, yeah. We could meet after I get my acrylics done.'

I've passed on previous shopping invites, fearing it would be too crazy an experience. But I can't stand another Saturday in which the highlight is watching Mum gloat while Eleanor proudly pulls a Victoria sponge from the oven as if seeing and smelling something freshly baked in our kitchen's a miracle akin to turning water into wine.

I'm slumped on the sofa eating toast, computer on my lap, lost in thoughts of what Dad told me the previous day when the chain of coincidences really dawns on me. First, the compulsion to re-read the letter I'd kept hidden for years, then Imogen's reference to Ashley, after years of honouring my taboo on any utterances of his name (unless suitably inebriated); leaving it firmly stamped into the mud. Then there was the resonance of her words about Ben contacting his mum, his need to 'know the truth'. And Dad's revelation.

It only takes a few keyboard clicks before I'm immersed in information about Ashley's accident. It was six months ago at a Reading theatre during a final rehearsal for a contemporary production; him and two fellow actors struck by some suspended staging. His injuries were clearly serious; he'd undergone several big operations. I think of Mum. No doubt she'd wished the equipment had been heavier. Clearly, she'd thought better of telling me.

I phone Sunny. It's a fortnight since my outburst and I'm keen to apologise. Although Imogen's adamant I've got nothing to be sorry for, should have 'given it to her with both barrels', my moral compass is guiding me in that direction; it's the right thing to do. I hate getting outwardly cross with people – even those well deserving of my wrath – fearful of upsetting them; and myself. Confrontation's even more challenging with Sunny, always so seemingly calm, hushed voice stroking her words, rounding the edges so they can't possibly be deemed negative or hurtful. Besides, she's not a bad person, I tell myself often. I shouldn't focus on her faults and foibles. She meant so much to Dan. 'I had to be her father and big brother when Dad was busy being a hippy, getting high on pot and pale ale,' he'd told me during one of his 'why was I lumbered with such liberal parents?' moments.

Yet, though I hear the apology in my head, I can't deliver it to my tongue. I end up telling Sunny I've got some cyclamen plants for her – a kind of implied peace offering.

'Super. I'll come over this morning then, if you don't mind,' she says.

It's not long before I hear the knock – an extended version, with extra taps. I wonder if it's some kind of Morse code, summoning evil spirits to punish me for evading my dead husband's wish.

After taking a deep breath that lasts the length of the landing, I'm forced to do one of her slow-motion blinks when, still in my PJs, I open the front door to Sunny. Winter sun and a very loud, tiered 'flower power' dress both scream at me.

'Hi, sweetie. Lovely to see you.' If Sunny's feeling any animosity it's well concealed, as always. She's on her way to the care home and thought she could take the plants. 'I'm going in early today – taking my violin – as Mick hasn't had many visitors this week, poor thing.' Her eyes slide slowly across my face.

Despite her delicate fingers, no one can press my guilt button as firmly as Sunny, I think, as we carry the plants to her car. She visited her dad almost every day, while Eleanor and I seldom went. Sadly, Mick had suffered several strokes, the latest leaving him unable to speak. It's why Sunny had stayed in Tetford. She hated stopping in one place for long, travelling for most of her adult life. (*'Travelling's so good for the soul, Carrie.'*)

I should visit Mick more. But things were strained between Dan and his dad – especially since his mum, Mary, had died – so we've never been close.

As Sunny squeezes the pots into the minuscule boot of her daffodil yellow Micra, I squint at the sun, checking no one's around to see me in my night attire.

'Mick will really appreciate these,' Sunny says. I smile. I still find it odd that she calls her dad by his name. Dan maintained it was the 'New Age thing'; she'd done it since her teens.

Eleanor greets us in the kitchen. 'I bought you a friendship bracelet, sweetness,' Sunny says, releasing her niece from a hug to rummage in the depths of her enormous patchwork bag. I'd love to see what's in there, apart from the natural potions, but it rarely leaves her side and she gets jumpy if anyone goes near it. I imagine a voodoo doll of me in there, or a stash of contraband goods: chocolate, Paracetemol,

Prozac, a Rampant Rabbit perhaps. 'A partially-sighted lady makes them in the flea market. Isn't it pretty?'

'Aww. I love these.' Eleanor holds the turquoise threads next to her scoop-necked top, the tight fit highlighting her newly-developed chest. 'Sweet, it matches.'

I whizz off to get dressed, returning to find Sunny in her favourite spot by the french windows. She often heads there, staring dreamily at the crab apple tree she adores. Unusually, she's put down her bag. On Dan's armchair. It's strange to see it there.

'I see your winter jasmine's flowering. Doesn't it look beautiful?'

I nod, unsure which one it is. As Sunny turns, she's distracted by something on the sideboard. I anxiously track her eyes to the newspaper article I'd printed out earlier and stupidly left there.

'Gosh. Is that someone you know?' Sunny's obviously read the headline – in huge print: 'ACTOR CRUSHED BY FALLING SET'

She blinks slowly, hazel eyes fixed on me.

'Yes, an old friend,' I say, dismissively. 'Went to the same primary.'

'That's awful.' She picks up the cutting, studies it. 'Gosh. Multiple fractures. Did he have any head injuries, I wonder?'

'I don't think so.' Yet if he had, Sunny would surely have a magic cream for them in her bag: '*It's totally natural, of course; rub it on that bruised brain tissue and those neurons will be firing like a Kalashnikov in no time.*'

Sunny leaves soon after, the rest of the day's tediously uneventful and, after tea, Eleanor and I go our separate ways, as we often do. I feel pretty dispensable, verging on invisible, in the evenings and most weekends. And the living room feels empty, the walls too distant, time too slow. Eleanor prefers to do her own thing, and firmly resists homework help, though I suspect I should be more insistent. Dan would be. But then she'd always accepted his assistance more readily than mine. I'd often felt she opened up to her dad more, too, though he'd assured me otherwise. I recall the time he'd tried to explain his cryonics decision. They were cuddled on the corner sofa, Dan stroking Eleanor's soft hand with his firm thumb. 'I think she understands,' he'd said after. 'She didn't say much.' I'm not sure what he'd expected of a nine-year-old.

As I search out a cake tin, my mind drifts back to Eleanor's pre-school days. I often felt like the baddie, the one who coaxed her to eat broccoli and tidy toys, or talked her out of watching *Jungle Book* for the twentieth time, and dealt with the ensuing strops. Dan would breeze in at about seven, just in time for the nice bits. 'Daddy, Daddy, can you read me a story, please, please, really big please?' Eleanor would race down the hall, limbs flailing and breathless with excitement, eliminating me from her radar. He'd scoop her up in his arms, a smile engulfing his whole face and a sigh of relief that he was home, at last, with his little princess. He'd lean over to kiss me tenderly; always ask about our day. And I'd usually get a remark about how lovely I looked – even when I was covered in crayon and chicken casserole. He was so patient; a doting dad, an attentive husband. I'd hear his voice, then Eleanor's excited interruptions – both snuggled on her bed, reading a story – as I picked up scattered dolls, her favourite jumbo pens and all the other mess we'd accumulated and stacked it in corners. I knew Dan would tidy it again later. We'd have a glass of wine and a chat while one or both prepared our meal. The evenings flew by.

Bored, I settle on the chaise to read Katie Strutt's column in my favourite women's magazine. Always a pick-me-up. There's an appeal for articles on dating experiences – a painful reminder that Gaz hasn't called; and of the previous, disastrous date. I'm tempted. I've tried writing a few things over the years. Most are tucked away, reserved for my own entertainment. I only showed one or two to Dan – whipping them away dismissively before his eyes had cast down the whole page – and rarely talked about my writing aspirations. I think he assumed it was just a hobby. I'd always thought he was right.

Once Imogen persuaded me to send off an article I'd written about competitive mums at the school gate, but several commissioning editors rejected it. I'd shared my dismay with Mark at work. 'You can't give up after one shot,' he'd urged. 'It takes persistence.' 'No', I'd told him, and convinced myself, 'presenting pitches to boring businessmen for Cullimore's is my calling'. That's what I was good at. Though maybe not for much longer.

I fetch a glass of wine and load Facebook. It's ages since Eleanor helped me create an account and post messages. I'd only sent a couple, but enjoyed searching out old friends. I'd looked up Ashley. Of course. He was the first one. I'd felt anxious, guiltily guarding the screen like an errant child, in case Dan should appear behind me; wondering if the cyber gods were watching in dismay.

Back then, Ashley hadn't posted anything. And there was no personal information – just his name alongside a photo of a little boy with messy blond hair, face painted like a lion; Ashley's young son, I'd assumed. All I'd gleaned was that he was still alive, that the many appeals for him to 'drop dead' I'd uttered in anguish two decades ago had not been fulfilled.

Locating Ashley's profile again, I find myself staring at a stream of 'get well' wishes. Clearly, not everyone harboured the hatred for him that I did. He'd replied, very briefly, to one or two. He was obviously on the mend.

A slurp of wine seems to trigger a blast of blood to the head. I can't stop myself, hitting the 'Add Friend' button. Butterflies tickle my ribs, their wings powering a wave of panic. Making contact – even now – is far more than he deserves. It's insane. Where's the resolve I'd shown when he'd tried to contact me previously?

I must have been about twenty-seven the first time, because Dan and I were still in our flat-pack flat, surrounded by all things Ikea. Ashley had somehow tracked me down through a friend of a friend. He'd sent a brief note, from an address in Fulham – he wondered how I was, would like to hear from me. Nothing more. I'd been tempted to reply, but resisted, tearing the note into tiny pieces. The second time (via an online friend tracking site), just after Eleanor was born, I'd given it more thought. I was at home all day, craving stimulation, senses dulled by the monotony of the nursing-nappy-nap-nipple cream routine. But I was afraid of discovering the truth, stirring up old pain, my curiosity not a match for the power of my grievance. Besides, what if Dan found out? I'd printed out

Ashley's e-message, to re-read, but, fortunately, Eleanor had projectile-vomited on it, bringing me to my senses.

I head to the kitchen, returning with more wine and extra courage. I'm going to send a message. It takes me ages to assemble the words. Eventually I settle on:

Hi. Heard about the accident – belatedly. Hope you're recovering well. Best wishes. Carrie

No kisses, no questions. I'd made it easy for Ashley to ignore.

I take a huge gulp of wine, pulse thumping; a strong, tribal beat. I shouldn't have sent it. I'm scared, yet foolishly excited.

I feel like I'm eleven again, after putting the mysterious '*C LOVES A*' note in Ashley's school drawer. Back then, I hadn't thought it through either. Mine was the only girl's name in Class 6R that began with a 'C'. *Miss Silly Socks! Yes Dan, I was even ditsy back then.*

CHAPTER 6

'So – our creativity, editorial excellence and expertise at Cullimore Corporate Communications will ensure your messages are delivered to clients with finesse and flair.' I clasp my clammy hands, taking my first proper breath for five, nerve-wracking minutes.

Scanning along the row of grey-suited men, all sat on the boss Pete's budget high-backed boardroom chairs, I'm relieved to note the smiles. There's even a flicker on Pete's face. His brows had been locked in a stern stare as I stood next to the white screen, legs planted as wide as my pencil skirt allowed, delivering the all-important pitch, just the odd tip of a supportive nod breaking his icy stillness.

'Great. Thanks, Carrie.' Pete slides a shaky hand across his bald head, eyes softening behind his rimless glasses.

The three men from Lorex, a medical and veterinary equipment supplier, nod and make pleasing noises. 'Well done,' one says at last, while the others shuffle paper, mumbling to each other. I switch off the equipment, scoop up my cue card.

'Tell Tash we're ready for coffee.' Pete stands, giving his testicles a quick but firm tweak through his trousers. I wince inwardly, as always, offering a damp palm to the trio before bowing out.

Back in the main office, I almost trip over the anticipation that greets me. Mark turns sharply on his swivel chair, hands clapped on his thick thighs, and Tash leaps up from her desk. Even Barbara has paid a rare visit from reception. She swipes off her glasses, letting them tumble on their gold chain towards her low chest, eyebrows raised and expectant.

'And?' Tash prompts.

'Did you balls it up, then?' Mark pulls a sardonic smile, pale green eyes wide with enquiry.

'A few stumbles, but I think it went pretty well. Thank God that's over.' Relief hits me in a sudden swell. The last three months had been difficult, Christmas and New Year passing in an anxious blur, preparation for the pitch constantly on my mind. I can't believe it's February already.

'Did Pete seem pleased?' Barbara asks in her cut-glass accent, hands on her heavy hips.

'I think so. He nearly smiled.' Barbara flashes a good-humoured frown, pushing a few strands of prim grey hair from her face. She's Pete's fiercely loyal and long-standing friend, so we rarely mock him in her presence.

'Well done, babe.' Tash claps excitedly.

'Thanks. He's requested coffee now.'

'I'm on it,' she says, neon-blue slingbacks scuttling off to the kitchen.

We call it the kitchen, though the title's far too grand. It's a windowless, glorified cupboard with one length of chipped worktop, a stained sink and a noisy fridge that smells of sick and is invariably empty but for a pint of milk and Barbara's plain yoghurt. Visitors are forbidden

66

to enter. So, as the most glamorous, Tash gets coffee duty, despite the fact she rarely reaches the boardroom without spillage or other mishap. Barbara's a great secretary but curt efficiency and cushioned shoes all the way.

'Let's hope we've done enough to impress,' Barbara says, heading through the door to reception, where she sits, like a minor royal, behind a huge glass desk, in a haze of polish and lily of the valley. The rest of us are the servants, tucked away in a square, dowdy space full of beige, beech and bulging box files.

When I'd agreed to deliver my first pitch, as a keen but green editorial assistant fresh from the local poly, I didn't envisage doing them twenty years later. The job was supposed to be temporary – I'd done unpaid work at Cullimore's during my final year and taken up Pete's offer of a short contract after graduating – while I decided what I really wanted to do. But I fell for Dan – a friend of Pete's son and working there to gain business experience – and stayed. Some days, I couldn't believe I was still there. There was only one filing cabinet that had served longer, with huge dents and runners that jammed – clearly ready to be decommissioned.

'You can relax now.' Mark interrupts my reflections. 'I've never known you get so worked up.'

'Well, Pete certainly piled on the bloody pressure, didn't he – all that talk about it being the biggest contract ever and desperately needing it? Talk about a biggie.'

'I hope you've done enough then.' Mark waves a finger in jest, head cocked. 'Or I'll be joining the travellers camped in my local field and living on economy beans.'

'Stop it!'

Although the redundancy threat appeared to have been postponed thanks to the graphic designer offering to work part-time on a freelance basis, we'd all had pay cuts and things didn't look good. I hadn't seen Pete this stressed since the council threatened to knock down our office complex and move us – and the other four businesses – to an out-of-town site a few years ago. It caused a huge furore, protestors declaring it another grievous assault on a terminally ill town. Pete was convinced the business wouldn't thrive there.

The only consolation of the cutbacks was that Mark, a trained journalist and brains of the outfit, was now the only writer, and editor, forcing Pete to occasionally let me loose on a few articles, albeit the 'lite' ones.

Pete's unrelenting pessimism aside, it seemed the company's survival really was in doubt this time. Barbara had a disabled husband to support and Tash had a big rent and even bigger personal maintenance expenses. I was particularly worried for Mark. He was still recovering from an expensive divorce, while his ex-wife refused to make spending cuts. Mark feared he may have to sacrifice seeing so much of his young son Jack if he was forced to relocate for a job back on newspapers.

'Seriously, I reckon the Lorex lads are signing on the dotted line as we speak.' Mark's muscular voice is muted by a chewy mint.

Tash totters in with a mug. 'You so deserve this, babe. And … wait for it …' She pulls her other hand from behind her back. 'Ta-dah!' It was one of Pete's posh gold-wrapped chocolate biscuits, reserved for clients.

'Thanks. Don't mind if I do.'

'Where's mine?' Mark asks.

'What about the flab?' Tash flashes a cheeky grin.

'It's shrinking.' Mark pulls his checked shirt tight over his belly, breathing in.

'You sure?' Tash grabs at his midriff.

'Cheeky cow.'

Tash giggles her way back to the kitchen, returning with a tray of coffees. 'Shall I lean over and flash the twins. It might help?' She lets out a guffaw as she leaves. Tash claimed her boobs were identical, disproving the theory that all women had asymmetrical ones. She had no scientific evidence, just a long list of men happy to take part in her unofficial survey.

'You didn't go for the whole cleavage thing then?' Mark nods to my cream blouse, buttoned to the top.

'No, I'm not that shallow. I wanted to wow them with my experience, charisma and our businesses credentials.'

'That's well and good, but a bit of tit goes a long way. And you've only got a bit—'

'Don't you dare, you rude bugger.' I lob a pen, hitting his chair as he spins.

Mark never fails to make me laugh – even in times of tension. He's become a great friend. Dan got on really well with him too. They shared a passion for flash cars and repetitive sixties music with jangly guitars.

I tuck my notes into a box file, slump in the chair and gaze out the window. The little old man with flyaway hair and a khaki anorak two sizes too big is sat on the bench beneath our office. He's there often, sometimes for hours, staring into the distance. I wonder if he's tapped.

Mark's phone rings. It's a client he's been chasing to interview. Crafty online activity's more hazardous now my desk's been moved; the screen visible to everyone. Pete's remarkably light-footed and has a nasty habit of appearing from nowhere. But I'm desperate to send a message to Ashley and, with Mark deep in conversation and Pete tied up with the Lorex men, it's the ideal opportunity.

I load Facebook, re-reading our exchanges. It had taken six weeks for Ashley to reply to my first message. I wasn't surprised and chastised myself daily for affording him the satisfaction of making contact, and for being bothered by his lack of response. I made all sorts of excuses for him, some decidedly weak: he was too busy, he rarely used a computer, the accident had affected the use of his hands. I concluded that Ashley clearly didn't want to rake over what had happened. Too much time had passed. I'd missed my chance. As it looked like there'd be no more messages, I wished I'd been more direct, gone straight for the jugular, asked why the hell he'd done it to me.

Then it came. I was eating breakfast, feet soaking in a mini spa, when his reply pinged into my inbox. My breath was snatched clean away, mouth paralysed in front of a slice of toast, as I spotted the little lion boy photo next to Ashley's name. I'd whipped my feet out with such speed and force that I tipped the side of the spa, slopping water over the red rug and turning it cherry. I had to read the message several times:

'Hi Carrie. Shocked to hear from you. Sorry for delay – computer died on me. Yes, on the mend thanks. Not quite the acting fame I wanted! Never want to see a pair of crutches again. Hope things are OK. Where you living? All the best. Ashley

There wasn't even the slightest hint of the grovelling apology I deserved. I was disappointed, allowing the anger to drift back momentarily. But I couldn't help feeling thrilled that he'd replied, at last. Everything inside fluttered in an overwhelming unison. I was nineteen again, the other twenty-three years hadn't happened; anger crushed by unexpected, inappropriate elation. Pathetically, I'd replied straight away:

Ashley, I'm still in Tetford – over 20 years now! Working in corporate communications. Yawn! Are you back on stage? Still in London? Carrie.

I had so many questions, all beginning with 'Why?' and ending with 'you gutless bastard', but I couldn't ask them. Not yet. Though he owed me answers. And an apology. In fact he'd owed me so much, and for so long, I doubted the debt could ever be settled.

After that, I'd checked Facebook several times a day. Nothing. Then, last night, I'd had another message. I was lying on the bed next to Mr Fluff – the evening sunshine lighting up his misshapen midriff – rehearsing my pitch, when it arrived. An internal buzz built to a ludicrous level, pulse thumping as I clicked:

Hi Carrie. That's a long time in Tetford. Great little place, though, don't blame you. Yes, I'm in London and back doing acting work. Also do photography – and a few crappy jobs when I get desperate. Surprised you didn't take up acting. You were great! Ashley x

Still no mention of what I really wanted to know. The massive elephant remained in the ether. I stopped myself replying straight away. It seemed overly eager, desperate perhaps – against the rules of e-messaging etiquette I suspected – and I needed to keep my focus on work.

I hear Mark laugh. He's still on the phone, scribbling shorthand notes. I can't resist. I type. It still feels too

71

daunting to directly ask the question I need the answer to, the one that seems to matter so much again. Instead I write:

Hi. Still in London, lucky you! I miss it, especially the theatres. The Rosehouse here has the odd decent production – probably not on your acting wish list though! Do you have to travel much? I took up am dram a few years ago but it didn't really work out. Did you ever take your driving test again? Hope your family are well. Carrie.

Despite a strong urge to tear into Ashley, I know I have to keep things friendly to keep the thread going. I want to know more about his life, whether he'd got his comeuppance.

Mark startles me with some loud hand-drumming on the desk. He often did this. Summoning his muse, I reckoned. I click off the screen, grab my biscuit.

'Yum. Bet you wish you'd had one?' I tease.

'I'm fine with my sugar-free mints. Anyway, I've got a piece of chocolate fudge cake waiting in my fridge. Actually, I lie, it's double chocolate.'

'You'll have to double the pace on the running machine tonight then.'

'Or just eat half of it.'

I chuckle. Mark had started exercising, joining Tash on her never-ending diet. He'd always kept fit playing rugby, his broad shoulders barging many a big-necked brute on the rugby pitch – hence the big tab of displaced cartilage on his left ear that Tash and I regularly flicked as we passed his desk. But he'd given up his favourite game after his marriage break-up three years ago and gained weight. He'd also turned grey. It was still a shock not to see the big nineties spikes, his hair now short, with a ruffled fringe that clearly got the gel treatment, though he vehemently denied it.

'Before you go, I've got two hundred tickets to sell for this auction, so if any of your rich friends fancy it?'

'Course. I'll ask the millionaires first, then work down.'

Mark was organising a black tie charity event. His younger sister had died of a rare form of brain cancer and he did lots of fundraising. Still several months away, Tash had already sorted us on to a table of six, with herself and whoever she happened to be dating, the graphic designer and his wife, and Mark and me. I was uneasy about it being a 'couples' thing. Sunny had made one of her comments after Mark had taken me out for a Christmas drink, leaving me feeling unusually sensitive. 'Just the two of you?' she'd enquired with wide eyes, after popping by to deliver Eleanor's present (a bag full of ethical make-up). Mark and I were friends. End of.

'Say bye to Tash for me.' I make for the door. 'Surely she can't still be in Pete's office?'

'Probably giving blow jobs.' Mark opens his mouth, pushing out his lips. I flick his ear.

★★★

It's an Eleanor somewhere around eight on the stroppy-ometer I get that evening. I'm stood by Mitsy, investigating the cause of a disgusting smell, when she crashes into the kitchen, chucking her bag with such a thump it sounds as if she's strapped a brick to it.

'Kendrick's given me a detention.' Her kohl-blackened eyes lock mine.

'Oh Eleanor. What for?'

'Wearing too much make-up and … calling Bethany a bitch.' I glare. 'Well, she is.' She yanks off her tie.

'So you deserve the detention. I thought you were friends again.' Eleanor and Bethany had a very on-off friendship. 'What's she done to upset you?'

'Well, right, this guy in our year fancied her and she didn't like him, but then he said he liked me and now she does and she had, like, a proper go at me in the form room – and it was so embarrassing.'

'When will you learn, it's not worth falling out over a boy?' I grab a cloth to attack a sticky stain on the island. 'Anyway, I didn't think Bethany's allowed a boyfriend.' Her mum has some strong beliefs and there's so much Bethany's not permitted to do.

'She's not.'

'It'll work out,' I say calmly.

'It won't. She's been a right—'

'Eleanor!' I want to chastise her, but her lip's quivering and eyes watery. She's clearly hurting badly, not just being cranky.

Bethany had gone to the same primary, they'd known each other for years, but they'd had a massive fallout in Year 5 when Bethany told everyone about Dan's post-death wish. They didn't speak for several months, and their friendship had been volatile ever since. Eleanor had been distraught. She'd arrived home hysterical, saying everyone at school thought her dad was 'weird'. 'That's a stupid, ignorant thing to say, just ignore it,' I'd said, trying to explain what ignorant meant whilst wrapping her in my arms in some vain hope of squeezing out the hurt. 'Your

74

daddy believes science can do some very clever things –
and it can, can't it?' I'd said. 'I don't know. I hate science,'
she'd replied, still sobbing uncontrollably.

Eleanor clashes a glass down on the ivory worktop
and pours a drink. I take a breath from the depths of my
diaphragm. 'Are you sure that's the only thing you're upset
about? You know, if you have a problem, you can always
talk—'

'Yes, for God's sake. How many times do I need to
say? Are you bloody stupid … or deaf or what!' She slams
the bottle down; an eruption of fizzy liquid soaks a pile of
mail.

'Eleanor. That's totally out of order.' I leave the room.
I don't want to lose my temper, make things worse. It's just
her hormones, I assure myself.

I can't do this single mum thing any more. I want you, Dan.
Eleanor needs her dad.

CHAPTER 7

The rip of the Merlot screw top follows the ping of Eleanor's microwave pasta meal by seconds the next evening. It's been a challenging week. I've earned it. I feel bad that we're not eating together – again – but I've planned to go for a drink with Mark and Tash. Besides, Eleanor likes to eat early these days, giving her more time to 'do stuff' – essentially lots of mindless messing with make-up, clothes and gadgets.

She used to do meaningful things like read and practise her clarinet but apparently books are for nerds and blowing a reed's a bigger turn-off for teenage boys than pubic plumage. She launched her fleeting musical career on the flute early in Year 5, swapping to the clarinet. 'Thin lips are better for the flute – you should play it, Mum,' Eleanor had teased, laughing heartily. At first, it sounded as if a donkey had joined her as she honked and squeezed out deformed notes, but recognisable tunes gradually emerged. 'That Yellow Submarine's got an unusual distress call,' Dan had joked once, while we proudly listened from downstairs, willing her to master it. Now the instrument rarely strays from its solid black case, which she often uses as a footrest.

I worry that she's lost her way a little, or rather she's

lost without the more steadfast parental sat nav – her dad – to guide her.

'You're an alcoholic.' Eleanor glares at my glass through lashes laced with mascara as I join her at the table.

'Don't be daft. There's a difference between enjoying a drink and being addicted.'

'Well, you enjoy it a *lot*.'

'It's been a tough week.' She ignores me. 'Do you mind if I pop out for an hour? Me and a few other *alcoholics* from work are meeting up for a post-pitch drink.'

'Fine.'

'Mark's picking me up at seven.'

Eleanor shrugs one shoulder. She's known Mark all her life. I've always imagined he's like a favourite uncle, someone who makes her laugh and might flirt with her mum after too much Cava at a family party. Yet I wonder if her view of him, and all bachelors or divorcees, has changed – how she'd feel if a stranger showed her mum some affection. A topic I lack the pluck to raise.

'Have you decided whether you're going to audition for *Fame*, darling?' Eleanor's drama club's planning to stage the musical.

'For God's sake. You've asked me that, like, a million times. I don't know.'

'What about Freya?'

'Duh! Course.' Eleanor's teacher maintains she has natural flair, but needs more self-belief. It doesn't help that Freya's stunning, with flowing, strawberry blonde hair, and enough confidence to fill the National Theatre.

'I'll have pudding later, yeah?' Eleanor shoves her plate aside and heads out.

As I sip my wine, braced to tackle the chaos in the kitchen, I think about how difficult things have been between us recently. It started in December. A painful awareness of the significance of the month – our second Christmas without Dan – combined with Eleanor's increased moodiness and my bout of winter blues produced some persistent heavy frosts. I tried to make it better. I bought a cracking Christmas, but it wasn't as jolly and bright as it promised on the tin. I went overboard with decorations, a real tree (Mark bought a twelve-foot monstrosity that was going cheap and had to hack off a huge chunk), loads of presents and enough food and treats for a plus-size convention.

Things were OK during the busy run-up and Mum and Dad stayed until Boxing Day. But then – on our own, festivities over, mince pies turning stale and crap on TV – the tension mounted.

I wonder whether we'll ever enjoy December again, or if the season has forever lost its sparkle. I hope not. Eleanor shouldn't be dwelling on loss and sorrow when others' thoughts are on gifts and glitter and what eye shadow shade's this season's must-have.

On New Year's Eve, two days after the second anniversary of Dan's death, she sulked in her room after pouring scorn on our boring lives – Freya was at a family party and 'everyone else was enjoying themselves' – leaving me to a plethora of snacks and a solo rendition of *Auld Lang Syne*.

I thought I was prepared for the teen trials, but Eleanor's turns are like one of those fair rides that swing stupidly high into the air, then plunge back down. And I'm the one in the back, taken along for the ride and stifling screams. I wish I could be firmer. Dan would do a better job; calm, consistently firm, but fair. But I'm so weak at times – evading situations and stern words I fear could end in a big clash, or turning them into a joke to lighten the mood. Conflict Dodgems – that was my favourite fair ride. Besides, I feel I owe Eleanor some leeway.

I'd even contemplated taking the pills again, after a few gloomy mornings that brought back some of the dark thoughts I'd had just after Dan died, those months when popping the foil on the anti-depressants became a morning ritual as necessary as the first two cups of Lavazza, when the pain in my head, and, strangely, in my body too, was numbed by the chemicals coursing through my veins. Unlike my caffeine addiction, no one, except Imogen and Dr Bell, knew about my guilty narcotic secret. A quick – private – fix. I'd kept the tablets in the inner compartment of my work bag, waiting until Eleanor left for school to take them. I felt weak and pathetic. I never imagined I'd need them. Nor did anyone else; *'Carrie seems to be coping well', 'She's still got her sense of humour'*. But a joke's a good cloak, as they say.

'It's so easy to get hooked on those things,' Imogen had admonished gently, urging me to ditch them. And, eventually, I did. I hated the dulled senses. I stared at things, but didn't really see them. I reacted to things, but didn't feel them. And it wasn't good for work. I needed some adrenalin to do my job, to perform. I flushed them down the loo.

The phone pulls me into the present. It's Imogen. She's had a big row with Ben – suspects he's running out of patience.

'It's the worse thing – having a ridiculously randy husband and absolutely no appetite. I'm not sure it'll ever return.'

'It happens to loads of women,' I assure her. 'Working when you've got two small kids is exhausting. You'll get your drive back.'

'I hope so. We almost never … do it. And when we do, Ben seems to know I'm just, well, going through the motions.' I'm surprised Imogen's divulging such information. She's never comfortable talking about sexual matters, coy even with me.

After the chat, I change my blouse, extend my top lip with the stay-all-day lipstick Tash has given me – red wine and a scouring pad are the only things that seem to strip it off – and I'm on my way back downstairs when Mark arrives.

He can't wait to show off in his new red Mazda MX5, head cocked as always, one hand on the wheel as he chucks it round corners, throwing throaty noises out into the narrow streets we speed down en route to his local in the next village. The radio's drowned out by the engine, but Mark must turn up the volume, as I'm suddenly aware of the strains of a familiar tune.

'Going too fast for you am I, Miss Scaredy?' Mark says, noting my grimace.

'As if.'

I try not to listen, but it's hopeless. Such a powerful song – a hit by The New Crew, the American boy band who'd turned me dizzy in my teens. I've only heard that track twice since I gouged my CD single with a compass and hurled it into the canteen bin at poly. Ashley had bought it for me. I'd played it over and over, knew every note, every cloying lyric; layered it with nuance.

'Turn this shit off.' I reach for the dial, stomach churning.

'Damn. I was so into that.' Mark tunefully hums the last line. 'I was a chorister, you know, before my b—'

'Stop! You bloody weren't. You were in the school choir.'

'We sang in church a lot – and I was lead treble once.'

'Only because the choir leader knew your mum.' Mark nods several times.

It turns out to be just the two of us at the pub as Tash has lined up a last-minute date. The pub's unusually busy and we're hemmed in, sat on low stools at a sloping table with sticky beer mats. Mark's forgotten it's quiz night. We aim for two quick drinks, so we can exit before the annoying man on the mic kicks off his questions. We share the opinion that pub quizzes are a form of slow torture.

Mark returns from the bar, throwing two bags of dry-roasted nuts on the table.

'What about the diet?'

'Didn't I mention,' he glances at his watch, 'it ends at 8.26pm. Besides, I must have pedalled to London and back on the exercise bike earlier. I've earned these.'

'Bloody liar.'

Mark pulls a crumpled flyer from his pocket. 'They're going to start comedy nights here on a Friday once a month. Stan Stead's kicking it off.' He smirks. 'If you fancy it?'

'What about Jack?'

'He's not staying with me on Fridays any more. Sue says he's too tired, Saturdays are better.'

For your ex-wife maybe, I think, scanning the sheet. But I don't say it. Mark would do anything for his little boy, Jack. Rightly so.

'Count me in then. I'm sure Eleanor won't mind.'

'Actually, I could sign Jack up. He's into telling jokes at the moment – most of them bum and fart gags.'

'Sophisticated, like his father,' I say.

The time passes too quickly and I'm soon back at home staring at my pre-packed chicken salad, another blurred wine bottle, and facing the prospect of several hours of TV on my own again. I need to start taking control of my life. I yearn for busy evenings, and even busier weekends, like we used to have – everything planned at least two weeks ahead.

Please come back and organise me, Dan. I can't do it. I need one of your 'to do' lists.

★★★

I have to keep rereading the message, letting the words work their way through a resilient barrier of disbelief:

Hi Carrie. Family well thanks. Yours? Cheers for bringing up the driving test – I eventually passed on the fifth go! Need a car to drive to regionals. Thankfully, back behind the wheel now. Been playing Duke of Norfolk in Richard III at a small theatre in Manchester. Not done The Rosehouse though. Your parents still in Surrey? If so, perhaps we could catch up some time – a good excuse for a trip to London methinks? Ashley x

'Doing a crafty bit of Facebooking were we?'

I hastily click off the screen as Mark walks back into the office, shuffling in my chair, fingers touching my lips and throat. 'Or has Tash got you on the dating?' Mark cocks his head cheekily, placing a coffee on my desk.

'Facebook. Guilty as charged.' I hold up my hands. Mark tuts. I still recoil when he mentions dating. I haven't told him I'm back in touch with Ashley – I've made Tash pinkie pledge she won't either – though I'm concerned he may have picked up a few threads of our kitchen chats, despite my attempts at discretion. I want to believe it doesn't matter what Mark thinks. He knows my history with Ashley – I'd confided in him during a lunchtime drink years ago. In fact, I'd told Mark more than I had Dan (Dan knew Ashley was a significant ex but I'd spared him the details) – and he'd surely declare me insane.

'Well, one of us has to do some work.' Mark drops noisily into his chair. I throw a pen, but it misses, hitting the bin. 'I've already got one, but thanks anyway.'

My eyes fix on the screen for the next few minutes, but my thoughts wind around Ashley's message and suggestion to meet. Had he meant it, or was it just a throwaway comment from the Crown Prince of Casual? Perhaps he did feel the need to explain himself; a scary thought – one I knew I'd struggle to shake off. And he was performing Shakespeare. Wow. *His was no 'pipe dream', Mum; you got that one wrong!* I wince as I recall how embarrassingly standoffish Mum was with Ashley, making it clear she didn't deem him suitable for her girl. I hated that she'd turned out to be right. Ashley brought the worst out in Mum. One of his alleged crimes was taking a year out, unmitigated evidence that he lacked direction – the eighth deadly sin in Mum's book. Of course, I'd turned out to be a sinner too. And she was dismissive of drama school. Acting wasn't a proper career, she'd informed me one day, dusting the mantelpiece whilst watching *Gone With The Wind* for the fifth time.

Once, after a huge row, Mum had declared Ashley 'a dozy drifter'. I remember Dad bursting into song: '*There Goes My Baby* – it's a song by The Drifters,' he'd clarified, 'a group in the hit parade in the sixties'. I was blissfully unaware of the irony of that song title at the time. Mum had put down her cleaning cloth, shooting Dad one of her sternest looks: 'Don't be so daft, Maurice.' Ashley was only twenty at the time. What did she expect, his whole life planned, career path definitively carved, investment portfolio filed, pension arranged? But Ashley shrugged off Mum's intermittently hostile attitude, always placid – and polite. Dan, by contrast, was perfect son-in-law material in Mum's eyes and the polished pedestal she put him on got loftier over time.

'Yes, yes, yes. Bring it on!' Tash is fist-pumping her way into the office, doing a celebratory stomp in purple slingbacks so neon you'd surely spot them from Neptune, and startling me from my musings. 'It's official. This party girl has a three-day weekend.' Tash's older sister, who shares a flat in Brighton with her gay best friend, was staying for a few days. 'Boom! We're going to have some fun.'

'Lucky you,' Mark says. 'Can't wait to see the state of you next Tuesday.'

'Oh, shit!' Tash stares at her mobile, then dashes for the door. 'I'll have to go. I've got both keys. My sister needs eyelashes and Immac for tonight and has got a right strop on – says she's a prisoner in the house. Such a drama queen. Can you cover for me?'

Mark and I do a belly laugh in stereo.

★★★

I'm distracted at my step class, head and limbs reluctant to coordinate. My mind's being dangerously over-exercised, grappling with the weighty implications of Ashley's message. It isn't long before Lady Lycra, our class leader, is on to me.

'Come on – you've got to earn the burn!' she yells, gaze lingering.

I respond with several vigorous steps, arms swinging. No one dared to disobey Lady Lycra. She looked like a Barbie doll – platinum ponytail scraped back off a ridiculously radiant face, cropped vest revealing a stomach flatter than a baking sheet and more bubble than a Sodastream – but barked orders like a Burmese brigadier. Somehow, her wide smile never faded, even when she was pumping holy hell out of her heavy neoprene dumbbells.

'Thought you'd get away with slacking, did you?' my exercise buddy Slim Kim, aka partner in pain, says cheekily, grimacing on her step next to me in bright red capri leggings that match her face. Her short vanilla curls are drenched with sweat.

'As if.' We both laugh, breathlessly.

Later, I'm hugging the laptop on the chaise longue, nursing aching muscles and eating crisps, when another message arrives – from Sheena:

Hi Carrie. How are you? How did the pitch go? Thanks for your message – I was touched by your support and concern, as always. Sorry I've not been in touch, we had a bit of an emergency here. Abigail was rushed to hospital with a burst appendix. She had a bad tummy after a party, which at first I put down to the usual – too much junk food and fizzy drinks! But during the night she was in agony, an ambulance took her to A&E and they operated immediately. She was in such a state for a few days, bless her. For the first time, I felt really angry with Geoff. While she was in theatre, I kept thinking 'how could you not be here for your little girl, you selfish man?' Thankfully, she's home now and doing fine – lapping up the attention, time off school, big sisters spoiling her. You know what 10-year-olds are like! Look forward to hearing from you. Sheena xxx

Poor Sheena. I could understand her anger. I'd felt it too. Days when it overwhelmed me, smothering all other feelings. How could the man who loved us, leave us? And with something we couldn't really comprehend? But most of the time I just missed him, and was livid with myself for being so bloody pathetic that I couldn't function properly without him.

It was difficult hearing how tough life was for Sheena; her situation so dire.

Through our early exchanges, Sheena had revealed her story to me, how she'd returned home from work one day to find a note on the kitchen table from husband Geoff, a sales rep, saying *'gone for a walk'*. She hadn't seen him since. It must have been well over a year. He'd had depression on and off and refused help, but hadn't appeared to be particularly down at the time. He'd taken the youngest of their three girls to school as usual and was planning to work from home. He wasn't there when

Sheena got back from her shift at the bank. He hadn't taken his BMW, wallet or mobile (which, strangely, they found in an empty plant pot at the bottom of the garden). 'Missing' posters were put up, hospitals, friends and acquaintances contacted and quizzed, the local area and his favourite haunts scoured. He'd left his passport and no money had been taken from their joint account since.

Several months after he disappeared, police received a report of a possible sighting. Someone matching Geoff's description, pale and rangy with wiry, grey hair and a beard, had been seen sobbing in a local park. Sheena was so full of hope. 'I just know it's him,' she'd said in an email. It wasn't. I cried for her. Yet Sheena was so strong. So positive. 'I have to be for the girls,' she told me often. 'Self pity's so destructive'.

I still found it impossible not to feel sorry for myself, especially when Eleanor stayed over at friends. Just recently, I'd had twinges of regret at not trying harder for another child. He, or she, would possibly be about nine now, still bouncy and excitable. There may even have been a third; at the 'wide-eyed and full of wonder' stage. 'Oh, you've just got the one,' other mums would often remark, with a sympathetic look, when Eleanor was little. But I had my beautiful girl, whom I loved with all my heart, and that was fine.

Dan and I were both keen on a brother or sister for Eleanor (I always hoped we'd have three children, possibly four) but after struggling for three years to conceive, we knew something was wrong. We'd had all the basic fertility tests – initially via the NHS until Dan had a run-in with a 'curt and condescending' medic and insisted on going private.

In the end, it was Dan who suggested calling it a day. No one had found any answers and more intrusive procedures looked the only option. Dan was happy with how we were – our tight little trio – and didn't want to put me through further pain and put unnecessary strain on us all. I agreed. I'd read the headlines: '*IVF ruined our marriage*'. I'd seen it tear the strongest couples apart. I didn't want that.

I never took the pill again.

Sadly, I never caught.

CHAPTER 8

'Tuck in, girls. Grandma will join us shortly,' Dad insists, pouring tea from a Royal Worcester teapot. 'There you are, young lady.'

'Thanks, Granddad.' Eleanor smiles sweetly.

We're sat at Mum's beloved rosewood dining-room table, Eleanor framed by a pair of busy floral curtains and big stiff pelmet overhead, the sun throwing geometric shapes on to the gold Berber twist carpet.

It's the third day of our stay and she's still agog, surveying a breakfast spread that would put some hotels to shame – a choice of cereals (in containers, 'boxes on the table are so uncouth'), grapefruit, melon, cheese, toast, various breads, and mini jams with swirly writing on the pots. This was before Mum brought out the bacon, eggs and Dad's home-grown tomatoes – some giant, misshapen hybrid variety with green and grey bruises he'd nurtured in his new ten-foot greenhouse.

Eleanor spreads a thick layer of jam on toast with a shiny knife. I gulp, uncertain I'll be able to eat, nerves filling my abdomen.

'Bacon's on its way,' Mum says, trotting in to fuss with cutlery, then retreating. She's never happier than when entertaining, particularly spoiling her loved ones. Yet her insistence on everything being 'just so' always makes her tense. She won't let me help, gets quite offended when I offer. Mum worries so much about Dad – and me – but it's her I'm concerned about. She seldom relaxes.

Dad hovers eagerly, trying to be helpful. 'Coffee's coming.' He skips round the table, drops into his carver chair. 'Tea for me, I think,' he declares, before bursting into song: '*Tea for two* …'

'Don't be daft, Maurice!' says a voice from the kitchen. We giggle and Dad drops his head in mock remorse.

'Oh, I forgot to say, we've got new neighbours at number 26,' Mum announces, sitting down at last.

'Have you met them?' I ask.

'Briefly – I don't think they're our type.'

Mum starts to loosen, shoulders sinking back into the chair, voice softening, as it always does, when she chats to Eleanor. They're going to a wildlife park. I'm going to meet Ashley, at a café in north London, before his rehearsal at a local theatre.

It's taken several weeks to organise and I've changed my mind more times than Mum's changed her bed linen, wrestling with doubts about the wisdom of opening up old wounds, whether I can face knowing the truth or even if his invitation to meet is a serious request. Eventually, I emailed saying I was visiting my parents and could catch a train into London. I'm petrified, fibbing to Mum, Dad, and Eleanor that I'm meeting an old sixth-form friend.

Yet I've convinced myself that it won't matter if seeing Ashley again turns out to be a mistake. We deserve a break. Eleanor adores her daft granddad and there are times when you need your mum, even though when you're one yourself you're supposed to be harder than one of Imogen's rock cakes left in the larder too long.

I set off before the others, leaving Mum and Dad disputing whether or not to keep the uneaten bacon, and Eleanor giggling as her granddad pulls faces behind his wife's back.

I sit on the train, questions and thoughts whizzing through my mind as rapidly as bits of blurred green and grey scenery flash past my eyes. Should I be meeting him? Should I confront him immediately? Would all the old hurt come flooding back? Was he going to tell me something I couldn't bear to hear? Would I recognise him? (the man pictured in the news stories was battered and bandaged). I wonder what age his children are, how beautiful his wife is, if he still drinks lemonade, whether his nostrils are hairy.

I'm worried he might think I've aged badly. I'd seen myself grow older in daily episodes, while Ashley will get the shock of a twenty-year visual fast-forward in one scan. I've found myself hovering by the mirror more – Eleanor style – convinced the creases by my mouth have deepened. Yet Ashley will surely forgive a few crinkles, I convince myself, recalling the state of his clothes, always scrunched up and shoehorned into that blue and red Gola bag he took everywhere.

But why should I care what Ashley thinks? I'm seeing him to confront him. It's answers I need, not admiration.

★★★

I climb off the tube, hemmed in by jostling bodies, most in a far greater hurry than me. Yet I can match their adrenalin, buzz for buzz, convinced that if someone touches me in the chest area, they'll get a life-threatening shock from all the nervous energy inside.

I decide to walk the final few streets as it's such a fine, sunny day – just a few fluffy clouds spoiling a smooth, cyan sky. Several black cabs hurl past, one blasting its horn at a group of excitable tourists straggling the road. I've forgotten how loud the hum of London is, with its confusing threads of noise; my eyes and ears on high alert. The air's hot, heavy and reeks of diesel.

Stopping by the window of an antiques shop to apply lippie and a top-up of perfume, I rummage in my bag for the scrap of paper I've scribbled the café's name on. I can't find it and have to text Ashley. Not a good start. He replies: '*It's Delish. See you in half an hour.*' He must have the time wrong. We'd definitely said eleven.

It takes me back to our student days. We were the dumb and dumber of logistics, Ashley often missing his connection when he travelled to visit me at poly, or me turning up at the coach instead of the train station to meet him. We regularly messed up social plans, both faffing over which party to go to, invariably arriving late, or at the wrong place, often without the cans of lager we'd bought. But I didn't care. I loved being with him. I thought he felt the same. And I stupidly believed we'd be Mr and Mrs Fuckwit forever. *Forever.* Just like the title of our song.

Delish is twice as trendy as anything Tetford has to offer, already full of chat, the heavy clank of crockery and all kinds of toasted and roasted smells. Low-backed red plastic chairs surround gingham-covered tables and confetti half-curtains made from sparkly red squares hang like vertical paper-chains in the quaint windows.

The only empty table's in the centre of the room. I sit, tentatively, feeling the full glare of the spotlight – and extreme stage fright. A striking waitress, with wolf eyes and multiple piercings, assures me she'll return when my friend arrives. Then he does.

It's the mousy hair I see first; the long fringe flopping over his face as he enters. He doesn't look over, so I watch as he turns to close the door behind him. He's filled out a little and I'm struck by the facial hair – which has a surprising reddish hue – but it's unmistakably Ashley.

He scans the room, sharp blue eyes quick to find me. He grins, lifts his palm in acknowledgement. I smile, gulp and wave back.

It's strange not to see him in one of his trademark crumpled plain T-shirts. It's what I'd pictured. He's wearing relaxed jeans with a linen shirt, cuffs folded back. I fidget as he approaches, hands wandering everywhere. His thumbs are hooked firmly into his front pockets, as always, splayed fingers hanging down. I think I detect a slight limp.

I stand, reminding myself to breathe as he lands a kiss on my cheek.

'Hey, great to see you.'

'You recognised me, then?' I fear it's the first of many stupid things I'll drop out, my tongue, as ever, loose with anxiety.

'Course.' He lets out a staccato laugh. 'You look great. Not aged a bit.'

I laugh nervously, half-expecting him to add, 'Age hath not withered ...' How he loved a Shakespeare quote, and spouting lines from famous plays, always with his tongue firmly in his cheek.

The waitress brings menus and we're both glad of the distraction. Ashley thanks her, then looks down at the single sheet. He's like a stranger, yet so familiar. It's the weirdest thing. His poker-straight hair's neater and shorter, barely brushing the top of his collar. Ashley was never textbook handsome, or stylish, like Dan. He was a little pretty, eyes framed by a canopy of thick lashes, and he had an inner confidence, a kind of nonchalance and effortless charm. I'd found him fascinating, and mysterious – a bit too mysterious as it turned out.

'The cakes in here are great.' Ashley shuffles in the chair, eyes passing quickly across my face before returning to the menu.

'Do you come in here a lot, then?'

'Not recently – I did a while back when I was in a production at the same theatre.'

I can't imagine eating. I feel sick with dread, wondering how this scene's going to unfold, whether I'll tell him what a heartless, gutless bastard he was, whether I'll fall to pieces.

'Just a coffee for me. You still into lemonade?' I've managed to get in the first reference to the past. He used to drink bottles of the stuff – always leaving them scattered around my room in halls.

'Yeah – not so much though. They do great cloudy lemonade here.' He flicks his hair and I glimpse a thin, L-shaped scar on his forehead. 'Actually, I think I'll have one. And …' he turns to the glass counter, ' … perhaps a flapjack. I skipped breakfast.' He looks at me. 'Actually,

94

forget the flapjack. Are you sure you won't—' I shake my head.

Ashley slides a foot out from under the table. He's still wearing beige desert boots. I want to let out a little laugh, but it's weighed down too heavily inside.

The strained small talk continues until the waitress brings the drinks. Ashley's expression changes, eyelids flickering, smile fading. He grips his glass with both hands.

'Look, about us, you know, the college thing. I didn't want to mention it on Facebook. I needed to tell you.' His eyes take time to find mine, as if stalling to recall rehearsed lines.

A wave of adrenalin frees my tongue. 'You mean why you left that weekend and then, with no explanation, I never saw you again?'

'Yeah, that.' Ashley's prominent Adam's apple rolls as he swallows. 'When I went that day I wasn't intending to … walk out on you, I mean … well, a few days after, I was contacted by Hayley, you remember …'

'Yes.' He'd finished with her after meeting me, though I often wondered whether she was still on the scene. I had no evidence – he assured me my suspicions were unfounded.

Ashley's gaze intensifies. 'She told me she was pregnant.'

I feel shattered; breathless. I don't know what I expected, but not that. So they weren't over. Was he still seeing Hayley while we were together? He must have read my mind.

'I hadn't seen her since you and I got together. I had no idea. I was completely shocked. A total mess. I thought

I'd have to make things work, to support the child.' I did the maths. He … she … would be twenty-one now. 'I quit drama school, got a job. But she lost the baby.' A pause. 'A stillbirth.' Silence. Ashley rubs his palms on his thighs. 'The baby had severe brain damage, it … she … couldn't have survived.'

'Oh no.' My throat feels like it's turned to concrete. I don't know how words break through. 'I'm sorry.' The waitress drifts over. She's forgotten to take the menus. Ashley waits for her to go.

'Of course, none of it's an excuse for not contacting you … explaining. I tried. I called a few times but couldn't speak. I was a coward. I didn't know how to tell you. '

'There's … always … a way.' I'm still tongue-tied, and my heart's melted the harder words I want to say.

'I know. And I understand why you ignored me when I tried to get in touch later.'

'Yes.' My voice is quiet. 'Far too late.'

'I know. It wasn't what I wanted. I couldn't handle it. Everyone was interfering, her parents, mine. I got dragged along.'

I can't get my head around it. Did I believe him? Could I forgive him? I wasn't heartless, but I wasn't sure any of it excused what he did.

'You remember Jono?' I nod several times, watching Ashley sip his drink. Jono was the one responsible for us getting together, Ashley's friend, a biology student at the same poly as me. He'd invited Ashley to a student party I was at – the first time we'd seen each other since primary school. 'I asked him to find out how you were, to … look out for you. I was going to come and see you at poly after

… the loss – the baby, but Jono saw you at an end of year party. You'd,' he hesitates, 'moved on.'

I cradle my coffee cup, welcoming a pause as Ashley stands to let a lady and her large shopping bags out from the table next to us. I feel dizzy, my mind frantically sorting through things to say.

So he had a spy. I can't recall seeing Jono after the 'split'. I'd heard through the grapevine that Ashley was seeing someone else. I'd sent a strongly-worded letter saying he should have had the balls to tell me. I'd called him a few times too, but he never answered. I hadn't moved on. There was no one else until Dan. Friends warned me to be careful that it wasn't on the rebound, but I'd laughed at them – it was over a year later, how could it be? Maybe my friends had been right?

Patchy images from that poly party emerge. The beach theme. Then I see it. I'd snogged the face off two different guys that night. It was my lager-headed way of dealing with the hurt and anger over Ashley. I'd spilled a bottle of cheap beer over the second one's Hawaiian T-shirt and, after being sick in my flip-flop, had spent a long night in the downstairs loo with a toilet seat and hula-hula garland as a pillow. Yes, Jono *had* been there. I remember. I was desperate to ask him about Ashley, but too afraid. Then later, feeling several lagers braver, I couldn't find him; he'd left. If only I'd been more persistent.

'It was a long time ago,' I say, as Ashley sits back down. He nods gently. I have the answer to the question I've been asking myself for twenty years. Why, when we'd been so bloody good together – or so I thought – he'd left me high and dry? But I don't know how I feel. Or what to say. I'd imagined that, if I ever got to tackle him, I'd rant, slap him, maybe bash out his brains with the complete works of Shakespeare; unleash all the anger and hate that had festered inside me.

'So are you with Hayley now?'

'No.' I urge Ashley to elaborate with my silence. 'I'm … married. We've been together, gosh … seventeen years.'

'Any children?' I regret the question immediately.

'No.'

'Oh … I assumed … your Facebook status, the photo of the little boy—'

'Oh, that's my nephew. Handsome like his uncle, isn't he?' He smiles at last. 'What about you. Any children?'

'Yes, a daughter, Eleanor – she's thirteen.'

'I was sorry to hear about your husband. I saw it—'

'Thanks. And for the card.'

A brief silence follows. I feel exhausted. Ashley looks it too, shoulders hunched over the table. We both seem to sense we've said all we can for now, that we must somehow drive away the dark fog that's descended over the bright furnishings in Delish.

I'm relieved when Ashley asks if I'll excuse him while he has a quick word with his friend – a woman with raven hair and purple lipstick who waves, rather sheepishly, as she joins the queue at the deli. I need time for it all to sink in, to begin the process of sifting through the wreckage, to discover which emotions remain, what I really feel.

Ashley's gone a while. His body language suggests she's a good friend, though she seems restless, fiddling with a huge silver ring, eyes constantly flitting over at me as they talk.

There's an aftermath of unease after his revelation, but when he returns we manage to lighten the chat, slipping into some of our old routines and behaviours, batting little funnies back and forth, me speaking a little hurriedly, Ashley more thoughtfully and listening in that detached, dreamy way of his. He tells me about the accident, the months in hospital, how he fractured both legs and a complex hip operation has left one slightly shorter than the other. He's more talkative than I remember. I'd always felt it was what Ashley didn't say that was more important.

We order a second drink and, with my curiosity at fever pitch, I ask whether his wife's in the acting business too. As always, he hesitates, widening his eyes before he speaks.

'No. She teaches – Year 4 primary.' A teacher's perfect for Ashley, someone to organise him, I think.

I tell him about my job – and lack of ambition. His CV's impressive by comparison and he's more animated, eyes flashing when he talks about his career, the challenging Shakespeare roles, several at regional theatres like Brighton, where he was Roderigo in *Othello*. A few years ago, he'd been a Hamlet understudy in a major 'Off West End' London production.

The work's unpredictable; he's had several, prolonged 'rest' periods, falling back on the photography and a few 'crappy jobs'. He couldn't work for months after the accident and wonders if his best acting days are behind him. I suspect he's being falsely modest.

'The photography's good. I'm happy to focus on this a bit more – excuse me for stealing one of your dodgy puns.' Ashley smiles, then looks at his watch. 'Alas, I'm going to have to shoot.'

I feel bound to oblige. I hold up my hands. 'No, don't shoot!' Yet I should be the one shooting you, I think.

Ashley grins. He's used to my stupid jokes, I muse, watching him finish his lemonade. They haven't got any more sophisticated, especially when I'm nervous. But give him enough lager and Ashley could be equally daft. I've never forgotten the time, at a party, when he donned a friend's leather jacket, slicked his fringe back using my cherry lip salve and serenaded me with a song by The New Crew – or TNC, as us fans knew them. Our friends were in fits. He strangled every note, grabbing at his crotch as his voice strained to reach the falsetto heights of Scott, my teenage crush. Ashley was no singer. And he couldn't have looked less like Scott – all dark, polished and Osmond-like.

It was the track I'd heard just recently on Mark's car radio: *I'll be Loving You (Forever)*. Ashley had dragged his hangover to town the next day and returned with a copy of the CD. 'I remember you telling me you'd lost this,' he'd said. 'And I know you still like them – secretly. I hope I didn't embarrass you too much last night. I was pretty pissed.' He'd put his hand on his heart: 'I promise never to sing along again'. That was one promise he kept. But the title of the song – he didn't keep that one. Perhaps it was the brackets. Damn those brackets.

'Don't be late, Bardie,' the raven-haired woman yells over. She's at the door waving a brown paper bag and grinning cheekily.

'I'm on it.' Ashley looks coy, hands fidgeting in his lap as he smiles back. 'Lily's one of the cast,' he tells me.

Wickedly, I wonder if they do more than just tread boards together.

CHAPTER 9

Mum serves up mashed potato that evening. It's delicious. It's hers that got me hooked. Real potatoes, a hefty dollop of butter; not a lump in sight.

At the dining table, I'm desperate to tell Mum how wrong she'd been to dismiss Ashley's ambitions as fantasy, and him as too idle to make it. 'I was right to be so excited and hopeful for him,' I want to say, as she sits, straight-backed, taking small mouthfuls of food. 'He's done Shakespeare – some major roles at impressive venues.'

But, of course, that day's assignment had been secret – though, earlier, when Mum asked if I'd had a nice time, and I'd given a brief, rehearsed reply, I was convinced she'd seen the fib etched on my face.

As the others talk about their day, Eleanor in fits of giggles recounting how Dad had dropped his Cornetto in shock when a monkey made a sudden run at the cage he was stood next to, I keep replaying Ashley's revelation, unsure what to make of it. He'd offered to walk with me to the bus stop, even though he was late for his rehearsal and it was in the wrong direction; then realised he'd forgotten his script. But he didn't seem unduly bothered, still taking things in his small, slow stride.

'It's been great to see you again, to have the chance to … explain; say sorry,' he'd said, as we stood near the queue at my stop. He'd leaned in, placed his hand behind my shoulder and kissed me on the cheek. It was the first time I'd smelled him. The first time I'd breathed properly perhaps. And it knocked my nostrils back – the same slightly peppery, warm scent but with a slight hint of summer sweat and some gentle deodorant I didn't recognise.

My response was partially lost to the rumble of traffic: 'Good to see you too.' I was facing him, a foot or so away, unsure what to say or do next. Reminding myself of the loathing I'd fostered for him, I was eager to reiterate that his explanation had come twenty-two years too late. But I couldn't. His parting words: 'Let's not make it so long next time.' I was taken aback. Would there be a next time?

Eleanor's voice brings me back to the table. She's moaning to Mum that her friend Bethany isn't allowed to go to the school disco. Her mum won't let her. Eleanor's gutted. They were 'all good' after their latest fall-out and had planned to go clothes shopping.

This news about Bethany's mum doesn't surprise me. She'd previously threatened to stop her daughter attending school assemblies because there was 'insufficient Christian content', and had refused to let Bethany have her tonsils out – something to do with avoiding medical intervention. Poor girl had months off sick from school.

I'd tried so hard with her mum, making conversation at the school gate when others sidestepped her, inviting her in for coffee when she dropped Bethany off at the house. She was always perfectly pleasant, but consistently refused my offers, preferring to keep herself to herself.

The mash is going down nicely, but I'm struggling with Mum's beef bourguignon, a loose knot still in my tummy.

'Had any more thoughts about moving?' Mum asks, noting my silence. Eleanor shoots me a frown.

'No, not really.'

'That's good,' Mum says, giving Eleanor a conspiratorial smile. 'It's a lovely place.'

Mum had never hidden her house envy. She'd yearned for a detached, but Dad hadn't earned as much in insurance as she'd hoped, so – unwilling to contemplate moving to 'a rougher area' – she'd had to settle for a smarter semi and posher postcode a few miles closer to Guildford. I'd loved our home, even if Mum hadn't. I wouldn't call mine a charmed childhood. I longed for siblings, the din and disorder of the family life my friends had, and often resented Mum's strict rules and fastidious cleaning regime, especially during our turbulent years when my difficult teens and her premature menopause collided and we clashed continually (that's when Dad bought his first greenhouse, a hormone-free haven where he nurtured prize-winning tomatoes; and whatever else he did in there). But I was loved and indulged, and our immaculate suburban semi was cluttered with happy memories.

After tea, I join Mum and her Marigolds in the recently renovated kitchen, the eighties limed oak cabinets replaced with a darker wood and huge swathes of heavily patterned tiles. I insist on putting plates away while she attacks the worktops with a giant bottle of spray. She has a heavy arsenal of cleaning fluids, all stacked in a huge basket under the sink and some so uber-powerful they'd render the mind of a sex pest clean.

Mum says I look much better than I did at Christmas, what a relief it is, how worried she's been. I'm touched. It strikes me how she's like one of the cleaning pads that seem to breed in her cupboards. Mum has a tough, sometimes abrasive, top layer, but beneath she's surprisingly soft. It's something I've only started to appreciate with maturity, and my own motherhood.

'How are you – I mean, really,' Mum asks, putting down the spray.

'I'm OK, on the whole. Just lonely.'

'I know.' Mum puts her hand on mine and I turn tearful.

'And Eleanor's growing up so quickly, she can be quite … combative.'

'I remember it well. You were no angel.' I smile. 'Would you like a drink?'

'A glass of wine would be great.'

Mum fetches a bottle from the under-stairs pantry. 'Eleanor says you drink every night,' she says, pouring it into a small glass.

'Not every night.'

'Your dad and I can make a bottle last a week.' I take the glass. 'Does your friend have a family?'

I panic, wondering for a second who she means. 'Yes. Two children,' I say, amazed at how convincing I sound.

'Are you going to meet up again?'

'Oh yes, probably.'

I stay up after the others go to bed, idly googling and

mindlessly hopping TV channels. I feel guilty when I pour the last drops of wine from the bottle. I think of Mum. Her disapproval. And Dan.

Dan was never a big drinker, but cut back drastically when his health crusade got serious. Around his mid-forties. I've never been the jealous type, but couldn't help suspecting an affair. His regime had become so rigorous and, at times, righteous, there surely must have been a trigger. It seemed universally accepted that the first sign of men playing away was a sudden upsurge of healthier eating, exercise and genital hygiene. I was in bits. Was he unhappy in our marriage? I thought the robust contentment was a mutual feeling. He'd always said he could never stop loving me, but what if he could? I'd never cope without him by my side. Imogen had virtually laughed in my face when I shared my concern. 'Don't be so sodding daft, lovely. He'd be one of the last men on earth to cheat,' she'd protested. 'He only ever has eyes for you – it's nauseating to witness at times.' I had to admit there were no other signs. Sex was great and he was still attentive, the one making more romantic gestures – even if the bouquets of flowers he brought home were often accompanied by a bunch of fennel or a bag of carrots.

So I moved to suspect number two: a mid-life crisis, or menoporsche as Imogen called it. Yet it certainly wasn't a textbook one. Other men waxed their backs or got a motorbike; they didn't overdose on lentils and lunges, or drink their own wee. Perhaps his was just an extreme case, possibly prompted by the slight bulge in the belly when he wore his favourite Fred Perry T-shirts, or my discovery of his first grey pube. He'd gone mad when I'd pointed out the lone silver strand one night. 'You shouldn't have told me!' He'd stared down in horror. 'OK, I'll pluck it out and you can forget it existed,' I offered.

Looking back, I'm not convinced it was just Dan being troubled by the middle years, a fear of losing the bounce in his bungee. He liked being in control, so it was no surprise he'd take on the ageing process. I'm sure there was more to it. His obsession wasn't helped by his business – selling health products and gadgets – and constant warnings about all the things that are bad for you. Like most people, I put my fingers in my ears and went '*la, la, la*' when I heard the latest bulletins about yet another thing you shouldn't eat, drink, touch or breathe in. But Dan took notice. It was OK to start with – cutting back, cutting down. Then he took it to extremes.

I could see that both Dan, and perhaps our marriage, lost a bit of sparkle. I can't pinpoint a moment when it happened. It was as if someone was gradually, surreptitiously, turning Dan's dimmer switch down. I looked at him one day – grimacing on his weights bench in the spare bedroom, forcing a sweaty smile through gritted, bleached teeth before declaring, breathlessly, that Eleanor and I should start watching the film without him as he still had some reps to do – and his whole demeanour looked more dull.

He was borderline teetotal in the end. Gluten, sugar, salt, dairy, meat – all on his hit list at one time or another. He even fussed over ingredients when we went to restaurants. Although I joked about it, it spoiled things a little. During one anniversary meal, he passed on dessert, peering righteously over a glass of fizzy water while I shovelled in banoffee pie washed down with wine.

A loud ping stops my thoughts – a junk email landing in my computer inbox. I decide to send a message to Sheena:

Hi Sheena. I was so shocked to hear about poor Abigail. How awful. Glad she's recovering well. I understand your anger. You've every right to be angry. Eleanor's thinking about auditioning for a part in Fame at school. Do you remember Bruno, Danny, Coco and co from the 80s TV show? And who can forget Leroy and his skimpy shorts. He could certainly throw his lunchbox around, couldn't he? Haha. You're not going to believe it, but I met Ashley today. I was all set to give him hell, but then he told me what had happened. Out of the blue, his ex-girlfriend had announced she was pregnant and he couldn't bring himself to tell me. He'd decided to stick by her, but then they lost the baby. One big, awful mess. It's crazy how one decision can change so many lives. He's hinted at meeting again, but he's married and, I'm not sure I forgive him for being such a bloody coward!? You're such a strong woman, Sheena. And you have three lovely girls to help you get through it. Carrie x

It's not until I'm in bed, a myriad thoughts whirring around my head and jostling with each other, that I note the absence of the Gola bag, always on Ashley's shoulder during his farewell routine at poly. 'I bid you adieu,' he'd say, pretending to doff his cap. Sometimes I just laughed at his silliness, others I tried to out-silly him with a reply like 'bless you' or 'no, I'm a Christian'. To think that the life of that carefree, dreamy young man, dossing with drama and getting tanked-up at parties, still drinking pop through a straw, had been shaken up and reformatted.

I think about our second baby – mine and Dan's –

that never came, then poor Ashley's that came but went so soon.

★★★

I'm startled by the phone. I'm in a light, busy-headed sleep. What's happened? Dad? Mum? Eleanor? I come to my senses – the soft mattress and strong smell of laundry liquid reminding me I'm at Mum's, all my loved ones are here; safe.

Fragmented memories of meeting Ashley float back as I grab my mobile from the bedside table. Yes, it *had* happened. I flick on the porcelain lamp, screwing my eyes shut at the shock of the bulb.

'Hi.' It comes out as a whisper. I haven't noticed the number.

'Ask me what I'm doing.' It takes several seconds to realise it's Imogen.

'What are you doing?'

'I'm bloody packing.'

'Are you going on holiday? It's a bit late.' I'm still dazed, mouth dry.

'No, I'm leaving Ben, taking the girls with me, that's what I'm doing.' Her voice has so many inflections, in odd places. Had she been drinking? Crying?

'Hang on. Why? What's happened?' I pull myself upright, tilting the plump Oxford pillow behind me and noticing the dark shadows at the edges of things in the room.

'Because I can't give him sex so he's looked elsewhere.'

'What. He's had an affair?'

'Well, who knows … no … bloody porn sites. Disgusting stuff.'

'That's not so bad is it, Imogen? I think all men do it.' I'm relieved it's not something worse.

'Totally disgusting,' she slurs.

'Have you been drinking?'

'Yes, lots. Totally rat-arsed.' This was the flip side to Imogen. No one could be as bubbly and upbeat as her without downers. Even the best bakers occasionally pulled a flat cake out the oven. Her lows were rare, but could be quite dramatic if fuelled by alcohol.

'Where's Ben. And the girls?'

'The girls are asleep. He's in Caen, staying overnight. With work – or so he says. Probably banging a prostitute, or one of his glam colleagues.' I gasp inwardly, shocked to hear her talk like this. 'Caught him on the laptop.'

'Oh … well—'

'I said, "Show me what else you've been looking at, you dirty bastard".' Imogen's voice is hard and spiteful. 'He wouldn't. So I looked anyway – though I wish I hadn't. It wasn't normal stuff. It was horrible, kinky, sordid things. Just horrid—'

'But that's the trouble with the internet, Imogen. Some sites just pop up …' I wince at my choice of words, '… and take you to others. Perhaps he didn't intend … but I think lots of people look at that stuff.'

'You didn't see it. Disgusting bugger.' I feel so sorry for her. Ben's timing is lousy. I glance at the alarm clock.

'It's so late. Why not go to bed? Think about things tomorrow when you're calmer. Talk to Ben when he comes home. You can't do anything now anyway.'

She sighs. 'Oh God, lovely. I don't know what to do. It's all such a mess. My fault. Fucking France.'

I try to be firm, think what she'd say to me. 'Look, get some sleep. I'll ring tomorrow and we can have a big chat.'

'OK. Sorry to wake you with this. You're such a great friend. Anyone else would be so pissed off with me.'

'Don't worry. I wasn't really asleep. Too much thinking. I'm at Mum's.'

'Shit, yes … oh sorry … I haven't even asked about Ashley. How was it?'

'It was tough, but—'

'So, did he explain? What did he say?'

'Yes, he did, but it's all very complicated. Tragic. His ex-girlfriend was pregnant. Sadly, the baby died.'

'Oh my God. So—'

'I'll tell you more in the morning.'

'How awful. So what—'

'I'll ring in the morning.' I'm unusually assertive. 'Bye.'

'Bye – and thanks, lovely.'

CHAPTER 10

Spring brings some early sunshine and thoughts turn to fancy dress. Mark hosts another charity event in the grounds of a friend's Victorian mansion and we all turn up as superheroes. Tash is Wonderwoman, Mark Batman, I'm Mrs Incredible (incredibly, I managed to squeeze into a small-sized costume I'd ordered by mistake) and Pete's Mr Invisible – failing to appear. We all suspect he knows his superhero days are done. 'Imagine Pete grappling his trussed up gonads all night in a tight jumpsuit,' Mark says, to a chorus of 'ewwws'.

We sweat in our costumes, munching canapés in the marquee and drinking 'super' strength cocktails on the perfectly-striped lawn, while a string ensemble plays action movie tunes. Before long, everyone's 'Pow', 'Fwap', 'Clank' and 'Boofing' each other and behaving like kids at a Smartie party. Mark trips over his cape after too many bat-juices and Tash takes out a plate of smoked salmon blinis with her right arm doing her best Wonderwoman twirl.

I'm driving to Sunny's, silently chuckling as I recall the events of that night – a happy distraction. Eleanor's in the back seat, sealed in by her headphones and teenage introspections.

The car radio cranks out a nineties indie rock track and it strikes me how much my thoughts have been on Ashley, as if the lid of the box containing past events, labelled 'done and dusted', has worked its way loose. My thoughts are mostly tinged with frustration and 'what ifs', tainted with regret.

Ashley has 'kaboomed' me over cyberspace, sending an email suggesting we could meet up again as two coffees weren't enough to catch up on twenty years. Feeling unsure, I sent an ambiguous reply, a sort of vague acceptance.

I'm always a bit tense going to Sunny's house, and carrying some extra guilt in my conscience clutchbag – because of Ashley – makes it worse.

Sunny called several days ago to tell me Mick's health was deteriorating. I decided I should visit, offering her a lift to the care home, expecting a 'no, the weather was sublime, the crocuses and wild primroses were in bloom, she'd prefer to walk'. But she said 'yes, that would be lovely' as she was pushed for time and her Micra was off the road – something wrong with the clutch. 'Of course, Dan sorted all my car issues,' she'd added. 'I can only wonder what it's going to cost to repair.' And I'd thought we might just have managed a Danless conversation.

As usual, there's no space outside Sunny's house. Hers is number 166 of around two hundred assorted red-bricked houses sitting behind cramped front gardens and shoehorned into a road that climbs and curls up a steep hill.

I park near the bottom, and while I try to relish the spring flavour of the surprisingly still warm day, the bursts of sun waking up a sleepy street and creating bright stripes

112

on the pavement, Eleanor moans with each step. She isn't wearing the right shoes for uphill walking apparently, though the expensive pumps she'd begged me to buy look perfectly fit for purpose.

Sunny apologises for not being ready. Her friend, a fellow traveller she'd met in Spain, has only just left. Eleanor and I sit on the sofa, taking in strong drifts of citronella, while Sunny, curls still damp, flutters around the living room in bare feet straddled by aubergine flares, rearranging furniture.

'We went to a folk music festival yesterday,' Sunny says, re-emerging from her treatment room with a cane chair. 'My friend plays the flute, so we took our instruments. It was wonderful to lose myself in music again. So uplifting. I was quite giddy when I got home.' She flashes her Madonna gap in a broad smile.

Eleanor hops up, heads to the bookcase. 'This is well awesome, is it new?' She's holding a large piece of rock with rings in vibrant blues.

'No, it used to be in my bedroom but I found I didn't fully appreciate it in there,' Sunny says, gently shaping her curls. 'The light's not as complementary.' Being settled in one place wasn't natural to Sunny, so she liked to keep changing her surroundings, said it made her feel more alive.

'It's agate,' Sunny adds, walking over. I'm desperate to say I thought it was a rock, not a gate, but I fear the puerile police would be on my tail and I'd face a long sentence. Miss Giggles would have laughed at that one though.

Sunny's tilting the rock, showing how the colours change as the light catches them. Eleanor's as tall as her auntie now, around five foot three, with a similar petite frame. Yet, with their heads almost touching, the contrast between them is striking – Eleanor with her perfectly straightened, chocolately hair and heavy make-up and Sunny's naturally tumbling curls and lightly-powdered face. I'd always thought the same seeing Sunny and Dan side by side. You'd never have guessed they were siblings. Dan essentially ticked all three of the tall, dark and handsome boxes (he scraped six foot stood ramrod straight in his Oxfords), and was pretty solid and robust, even before the muscles expanded. Sunny was more delicate, like their mum, one of those people who appeared to have extra bones, little knobbly ones that protruded and stretched her skin.

'Could you go and see if Blossom's still on my bed, sweetness?' Sunny asks Eleanor, returning the rock to the shelf. 'If she is, I won't need to shut Daisy in the treatment room. I don't like leaving the cats together when I'm out. Daisy likes to torment Blossom.'

'Sure.' Eleanor heads up the twisted pine staircase.

Sunny disappears through the archway, returning with a violin case and fringed suede boots. 'Yes, the festival was just the tonic I needed after seeing Mick.' Her smile wobbles, a hint of discomfort beneath the composure. 'He's had a bad few days. I truly hope I'm wrong,' Sunny says in an undertone, 'but I sense he's giving up a little.'

'Oh dear, really?'

'Yes. He looks so weary and finds it difficult to shuffle around without help.' Sunny's eyes flutter, as if batting away invisible tears. She props the violin against the wall, next to two others. 'I still find it hard to accept that he can't speak. He gets so frustrated, poor soul. You know Mick, how he loved to talk.'

Eleanor's pumps pound down the stairs. 'Blossom's on the bed. I've been stroking her.' She heads off to find Daisy.

'It's what helped me to accept Mick going into Beeches Green; knowing that he'd have lots of company,' Sunny continues. 'Several of the staff have a really positive energy, but I feel the care's sometimes lacking. And it's so frenetic.'

'Really? That's a shame.' I'd always thought it had a warm, cheery atmosphere, considering how ancient, ill and cantankerous most of the residents were, but feel I have no right to say so.

'Anyway, we must keep positive.' Sunny's facial switch flicks back to serenity setting. 'I'll just fetch some massage oil.' She heads upstairs, gliding noiselessly.

I feel sorry for Sunny. She's devoted to Mick, and I know how difficult it is for her. Mick coped well living alone for several years after his wife Mary died, and even after his first stroke doctors predicted a good recovery, that he'd regain his independence. But after Dan died, Mick suffered a second stroke and Sunny's temporary return from her travels became permanent. She'd made huge sacrifices, suppressing her lifelong wanderlust, and dutifully visited her dad in the home – rarely missing a day.

Dan had very occasional contact with his parents. He tolerated them for Eleanor's sake. He'd despised his dysfunctional upbringing and Mick and Mary's hippy lifestyle. He wasn't surprised his dad had suffered a stroke, with all the drugs and booze he'd consumed. It was almost as if Dan felt he'd got his just deserts. Sunny, on the other hand, embraced her unconventional childhood. 'I know I was very small when our parents were into the hippy lifestyle, but I have so many happy memories. I loved the freedom, the fields and the fresh air,' she'd told me during a short stay when Mick had first fallen ill and she'd flown back from Greece. Mick was no angel, but he had a big heart. She wished Dan could have seen the best in him. It was the closest she'd every got to criticising her darling Dan.

'OK, I think I'm ready now.' Sunny's back, bag firmly on her shoulder. 'I'm doing a treatment later – bit of an emergency.' She turns towards the door; halts. 'That reminds me, Carrie. I had a new patient the other day who used to work for Dan. Michael Whitley … or Whitfield? Charming man.'

'Was it Michael Whitham? Really big fella, very tall?'

'Yes.' Sunny stares past me. 'He was so shocked to hear about Dan, said he didn't know many people who looked after themselves better.'

'That's for certain!' As soon as I say it, I know it's come out wrong.

'Well yes, but … he did it for you. For the family, and because … ' Sunny stops, shoots me an uncharacteristically stern look, then turns away.

I hop on my Conflict Dodgem, breathing deeply, silently puzzling over what she'd meant, and what she was about to add before silencing herself. I certainly never pushed Dan to keep himself in peak condition – not like some wives. If anything, I was the one under pressure. I couldn't let myself turn into a middle-aged munter with such a fit husband. I'll never forget what Slim Kim said after Dan had picked me up after step class one night. It was summer and he'd been exercising, so he was wearing short shorts and a clingy vest. 'Your hubby's such a dish. I wish mine looked after himself like that,' she'd declared, lips pulled in a 'phwooaar' pose. 'His Nibs is so fat he looks like he's swallowed our Chow, and he's got enough back, crack and ear hair to knit an Afghan.' I'd creased. She was right. Dan was a dish indeed – albeit a very low-fat, sin-free one – and I'd appreciated the fruits of his labours. I'd never stopped fancying him.

'Shall I shut Daisy in too?' Eleanor appears through the archway.

'No, that's fine,' Sunny says. 'She likes to wander if Blossom's out of her way.'

It dawns on me that Sunny and I are like her two cats. Sunny's Daisy, the wanderer, all soft and fluffy but not quite what she appears. In the same room, we made each other's backs arch. But I invariably yielded, like Blossom, so although we stiffened and spat a little, we didn't reach the full-on fighting stage.

★★★

'Mick will be so pleased to see you both,' Sunny says, giving Eleanor a big squeeze as our feet crunch across the gravel drive that sweeps up to the converted Edwardian house, patches of pale blue paint flaking around its sash windows. 'You should see how his face lights up when his friend's granddaughter visits.'

We find Mick sitting in a high-backed green chair in the communal area, with its worn carpet and peeling striped wallpaper. It's lunchtime and the room's full of clatter and gusts of cooked cabbage and mildew. The only other face I recognise belongs to a lady with a wispy white fringe and hunched back sat by the window. A friendly old thing, a costume brooch always pinned to her cardigan, she's convinced it's a luxury hotel. Last time Eleanor and I visited, she'd boasted about her daughter's success as a film director, which paid for the accommodation. In fact, her daughter directed sales on Morrisons' fish counter. Yet she was so convincing; worthy of an Oscar.

Mick looks gaunt and unshaven, his smoky-grey hair thin and lacklustre, though the old twinkle lights up in his mahogany eyes at the sight of Eleanor. A broad, toothy smile stretches the deep dimples that accentuate his resemblance to Dan.

'Baarr aay,' Mick says, beckoning his granddaughter for a cuddle.

'Hi, Granddad.' Eleanor throws herself at him, settling on a frayed chair by his side. I lean over, kiss his scratchy cheek.

'You look tired,' Sunny says, pulling up two chairs to face him. 'I'm sensing you didn't have a good night's sleep, sweetness. It's not surprising in this place.' She takes her dad's hand.

'Yaaam.' He drops his head to demonstrate his fatigue, following it with an impish, one-sided smile. It's a good job his face is so expressive, now his tongue's been taken.

While Sunny tells him about the folk festival, and Eleanor talks about school and drama club, I watch a tiny

118

lady in a brown woollen hat knitting the longest scarf I've ever seen.

A young woman wheels in a trolley, handing Mick a bowl of ice-cream, which he balances precariously between his frail legs. He refuses Sunny's offer of help, so we watch nervously as he carefully negotiates each mouthful, at one point dropping the spoon and looking agitated when Eleanor bends to pick it up.

The old lady by the window catches my eye. 'I'm off to the theatre tonight.'

'Lovely,' I say, nodding.

'You're not. It's bingo,' a skinny woman to her left snaps. Eleanor looks at me and we snigger. Sunny nobly ignores it.

'I've got some lavender oil to massage your feet – see if we can reduce that swelling.' She taps her dad's knee. 'Sadly, I haven't got time to give the woman who does all the knitting a hand massage today.' She pulls a bottle from her bag. 'I wish the carers would help him get outside into the grounds more.' She looks at her dad. 'You've always loved being outdoors, haven't you, in your element camping at all those festivals? Saying that, Dan and I did too. Making dens in the woods. Do you remember when I got lost and neighbours had to help search for me?' Mick waves his fist, feigning anger.

Sunny grabs a stool, gently raising Mick's legs and removing his socks. The bulging flesh around his ankles is streaked with thick purple veins.

'Oh dear. No dancing for you this week.' I give his shin a gentle tap. Mick smiles, wiggling his upper body, dad-at-a-disco fashion.

As Sunny rubs her thumbs up and down her dad's ankles, telling us how there should be a quiet room as it was 'impossible to get a sense of calm in here', a male carer with a dazzling ginger beard and wiry hair comes over to take Mick's bowl.

'Three female visitors today, Mick, you lucky thing.' The carer stands by Sunny, hands on his wide hips, transfixed by her ritual.

'You're not usually in on a Sunday,' Sunny says.

'The deputy manager's in Spain.' He glances at the noticeboard. 'Vejer de la Frontera.'

'Oh, I know it well. I spent several weeks there while travelling through Europe,' Sunny says. 'A beautiful Moorish hilltop town – full of wonderful, vibrant colours and the smell of pine forests. On a clear day, you can see the coast of Morocco.' Her eyes widen, as if in a trance. Something has stirred.

'Bet you wish you were there now,' the carer says. Sunny doesn't reply. 'Wish I was. Are you bringing your fiddle in again next weekend?'

'If you'd like me to.' Sunny blushes, rubbing deep into the tissue on her dad's ankles. I'm convinced they're flirting.

'We love hearing Sunny play. Last weekend, Mrs Blake cried all the way through *Danny Boy*. Oh yes, the doctor's prescribed some new water tablets and sleeping pills.'

'Oh, more tablets.' Sunny sighs. 'I'd really rather he didn't have sleeping pills. There's a herbal remedy on his locker. It contains valerian root and passionflower, both are great for aiding sleep naturally.'

'Well, I suggest you chat to the doctor.' The carer taps

Mick's shoulder. 'I bet you'd prefer a pint before bed, eh, to help you sleep?' Or maybe some pot, I think wickedly. He gives Mick a playful punch, walking away. 'How's that scarf coming along, Vera?' he bellows. 'Is it time to call the *Guinness Book of World Records*?'

'OK, let's put your socks back on then, Dad,' Sunny says.

Eleanor and I both stare. She never calls him dad. Always Mick.

Mick jerks his leg, some kind of spasm perhaps. For a moment, I think he's going to kick her. Sunny looks strangely uncomfortable.

'Gosh, what was that about?' she says with an awkward smile. 'Did you want me to carry on. I'm sorry, I'll make it a longer massage next time.'

Yes, what was that all about?

CHAPTER 11

If only ripping it up would rid it from my mind. I stare at the mess of torn newspaper scattered like black and white confetti on the breakfast bar and floor beneath me.

A few bits of paper float in my bowl of cereal. I bash them with a spoon; several drown. My appetite's abandoned me. If only I'd cancelled Dan's weekend newspaper delivery, I chastise myself, then perhaps I wouldn't have seen it.

But it's too late. That day's front page headline, now in tatters, is still there – in bold – in my mind's eye, and emblazoned on everything I look at:

AGEING POP STAR'S ULTIMATE COMEBACK
Bryan Flint pays £2 million to 'live again'

There was a photograph of the star, now aged sixty-eight – taken after a recent facelift by the look of his too smooth, glossy skin and stunned expression – and a two-page article about how the old rocker had announced to the world that he wanted to be cryonically preserved. He'd donated two million pounds to research into improving human preservation techniques.

But my eyes had fixed on a panel down the side of

the second page, and a far more familiar face. Dan, pictured in his favourite grey Italian suit and pale pink tie, had stared at me from under a smaller heading: *Other cryonics enthusiasts who've dug deep to donate*. The caption: *FROZEN ASSETS: Tetford businessman Dan Colwell handed over £200,000 before he died*.

Anger's constricting my breath. Why had they raked up Dan's case again? And how had they found out about his donation? Only Imogen and Mark knew. I'm not sure we'd even mentioned it to Eleanor. Dan didn't want it to be common knowledge. It was a personal gesture, not one for the public domain, unlike his company's charity donations – all recipients universally accepted as worthy causes, and great for PR, his acts of kindness carried out with a loud fanfare, official photographer and a tip-off to the local news.

Wondering if a distant thud is Eleanor stirring upstairs, I frantically gather the shreds of paper and push them deep into the bin. I don't want Eleanor to see it. It would upset her so much, like the previous stories. Yet I know it's hopeless – destroying one newspaper won't hide the headlines, shield her from gossip.

I'm in two minds about phoning Imogen, burdening her at this difficult time. Following the porn episode, she had another row with Ben, ended up taking the girls to Brittany to stay with her sister for a few days. Imogen was convinced their issues must signify some huge, insurmountable problem in their marriage. It all seemed so drastic to me, a truly uncharacteristic overreaction for Imogen, always so considered and sensible, and I wondered if she was withholding some vital information. Had something else prompted their move abroad? A sexual misdemeanour in Britain by Ben perhaps? Yet Imogen would surely have told me. We shared everything. Maybe she was having some kind of meltdown, her superpowers flagging? Not surprising with what she'd taken on.

I have to call. I stretch across the chaise longue, the red leather still pristine and retaining its rich, oily smell. I think of Dan. 'It's going to be a "chaise longue" one!' he'd tease when I settled there for my more epic chats, arching an eyebrow at Eleanor.

I'm so glad to hear Imogen's back home – and no longer threatening to leave Ben. But things are still tense between them. She fears the girls are picking up on it. I'm desperate to see her. There's a possibility she'll be flying back to the UK for a meeting, so fingers crossed.

I tell her about the headline. She got up early to work – hadn't heard any UK news.

'Bloody hell. Not again. Can they really just keep printing stories without speaking to you?'

'It appears so. I know Dan didn't keep the cryonics thing a secret, but he was discreet about the donation. So much for that!'

'I thought donations like that were confidential.'

'So did I.'

'I'm sure Mark wouldn't have told the press – and no one else knew, did they? Did Dan tell Sunny?'

'Not to my knowledge.'

After hanging up, I call Sunny, telling her Eleanor's landed the part in *Fame* she wanted, how proud I am. Sunny's stoked, requesting a ticket to see one of the performances. She talks about two new patients she's taken on. I cut in.

'Have you heard the news story, about Bryan Flint … the cryonics thing?'

'No.' Sunny sounds genuinely surprised.

'It's on the front page of *The Daily Press*, mentions Dan donating a big sum of money to fund research.'

'Gosh. Is that true?'

'Yes, but he didn't want it to be common knowledge,' I say, rather pointedly.

'I had no idea … he didn't mention it to me.' Sunny sounds deflated, voice weak. So it wasn't her. 'Did you know they were going to run the story?'

'No.'

'Did they mention your … position again – not signing up.'

'No – why would they?' I snap.

'It's just … well, they've always mentioned it in previous stories and I wondered—'

'No.'

Sunny has the sense to move on, returning to work chat, but my head continues to contemplate who the culprit could be.

The next day at work, I scrutinise colleagues' faces, try to guess who's heard the news. I'm pretty sure Pete has – his eyes dart more than usual as he briefs me about several new tasks. Barbara has, too, I surmise, as she does the opposite, giving me what appear to be sympathetic stares. Tash is clearly oblivious – there's no way she'd be able to resist mentioning it.

It's a relief to finally discuss it with Mark, who makes

an excuse to get me in the kitchen mid-morning and comes straight out with it.

'Can they just keep writing what the hell they want – regurgitating stories?' I expel a loud sigh, throwing a teaspoon into the sink.

'Well, yes, pretty much.' Mark takes a swig from a bottle of sparkling water, letting out a grunty belch.

'I wonder how the bloody hell they found out about Dan's donation? I'm pretty sure only three of us knew – and Imogen's in France.' I try not to sound accusatory, ensuring my eyes skirt his.

'You don't think I … ?' Mark stops drinking, eyebrows raised. I hesitate, but he jumps back in before I can think, or speak. 'Bloody hell. I'd hope that wouldn't even cross your mind.'

Sadly it had. Only fleetingly, against my will – and just because it couldn't be anyone else. But I'd arrested the thought immediately. There's no way he'd do it. And then I'd been upset with myself for thinking otherwise, even for a second. What was happening to me?

Mark reads into my silence, clearly unconvinced by my emphatic shake of the head.

'That's a bloody smack in the face, that one.' I try to force a dismissive laugh but tears well. 'Sorry, but, come on – really!?' He marches out, shuts the door.

I've seen Mark moody before, but the rest of the day's different. Even Tash picks up on it. Was he OK? She pesters him relentlessly. While I'm in the kitchen, he leaves for an interview without saying goodbye.

That evening, I'm still giving myself metaphorical kicks for how atrociously I'd handled Mark, possibly jeopardising my relationship with one of the most important people in my life, when I receive a call from a *Tetford Times* reporter tasked with doing a local follow-up on the pop star story. He wonders if I want to comment – particularly in relation to Dan's donation.

'Who told the press about that?' I squeeze my spare hand into a fist so tight it cuts off the circulation in my fingers. 'My husband was very clear on it not being made public knowledge.'

'These things tend to get out, Mrs Colwell,' the reporter says. 'It may well have been the research foundation themselves.'

'I'd rather you didn't run the story,' I say, impressed by my audacity and determined tone. 'I have a daughter, it was two years ago – we don't want to keep seeing—'

'I appreciate what you're saying, but it's not my decision. I can pass on what you've said to my editor but …'

I stop listening. I swallow my anger, put down the phone and close my eyes to block the tears.

Dan's story will be resurrected in the local paper tomorrow – and along with it all the hurt and anguish it stirred in Eleanor and me – and there's not a thing I can do about it.

CHAPTER 12

'They must be short of news.' Mark and I stand by his desk, leaning over a copy of the *Tetford Times*. Dan's donation's the lead story on page five.

'Yes, always.' Mark folds the paper.

'I'm so sorry about … Dan's donation … what I implied. I really didn't mean to,' I say, as Mark flicks through the pages of his reporter's notebook. 'I think I'm losing the plot.'

'Look – no more bloody apologies. All forgotten.' He taps his pen on the desk. I hope he *has* truly forgiven me for my stupid semi-accusation.

'I can't believe Pete hasn't heard about the Lorex contract,' I say, heading to my chair. 'Do you think it's a 'no' and he's not telling us, because he looks so miserable?'

'No. He says they've delayed the decision. Something to do with a big project they're working on. We may not hear for a few months. I hope the business can hold out.'

At home, I get a message from Ashley saying he's staying with a friend in Cherlsbury for a few days as he's secured an audition for a part in a restoration comedy. As it's half way between us, perhaps we can meet. I decide I can't evade a straight answer any longer, so agree in principle. I just need to sort a day off.

Hearing Eleanor's key in the lock, I guiltily snap the laptop shut, slide it under the duvet and jump off the bed. The previous evening, Eleanor had rightly called me a hypocrite after catching me unawares next to a pile of women's magazines, legs curled up in slouchy leggings, computer snuggled by my belly like a comfort blanket. 'You moan at me for always being on my gadgets. He-ll-oo,' she'd said, elongating the word. I couldn't deny it.

'Hi. I'm in the bedroom,' I yell. There's the usual reverberating thud of her schoolbag hitting the oak floor in the hall, a few footsteps – then nothing. I find her in bed, head buried beneath the duvet.

'Eleanor, what on earth's the matter, darling?' I try to pull off the cover, but she grips it tightly.

'Go away.'

'I'm not going until you tell me what's the matter.' I perch on the bed. 'The first rehearsal wasn't that bad, was it? Have you got another detention?' Silence. 'Did they run out of ham pizza at lunch again?'

'Shut up, Mum, you're not funny.' A muffled voice rises from under the cover. Seconds later, Eleanor sits up, dragging two index fingers across the tears under her eyes.

'It's the newspaper stories. About Dad – the donation thing. This new guy who everyone hates had a go in English about it. It was beyond cringe. He asked if I was going to join Dad – maybe they could make space in the school freezer. Amy said Bethany told her that her mum had said it was 'immoral' but when I asked Bethany, she denied it.' I lean over to wipe a wet black smudge from Eleanor's cheekbone. She pulls back. 'He was humming the song from *Frozen*, then Mr George threw him out. Mr

George had a little chat to me after, because I got really upset.'

'Do you want me to go into school?'

'No way. You'll just make it worse.'

'It will be forgotten in no time.' I pull Eleanor into a hug, landing a crafty kiss on her wet cheek. 'I know how you're hurting. If it helps to talk – I'm here to listen any time. It helps me too—'

'Mum – not now.'

'OK. Love you.'

'Love you too.'

'Cheer up, and I'll see you downstairs later. How about you, me and Mr Fluff have a big cuddle on the sofa and watch *Corrie*?'

Eleanor looks disgusted. 'Mum!'

Days after I've assured Eleanor – and endeavoured to convince myself – that the donation story would soon be forgotten, the *Tetford Times* run another story. A local charity leader has hit out at narcissistic, wealthy people 'wasting' their money on self-indulgent whims when there are so many good causes desperately in need of funds. He's scathing about pop star Bryan Flint, but also implicates Dan. The claims have proved controversial, prompting a flood of readers' letters. Everyone has an opinion, it seems.

'But Dan's company gave thousands to local charities. Why didn't they tell readers that?' I ask Mark, who's reading the story on my computer screen.

'Um, they sort of allude to it. Remember, they don't like facts to get in the way of a good story.'

'I don't think I can stand this any more.' I take an audible breath, feel my throat tightening, eyes stinging.

'I think you should ask for an apology, and maybe a follow-up story about Dan's charity donations. Balance things out. Local papers are usually pretty fair about these things. It's worth speaking to the editor.'

'Yes, but … it's just another story then, for Eleanor to face. Maybe it's best to leave it. Oh, I don't know.'

Mark curls his meaty hand over my forearm, giving it a firm squeeze. 'It's up to you. Do you want me to contact the paper, see what I can do?'

'I think so.'

'No worries.' Mark tilts his head, smiling softly.

'I don't deserve you,' I say.

'That's true.'

Back at home, a message from Sheena lands on my laptop:

Hi Carrie. I can't believe what Ashley told you. So sad. But at least now you know. Did you decide to meet again? Your last message made me laugh out loud. Yes, I remember Leroy – and those shorts! I must confess I bought the soundtrack album (from Woolworths). Hope Eleanor went for it! The local newspaper's planning another appeal story for sightings of Geoff – fingers crossed. The girls keep nagging me to go out, but the invites aren't exactly flooding in! We make dinner party conversation awkward, don't we? Like you, counselling isn't really for me, but my friend knows a life coach, so I'm meeting for a chat over a glass of wine. Worth a try? Must go, daughter number 2 needs homework help. Sheena xxx

Every day was stomach-churning for Sheena, I think, head hanging over the sofa to swipe biscuit crumbs into the thick tufts of the rug. But she saw the media in such a positive light. Her allies; potential saviours. It's an industry I'd love to work in, yet I was seeing a different side, beginning to view them as an adversary.

I'd shaken off all the early sensational, insensitive headlines. Back then, all I could think of was surviving without Dan and making things better for Eleanor. But I still remembered them; and, recently, with increasing clarity.

One particular gem was: *Over My Dead Body. Wife Refuses to Join Hubby in Freezer*. I'd only spoken, briefly, to one local reporter – the rest was scraped off loose tongues or concocted from hearsay and speculation. I'd taken great pleasure in wrapping potato peelings in those headlines and stamping them into the bin.

I can't resist skimming the latest *Times* article again, finding myself immersed in the online comments. A few are positive, several writers saying they'd sign up for cryonics if they could afford it. One relished the anticipation of 'seeing the wonders of the future'. But most were scornful, some scathing, spiteful, describing cryonics as selfish, ludicrous, deluded, greedy – even vile and deeply creepy. '*It's a scheme to part the gullible and their cash.*' '*Evolution needs fresh life, nobler people with more commitment on this planet, not retreads on worn tyres.*' Some cracked jokes – about staff unplugging the freezers to charge their phones, the bodies ending up as porridge or expensive hamburger, or what movie star they'd prefer their spouse to come back as.

I've heard about internet trolls and assume many are just that – people deliberately trying to provoke a reaction with inflammatory remarks, hiding behind the mask of virtual anonymity.

Stupidly, I watch an updated version of the *Cryonics Emergency Procedure* video on an official website, and wish I hadn't. Later, images of what I'd seen keep hurtling across my mind. Sometimes, the corpse the trio of masked men are preparing for preservation is a dummy, others it's real – it's Dan's. It reminds me of the nightmares I had after the memorial service. Back then, I'd blamed the anti-depressants.

I try to lose myself in a magazine, but Sunny phones to express her outrage over the charity story.

'Dan had such a generous spirit,' she says. There's no way she's going to let people think her brother was less than charitable. I explain that Mark's sorting it – he's the expert – but, no, she's resolute; she's going to put the record straight. I think she feels I should be ranting and raving, making more noise in defence of Dan's honour, rather than getting quietly upset.

As far as tonics go, they don't come more potent. I have Imogen sat opposite and a huge slice of chocolate and toffee pecan cake right under my nose. It's been worth enduring a tedious drive through heavy traffic to Heathrow airport, dodging impatient sunseekers and recklessly wheeled suitcases in an arrivals lounge with the air con set to Arctic chill – just to see her huge, infectious, gummy smile. Shame it's only for a couple of hours.

133

We're sitting by the window of a crowded café in Terminal One, watching the mayhem and madness of departures, flustered travellers fretting beneath flight information screens and joining queues that never diminish, while immaculately dressed women clip-clop across the concourse in shiny red shoes and matching lips and neckerchiefs to aid and appease.

'You look really well,' I reiterate.

'Thanks, lovely.' Imogen beams. Her hair's a brighter chestnut, the fringe short and showing off tinted brows and eyes shaded in two tones of green. She removes her tailored jacket, revealing a striped top.

'Where are the onions?'

'Funny,' she says. 'I think horizontal stripes are a mistake – they make you look bigger apparently, not good when you've being enjoying French food a bit too much. It's why I wore a long top, means I can undo my skirt and breathe.' She fumbles at her waistband, expels a force nine gust of air. 'Phew, that's better.'

It's not long before she asks about Ashley. 'So are you going to meet him again then?'

'I think so.'

Imogen's shapely brows take flight. 'I wonder whether he'll tell his wife he's meeting a significant ex?'

I'd wondered the same. I shrug. 'I feel guilty asking for a day off when I've just booked a week so Eleanor and I can escape somewhere sunny.'

We talk a bit more about all the media madness. Then I get out the letters.

'Look at these.' I watch Imogen's eyes pop, jaw slackening as she reads. Two begging notes. One's professional-looking, on thick paper, with logos and several different typefaces, from a charity appealing for funds to send aid workers to Africa. The other's badly typed on a thin, crinkled sheet, littered with errors, from a man desperate for a life-saving drug.

'Sodding hell. So they assume Dan's donation means you're loaded and can ...' She stops. 'What a cheek! And how did they get your address?'

'I'm not sure. I have another pile of post I haven't opened. I think there's more. The thing is, although it makes me cross, they're probably genuine requests, and I feel really bad—'

'Whoa, stop there.' Imogen holds up the letters, ripping them straight down the middle, then throws them on to the tray by her feet. 'Your local paper has a lot to answer for.'

I relay how Sunny's efforts to get an apology have been fruitless. She'd turned up at the newspaper's offices demanding to see the editor, but been fobbed off by his deputy who'd defended their right to quote people's opinions, however controversial. He maintained the story had been balanced, suggesting she write a letter for them to print. But Mark had fared better. He'd got access to the top, persuaded the editor, in lieu of an apology, to run a small story – not another big headline, he assured me – defending people's rights to donate their hard-earned cash to whatever they wanted and highlighting Dan's donations to good causes. Lots of people had contacted the newspaper voicing support for Dan and others like him. One woman had happily confessed her intention to squander her whole estate on cruises before she died, determined to enjoy every penny. Hopefully, that would be the end of it all.

'Anyway, how are things with you?' I realise I've hijacked the conversation and, as our cake has long departed and my Americano's a few degrees from iced coffee, it's clearly been a long time.

Imogen tells me she's started French lessons, Katie has a full set of teeth, Laura's taken up ballet and insisted on wearing her tutu to the Super U, practising her steps down every aisle. And, after exchanging several letters and emails, Ben's arranged to meet his biological mum, in Ireland. He's excited, but very nervous.

'I thought it might be a distraction,' she says. I knew there was a 'but' coming.

'But he's insisting we see a sex therapist,' she says, voice hushed.

'Really. Are you OK with that?'

'Not really …' she leans in, voice barely audible, '… talking about my sex life in front of a stranger fills me with dread – but I guess I should. I owe it to Ben to try. Things aren't getting any better. In fact, the longer it's gone on, the bigger deal it seems to be and the more pressure I feel. I can't do – it – at all now.' She fiddles with her gold pendant. 'Our first session, with Genevieve – I insisted it was a woman – is on Friday.'

'I'm sure it will help. You'll be OK. Lots of couples go through it. Having children changes things, you just need time.'

'I hope so. If it takes much longer, Ben will certainly be off with some Parisian nymphomaniac; if he isn't already. And you'll have three new lodgers.' Imogen giggles nervously. I rest my hand on her wrist, watching her chase cake crumbs with a fingertip.

Although it's ancient history, I've never been entirely convinced Imogen's totally over Ben's misdemeanour when they were first together. He'd got off-his-face drunk at a nightclub and slept with a mate's girlfriend. They were both distraught, Ben deeply regretful. They parted for months, but got back together. I'd seen hints of Imogen's insecurity and a thin jealous streak, though she usually hid both well beneath her bubbles, leaving everyone to assume they possessed the perfect recipe for relationship success and their sex life must be as steamy as her treacle puddings.

Ben oozed charm, with his permanently tousled hair and melodic Irish voice, and women loved it, one or two perhaps misinterpreting friendliness for flirting over the years, though I'd never seen him cross the line.

I recall one of Imogen's dinner parties when the super skinny wife of Ben's colleague had overdone the Pinot and flirted outrageously with him. She'd sat next to him, giggling through whitened teeth at every word he uttered, nudging him with a toned arm; even pawing his sleeve a few times. Imogen didn't say anything, but I watched her simmering. Her revenge was sweet. The flirty female got the only soufflé that hadn't risen – served with a sugary smile, of course.

I'm concerned the problem in the bedroom is reigniting Imogen's old anxieties.

'Come on – who's being a daft mare now?' I ask, as Imogen stacks her plate on mine. 'Anyway, Eleanor and I want a holiday in Reims. You can't come back.'

137

CHAPTER 13

A noisy crew of hollering workmen with hefty power tools, all wearing matching low-slung grey trousers and showing several inches of arse-crack, greet me as I open the pencil pleat curtains on a misty May morning. A drunken motorist has knocked a street lamp askew and it clearly takes four burly blokes to dig out the foundations and realign it. I look up at a feathery chrome sky that could go either way, just like my day ahead.

A monobrowed weatherman appears on the TV as I dress, promising an abundance of spring sunshine in Cherlsbury, the Cotswold town where Ashley and are meeting. I'm only marginally less nervous than before the previous meeting, I think as I pull on a cami top, trusting the forecast.

Pete agreed to give me a day off, despite it turning into a last-minute request. I dallied for a couple of weeks, unsure whether I had the courage to go through with it. 'Take your time owing now, because we're going to be busy bees if we get the Lorex contract,' he'd said in an almost optimistic tone. Yesterday, Tash kept referring to my planned outing as a second date and I had to correct her. 'He's married. We're just meeting for lunch. We have – unfinished business; a few more things to talk about.'

'Of course.' Tash raised one razored eyebrow.

I'm emptying the dishwasher when Eleanor shuffles in, one arm gripping her tummy.

'I feel really sick – and I've got a headache.'

'Oh dear.' My first thought is: 'Not today! I can't meet Ashley if Eleanor's too ill for school'. My second is that my first should have been 'My poor daughter, what if it's something serious', and my third 'I must be a bad mother because of my first thought'. I feel Eleanor's forehead, trying to make amends for the badly prioritised thoughts.

'You're not overly warm, darling.' She looks normal – well, what passes as normal before she hits the bathroom; dozy, dishevelled, eyes barely open ('like pee holes in the snow' as Dad says). No rashes. No smell of bile on her breath. Nothing obvious. But she's still in pyjamas, a clear sign she's planning a return to the duvet.

'When did it come on?' I try to hide the disappointment, but not the concern.

'I don't know,' she growls. 'Duh, I was asleep!'

'Why don't you try some breakfast? Might make you feel better.'

'I don't want breakfast.' She climbs on to a stool, slumping like a rag doll, head against the breakfast bar.

'I'll get some painkillers. They may help the headache at least.'

'OK.' A muffled voice rises from between her arms, which have formed a barricade around her head.

I fetch the pills from my bag, desperately wondering what else I can do – one of Sunny's natural remedies; pray, perhaps?

'Have you actually been sick?'

'No,' she says, with a whimper.

I pour a glass of water, watching her grimace and gag as she swallows the tablets, then slump again. I'm distraught. All that planning and anticipation for nothing; arranging for Eleanor to go to Bethany's after school and telling another fib about who I was seeing.

It's a hopeless prospect. I'll have to cancel. 'Shall I phone the school then, tell them you're too ill to go in? You'll have to stay in bed though – no TV.'

'Yes.' The stifled voice again.

I can't believe this is happening. Ashley may not be able to rearrange. He may not want to. I can't ask Pete for another day off any time soon.

In my rush to fetch the phone, I trip over Eleanor's trainers in the hall and do a clumsy forward hop, letting go of a few expletives and landing inelegantly, but safely, a short distance ahead. I glare at the trainers.

Then I remember. Eleanor has athletics trials. Eleanor despises athletics; running fast is 'painful and pointless'.

What an actress she's turning into. The devious little …

★★★

'What a gorgeous day.'

''Tis quite splendid, I concur,' Ashley says with a wry smile, taking a big swipe at his raspberry ice cream with a pink-coated tongue.

We're sat on a grassy bank in a beautiful park filled with exposed flesh, espadrilles and skippy excitement over the burst of surprisingly hot sunshine.

The park's lined on three sides by elegant, balconied white houses posing behind shiny black arrowhead railings, and, at the lower end is a little wooden refreshment kiosk with a striped awning and packed picnic benches.

I'm devouring a giant tub of rum and raisin ice cream, legs outstretched on the perfectly clipped grass, catching drifts of sun cream and squeals from a huddle of high-spirited students on a blanket nearby, starting to feel truly relaxed and wishing I didn't have to drive home so soon.

Ashley's leant back on one elbow, a long scar on his upper arm prominent under the sun's glare, its edges dark pink and puckered. My eyes rest on the familiar carpet of downy fair hair on his forearms, and I recall, with a rush of adrenalin, how it felt beneath my wandering fingertips. I avert my gaze.

We've both fallen a little quiet, sedated by the lovely long lunch taken on the terracotta-tiled terrace of a smart French bistro opposite a row of smart shops with pretentious names in elaborate fonts. I'd arrived late and apologetic. Eleanor's little act to try to skive athletics had ended in a verbal battle – she still insisted she really did feel unwell – and then a deliberate 'go slow', which meant she missed the first lesson at school, I got stuck in a rush-hour jam, was late for my hair appointment, then couldn't find anywhere to park when I finally reached Cherlsbury. But Monobrow Man had been right. A few miles before I exited the motorway, just as Oasis were belting out *Don't Look Back in Anger* on the car radio and I was smiling inwardly at the irony of the song, intense golden rays bullied their way through the pale grey clouds.

'Have you got any photos of your daughter?' Ashley sits up.

'There's a few on my phone.'

'Do show, then. I want to see if she looks like her mum.'

I smile. I've softened – just like our ice creams – unable to stay frosty with Ashley for long. I'd tried in the bistro; a few initial terse, brief responses to his questions in a bid to make it blatant that instant forgiveness and unflagging friendliness weren't on the menu. He'd remained sedate and courteous, gradually winning me over with his easy chat.

I hold my mobile between us, clicking through the images. Some are from another life, it seems.

'That was last year,' I say at last. 'She's changed a bit lately – wears more make-up, frowns more, has grown her fringe and a bad attitude—'

'She's very pretty.'

'Yes, she's lovely, though it's hard to convince her of that these days, teenage insecurity and all that. She thinks her best friend gets all the boys because she's prettier, cleverer, more confident, less spotty – the list goes on.'

A Toy Story football hurtles across the grass towards us for the third time, hitting Ashley's chest. He grins nonchalantly, rolling it steadily back to the uncoordinated toddler whose tiny legs are lost in oversized shorts. The boy's mum mouths an apology.

'Who do you think she looks like?' Ashley sniffs loudly – an old habit.

'She's a mixture really, probably more like her dad.'

'How has she taken it – you know … losing him?'

142

I'm surprised by his directness. 'She's coped fairly well. She hates talking about it though. I've tried hard to get her to open up.'

'I hope you don't mind me mentioning it, but I saw your husband in the newspapers again.' Ashley lifts his sapphire blue T-shirt, hooking one thumb in the front pocket of his cargo shorts.

'Yes, it's really upset Eleanor. Poor girl's been teased at school. I've had loads of begging letters …' Ashley pulls a deep frown, '… and you should see some of the online comments about cryonics. I just hope Eleanor hasn't. Some people are quite vicious.'

'Really – how?'

'Oh – where to start? My husband's been labelled a loony, and cryonics a crazy con. Some of the attacks have been pretty personal. One guy said it was a big scam, a tax on vanity and that the last thing the team preparing my husband's body did was stick a note on his forehead saying '*Mug*'.'

Ashley slowly shakes his head. 'Morons. I wonder how much those people really know about it.' He pauses. 'I quite like the idea – seems worth a punt. Scientists can do amazing stuff now, with stem cells and such. Impossible things are becoming possible.' I stay silent, intrigued by his reaction. 'I'm guessing you don't share your husband's desire then?'

'No. But I respect it. I just wish others did. Dan wasn't eccentric, or a sci-fi nerd. He was pretty clever, down to earth.'

'I guess it's something we've all thought about. Being invincible.' Ashley gazes into the distance. 'I was

143

desperate to be Superman – dodging that kryptonite. I can understand someone wanting to live again, or forever. If you enjoy life, why wouldn't you want to? You spend years learning and progressing, death seems a waste.'

'It scares me a bit.'

'Why?'

'I don't know.' I take another spoonful of rum and raisin. 'Probably, because I don't understand it – science baffles and scares me in equal measure. And I'm a bit squeamish about death … corpses and all that.'

'I know what you mean.' Ashley knocks off some grass stuck to his scar. 'I'd never really heard about cryonics until I read … well, not a real case.' A pause. 'I don't get the science.'

'You and virtually everyone else, it seems. Even the experts can't agree over whether it could work. Many say neurons are destroyed by freezing, cells would turn to mush. My friend Tash said she'd worry about waking up looking like a pork scratching. She can't bear going a few days without being exfoliated, let alone decades.'

Ashley lets out a suppressed laugh. 'I don't like the thought of having to die over again though, and …' he squints into the sun, eyes taking on a metallic sheen '… what about the soul?'

'Hmmm. I'm not sure there's a place for spirituality in cryonics.'

'Are there many people who want to be preserved then?'

'Oh yes, Dan won't be lonely in the freezer – he's in good company,' I say, putting down my tub and wiping my hands on my linen trousers. 'Rumour has it a few celebrities are already in there, and music mogul Sam McDowell's supposedly booked his space – although I'm guessing he'll want to be on the top shelf and have piped music.'

Ashley grins. 'Does it cost a lot?'

'Yes – an arm and a leg … and a head … and a torso …' I stop. 'Sorry that was a cheap shot. Dan had his own business, the money wasn't an issue – as you may have read.'

Ashley takes my empty tub to the bin. 'Sorry for all the questions,' he says, ambling back. He sits, legs crossed like a primary pupil on the carpet at story time. 'It must be a tough thing to deal with, and all the publicity—'

'Yes. And Dan's sister's been a total pain. She thinks I should sign up, too, to please him. It's what he wanted. She makes me feel guilty and … it's as if she thinks I should stay forever loyal to Dan, just in case he comes back.'

'That's not right.' Ashley's eyes narrow to slits.

'I know, but it gets to me at times. But then …' I hesitate, 'anyway, let's change the subject?' I wiggle my legs – they're starting to cramp. 'Have you prepared for your audition?'

'Course … sorry. Not really. Alas, I don't do preparation very well.'

I nod, recalling how much he procrastinated over learning lines, annoying lecturers with his frequent absences and late assignments.

'How about your wife? I suppose she has to do lots of preparation, and lesson planning?'

'Yes, she's very organised.' I wait for him to elaborate. 'We're not really together any more. We've been separated for a while, hoping to work things out. But …' He stops.

145

I'm convinced raisins are racing around my chest. He rubs his thighs. 'Both want different things, I guess.'

I lean back on the grass while Ashley tells me how his wife had never really been keen on the acting. 'She'd prefer me to get a proper job, so we can get a mortgage and a better house. She hates renting. To be fair, she's worked damn hard to qualify as a teacher – she was a classroom assistant before. It's not the easiest role, being married to a struggling actor. There's lots of time apart, no stability. This year's been rough with me out of action, and all the operations.'

'Yes. I can imagine.' But I couldn't envisage Ashley giving it up. Over lunch, he'd told me how nothing matched the feeling he got on stage. 'There's raw fear, but then the biggest buzz,' he'd said, eyes blazing with fervour. And I couldn't imagine a wife being other than preposterously proud to be married to a talented actor. I'd be happy to shout it from my rented rooftop.

But it wasn't just that. I persist with the questions and eventually prise out of him that he'd become keener to have children, especially since the accident, while his wife seemed less so. She'd decided to focus on her career, determined to be the one earning the reliable income. Her ambition was to be an assistant headteacher before she turned forty. She was thirty-six.

'I think we could have worked something out if we'd both wanted it enough and things were …' Ashley shuffles. 'I think I knew early on that things weren't right, but I didn't want to … walk away …' He picks at the grass.

Again! I think. *Say it*! So he could walk out on me, a smitten, obliging girlfriend, but not on a selfish, malcontented, resentful, controlling wife. But they were married, weren't they? And we'd only been together for seven months. It was right that he'd tried to make his marriage work.

I try to appear sympathetic about his separation but a voice in my head's saying 'serves you right' and, at the same time, I can't stop inappropriate thoughts in their tracks. Ashley's available. Did that change things? Then a sweep of despair. Ashley wants the one thing I can never give any man – a baby.

I fold the thoughts away; try to steer my mind in a different direction. After what he did to me, why should I care about his desire for a child, or his marital situation?

Ashley's subdued after his revelation and I'm still wrestling with several inner voices as we sit on a Cotswold stone wall by a glistening pond jewelled with sunken coins and topped by a cascading fountain, debating when I should leave and how long my journey back will take, both reluctant to be decisive, as always.

Ashley reaches out, flicking water at me. I feel a few cold droplets cling to my clammy cheek.

'OK. Have that.' I plunge my hand into the pond, splashing far more water than I'd intended. One side of his T-shirt is soaked.

'You really shouldn't have done that.' He grins mischievously, grabs my arm and grapples me to the edge of the water, pretending he intends to throw me in. I go to pull away but his arms lock me in. Then he kisses me.

CHAPTER 14

It's hard to focus after the fountain incident. Simple tasks prove painstakingly difficult, with a mind so delirious and distracted. This morning, I found my car keys in the fridge. Last night, still disorientated by the twists and turns of the day, I smothered my face in lemon foot cream, mistaking the yellow tube for my new moisturiser. I went to bed with a burning forehead, one shade short of strawberry.

The kiss has stirred up so many emotions – passion, excitement, confusion, guilt, betrayal – and endless questions. Should I have resisted? Was it significant? Could it ever lead anywhere? Did we look like a couple of sad oldies who should know better than to pucker up in public in the daylight? Did my breath smell of rum and raisin?

Over breakfast, I give myself a strict talking to: 'It was just a spur of the moment thing. We were splashing each other in a fountain on a glorious spring day in a picture postcard park; he'd have snogged an octogenarian with halitosis in such a perfect setting. It shouldn't have happened. It can't mean anything. We have a tarnished past. I can't trust him again. He has an estranged wife. He wants someone to start a family with – your baby days are over. Then I try to eject those thoughts, keen to enjoy the buzz and thrill – two old friends whose company I haven't shared for so long.

Several episodes of extreme daydreaming later, a pile of post thumps through the door. Casting aside the usual junk, bills and credit card inducements, I see an envelope addressed in erratic, spidery writing I don't recognise. A local postmark. I stare; handwritten mail's such a rarity. I'm not expecting anything – perhaps it's an invitation, or an early birthday card for Eleanor from a distant relative. Not another begging letter.

I tear it open. Inside is a single sheet, blank but for a few words in the centre, in huge, bold type:

'Your husband's a selfish freak. Give money to the living, not the dead.'

I wrench up my stomach muscles in a gasp. I'm sickened, imagining the sender, wicked and spiteful, bent menacingly over the keyboard, bashing out each letter, concluding the mission with a resonant cackle. Beneath the writing is a horrible yellowy-brown stain.

I'm startled by the phone, standing rigid for several seconds, legs unwilling to move. This person knows my address, perhaps my telephone number, too. I answer. Relief. It's a *Tetford Times* reporter.

'I'm putting the story together about local charitable donations – and your husband's generosity – and wondered if you wanted to comment,' says the cheery male voice.

'Not really.'

'OK – just wanted to give you the opportunity, that's all. We've got some good quotes from your husband's former secretary …' he pauses, '… Kirsten – saying what a generous man he was.'

'Oh … really.' I wonder why they'd contacted Kirsten. It's a long time since she'd worked as Dan's secretary. She'd left a couple of years before he died to look after baby number four.

'I think she felt a bit bad – wanted to make amends,' the reporter adds.

'For what?'

'Oh, didn't you know … for … letting the cat out the bag, telling the nationals about your husband's donation to that research trust.'

'Oh, really.' My mind's spinning.

I make a detour on my way back from work. I sit for ages, staring across the busy road through a wet window, watching between cars parked along the edges of neat driveways and tiny trimmed lawns, as neighbours come and go – a suited man dashing home under a giant golfing umbrella, a postman dropping a pile of letters on to a rain-soaked pavement – willing myself to knock on the door I assume is still Kirsten's, to confront her, but unable to. She may have moved. Besides, what would I say?

Tired of craning my neck, I'm daydreaming at the dashboard and think it's my Conflict Dodgem arriving when, from the corner of my eye, I spot a boxy blue car pull on to her drive, narrowly missing a neglected planter spilling over with a tangled shrub. The side panel on the car's passenger side is grey and unpainted, with white splodges across the door.

Kirsten climbs out, auburn hair drawn back in a loose ponytail, huge hooped earrings dangling. A blonde girl and a smaller boy in bright trainers join her as she fumbles in the back seat and pulls out a sleeping infant. It must be baby number five; the bump she was carrying when I saw her in the street a few months ago. I gulp. I can't do it.

I watch from a distance as Kirsten fumbles in a rucksack, then unlocks the door and walks in, toddler draped around one hip, fidgety girl following behind.

I stare ahead again, distracted, half watching an estate car trying to squeeze into the space in front of me. The rain's eased, just gentle flecks filling gaps on the windscreen. I should go.

Moments later, the driver makes his second attempt, bumper inching closer. I hear a bang. I jump, heart tripping.

I expect the man to leap out in horror, but the car's still moving, approaching the snug gap from a different angle. I turn to my right, so startled at the sight that I gasp loudly.

It's Kirsten, freckled face up close, chest pressed against the side window, waving with one hand, grumpy boy grasping the other. I lower the window.

'Hi. Thought I recognised the car,' she says. 'Surprised to see you.'

'Hi, Kirsten,' I say in a carefree voice, feeling foolish, mind frenziedly searching for a reason to be there. I glance at my open handbag on the passenger seat. 'I was driving … my mobile rang … thought I better pull over to answer it. Anyway, how are you? Looking well.'

'I'm fine, ta. Busy. My baby girl's teething and this one's having tantrums.' She lifts her straight eyebrows skywards. The bleary-eyed boy's clinging to her jeans, dark hair dishevelled. 'Although he's four in a few weeks, so he should be over it.' She smiles. 'He's just woken up –

being a proper Mr Grumpy Pants, aren't you?' She tickles his chin.

The boy can't resist a smile, turning to give me a bashful stare. He has little dimples and tiny teeth. Kirsten tells me she has an interview for an admin job tomorrow. She hasn't worked for a few years and it's doing her head in now. She's recently parted from her boyfriend – needs the money.

'I better dash.' I cast an eye at my watch. 'Great to see you. Take care.' Adrenalin coursing, I pull away from the kerb in haste.

At home, Imogen isn't answering her phone, so I send an email to Sheena about the nasty note and what the reporter revealed. I tell her about Ashley's separation bombshell, how much I enjoyed his company and how we'd slipped so effortlessly into our easy chat. I confess to the kiss – that I still found him attractive – and the strength of my guilt.

I decide not to mention the letter to Eleanor. She comes home fretting about her fourteenth birthday plans, even though it's several weeks away. She doesn't want a party, just three friends over for a pamper evening and sleepover. It had taken Eleanor ages deciding who to invite, but after saying 'yes' Bethany had changed her mind about staying over, and now said she couldn't come at all because she was visiting relatives.

'I think she's lying. I don't think she's allowed,' Eleanor says, squeezing a spot into the hall mirror.

My mind dips in and out of the TV programmes I try to distract myself with that evening. I've searched out Dan's old contacts book and found Kirsten's number.

With a little Dutch courage, and Eleanor in bed, I tap in the numbers.

'I've just had a call from a reporter from the *Tetford Times*,' I fib, squirming at how ridiculous my fib is. It's ten o'clock at night. 'He mentioned that you told the press about Dan's donation.' I feel so silly, as if she'd miss the coincidence of my appearance in her street for no apparent reason earlier.

'Yes, I did – accidentally,' she says. She'd seen some paperwork at the office regarding Dan's donation. 'This newspaper guy – from *The Sun*, I think – tricked me, said he had a list of people who'd given money and asked me to comment. Turns out he was lying, that Dan's donation was just a rumour.'

I want to know if she was offered money from that rascal reporter in exchange for her snippet of information. Finances must be tough with five young children and no partner. But I can't bring myself to ask. It won't change things. I'm amazed I've been brave enough to ring in the first place.

'These are on me, for being Mrs Patience while I faffed over dresses.' I place two giant slices of chocolate and hazelnut brownie on the table.

'Ta-dah! Don't mind if I do.' Tash eyes hers with a look of pure lust, nibbling it in a rare silence.

Farello's is my favourite café. Although below ground and a little cramped and devoid of natural light, it's full of rustic charm, from the wobbly wooden tables to the mix and match crockery and sloping shelves stacked with authentic Italian products. The owners, a family of excitable Italians, constantly collide and bicker in the confined space behind the counter, but the coffee's perfect and stars of the show are the cakes, housed in a rotating glass cabinet covered in the breath marks of drooling customers.

'Buongiorno,' Nonna, the impossibly short and rotund matriarch of the family, says as she marches past, her tiny head partially obscured by a stacked tray. Sweeter than one of her family recipe panettones to customers, she snaps orders to her relatives with an edge harder than the rind on a wedge of Parmesan.

'Oh my good God. This is so yum – though I shouldn't be eating it if I'm going to get into that dress,' Tash declares, face turning from delight to despair.

She'd bought her dress for the charity auction long ago but, tired of helping to choose mine, had tried on more, ending up with a stunning knee-length blue one that clung so closely to her curves it looked like a silk condom. I'd taken an age choosing between my final shortlist; if indecision were ever declared an Olympic sport, I'd be on the podium for team GB.

'Don't worry,' I say. 'We burned off some serious calories walking between each shop.'

'Good point, babe.' Tash pulls tiny pieces from her brownie with freshly manicured plum nails, savouring every crumb.

'There's no need to be quite so careful. I think your nails are dry now,' I say. Tash laughs – loudly – drowning out the clash of china and aggressive hiss of the coffee machine. Nonna Farello stops to give us a stare.

'I always eat really yummy things like this, makes them last longer,' Tash says. 'How gorgeous is your dress? I'm not gonna lie, I've never seen you look so stunning. You'll need some killer heels, though.'

'You know I don't do really high ones.'

'With that dress you so have to. Lowies are illegal!' Tash looks indignant.

'Don't tell me, you'll be wearing slingbacks with yours?'

'Cheeky cow! Actually, I'll need new ones. I don't have that shade of blue.'

Shopping had kept my mind off the kiss, but it hurtles back into the centre of my thoughts, bringing a burst of adrenalin that, when mixed with caffeine, feels on the edge of lethal. I watch Tash lick the last traces of chocolate off each shiny fingertip, debating whether to tell her. I decide against it. I'd mentioned the letter earlier and, while appalled, she'd been more shocked that it had been posted: 'Do people even send letters any more?'

'I better go easy on the croissants in France next week,' I say. 'I probably should have waited until after the holiday to buy the dress – in a bigger size.'

'Just have lots of sex while you're out there. That'll keep the weight off!'

I scowl. 'So how's your sex life?'

'Pretty good. I've got two dates next week, and one the week after – so far.'

'Have you ever considered a dating detox? You're addicted.'

'Are you for real?'

I shake my head. 'You're a hopeless case.'

Tash checks her teeth in her compact. She's so attractive; and always out and about. She doesn't need the amount of cyber assistance she seeks. But she's hooked on the whole online dating process, loves filtering out the 'fitties' from the numerous 'fuglies' (her word), wasters, geeks, creeps and sex-starved husbands, then flirting electronically for weeks, so both parties are armed with the minutiae of each other's lives and personal preferences before clapping eyes on each other.

And her attitude to sex is beyond casual. I'd lost count of her boyfriends, mostly one-nighters on her long 'cop and drop' list, though she tries to assure me she's hunting for Mr Right – just having fun along the way.

I hadn't slept with anyone other than Dan since I was twenty-two and only six people before him. Two were drunken one-night stands. Although I don't share Imogen's rather prudish view of sex, some of the content of Mum's lectures on the evils of promiscuity filtered through (thankfully not all of it; her moral compass led her so far north she was at risk of hypothermia – Dad once telling me the fridge had frosty drawers 'just like your mum') and I didn't sleep around willy-nilly like some friends at poly.

'I've been messaging Seb for a month now – I've got to know him well, he's lovely,' Tash declares.

'So what's his view on euthanasia?' I ask facetiously.

Tash gives me a questioning stare. 'I don't know – but he's got eight tattoos, a nipple ring and loves *Top Gear*.'

Several stunned faces look over to locate the source of the shriek.

CHAPTER 15

It's great to cross the Channel, say goodbye to the changeable May weather, leave my confused, cloudy life behind, and escape to a world of sunshine and blanket brightness.

I spend the first day staring at clear skies and sharp scenery, though I can't shift the haze that descends on my mind when I think about Ashley, and seeing him again.

Since the fountain episode, we've both managed to dodge direct references to the kiss with great prowess. He's texted several times, telling me he had a great afternoon in Cherlsbury and hopes we can do it again soon. I echo his sentiments. But we've made no plans – leaving it in a veil of vagueness. Ashley was tied up helping his wife's friend to run drama workshops in schools; the perfect excuse.

Then he calls to say he's landed another audition next week, not too far from Cherlsbury, and perhaps we could meet there again; a proposition that sends my stomach spinning ahead of me down every aisle of the local supermarché as Eleanor and I pack a trolley with far too much French food, bickering along the way.

It's only after it sinks in that I start to fret, both about meeting, and why he's being so uncharacteristically decisive, concerns I share with Imogen over the phone.

'Perhaps he wants to tell me face-to-face the kiss was a huge, impulsive mistake – the intense heat had seared his sanity, combusted his common sense – or that he's trying to make it work with his wife and she's threatened to staple my nipples to Class 4's wall display on UK landmarks,' I said.

'Perhaps he's just really keen to see you, and found a way.' Imogen's words send my stomach whirling again.

It's on our third glorious morning in the French Riviera that courage comes. I decide to say 'yes' to Ashley, even if it means pulling a sickie. I send the text, then brace myself for more bravery.

I'm sitting opposite Eleanor at the ornate iron table on the upper terrace of Villa Mas Thiel – our haven for the week – sniffing in the sweet-scented jasmine and staring out over a gorgeously glistening bay framed by the majestic Esterel Mountains.

I watch with a smile as Eleanor dabs chocolate spread on to a croissant, taking a gigantic bite before it melts in the scorching sun. I'm relieved to see her eating well as she'd clearly been on a picky, pre-holiday diet, despite denying it vehemently.

'You know the boy who was Joseph, in my school nativity …' I wait for Eleanor to look up, '… well, we're back in touch.'

'How?' She forces the word through a mouthful of flaky pastry.

'Duh! Faceook. We're going to meet.' I don't mention the previous two encounters.

'Really?' She sneers.

'Yep.'

'Like a date?'

'No, not really, not like that.' I flick at the dry flecks of croissant stuck to my lips in the heat. 'We used to go out when we were students. He's married.' Well, he still was legally.

Eleanor eyes me suspiciously. 'Were you … together … for, like, a long time?'

'Not really.' I shift in my seat. 'He's an actor,' I add breezily, glancing down to admire my new jewel toe sandals.

Her eyes light up. 'On TV?'

'Theatres.'

'Oh.' She looks unimpressed, twitching her nose and turning her attention back to the croissant.

It isn't spoken of again, but I spend far too much time during the rest of the week watching the whole world turn soft and soppy in the sun and wishing my holiday had come with that bonus. There are loved-up couples on the beach, on benches, in restaurants and bars, even in the queue at the boulangerie. Then my daughter joins in. She befriends two sisters from a family in a nearby villa and, before long, several fidgety, hair-obsessed, metrosexual boys with co-ordinating floral shorts and backpacks tag along. Eleanor spends her time 'hanging' with the new gang – leaving me to solo sightseeing and sunbathing – or daydreaming, moodily, about Charlie, who's 'so not a boyfriend, just a friend' but whose hand she's clearly holding before dropping it in a flash when I turn up, unexpectedly, at the shared pool one afternoon.

I lie on my sunbed for hours, moving in and out of the shade, fantasising about meeting a French film star who'd declare love at first sight over a steak hache, insisting that Eleanor and I leave England behind and move into his eighteen-bedroomed chateau where I'd pen a magazine column about my glamorous life.

One lunchtime, as I dine alone outside a café in a cobbled street, wearing a creased sundress and no bra, I'm convinced a swarthy stranger in aviator shades is giving me the eye – shooting me several huge smiles in-between spells of expressionless gazing. But minutes later he's joined by a big-lipped, pencil-thin woman so glam I expect a style team and film crew to descend. That afternoon I buy a whole collection of exquisitely tailored summer clothes I suspect I'll never wear.

I also suffer my worst attacks of body insecurity, probably due to spending far too much time stretched out in the sun, reading about the lives of D-list celebrities existing on fresh air and coffee enemas, and staring down at the sides of my exposed thighs. I'm seriously troubled by the unsightly patches of orange peel – which have turned from ripe mandarins to dehydrated Jaffas since I last wore a swimsuit. So much so that I find myself reaching for my tie-dyed sarong every time Monsieur Maintenance – a middle-aged man with close-cropped, grey hair and pointy ears who fishes insects and other debris out of the pool each morning – is in the vicinity.

Ironically, it's while I'm lying by the pool rubbing on some new cellulite cream (I've succumbed to the French 'superieur' marketing) – scared that I may get dragged down a lotion- and serum-covered slippery slope to collagen city, where I'd join the millions of women on a relentless, painful and costly anti-ageing crusade – that

Mrs Lilo, the rotund mum of one of Eleanor's holiday friends – asks if I diet because I'm 'nice and slim'.

'Not really. I try,' I say, embarrassed, 'but I like food too much.' I look round to see her flat out on her inflatable, downing another mini pain au chocolat in two bites and chasing it down her fat neck with a glug from the family-sized fizzy pop bottle she keeps by her side.

I spy Monsieur Maintenance on his morning pool patrol and wrap up my thighs.

'I think he's got the hots for you,' Mrs Lilo whispers. 'Look – he's using the net to cover his boner!'

I roar, but her comment prompts him to crop up in several of my daily daydreams.

In the end, I come back from our break without any romantic anecdotes of my own, but with a great tan, some miracle cosmetics, a whole new wardrobe and some sassy lingerie.

And I return with a clearer mind and a strong sense that it's time to take control. A fresh start. As I weave my way around a slouching, lovesick daughter with post-holiday blues, I mull over my job options, deciding to be proactive about moving on.

Then, I get a call from Mark. He's seeing a local landlord about arranging a charity comedy night. I agree to meet for a drink, an excuse to escape the dirty laundry and filthy looks from Eleanor. Mark looks different, arms more shapely in a fitted polo shirt, the soft contours of his face tighter. He has one of those faces you'd instantly recognize in a baby photo line-up, that make you want to grab his cheeks and say 'choo-chi'.

Mark returns from the bar, placing a large glass of red

on the table. 'Here, get some proper cheap plonk down your neck; give yourself a break from all that expensive French stuff.'

'Great. And nuts, too. You spoil me.' I watch Mark drain a third of his pint in one swig. 'You've lost weight. Looking good.'

'Tash has been strict with me. While you've been enjoying all those croque monsieurs and crepes, I've been living on low-calorie wraps and rice cakes. Still, I'm treating myself to a super saver away day to Weston-Super-Mare next week. Might even buy a sandwich and crisps on the train.'

'Pensioner special, is it?'

'The cheek – there's only four years between us, remember. No, I'm taking Jack, and a few of his collection of plastic dinosaurs apparently.'

Mark's smile fades far too fast, a faraway look creeping across his face. I've considered telling him about Ashley, but I sense something's troubling him and think better of it. I find myself studying his expressions and gestures, hunting for a subtext in his words and silences.

I decide to ask, and he tells me. His wife's planning a move to Somerset with her new partner.

'It's not definite, though,' I say, trying to bring comfort. But Mark thinks it's highly likely.

'The hardest thing's knowing that another man will see more of Jack than I do,' he says. 'I'm not sure how I'm going to deal with that.'

'Things will work out.' It seems such an inadequate thing to say.

'By the way. I know it's short notice but I have a couple

of spare tickets for the auction if you know anyone who wants them.' Mark drums his fingers on his glass. 'One of my friends has just had a colostomy bag fitted and doesn't think he'll be up to the five courses. Wimp!'

I throw a peanut into his pint.

★★★

'You've obviously packed Freya's clothes in here, too,' I say, dragging a stuffed suitcase to the front door. Eleanor's tying the laces of her new multi-coloured pumps.

'You're funny.'

I'd barely pulled the last load of holiday washing from the machine and rid my nose of the reek of French flip-flops when Eleanor received the invite to join Freya's family in Madeira. It's the first time she's been away for longer than a night without me.

At first, I was reluctant to let her go. It over-runs the break, so she'll miss two days of school. Freya's mum had popped round to discuss it, assuring me the girls would be kept on a tight rein. I felt I could hardly refuse. It was only for five days. Eleanor was almost fourteen and I dreaded how sullen she'd be if I said 'no'. She'd been raging with hormones since her French frisson.

'Now, are you sure you've got the suncream? And don't forget your money should be in your hand luggage, and—'

'God, Mum. Stop stressing me out.' Eleanor visibly clenches her muscles, sighing so heavily into the mirror it creates a large patch of mist. 'You've asked me that like a hundred times!'

With Freya and her mum at the door, I squeeze Eleanor in a tight hug, taking a noseful of her sweet scent I hope will last the week. She releases herself from my grip with an air of hurried excitement, not a trace of trepidation in her body language.

I call Reims to seek Imogen's reassurance, whilst attempting to down a bowl of reheated lazy mash balanced on my lap. She thanks me for the bouquet of her favourite pink tulips I sent in a bid to lift her spirits.

'Eleanor'll be fine,' she says. 'I'd pack my two off in a heartbeat, if only anyone was brave enough to take them for that long.' Imogen's baking. Her roulade had held its own against the upturned nose of her French neighbour and competitor in a dessert duel. Pernickety-tongued tasters had declared them both 'magnifique', so it was to be profiteroles at dawn for the decider. I chuckle through a mouthful of mash. Few things get Imogen more enthused than food. She sounds more upbeat, her bubbles resurfacing. I'm hugely relieved.

Then she tells me Ben's meeting with his mum went well. They'd connected immediately. 'He said she was so scared that he wouldn't be able to forgive her for giving him away. But, like he said, she was really young. Her parents were threatening to throw her out if she kept him. She didn't have a lot of choice.' His mum was planning to visit France to meet Imogen and the girls.

'I'm so glad it's working out for him. I can't imagine what he must be feeling.'

'Yes.' Imogen stays silent for several seconds. 'So, are you all set for your date with Ashley?'

'Yes, though I'm still in two minds.'

'Look, lovely, you were full of it after meeting him last time. You can't leave things dangling – again. You'll regret it.'

'Yes, you're probably right. But it's all a bit scary. We had a great day in Cherlsbury – maybe we should leave it there; too much water under the bridge and all that,' I say. 'Aww. One minute I dread him telling me we can't see each other again, the next I hope he does – to make things easier. I'm still angry about the past, I still think about Dan, about betrayal, and … sometimes I feel I'm beginning to get to grips – moving on – and then something happens, like the news stories and that awful letter, and I feel I'm back where I started. It's starting to feel like a curse.'

'That's stupid talk!' Imogen reprimands rather tersely. 'You have to go with your gut. There will always be reasons not to do things. You may not be able to forgive Ashley; you two may not have a future as friends, or anything else, but remember what evasion did twenty-two years ago. You probably need to chat some more, either way. I'm discovering how important talking is in these sessions with Ben.'

'So, how are things?'

She lets out a sigh so long she sounds like a phone perv. 'Oh, I don't know – thanks for sending that article, by the way. You're so thoughtful. It helps to read about others in the same boat.'

'Imogen,' I urge.

'The sex therapy sessions are going OK, I guess. We've talked, Ben's made lots of declarations of love, and I've squirmed a bit – and cried a lot.' I'm braced for the 'but'. 'But it's not really helped things in the bedroom yet. Ben's feeling so neglected. I've tried, we've, you know, dabbled, had a few starters, but … I've still got no … urge … I just think there's something really wrong with me … us …'

'Oh Imogen, there isn't. It's so common. You just need time.'

'Yeah – and a lorry load of female Viagra!'

I laugh, and picture the wrinkled nose I miss so much.

CHAPTER 16

I struggle to adjust to the new sense of prolonged loneliness in the house. I make lots of noise – leaving the radio on, banging doors, clanging crockery – to block out the eerie silence. I even resort to inane humming and chatting to Pepsi each time I pop into Eleanor's empty room, feeling her absence so acutely it's like another bereavement.

My erratic emotions are disconcerting. The second day after Eleanor leaves for Madeira is the worst. I have a hectic-headed night, chasing sleep but only catching it for brief intervals – then wake up feeling flat, as if my copy of the world has turned a faded black and white again. Life's lost its texture.

The following day isn't much better. I watch a heart-wrenching programme about a severely disabled boy without shedding a tear, laugh like a lunatic at a mildly amusing advert, then sob when I drop a plate of mash. It scares me. My emotional dial's malfunctioning – swinging wildly between high and low settings, while the medium's defunct.

I recall reading an article that warned against racing to leave grief behind because it could catch up with you all over again. Perhaps it's that. Had I tried to hurry the healing? Yet mine was turning into a marathon, with hideously high hurdles and other obstacles. Would I ever reach the finish, I pondered, while there was a chance I could look back and see Dan at the starting line, breaking into a sprint to catch up with me?

I wonder whether the depression could be descending again. Yet I manage to get out of bed with the alarm and don't sob into my bran flakes. I crack the odd joke. I function fairly well at work.

Imogen dismisses my worries. 'Don't be so hard on yourself. Of course, you're still going to have highs and lows,' she says. 'I wonder if I need mood stabilisers. I came back from holiday so positive,' I say. 'Grief is complex. And you're dealing with so much. You just need time. Your daughter's just gone abroad without you for the first time. That's a tough one for any mum.'

I'm pretty sure Imogen's right – it's a wobble, not a tumble, and I can stabilise myself. I just need to hear it from Mrs Sensible.

I feel heaps better the next day. I go for a long walk. I see things, and feel them – the sunshine flickering on my face, bursts of light that shine on candy-coloured summer blooms. I have a rush of maternal compassion when I see a toddler knocked off his feet by an exuberant dog, fighting the urge to rush over, push mum aside, and scoop him up in my arms. I tidy the living room, even throw a few things away, and have several long sessions on the computer searching for jobs. I find a few with potential, and one that really grabs my attention. I feel quite excited.

It's when I'm putting out some bottles for recycling that I notice a long, thin scratch along the passenger side of my car. I wonder if it may have happened in the airport car park and I'd failed to spot it previously. Surely not. I definitely haven't scraped it whilst driving.

I decide to go into the garage to see if there's anything I can use on it. Dan used to talk about polishing out surface scratches with something called T-cut, although, up close, the damage doesn't look superficial.

It's strange to see the electric door slowly rise to reveal Dan's man den, where he worked on mechanics and, occasionally, his muscles. I rarely ventured in there.

It looks so vast and empty without the cars, the bitter smell of oil out of place with no engines to linger beside. I'd dreaded going in there so much after Dan died that Mark had stepped in to clear it. He'd sold Dan's two remaining cars – the Audi he used for work and his 'fun' car, the old MG – and sorted through the paperwork neatly filed in cabinets and trays along one length of the bare bricks. I'd invited Mark to help himself to Dan's exercise equipment – feeling guilty that he'd jarred his back moving it from the spare bedroom for me. Mark took some weights, declaring the rest a bit 'hard core'.

He was right, I think, glancing up at the heavy metal pull-up bar suspended from one of the rafters that Dan used to hang from, building his latissimus dorsi *('It's the largest back muscle, Carrie')*; before he dislocated his shoulder – twice.

The old purple aerobic step Dan bought when I started classes was tucked in the corner, used only by a few spiders caught up in cobwebs. I'd been a fitness tart before finally settling on the step sessions. I'd tried everything – aerobics, aqua fit, tums & bums, pilates – but rarely lasted long. It didn't take much for me to quit. I loathed exercise.

But I'd finally come to the sad realisation that I'd have to make a token effort if I wanted to eat chocolate and spuds and not become Carrie Chubby-Chuff.

Dan was deluded, believing that as I'd finally found an activity to stick at, I'd be keen to exercise at home, too. He did it most nights, usually in the spare bedroom, where he also waded through work he brought home from the office. It was his favourite space, a wide, picture window overlooking the garden and distant, patchwork fields beyond. He loved to stare at the tranquil scene as he huffed and puffed on electronic equipment that banged, bleeped, whirred and whizzed. But I lacked the discipline, and willpower. I'd even tried putting my exercise step by the kitchen door as a prompt, but it didn't work, even when I tripped over it. However, I did discover how handy it was for reaching the cake tin in the highest cupboard without straining any muscles. No, I was too lazy for daily exercise, and too lazy for garages. I'd never once put my Toyota in there.

I can't see anything for repairing scratches. I flick through a small pile of papers that lie in the bottom of a three-tier letter tray. A few lists remain, several tasks crossed out, others left – never to be completed. I need one of Dan's lists. A definitive list of things I need to do to get my life in order. And just a dab of his determination.

Our old willow picnic basket's still tucked in the corner. I open the dusty lid and out pops a potent memory of when Dan bought it, for our first trip out together in the MG – a surprise he'd sprung on me, no doubt one he'd spent weeks planning. He was so much better at the romance thing than me. I had regular romantic thoughts,

170

but fewer deeds. It shamed me now. Dan had claimed to be working that day, arranging for Eleanor to go to Imogen's so I had some 'me' time. But he'd arrived home just before lunch to take me out in the new car. We stopped off in a beautiful spot called The Beacon. Dan opened the tiny boot, pulling out a blanket and the tawny brown basket, with its robust leather straps and posh striped lining. Inside were proper plates, cutlery – even napkins – and all my favourite foods: potato salad, chicken, various cheeses and chocolate brownies. He'd even organised the weather, a beautiful blue-sky day; now with an added glow of rose-tinted retrospect perhaps.

We'd talked, about work, and Eleanor – always Eleanor – how we missed her even after just a few hours. We reminisced. We cuddled. We laughed. Dan's eyes grew excited as he filled me in on the history of the site, how it was an Iron Age Hill Fort and 'blah blah, blah'. Eleanor must have been about five or six then. It was before Dan's bid to keep healthy got really heavy. He was still indulging now and then, treating himself.

I pick up the basket, wondering whether to keep it. I'd never use it. Picnics had to be planned. I put it down, opening the door of a big metal cabinet, expecting more echoes and emptiness. But there's a laptop, an old one I'd hardly ever seen Dan use. It looks so bulky, already an ancient relic. I take it inside, place it on the sideboard. I'll ask Mark to clear it. It may be useful for someone, or to recycle.

It's after lunch before I look at the day's post. Ripping open the envelope of what I assume is a third piece of marketing mail, I get an unpleasant surprise.

It's another anonymous message, one shocking sentence in the centre of a crumpled white sheet, in that same bold type:

'Only the wicked want to cheat death – they fear what awaits them.'

The address had been typed on the envelope, not written in spidery handwriting, but it's surely from the same person. I feel a little spooked. It wasn't a one-off. Maybe I should report it. I'm on my own. This person really wants to upset me.

In the shower, I wipe my hand across the misted screen and have a moment of clarity. I'd already started looking for a new job; now I can see number two on my mind's mission list forming in a clearer typeface: *time to move away*. For a while I've thought, in a vague, unfocused way, that putting the house on the market could be a good idea; a smaller home, new surroundings, a new beginning. I miss London, though France is tempting.

Until now, I've been unsure about it, scared even, but later that day I'm in the estate agents' on the High Street speaking to a slightly pushy sales manager with stencilled slug eyebrows, and three days later, a valuation has been done, the sale board's up, Eleanor's in a sulk and we're preparing for strangers to ring the doorbell.

★★★

Pete marches through the door, just as I grab my new ponte jacket, ready for a sharp exit.

'At last – they've confirmed. We've won the Lorex contract,' he declares, saggy cheeks lifted with his first full

172

smile of the year. 'We've all got jobs for a little longer.' I feel a surge of guilt I'm convinced has spread across my face.

'Yes!' Tash jumps from her chair, clapping. 'That's so brilliant.' She wraps me, and the jacket, in a long-clawed bear hug. 'Whoop whoop for Carrie.'

'It was a team effort, but yes ... well done,' Pete says, looking bemused by Tash's outburst. The phone rings in reception, a great excuse for him to exit. He tweaks his testicles, then strides out, still smiling.

Mark's out interviewing and Barbara has a hospital appointment, a women's problem she's keen to keep to herself. 'I think she's got that bladder thing, you know that old ladies get when they leak wee,' Tash conjectured in the kitchen earlier. 'Not being rude, yeah, but her chair smells a bit – 'off' – sometimes when I sit there.' 'And I'm supposed to be the one with the olfactory that works overtime!' I'd said, gesturing to my nose. Tash had looked perplexed. 'Don't throw those big science words at me, you know I got a D in Biology.'

Tash shrieks, startling me. 'The others will be so stoked.'

'Barbara might wet herself when she hears the news,' I say.

Tash laughs. 'Yay. I can get one of those sweet little Fiats now. And we can all celebrate by getting smashed at the auction. Maybe Pete will get a few bottles of bolly.' She combs her fingers through her hair, whilst speed texting with one thumb.

'The only fizz we're likely to get is value lemonade,' I say, stapling some documents. 'Still, at least he's happy and, hopefully, the business is safe.'

'You OK, babe? I'm not gonna lie, you don't look that pleased.' Tash sits, peering at me through her lashes, the twins staring up from a low-cut top.

'Just being moody. I've been looking at other jobs,' I blurt.

'Nooo. You can't leave.' Tash puts on an exaggerated pout, holding the pose for several seconds. 'And ...?'

'I've found one for a staff writer for a women's magazine. And another working as an assistant arts manager for a small group of theatres. I doubt I'll get a look in and—'

'Both sound great, babe. Have you applied?'

'Not yet.'

Tash's phone rings. She picks it up with an exasperated sigh. I pack my bag. The magazine job sounded perfect. It was based in Birmingham, the advert stating no experience was necessary for the right person and requesting samples of writing. I'd brimmed with skippy excitement, then crashed down to earth, hitting several sensible planets on my way. *Stupid woman. You're forty-two – you've left it far too late.*

Tash slams down her phone, cutting through my uncomfortable reverie. 'You so should apply.'

'I will. Don't say anything. Besides, I'll probably still be here until I retire.' I head for the door.

'Pinkie pledge.' She holds up a polished little finger to seal her promise.

★★★

An irritating pop tune's blasting out from a little black box on the kitchen table when I get home. I bust some of my eighties disco moves as I enter the room, the ones that are 'soo cringe' if I ever dare to do them in public. Eleanor looks up from her magazine, giving me a look that would make a rugby player's studs look clean.

'We won that contract.' I throw two thumbs into the air.

'So that's why you're in a stupid mood.' I flash a cheesy smile. 'That's great, Mum. Hashtag proud.'

'Thanks, darling.' Taken aback, I go to kiss her and she happily lets me.

I've obviously been forgiven for putting the house on the market, though I think Eleanor's fairly confident the move won't happen as I haven't looked at any properties, or even decided where to move to.

Eleanor disappears upstairs for ages, returning in red skinny jeans and full war paint. I'm not sure who she wants to impress more, any teenage boys who may be at the cinema later, or her maths tutor. It's hilarious to witness how sweet and obliging she is around him, even when doing algebra, which she hates more than the pink sparkly pyjamas Grandma gave her for Christmas. She'd protested about the idea of a tutor when Dan raised it, but within minutes of seeing him – tall and trendy with boyish looks, messy hair and man bangles – she'd been converted quicker than one of her fractions. It was bizarre to watch your daughter building up a repertoire of flirting techniques way in advance of your own.

I tuck myself away upstairs during Eleanor's maths session, taking my laptop and a bottle of wine. Cutting back on alcohol was third on my invisible mission list, but it could be deferred for a few more days.

I don't expect any e-messages from Ashley. I had one a few days ago confirming our plans for Monday and telling me he'd turned down a night out with friends to prepare for his audition. But I check anyway – with a wrench of disappointment, as always.

I force myself to fill out the arts job application and have just filed it when a message pings in from Sheena:

Hi Carrie. How was the holiday? Plenty of sunshine and relaxation I hope. I can't believe someone would send that disgusting note. There are some sick people out there! Have you reported it? You shouldn't feel guilty about Ashley. You've been through a lot, he's separated, you clearly still have a strong connection and owe it to yourself to enjoy it. A strange thing happened earlier today. I found a message on the answerphone and a voice said: 'This is Geoff … sorry … this is a message for Geoff Caddock. His car's due for a service.' The sound was muffled and, for a second, I thought it was him. It knocked me for six. I may end up going totally mad at this rate! Still – good news at work. They've promoted me to senior mortgage advisor but agreed to cut my hours so I get to spend more time with the girls! Win, win. Sheena xxx

I intend to search out some old bits of writing to see if there's anything I can polish for the magazine job, but find myself staring out the window and thinking of Sheena.

After the tutor leaves, I question Eleanor about the session and she's terse as usual. 'If you must know, we looked at balancing equations and a negative 'x' – like you'd understand.' Mark knows all about a negative 'x', I think ruefully.

Minutes later, the doorbell rings and Eleanor dashes past me in the hallway, barging me with her bulging backpack.

'Hi, Bethany!' I yell, as Eleanor yanks her friend away.

'Hey, Mrs Colwell.' Bethany turns, braces blinking in the evening sun. She's so much younger-looking than all the other girls, still stick thin and flat chested, with short beige hair in a pixie cut.

'Where's your mum?' I can't see the car.

The two girls are already away down the drive. 'She's parked just round the corner,' Bethany yells.

'Have fun at the cinema, you two.'

'We will,' Eleanor hollers impatiently.

Later, so bored with my own company that I'm rearranging the crockery cupboards, I remember the CD I'd ordered. It's still in my handbag, unopened. I tear off the packaging, unable to suppress a smile at the sight of the cover photo. I used to be one of those sad fans who knew more about the band members than some of their family did: their favourite foods, hobbies, pets (one kept bearded dragon lizards in a tank in his bedroom), vital statistics, crushes.

I put the CD into the music system, selecting *I'll Be Loving You (Forever)*. It was a slow track, one of those end-of-the-disco, smoochy ones with potential for some sly tit touching, maybe even groin groping if the dance floor was sufficiently crowded and dark. I stand at the french windows, staring plaintively at the neat criss-cross shadows of the trellis on the lawn as the moody melody washes me with bittersweet memories.

'That's so loud!' I jump from my trance to see Eleanor sneering at the CD cover. I turn down the music.

'Did you have a good time?'

'OK, I suppose.' She shrugs. 'Who are they?'

'A boy band I used to like.'

'Did they even have boy bands in your day?'

'Yes – and they could sing.'

'Yeah, funny. They look so lame.' With that judgement, she flounces out, leaving me with my musical musings and to lick some very old, deep wounds.

CHAPTER 17

In the end, I pull a sickie. Far from stopping the white lies, they spring to my lips far too readily; the guilt of being untruthful to Pete adding to the stress of seeing Ashley.

We agree to meet in an old-fashioned tea shop in Cherlsbury, with a façade that belongs in a Dickens' novel, a basket bicycle leaning against the bowed white window, customers framed in its leaded squares.

Ashley's late this time, and I'm jumpy with each chime of the café door. Yet it turns out I've got worked up for nothing. He strolls in, all smiles and, although a little stilted at the start, conversation soon flows, with much less awkwardness than we'd left by that fountain, and no mention of regrets in relation to the incident that rendered us both unable to utter a whole sentence immediately afterwards.

It felt like two old friends catching up, albeit one's holding a new patent handbag in one hand and hopelessly trying to grip a grudge firmly in the other. Imogen's right – again – its good to talk more, to revisit our student days and fill in a few details about our lives since, adding colour to the quick and rough sketches we'd drawn for each other.

Ashley thinks his audition, for an autumn production of *As You Like It*, went well, though competition was fierce.

Sadly, our time together's cut short. We're sat in the sunny window seat, elbows constrained by the compactness of the pine table and delicate, fine bone china, and the volume of our voices by the proximity of customers, when Ashley gets a call – a last-minute request to do a voice-over for a sick friend. He dallies for ages.

'You can't turn it down,' I say.

Ashley screws up his nose, tells me it's for a national TV advert for injury lawyers.

'Oh my God, of all the people!' I exclaim.

'Ha, only joking – it's a solar panel ad for local radio.' He adopts a pompous broadcast voice. 'Are your bills going through the roof …?' I laugh, pinching my nose to suppress another hay fever sneeze.

Ashley turns serious. 'I guess the money's good for very little effort. It'll help pay a few bills, maybe keep the rust bucket on the road a little longer. But I don't want to mess you around – go so soon.'

'Don't worry – honestly.' I'm not sure I sound convincing.

I've brought the letter I keep hidden in my jewellery box. I'm not sure why; perhaps in case he'd planned to hit me with bad news, so I could respond with a vengeful, emotional stab. It doesn't feel right, but I can't stop myself. I pull it from my bag, ignoring the voice urging me to resist, the surge of dread.

'Do you remember writing this?' I hand the sheet across the table, pen now faded in the deeper creases left by constant folding and unfolding. A wobbly smile forms as I follow his eyes along the opening words: *To My Leading Lady*.

He scans in a stretched silence and I shuffle uneasily, tugging at my tunic.

'Wow, yes, I do now,' he says.

'It was when I had glandular fever.'

Ashley nods, reading on. He'd sent two letters. I was ill for weeks, and he had assessed college performances – couldn't risk catching it – so we didn't see each other. He'd told me he missed me terribly, but loved being on stage with such talented fellow students. 'This is absolutely what I want to do,' he'd declared with more conviction than ever before.

Dan had found the letters when we moved house. He wasn't cross – he'd mocked the smattering of Shakespearean language – but I'd felt bad about keeping them, so threw one away and found the hiding place for the other.

Ashley's squirming, mouth pulled askew. I will his eyes to linger on the last two lines. He'd called me '*my love*' and signed off '*yours for eternity*'. Words he'd uttered before, but for me, the print gave them power, and permanence. Yet it was only about a month later that he disappeared. In the margin, I'd written '*Fucking Liar*' in huge, dark, angry felt-tip capitals, but scribbled it out later. You could still see it if you looked hard enough.

Ashley hands back the letter with a roll of the eyes, a little shamefaced. I feel cruel, unsure why I've shown him, what I hoped to achieve.

'What a jerk I was. I'm amazed you kept it.'

Feeling ashamed, I make no comment, nudging the conversation swiftly on with inane chat about the antiquated décor.

Ashley leaves me with cash to settle the bill, and a kiss on the cheek. We talk about seeing each other again. Nothing concrete, nothing that can't be wriggled out of, just a motion 'in principle', subject to indecision and procrastination. Maybe I could go to London, or he could visit Tetford, or meet in-between? The multiple choice thing again. Ashley stands to go.

'Maybe you could check out my new flat.' As soon as I nod, I realise what a biggie that option is.

★★★

'So how did it go with Bradie?' Tash stirs the coffee, a chance to check out the nails, bedecked in red, with blue tips.

'Not Bradie, Bardie, you know, Shakespeare, The Bard.' I chuckle.

'Oh – got you.'

'Yes, fine – though he had to dash off early. He's invited me to London again.'

'Oh my God. Are you going to go, you naughty lady? I wonder whether he'll tell his wife he's meeting an ex? I bet he won't, the sly dog.'

'They're separated.'

'O-o-oh.' Tash grins stupidly, returning the milk to the fridge.

'Back to work, slackers!' Mark's voice carries through the gap in the half-closed kitchen door. 'And mine's white with sweetener.'

'Cheeky bugger. How about a "good morning" before making your demands?' I put my head round the door, but he's gone. I wonder if he's been listening to our conversation.

The fact I've kept quiet about my meetings with Ashley is troubling me greatly. What started as a small omission now feels like a big deceit, though I suspect Mark knows something, maybe overheard one of our kitchen chats. His ears are constantly pricked up – like a German Shepherd at a crime scene.

I take a coffee to Mark. He's back from interviewing a client, looking dapper in a linen jacket. He chucks his notebook on to his cluttered desk, knocking over the framed photo of his son Jack in a triceratops costume.

'Got anything in there that's laced with chocolate and stuffed with caramel and nuts but only has three calories,' I say, pretending to peer into his leather case.

'Sorry, no can do. I've got a low-fat crispy rice bar, though. A quid to you.'

'Keep it,' I say, smiling.

That evening, I find myself working ludicrously hard during my step class, the pounds I've gained since buying the dress for the auction driving me, the thought of my dimpled thighs wrapped in tight teal generating extra, fear-fuelled aerobic energy. I'm certainly 'earning the burn'.

'Bloody hell, Carrie, you been on the Red Bull?' Slim Kim's huffing on her step next to me, desperate to keep up.

'Nope.' I try to smile. The new recruit, a chunky girl with a glamorous up-do and pretty heart-shaped face, looks over as she takes a protracted mineral water break, holding her sides with a grimace.

Lady Lycra gives me a little nod as she sets the pace out front, eyes flashing with amazement at my effort.

'Step it up and beat that fat. Hard and fast is where it's at,' she yells in time to the bouncy music. Even the Fit Twins – both gay, astoundingly buff and fiercely competitive, always trying to out-exercise each other – have broken into a glossy sweat.

'I shouldn't have had that big dinner,' Slim says, holding her stomach and lagging behind the beat.

'You doing the wrong kind of pumping?' I ask. She smirks. She'd been caught out once during an unexpected silence in a 'techno track'. Never lived it down. 'Thank God for the … blaring music then,' I say, straining to talk.

'Damn you, Mum, for the inherited cellulite,' I mutter through gritted teeth, ogling our leader's thighs – so tight you could bounce toffees off them – as I thrust my torso this way and that in response to her orders. I wonder whether some of my effort's for Ashley.

Eleanor's sat on her bed pulling faces into her mobile, cosmetics littering her gingham quilt, when I sashay into her room in shiny teal.

'God, I've got so many spots,' she fumes. 'I hate my skin.' She did seem to be getting more, proper custard tops, not just the usual clusters of red and black dots, but I'm not about to say it.

'You can hardly see them,' I fib. 'So – what do you think?'

'Wow. That looks well nice. Colour's cute.'

'Thanks, darling.' I stand at the mirror, turn this way and that, wondering what my Spanx will bring to the party. Snorting some acrid air, I turn to see Pepsi whizzing around on his wheel as if in training for a rodent run.

'That cage stinks again. I had to go mad with my new pomegranate and pine spray up here this morning. You need to clean it more regularly.'

Eleanor plays deaf. I retreat.

I've decided on a topic for a new article to send with the magazine job application, but can't find the creative energy. Instead, I email Sheena, assuring her she's not going mad mistaking the voice on the answerphone for Geoff, how I'd thought I heard Dan moving around the house several times after he'd gone, and once was convinced I'd heard him speak. I congratulate her on the promotion and tell her about my moodiness, the job searches, meeting Ashley, the upcoming auction and how Eleanor's been playing the diva since landing her acting role, demanding bottled water for one rehearsal and yesterday announcing she couldn't go because of her spots.

Then there's another 'silent' phone call; the third that day. I had two yesterday. The pattern's the same: 'Caller unknown'; I pick it up, an eerie silence the other end. A purposeful rustling follows and the faint but protracted sound of expelled breath – then the call ends. I'd assumed the first couple were junk calls, but now I know they're not.

Someone's listening in silence to my pleas:

'*Who is this?*', '*Why are you calling?*'

★★★

'Congratulations, troops. Tuck in,' Pete says, as we gather in the boardroom to celebrate the Lorex contract, gesturing to the spread as if he's laid on a royal banquet.

Forget ice sculptures and diamond-encrusted napkin rings, we have Pringles and onion rings. Mrs Cullimore has made a cake and Barbara's brought in a variety of unidentifiable fillings wrapped in filo. It's not lavish, but none of us have worked for extravagant publishing houses who throw in bonuses like bi-annual botox or Harrods hampers and appreciate that for Pete, and given the circumstances, it's a generous gesture.

'I should have worn my tux,' Mark whispers as we toast our success. I titter, trying not to spit out a mouthful of Asti.

Despite the levity, there's such genuine jubilation I feel like an impostor – like the time Ashley and I turned up to the wrong party at poly, deciding to see how long we could stay before someone realised. It was several hours.

I *was* pleased about Lorex, but primarily for everyone else. Saying that, Cullimore's was comfortable and familiar, made me feel secure, though it wasn't what I'd choose; like a good support bra. And my wonderful colleagues had helped me through the previous two years. I feel guilty and ungrateful, compounded by the fact that, by some miracle, I've sent the magazine job application and, judging on the positive reactions of people who've viewed the house so far, may be moving away.

I've lost count of the number of times I've 'nearly' applied for editorial posts, courage abandoning me at the last minute. I can't believe I've really done it, for once eschewing excuses and distractions to write a short piece about being a single parent and tidying up a few old articles – though I don't hold out much hope.

Work passes in a blur for the next few days, spirits lifted by the Lorex triumph soon grounded by the pressure of a heavy workload and Pete's admission he's been 'screwed down on price' to secure the contract so we we're not out of danger, especially if we don't deliver. He can only draft in one extra freelancer, leaving Mark to gather almost all the editorial for a thirty-page staff magazine.

Then Tash spies a mystery visitor leaving Pete's office, describing him as mean-looking with dark, greasy hair; and dressed in black.

'A friend of ours, perhaps,' Mark says. His cryptic comment's met with bewildered stares. 'Perhaps Pete's joined the Mafia,' he adds. We speculate about possible plans to sell the business to some shady media man.

I'm apprehensive when, soon after our usual Monday meeting, Pete calls me back to his office.

'Carrie, you're obviously going to head up the DVD project. They'd appreciate an initial call from you,' he says, shoulders hunched over his large notepad.

'OK.' I'm reassured that work's continuing as normal, but rattled by his use of the word 'obviously'. Keen to ease Mark's load and get some practice in, I tentatively offer to write a few articles. Pete commends my idea, allocating me several, small 'filler' stories, though I'd hoped for a proper feature that required research skills and several face-to-face interviews – something challenging and substantial.

Back in the office, Mark greets me with a gruff groan, hands locked on his head as he stretches back in his chair. I try to engage him in conversation but he's unusually grumpy.

Later, demanding he take a break, and concerned his joke tally has dropped to a dangerously low level, I lure him into the kitchen with coffee and a contraband chocolate biscuit, offering to help him search out the final few business sponsors for his charity auction programme. The event is two days away. He needs to get it printed urgently.

'Thanks, yeah, great. Sorry I've been a bit of a moody git, but—'

'I know – hideous workload, no time for idle chit-chat.'

He tells me his wife's becoming increasingly difficult and obstinate, insisting he collect Jack at a set time, then changing her mind at short notice or leaving him waiting outside the house for hours. And she's definitely moving away.

'Anyway, enough about her. So what's new in your world?' Mark asks.

I mention the second nasty note, and the strange calls. I wonder if the scratch on the car's related. He's concerned, as Imogen had been, advises me to log everything; details, times. Take photos. I don't want to report it to the police, but maybe if it continues I will.

'And I've put the house on the market,' I add.

'Bloody hell.' He freezes, mug mid-air. 'Everyone's at it. Where you going?'

'I don't know.' I toss the teaspoon into the sink.

'Are you staying in the area?'

'I don't know.'

'You mentioned France before, joining Imogen. Strewth, don't say you're off to Oz.'

I shrug, with a half smile.

'Do you really want to move?' Mark's head is cocked, eyes glazed from staring at his screen.

'I don't know. Bloody hell, this isn't one of your interviews.'

'It's a good job. It wouldn't be much of an article.'

I tut, flicking Mark's cauliflower ear as I head for the door. He flashes one of his soft smiles that saturate his eyes. He's right. I realise I'm making decisions about moving on, yet I'm not fully convinced by them.

Back at my desk, I read an email from Sheena. I know it must be important, so soon after her last one:

Hi Carrie. It's hilarious Eleanor's playing the Diva – 13-year-olds are funny, aren't they? Daughter number 2 has announced she has a boyfriend, although they never meet, just send texts with XXX and some sort of code. I had a reporter from the local newspaper here as they're doing a follow-up story about Geoff. She was pretty tactless, digging over the same old questions, then had the cheek to say she understood the police assumed someone was dead if they'd been missing for more than three weeks and did I agree!! Let's just say, I was very curt. As you know, I've tried to be honest with the girls about Geoff's disappearance, yet keep them optimistic, as I am, about his safe return. It's been nearly 17 months (507 days) but I still strongly believe he'll come back to us. Sheena xxx P.S The girls insisted I go to a colleague's leaving party tonight – daughter number 1 is babysitting!

It's shocking to see it written as a number – 500 days of not knowing. 500 days of the kind of anguish that would destroy lesser mortals than shatterproof Sheena. For the first time, I imagine her face. She has fine hair, recently turning grey, with a soft fringe, gentle smile – and small, steely eyes. For the first time, I want to see her, and hug her. And, not for the first time, I want to inflict physical pain on a newspaper reporter.

Driving home through hard rain, so tired of the route that I welcome the challenge of misty windows and heavy, wet streaks that obscure my view and exhaust the wipers, I promise myself I'll launch straight into the sponsor search when I get back. Mark was joining me later. There'd be no distractions as Eleanor was staying late at school. Performances of *Fame* were imminent, her anxiety was building, moods mixed, and she was spending so much time rehearsing, I was considering sending her to school with her onesie and microwave porridge.

As I imagine her name on a huge billboard intermittently blurred by a wet windscreen, the irony of the lyrics of the musical's hit song strike me. I'd heard Eleanor belting it out repeatedly in her bedroom: the bit about living forever. Luckily, Dan had passed on the flying bit.

Poor Eleanor had to sing those words on stage. Maybe I was being stupid, but I imagined her fellow thespians nudging, smirking and whispering in the wings when she did so. I dreaded the thought that she might be subjected to more taunts and teasing. I needed to try talking to her again. I still didn't know what Eleanor really thought about cryonics now she was older. I'd given up asking as she stiffened and seethed when I raised it, but I knew I had to find the resilience to break through.

I'd made no attempt to hide my views on cryonics from her: how it didn't really appeal to me, I was a little bemused by it but keen to support Dan, and how the latest media stories – particularly people's reactions and responses – were making me angry and defensive.

I was desperate for all the publicity and drama to stop, so Eleanor could have time and space to make up her own mind. I hoped it wouldn't become a stigma that could damage my daughter in some profound way in the future – causing deep, emotional scars – or be a burden that would follow her everywhere, attracting intrigue and derision; the daughter-of-a-weirdo. If it was eternity Dan craved, he may have got it. 'The dad in the freezer', then in the future 'the granddad … the great-granddad …'

I swing into the drive with a gasp. Two strangers are standing by the front door, a suited man staring at the car, a woman on her phone, one hand on the hip of her patterned jeggings.

Of course. I'd agreed to do an unaccompanied viewing as the estate agent was busy. It had slipped my mind. I close my eyes, letting out an exhalation of despair as I tug on the handbrake. Something else I've messed up; my life still so disorganised, a tangle of threads that begged for Dan's touch to unravel.

The couple accept my apologies for the late arrival, and the untidiness of the house. They appear to love it, the woman gushing in every room, nudging her husband and flashing consultative glances. They have four children and three dogs; the space is ideal.

Yes – this house is perfect for a lovely, large family, I think, with regret after shutting the front door on their smiles. They coveted my house, and I coveted their family. I realise that not only had I made zero effort, as with previous viewings – no decluttering, vases of flowers or baking smells – but I'd found myself scratching around for negatives, telling them about the distant road noise when the wind was blowing in an easterly direction and that the automatic garage door sometimes stuck.

Do I really want to move?

CHAPTER 18

Catching sight of Dan's old laptop charging on the sideboard, I can't resist powering it up. On the screen sit a few work-related files and documents, gathering data dust, and stuck beneath the keyboard is a faded yellow Post-it note with what looks like some passwords. Good old organised Dan. He loved a Post-it, deriving such satisfaction from ticking off listed tasks, preferably in order.

I imagined I'd still find Dan's Post-its cropping up in odd places for years to come, like dog hairs at Auntie's bungalow long after her schnauzer departed.

I remember teasing him about wiping out a huge swathe of Nottingham forest for the squillions of Post-its he got through.

'Still not enough of them to cover your mouth though,' he'd retorted. I roared at that one; cheeky bugger. Dan often stunned me with a perfectly timed gem, and he pulled the odd, impressive ruse, like convincing me his health company was testing a tablet that could make your armpit sweat smell of lemons; naturally, of course. I'd been unusually gullible to swallow that one, though it was washed down with a huge gulp of wishful thinking. I had a strong aversion to body odour.

I scroll through Dan's internet history; mostly motoring and healthy living websites. I'm about to click off when I stumble across a forum. *Dan on a forum. Surely not.* The link leads to a cryonics website.

Typing in several passwords, I'm soon in the middle of a conversation between Dan and someone called '*CrykeyMoses*'. It's so strange reading Dan's words. I used to hear his voice clearly in my head, but just recently I'd had to strain to recall it, desperately willing the sound to form in my inner ear. Reading his words is like having Dan back in the room. I hear his inflections, the clear tone and slight hint of a Midlands twang. Yet he's playing a slightly different character with his online acquaintance, dropping in slang I never heard him use, an exaggerated informality.

Then I read something I wish I hadn't.

CrykeyMoses has posted: '*Your Mrs still not into the freezin' thing bud?*'

Dan: '*No, she doesn't get it.*'

CrykeyMoses: '*What's with women not getting it? Has she seen the training video?*'

Dan: '*She's not really interested, mate, doesn't take it seriously. Everything's a joke to her.*'

My heart's pounding through my blouse. My eyes race on, but the subject changes, Crykey asking Dan how much he can press on the bench and if he's still on the strict diet. Dan's reply certainly impresses.

CrykeyMoses: '*Shit – you've got some serious stamina bud. That should sort out your little problem. If not now, you're sure to come back as a stud! Saying that, you'll live forever at this rate!!*'

I check the date of the messages. April. About eighteen months before Dan died, just after our fantastic Easter break in Rhodes. The weight of his words in print pains me. What was Dan's 'little problem' Crykey had referred to, and why the 'stud' reference? It made no sense – and from a virtual stranger. Dan's comment about me not taking anything seriously was harsh; unfounded. I might have made a few jokes, but I'd tried to listen. I certainly didn't discourage him. I was just mystified by his cryonics wish. In my defence, I really didn't think he'd go through with it.

I *had* watched the training video. Most of it. It's true I was reluctant. Selfishly so. I just found it hard to digest. *'Once a person's pronounced dead, it's essential that the preservation procedures begin immediately'* the voice-over had explained in a dry monotone. Then a dummy, called Bill, was shown being manhandled in a bath in the back of a van. There was lots of machinery and equipment, and urgent voices talking of stabilising medications and something to stop the blood clotting. At one point, I almost laughed – it seemed so amateur, like a spoof. At another, I wanted to look through my hands, like when I was a kid watching the hacking scene in a horror movie. I was alarmed, thinking: 'they could do this to my husband one day'. I had to walk away. I preferred not to see the rest, though I'd made myself watch it since.

Shunting the laptop aside, fingers between my eyebrows as if to soothe the hurt, I recall what happened after I'd stopped watching the video. Dan had followed me into the kitchen. I was feeling emotional, trying not to cry. He'd come behind me at the sink, giving me a big squeeze. 'You should have seen it to the end, Carrie. I really wanted you to know what happens. It's important.' 'I saw most of

194

it,' I'd said, chewing my cheek. I didn't want a row. I'd do almost anything to avoid that. I was determined not to allow the cryonics to come between us. 'OK. Well, I'm not fetching Eleanor for an hour, so we have some spare time,' Dan had said. Then he'd blown a rasping kiss on my neck, pulled a wide smile and, in that moment, his eyes melted the hurt. 'Let's go and say hi to Mr Fluff then.' He'd held my hand. His felt so strong and safe. I knew we'd work through it. He turned to me. 'Woof'.

★★★

I kick at the sign, surprised at how loose the wooden post is in the dry soil of an abandoned border at the edge of the drive. It slopes, then falls.

I look around – make sure no one can see me – then give it an extra, gratuitous blow that dents the patent-leather toe of my work shoe, making me wince. The sudden surge of anger and frustration stuns me, triggered, in part, by Dan's comments about me not taking things seriously, and by my inability to take control of my life; my pathetic inadequacy. *I* was the joke – dropping through each day in some kind of free fall, with no real grip on things.

I straighten the post along the ground.

My home's no longer for sale. *Our* home.

Inside, I call the estate agent, ask her to cancel viewings for the foreseeable future. I apologise. I need time to reconsider the move.

Mark's supposed to refuse my offer of alcohol when he arrives, so I won't be tempted. Within minutes, we're both hanging weary heads over large glasses of Merlot, already partially drained.

He joins me on the sofa, jangly music on in the background, as always, in his honour. He's lost more weight and wearing a fitted pale green shirt that sparks a vivid memory. He wore it the night of his ex-wife's thirtieth birthday party, when she spent most of the night drooling, drunkenly, over one of her devilishly handsome solicitor colleagues. Mark left early after they rowed, a little publicly, in the foyer of the village hall.

'I see the "For Sale" board's down.' Mark drags the coffee table closer to spread out his paperwork, releasing a breeze of his citrusy cologne.

'Yes, for now. I'm not ready.' I flush inwardly.

I listen while Mark moans about his workload. I refill the glasses.

Selfishly, I know I can't concentrate on our task until I've told him about the forum. He's the wordsmith. What did he read into it?

'It's just manter.' I arch an eyebrow. 'Male banter.'

I smile. I want to ask Mark what he makes of the stud comment, if Dan was perhaps having an affair. Mark wasn't what I'd consider a best friend, but close enough that Dan may have confided in him. But I can't. It seems such a silly question to arrive at. A big leap. And poor Mark was cheated on – twice – by his wife, so it would be tactless. He'd forgiven her the first time, she was quite a bit younger, more foolish, but the second time he threw her out.

'People write all sorts of crap on these things.' Mark looks earnest.

'I know. It's just upset me – and the bit about taking everything as a joke …'

'There are worse crimes.' Mark reaches for his computer. 'Look, do you want to do this another day? We don't have to—'

'No. I'm fine. Let's do it. Pass the phone. You Google, I'll call.'

Mark places a warm hand on mine, grips it. 'If you're sure.' His face holds a tentative smile. My pulse feels heavy as I stare into my wine. Mark leans closer. 'Look, Dan adored you,' he says, banging his nose, playfully, against mine.

'I know.' He releases my hand. For a fleeting moment, I'm disappointed. I missed affection.

'And who wouldn't want to come back as a stud?' Mark adds. I take a sharp breath at that one, masking it with a playful thump on his arm.

I watch Mark click and browse. His joke knocks me back to about six months ago, at his local. Tash was there, we'd all got stupidly tipsy and I was recalling how difficult it had been to decide what sort of memorial, if any, to have for Dan. The vicar had been so patient, despite the fact that I'd blubbed throughout our meeting and blurted out that I rarely went to church any more and wasn't sure I could call myself a Christian, or what I really believed. Undeterred by my agnosticism and brazen confession, the vicar had suggested that, in the absence of directives from a loved one – and in such exceptional circumstances – it was about what *I'd* like, perhaps a low-key service for close family and friends to pay their respects.

'Dan barely stepped foot in a church growing up and we only went together to get married and support

Eleanor at school events,' I'd said to Mark, slurring my words. 'Anyway, hadn't he decided to put faith in the scientists?' 'I think you did the best thing,' Mark had said, with a reassuring smile. 'Definitely, hon,' Tash agreed.

I'd then confided how hard I'd found choosing the music. *Unchained Melody* had sprung to mind, because Robson and Jerome were constantly spreading full-fat cheese on the song on the radio when Dan and I were first together. It was our little tune. But at the time, I knew I couldn't bear to hear it. Mark had chipped in, quick as a flash: 'Maybe you should have gone with ColdPlay?' I actually missed the joke for a moment, even though Tash tutted and scowled as he grinned cheekily, head cocked over his fifth pint. 'Hang on,' he'd added, 'what about *Freeze A Jolly Good Fellow?*' I laughed, but even through the beer barrier, I felt the blow. I was upset, though I didn't let on. Mark was a little drunk. I usually appreciated his sense of humour. Tash had struck him on the shoulder, spilling his pint. 'You're awful,' I 'd said. 'Sorry, a bad one ... out of order,' he'd slurred.

At work, he'd apologised again. He was concerned he may have upset me. I fibbed; assured him he hadn't. Had Dan talked to him about cryonics much, I'd asked? And what did he really think of it? Mark said yes, he'd discussed it with Dan, but not much. But he'd done his own research; wasn't convinced the science was there yet. 'It's definitely not for me,' he'd said. 'Look, Dan was a great friend. We shared an enthusiasm for sixties music and Maseratis. But cryonics – I'm definitely not with him on that one.'

'You sure you're up for this?' Mark interrupts my reverie.

'Course.'

We're still searching when Eleanor returns from her *Fame* dress rehearsal. Although she's polite to Mark, says her scenes are 'going OK', and laughs at his short melodic burst of the show's title track, I know she's trying to mask a bad mood. I follow her to the kitchen.

'Freya always tries to make me look stupid, so she looks good. I frickin' hate her so much sometimes!' she tells me, after my third attempt to find out why she's upset.

'What's she done?'

'We were walking down her road and Lewis, like, came out to talk because he lives close, and said his brother had just squeezed a spot on his nose and Freya said she rarely got any and I wouldn't let her pop mine. So he was, like, staring at my chin then, just when my skin's so bad. It was so embarrassing.' Eleanor yanks off her school tie.

'Your skin's not bad, just a few little spots. I'm sure she didn't mean to upset—'

'She so did. She always does it, when I like someone or they like me. She's a b—'

'Stop! Well, maybe you should try doing the same to her?' I say, aware I've strayed from the textbook advice to 'turn the other cheek' 'If a boy likes you, a few zits won't put him off.'

'I'm never speaking to her now.' Her mouth's bunched into a miserable mass.

But she can't suppress a grin on hearing Mark's triumphant 'Yes!' from the living room. I give Eleanor a squeeze and leave her to cool.

Mark has sold an advert to a local builder and found another firm to approach.

'Let's give these a go. You ready to turn on the charm?'

'Watch and learn!' I say, picking up the phone.

But then it rings.

I answer it.

Silence.

Rustling.

Then more silence.

CHAPTER 19

'So are you and Mark going to have a cheeky little one-nighter?' Tash slurs the question, standing next to me in the opulent washroom, eyes double-glazed.

I place my hands under a gleaming gold tap, addressing her in the illuminated mirror. 'Nope.' I exaggerate the 'p' sound.

'Aw. You get on soo well. You're both so funny. You should get it on.' I chortle. Tash is bent double, pulling off a shoe to check for damage. 'Ow, bloody things.' She squeezes it back on with a grimace.

It's the night of the charity auction. She's donated a fair few liver cells to the cause and just collided with a waiter after zigzagging across the rich mahogany floor of the Regency function room, falling off one of her six-inch-heel slingbacks and cutting through the strains of civilised chatter and clink of expensive crystal glasses with a deafening guffaw. Heads had swivelled to check out the commotion and one haughty lady – chest hidden under jewels so big and sparkly they were hypnotic – shot a stare that threatened to melt the swan ice sculpture perched on a tiered glass table nearby. Fortunately, the waiter, a short lad with a tall quiff, had managed to stabilise his stacked tray, averting the danger of creating a second drinks fountain.

'You could have comedy babies,' Tash says, lips pulled askew to check her teeth.

'Stop!'

'Just saying it how it is, babe.' She fumbles with the zip of her make-up bag. This paint job's going to take a while.

Mark and I do have a special bond, I muse, wiping off mascara that has run with all the evening's hilarity. It's been a fantastic night; unforgettable. Despite the responsibilities and distractions of being the organiser, Mark's been wonderfully attentive – smoother than his silk lapels. His tuxedo's turned him into Captain Charm.

His isn't the only transformation. The venue's full of old-fashioned chivalry and beautiful people. Dapper men in fitted suits and women draped in rich silks and velvets, dripping with Chanel No 5, sit next to tables laid with crisp, white linen and dazzling cutlery, poised and polite beneath ornate ceiling roses and chandeliers.

Even the live band's perfectly polished, though Mark's attempt to teach me to jive was the point at which the sophistication stopped. It was riotously funny. I was so bad, hindered by the four-inch heels Tash had coaxed me to buy. The saxophone player had stopped several times to snigger over his reed. After I'd tangled my lower legs around his for the hundredth time, Mark had congratulated me on 'putting the prat into Latin', dragging me back to the table, where Tash greeted us with her seal clap, tears of laughter rolling from her smoky eyes.

It was just the tonic we all needed with such a tense atmosphere at work and continuing uncertainty over the business's future (Mafia Man had paid a second visit and Pete had been off sick for only the second time in twenty years). The abandoned calls were troubling me, too, and I'd dwelled on Dan's online comments for days, perhaps getting more upset than I should have been. 'I think you can take what people say on these chat sites with a hefty pinch of salt. It's just faceless banter,' Imogen had said. 'Dan loved you to bits. It was blindingly obvious.' 'Yeah. I'm overreacting,' I'd said. I had to agree the stud comments were ambiguous.

I couldn't help wishing Ashley had come, wondering what he'd look like in a dinner jacket. I've never seen him in a suit and only once or twice in a shirt – certainly not a crisp, crease-free one.

Tash pulls me back into the moment. 'I've got a bloody kink!' She scowls, dragging her fingers impatiently down one side of her lustrous hair.

'Oh no. Disaster.' I mock her reflection as I dab on powder.

'It so is.' Tash frets and huffs a bit longer, then turns to me. 'What do you think our babies would look like, you know if Ryan and I made them?'

'Gawjuss, obviously,' I snigger. 'Straight from the cot to the catwalk. I can picture them in designer romper suits, with infant fake bake and baby sling-backs. Have you got something to tell me then?'

Tash looks bemused, facial muscles loosened by alcohol. 'No, what … oh, you mean, like am I preggers? You're joking right? Course not.' She laughs. 'My sister's so obsessed with getting pregnant. Thinks her clock will stop tick-tocking soon. But she can't get a boyfriend. She's—' Tash twists her face, as if she's about to say something shocking, like 'a bit of a bunny boiler', or 'into witchcraft'. Instead, she gestures to her belly: '… a bit fat.'

A titter turns to full-on laughter as I watch Tash try to apply more shocking red lipstick; how much concentration it takes to avoid decorating her teeth. I've reapplied mine countless times, depositing my lip print on several cheeks and crystal tumblers, leaving it looking thin and pathetic in a sea of impressive trout pouts on display next door.

'You've been with Ryan for a long time. Must be nearly three weeks,' I say.

'I know. It's insane. I can't actually bloody believe it. He's cute though.' Tash flings herself at me. 'I hate it when you're not drinking. You so should have stayed. I'm sure Mark could sneak you into his room.' She pulls back, tottering.

'Go on, you could have a crafty shag – all for charity.' She shrieks and a woman with loose curls and a sequinned shawl, washing her hands in the next basin, glares and tiptoes out on ice-pick stilettos.

'Stop right there, Miss Piss-Head,' I say. 'I'm going home as planned. End of.'

It was certainly a change to be the sober one – and a little alcohol may have taken the edge off Tash's volume. She'd heckled throughout the auction bids, almost agreeing to pay two grand for a guitar signed by some D-list rocker. Mark had eventually cast etiquette aside, put her in a headlock and slapped his silk napkin over her mouth.

Everyone else on our table was staying, and who could blame them. As well as landing impressive freebies like drinks fountains, Mark had secured a massive discount on the rooms, bagging a few of the Queen's Hotel's prime five-star suites for the price of a box next to the boiler room in a budget hotel. But I'd decided to opt out of all that opulence, even though Eleanor was stopping overnight at Sunny's. It didn't really appeal. Besides, I'd decided to drive home, so I couldn't drink. It was time to finally do something about my wine intake. I suspected it wasn't helping my erratic moods, furring up the common sense cogs in my brain.

When I finally decide to leave, Mark insists on escorting me. He's clearly rewarded himself for a successful evening with a few strong spirits. I get a potent whiff of whisky, his body heavy as he drapes his arm around my shoulder, walks with me to the gleaming reception area.

'Fancy a coffee before hitting the road? They do Lavazza – I've checked! And that sofa has our name on it.' Mark gestures to a huge, wing-backed chesterfield, next to the Cotswold stone fireplace.

'I think I'd better head off,' I say brightly, trying not to appear rude or ungrateful after his efforts with the gallantry all evening. 'I feel really … tired.'

Mark gives me a squeeze, one arm held tight around my waist. 'Shame.' He kisses the top of my head. I sense his silent stare, an unexpected tenderness in his grip. My pulse quickens. I'm reluctant to meet his gaze, his lips so close. It could be so easy to be dazzled by the heady atmosphere, the richly romantic setting of this 'other' world, to do something foolish, maybe slip through that mates gate. Yet I'm sure we both know the lock's secure, that we can't venture beyond the safe environment of our treasured friendship.

Mark loosens his grip. I cast him a sideways glance. 'It's been a great night,' he says, smiling broadly. Those lips had taken part in so much banter with Dan, they'd uttered so many consoling words to me, poured out so much advice, amused me so often.

'Bloody fantastic,' I say, easing myself away. I hastily unzip my clutch bag, pulling out my keys to make my exit intentions clear.

For a second, I dare myself to say, 'I'm seeing Ashley'. If there are any foolish, whisky-induced amorous thoughts, that would surely be the easiest way to banish them. But it would be cowardly, ill-timed, cruel perhaps. Unnecessary, surely? I don't need to spell it out. Mark knows what we are – great friends and colleagues, a strictly professional double act; Mr and Mrs Mirth.

He cuddles me close again, hand stroking the curve below my waist. His eyes find mine.

'I must say, you look stunning tonight, the best-looking woman in the room.' As if sensing my unease, he pulls himself upright. 'Well, second best, or perhaps third, actually fourth because there was that brunette on the next table with the massive tits …'

I thump him; laugh nervously. 'I'm being serious,' he says. All traces of jollity fall from his face again.

'Hey.' A loud voice startles us both. A man in a white suit, with a slick comb-over, is by the front desk. 'You leaving, Mark?' he yells.

Mark holds up a stiff palm. 'Wait one minute, Carrie.' He shimmies over to the guy and I hear him explain that 'no, he isn't leaving', he'll be back to chat shortly. Then a young couple passes in front of them, canoodling and chatting loudly, and I lose Mark's voice. He must crack a joke, because they both laugh, look my way.

I feel cross. I'm not sure why.

My mind shouts over to him: '*Oy Mark. Did you hear the one about the widow whose husband's corpse was in a freezer in Arizona?*

'*She's giving you the cold shoulder!*'

★★★

It's great to wake up headache free, and with the ability to recall last night's shenanigans with the kind of clarity a peeping Tom yearns for.

Through this crystal-clear cerebral screen I replay the final scene with Mark, wondering whether I misread things, and how much whisky he'd had.

'Mark, you're such a great friend,' I'd said, before leaving, with as much seriousness as I could muster when facing a master jester. I'd tried to verbally underline the last word.

I think he knew what I was really saying. He knew me so well.

'I'm better than great. I'm frickin' fantastic, me,' he'd said, doing a kind of elaborate foppish twirl with his hand, then pointing to himself.

Driving home through twisting moonlit lanes, I'd reflected on what a superb night it had been. I felt so uplifted; more alive, senses stirred. If things had been different, could Mark and I ever be a serious duo, I'd pondered, almost missing a sign and swerving on to a deserted B road, the car headlights exposing mysterious dark shapes as hedgerows. My alcohol-free recollections were pin-sharp, but, for a while, the edges of my feelings were blurred.

The high heels have left their mark so, before breakfast, I soak my sore, pinched feet in the washing up bowl – still in my dressing gown, with bed-head hair and skin streaked with last night's makeup. I consistently neglect to remove it on late nights, then regret it. My idleness puts brown stains on the pillowcase and probably years on my face.

I get a text from Ashley. He's looking forward to tomorrow, he 'might even tidy up!'

Spotting my laptop, concealed under newspapers and documents on the table, I'm compelled to switch it on – ignoring my own pre-breakfast computer curfew.

I send an email to Sheena, ask about her night out. Having a daughter who can babysit's great, she should make the most of it. I hope the 'update' story will help to find Geoff. I'm glad she gave that journalist what for. Mark says most reporters hired on local newspapers these days are young and inexperienced – all part of the cost-cutting. Still, doing a little research wasn't difficult! I tell Sheena about the auction, that I didn't drink a drop and was determined to continue curbing my alcohol consumption. I could do with a drink tonight though, as I'm seeing Ashley tomorrow. At his flat. I'm getting nervously excited at the prospect, now it's so close.

When Sunny tappety-taps on the door and 'hi, sweetnesses' me later that day, I don't bristle in the slightest. Nothing can ruin my mood. I'm determined to relish the elation the previous evening has sparked – my eyes and emotions back to a normal setting – and the anticipation of what the next day may bring.

Eleanor's in surprisingly good spirits, too, and can't

wait to show off the boho braid Sunny's given her. It circles right across the top of her forehead and down the back.

'Reminds me of the crust on a Cornish pasty,' I say. She giggles, bounding out of the room.

Sunny sits at the kitchen table, despite the muddle, spindly fingers cradling a cup of tea. She doesn't like being elevated on the chrome bar stools by the island, something to do with feng shui, no doubt. She quizzes me about the auction; tries hard to persuade me to have a foot massage. I decline, reminding her (again) how ticklish my feet are.

'Why don't you try this?' She plucks a tube of cream from her bag, bangles jangling as she hands it to me. 'It contains peppermint oil and shea butter. It really does work wonders.' I take it with an appreciative smile.

Sunny's discussing Mick's declining health when Eleanor marches in to ask where her striped top is and then, after I inform her it's probably in the ironing pile, flounces out, declaring that her clothes are 'never ironed when she wants them' and I'm 'proper lazy sometimes'.

I can't take a passive ride on that particular mood swing, especially as it's witnessed, yet again, by a straight-faced Sunny. I follow Eleanor upstairs, inform her how rude she's been, inviting her to do her own bloody ironing.

'Well, thanks for the tea, but I should be going,' Sunny says on my return, grabbing her bag. 'I'm doing a treatment shortly, on a lady who's just been diagnosed with cancer and suffering extreme anxiety, poor thing.'

'Oh dear.' I watch Sunny drift across to the door. 'Thanks for having Eleanor.'

'Oh, she's such a pleasure. Never any trouble … to me.' I grit my teeth behind a smile.

With Sunny gone and Eleanor sulking, I reluctantly do some ironing, made slightly more bearable thanks to catch-up episodes of a new sitcom.

I'm sorting some old clothes to fill a charity bag when Eleanor joins me and, clearly feeling some remorse for her 'you're a bad mother' outburst, offers to help choose which clothes to donate.

'Can Freya come over later?' Their Zitgate bust-up, that was going to be forever, is clearly already behind them. I nod.

'You two friends again then?'

'Course. Bethany's being weird, though. She's so moody.' I raise my eyebrows. 'Says her mum's not well. I don't know what's wrong with her.'

'I hope it's nothing serious.'

Eleanor sighs. 'Suppose I better do my history homework. We've got to do some research on Hitler.'

'Hitler was a vegetarian, you know,' I declare, pulling off a flimsy top and flinging it on the large reject pile. I'd picked up that pearl of historical wisdom from Dan, one of the few I'd retained. Eleanor lifts one eyebrow sardonically. 'And he only had one testicle,' I add.

'Please, no!' she scolds, elongating the words.

I sing, head swaying from side to side as I conduct myself: '*Hitler has only got one ball, the other is in the Albert Hall, His mother, the—*'

'Mum!' Eleanor can't suppress a small grin.

God, I'm turning into my dad.

CHAPTER 20

It's Monday morning and I feel ridiculously energetic, as if I've had a shot of adrenalin intended for a large African mammal. In terms of biggies, the day's dangerously obese.

The enormity's not only affecting my mind, thoughts jumping in all directions, but has sparked an urge to do the more demanding domestic deeds I usually find any excuse to evade.

I end up with a white stripe down my blue leggings after bleaching the toilet and manage to dust a family photo off the wall, the glass shattering on the hall floor that I've just vacuumed with vigour. Even Pepsi's stunned by my housework frenzy, sniffing suspiciously as he re-enters his pristine cage.

The train trip passes slowly. I sip rank railway coffee and scan magazines to sedate the butterflies, but my mind wanders wildly, forcing my cerebral sat nav to constantly recalibrate. Maybe it's the journey triggering them, because the thoughts aren't exclusively about the day in store. I think about the last few weeks, the news stories, nasty letters and cut-off calls, work, the move, Eleanor, Mark, Sunny, and Dan; always Dan.

Several times, I try to make eye contact with the man sat opposite at our sticky, grey table, but he's engrossed, fat fingers clicking relentlessly on his laptop keys. I yearn to know who he is, where he's going. He looks like a Clive. I imagine he works in an insurance office and drives a Ford Focus, probably in silver, maybe dark blue. And he always cleans it at the same time on a Saturday, before checking the football scores.

I comment on the coffee and he flashes a feeble smile. Then his head drops before I can engage him further. He clearly doesn't want to chat. I have to be content with staring at the top of his balding head, which, as the journey progresses, begins to resemble the face of Jesus – a hairy bit in the centre of two widow's peaks forming the Messiah's beard, the bald circle in the centre, his face. Was I having some kind of conversion on the rail to St Pancras? I wondered.

Ashley's flat is on the third floor of a red-bricked building above a ragged row of shops that smack of desperate times and drastic measures. I enter through a peeling green door between a boarded-up Italian restaurant and an archaic curtain and bedding shop that promises '*Every Item Reduced*'.

My legs feel weak and wobbly as I climb a set of white stairs, staring down at the threadbare runner. I take a deep breath, pressing firmly on the bell by the door at the top marked with a faded number 3.

Ashley greets me with a wide smile and slightly damp hair that clings to his cheekbones and, looking relaxed, thumbs hooked in the front pocket of faded black jeans, leads me straight into the living room.

It's surprisingly large and reassuringly untidy, with mismatched furniture and three pairs of near-identical desert boots huddled around a brass floor lamp in the corner. Yet it has a homely feel, the rustic wooden floors covered in a huge black rug, cushions bundled on to a scuffed brown leather sofa and a collection of black and white photos, some hung, others propped against the wall.

'Nice place.' I shift aside a London bus cushion to sit on the sofa. 'Smells lovely,' I add with a wry grin, nodding to the plug-in I've spotted by the lamp. 'Linen and Lilac, if I'm not mistaken.'

'Thanks.' He doesn't smile, and I'm not sure he gets the joke. I can't believe Ashley Baird's got a bloody plug-in – he's the one who's had the conversion! He'd ridiculed my air freshener fetish at poly, swearing he'd remain forever loyal to the humble aerosol and never succumb to the latest gel fragrances I was being lured by – always one tucked in my knicker drawer and several others hidden away when he visited as he found the smell too strong.

'It's all right, isn't it?' Ashley fetches a pair of boots, chucks them by the chair. 'Good space. And light. Best I could afford round here. Rent's still hideously high.'

'I bet it is.' I wonder what his other home's like, whether his wife will stay there.

'There's a small kitchen through there.' Ashley points to a door next to a pair of dirt-brown curtains with insufficient gather. 'And two bedrooms.'

My eyes scan in silence, stomach still tight. It's like a larger version of his student room, though less messy and minus the lemonade bottles. A camera and other photography paraphernalia are spread across a smeared glass table and there's a musical keyboard next to a cluttered desk in the corner.

'I didn't know you played?' I say at last.

'Taught myself a few years ago. I can play a mean *Blue Moon*.'

'Any other songs?'

'No – just the one.' I chuckle.

While Ashley makes coffee, I survey the photographs. They're all acting related – striking theatre façades, shiny stages, groups of heavily-painted strangers oozing confidence and loving the camera. I recognise the black-haired woman with the purple lipstick from the café. Lily. She's in several shots. She seems to be giving the man behind the lens a special, knowing look. Jealousy creeps up on me. Would she be mum to the baby Ashley wanted? She was young, beautiful, talented; good genes. Or would it be one of the other glamorous actresses pictured?

I move to the far wall and there, under a strip light, is a photo of Ashley draped in black with white ruffles around his dark throat, his shadowed face stern and staring at a skull, its eerie crevices highlighted in the glow of an intense spotlight. He looks so convincing as Hamlet, yet so different. I'm mesmerised.

My eyes travel along the wall to a man with a long, dark beard, wearing an over-sized coat and fedora hat. He stares into the camera, shrugging with outstretched arms. His gesture could be directed at me. '*What you doing here?*' the stranger asks. I shrug back.

I'm startled when Ashley appears. I fiddle with the collar of my chiffon blouse, hand unsteady as I reach for my coffee.

'Did you take these?'

'Most of them. My little sideline.'

'They're really good. Clever bugger.'

'Cheers. I'm getting better. I'm doing some photography for a hotel brochure. A bit beyond my comfort zone, but with the acting work looking quieter in the months ahead, it's worth a shot.'

After coffee, and much indecision and debate, we settle on the idea of lunch in a nearby Turkish restaurant, followed by a guided walk around the area.

I emerge from the dark basement into the brightness of a warm but blustery day feeling light-headed. I'd let myself get carried away with the conversation, the cabernet sauvignon I'd intended to ration, and the cloudy raki the proprietor persuaded me to try. We'd both over-indulged, notching up a massive bill. I'd insisted on paying. Ashley put up little resistance.

I can tell he's tipsy, too, eyes dulled, gait even more relaxed and limp less prominent as we amble through the town past some stunning period houses with premium price tags and, according to Ashley, celebrity owners. I laugh as his fine hair's repeatedly blown across his face in the strong breeze. Our conversation turns to Ashley's run of school workshops.

'They were exhausting,' he says. 'I might take back what I said about wanting children. They're bloody hard work. I'm sure Eleanor's the exception,' he adds. I shake my head emphatically. 'And my nephew, of course. He's a star, though he's really unwell at the moment.'

'Really?'

'Yes. Waiting for a liver transplant.'

'Aww – no. You didn't say. Is that the little lion boy?'

'Yes. I don't see much of him unfortunately. My sister

lives in Yorkshire. He's had several ops, they thought he'd be OK, but his condition has worsened. They're waiting to find the right match. There's an average three-month wait, even for children. You can't believe it in this day and age.'

'Poor little thing. And your sister. There can't be anything worse as a parent than having a sick child. I feel so lucky.'

Ashley nods. 'I'd really like to meet Eleanor.'

'I think she'd like to meet you. She'd be star-struck.'

'Hardly.'

'So, any news on the acting?'

'Well, I missed out on a recall for *As You Like It*, but I'm going up for several other roles so it's no great tragedy.'

'I thought it was a comedy,' I say. Miss Giggles guffaws.

'Oooh, that was bad.' Ashley narrows his eyes. 'I've been offered a minor role in *Macbeth*, but that's not until the winter.'

'Wow, I did that for GCSE English,' I gush like a schoolgirl. 'What part?'

'Lennox, a nobleman.'

'I don't remember him.'

'Exactly.' Ashley shrugs.

'Anyway, I thought you're supposed to call it the Scottish play, not—'

'I'm not superstitious.'

'I am – I think. You've had enough bad luck. I'm thinking stage equipment here,' I say, buttoning my thin cardigan against the gusts.

Ashley speaks in a menacing monotone, eyes widened in a spooky stare: 'Let's hope I'm not forever cursed.'

'Fingers crossed,' I say.

'Very funny.' Ashley pauses. 'My friend has set up a new theatre group and I'm in his rather trendy take on *1984*, starting in two weeks. Got to use your contacts where you can.'

'That's great. So the career could be taking off again.'

'Well, it's only small theatres, but it's a six-week tour. Should be fun. It has lots of nudity – not me, I hasten to add.'

I try hard not to imagine that one. 'I might book some tickets in that case then.'

'Fair play, he's banking on people reacting like you, booking tickets once they hear there are fit, naked actors in it.' He flashes a sardonic smile.

'Do you come across the same people at auditions?'

'Yes, there's one guy – hugely talented, handsome, rugged, booming Brian Blessed voice; you know the type. But, alas, he got food poisoning from the buffet after the last night of a production of *Antony and Cleopatra* and could be out of action for a while.' He stops walking, hands held up in surrender. 'I didn't make the sandwiches. Honest.'

'I put laxatives in Dan's food once.' The post-wine slack tongue syndrome again.

'Really – for a joke?' Ashley looks bemused, jaw set at an odd angle.

'Well, sort of. I was fed up with his fussy eating. He'd refused some rice just because I'd put ordinary instead of sea salt in it. So I put some laxative powder my mum had left behind in his dhal. Funny, he could taste the wrong salt, or half a grain of sugar, but not the laxative.'

'And did it have the desired effect?'

'Not at first. But after I'd done it a couple more times it did.'

'Wow. That's a wicked streak I didn't know you had.'

'I read about a woman who put bug poison in her husband's porridge after he did the dirty with her sister on the rattan sofa in their conservatory. He was really ill for weeks,' I add.

'Poisoning – very Shakespearean.' Ashley forces a chuckle through the shock his acting skills can't conceal. 'What other villanies do you possess?'

I titter. Damn that raki! I'd tried to make it sound like a big prank, but I sense his disapproval and regret it.

'God, you must think I'm some mad bunny boiler type. Don't worry, I'd never have done the poison thing. I felt bad enough about the laxative.'

'They say we are all capable of evil thoughts, but only rarely of evil deeds; we can all do good deeds, but very few of us think good thoughts … or something like that.'

'Shakespeare?'

'No, my mate Brooksie.' He flicks a grin. 'Any other confessions?'

I can't stop myself. 'Yes, I also ruined Dan's best Italian shirt, ironed it on the hottest setting. I stopped short of cleaning the toilet with his toothbrush, though I know that's a popular one.'

'Bloody hell.' Ashley taps an index finger on his lips. 'So – remind me to never let you cook, or do my ironing. And I might just hide my toothbrush when you're around.' I shudder at the thought of seeing his toothbrush again. Why had he mentioned cooking and ironing for him? He glances down at his chest. 'Actually, most of my shirts don't need ironing, and this is my only Italian one, by that great fashion designer – Marko Prima.'

I slap him, playfully, and he grabs my hand – and holds it.

★★★

We find ourselves in Ashley's bedroom within minutes of returning to his flat. It had all started with the hand-holding. Neither of us let go as we walked the final few streets in silence. We kissed behind the door of his living room, his eyes flashing those familiar, intense stares, our lips already loosened by alcohol, now softened by lust. We didn't speak, both consenting with looks and gestures. Both overpowered by something way beyond sense. The power of past attraction must have pulled us through the living room and into here, as I can't recall our steps.

I note another pair of brown curtains, the absence of the piles of creased clothes I'd expected. The Gola bag's in the corner. I smile inwardly.

Ashley sits on the bed, its iron frame pushed tight against the window wall. He pulls me next to him. The curtains are only partially drawn, putting us in shadow. I hear the hum of traffic in the street below, a singing siren in the distance. I stare down at his New York skyline duvet.

'Bad, isn't it?' Ashley's tracking my eyes, trying to grin. 'I got it in the shop next door. It was all they had without flowers on.'

My smile's shaky and he wraps his arms around me, pulls me tighter to his chest. He raises my chin, eyes locked on mine, fingers tracing the curve of my shoulder.

'I'm sorry.'

'What for?' I know, but I need him to say it. Again. And again.

'For what I did; for ruining us. I hope you can forgive me.'

I can't find words. I sigh into a silence that presses down on us like a lowered ceiling. I know what's going to happen. Shamefully, I've imagined it many times. And in that moment I want it more than anything. I block thoughts of Eleanor from my head. But Dan's image comes. *No! Sorry.* I shoo it away.

I hear Sunny's voice: 'You two could be together again.'

Which two?

We can't!

We bloody well can't!

CHAPTER 21

'So you copped off under the Empire State Building then!' Tash beams at me during our coffee-time kitchen chat the next day. 'Even I can't beat that one.' She shrieks.

'Sssh!' I flap my hand. 'And don't spoil it with your slutty smut.'

I'd intended to keep tight-lipped about it, but Tash is relentless. She's worn me down.

'I think Carrie's been a naughty girl,' she'd said, with a saucy grin and prolonged flutter of the lashes when I'd first arrived – late and flustered after oversleeping. Mark had heard, and although I'd finally gathered the pluck to tell him I was seeing Ashley, I was mortified, blushing beetroot.

Tash grabs the kettle. 'So is he still in good nick – you know, down below and that?' I glare. 'Was he hairier? They say men get more body hair when they're older, and it grows in odd places; even inside their bums.'

'Oh my God, Tash.'

'It must be so weird, having sex with someone again after so many years. I can't imagine shagging Chris in twenty years' time.'

'Knowing you, it'll be a miracle if you're doing it in twenty days' time.'

'Ouch. Cruel,' Tash says. 'I think you might be surprised. Chris and I have really hit it off.' I roll my eyes. It's only a couple of weeks since she split with Ryan. 'And I didn't sleep with him on the first date. That could be, like, a sign.'

Admittedly, when she'd told me about the bonk-free first meeting I *was* amazed, but assumed it had more to do with a run-in she'd had with a weirdo who locked her in his flat, demanding she stand in her underwear and heels while he fed her Revels; she was exercising some caution at last.

'And we're going on holiday on his parents' boat when I come back from Turkey. That's three weeks away. Aw, I'm so excited about Turkey. Shame I have to finish a pile of work before I go.' Tash's hot fuchsia skater skirt twirls as she turns to the fridge to get milk. 'So – is it serious with you now then, babe; with your Joseph?'

'Well, yes, in the sense that things have clearly … progressed.' I swallow down a surge of nervous excitement that takes my breath. 'But I'm not sure, in terms of it being a proper, couple thing. It's early days – and there are more hurdles than on an Olympic track; what happened before between us, there's his work in London, his wife, my work here, and Eleanor, a little matter of trust, and besides—'

'Don't think about that stuff, babe. Just enjoy it. And keep putting the orange peel cream on those thighs.' Tash totters out, sniggering.

I stir my coffee with a smile, imagining the bedroom scene replaying in the central spin of the liquid, the dazed dizziness returning. Tash is right. I'm in danger of allowing myself to spoil things. The thrill that accompanied me on the train home from London had abandoned me as I'd stepped through the front door, taken over by a sweep of remorse that I couldn't shake off.

I'd desperately wanted to call Imogen, but knew I needed to get my head around it before I wrapped it with words. I had a bath, adding my favourite sandalwood scented salts, keen to let the warmth and excitement of the day's events wash over me, the recollections making my skin tingle, body twitching with tiny darts of delight as the bubbles whirled and popped around me.

Then I'd spied my robe, hanging alone on one of two brass hooks on the bathroom door and the self-reproach came trickling back. Later, passing Dan's photo on the sideboard, I'd found myself uttering an apology. How was it possible to feel so exhilarated, yet so regretful, to swing so wildly from one state to the other?

When Eleanor had returned home, bleary-eyed and moody, she'd been keen to retreat to her room and I was relieved. I was lost in a mess of guilt and elation. My conscience dragged my inner turmoil around the kitchen, armed with an all-purpose cloth and some Mr Muscle. I cleaned and tidied, then cleaned some more. Then I made Eleanor's favourite tea.

'Lush.' Eleanor grinned at the sight of the piri-piri burgers, battered onion rings, oven chips and cheesy coleslaw that greeted her. Her eyes cast wildly around the room, noting the transformation. Yet they appeared to miss the shame etched on my face. Clearly, I still looked like the same mum, not the guilt-stricken widow who'd just had sex with her ex from prehistoric times and was serving junk food to her daughter to make herself feel better.

'Thanks. Wowzer! You've proper tidied up,' Eleanor said, crashing down to eat.

'Don't say it as if it's a miracle.'

'Well, it kind of is.'

'Anyway, it's tidied up properly,' I corrected. Eleanor groaned. She was right, I seldom tidied and cleaned the kitchen that thoroughly. Yet it had been surprisingly therapeutic.

I was sure I could sense Eleanor's silent scrutiny when she'd asked about my day, and I cagily confirmed that it had been simply 'OK'. I'd gone to bed early, but woken in a sticky sweat after watching the chest of Dan's corpse being punctured by a masked man with a giant needle, while another medic shouted frantically: 'Stop! He's not dead'. With that, Dan's eyes snapped open, and so did mine.

I stop daydreaming and take a coffee to Mark. He thanks me, though his eyes barely stray from the screen. Things had seemed a touch strained between us since the auction. He'd cancelled our plans to go to the pub comedy night because he was feeling unwell – and, work stress aside, he seemed a little distant and distracted. It was just small things. Maybe I was reading too much into it, but there seemed to be less chat, fewer friendly gestures, the tiniest blip in our shared wavelength and easy companionship.

We work on, mostly in silence, and I manage to get a lengthy marketing report completed. Before leaving the office, I ask Mark if he'd like to come over for something to eat one night. I'm so glad he accepts.

Relishing the light evening, I take a detour on my journey home, driving down a road lined with trees abundant with vibrant white and pink blossom. It reminds me of the candy floss at the fair that visited every summer when I was a kid, and of my pal Jo, whose cousin worked on the waltzers and used to give us free rides, spinning our car until our shrill screams subsided and we clutched our heads and turned green.

As I raise a grateful hand at an elderly driver who waves me on to the busy A23, pleasuring my nostrils with the Elmo air freshener hanging off the rearview mirror, I think of Ashley and find myself beaming. A proper, natural smile – lit from the inside – not one of those overcast ones you force on to your face.

I drive to the garden centre, buy a dozen trays of vibrant summer bedding plants – petunias, marigolds and several other striking pink and purple blooms the man recommends – to fill the borders at the top of the driveway. I can't stand to see them bare any longer.

Back at home and Mum's left a rambling answerphone message wishing Eleanor luck for her final show. She'd rushed Dad to A&E with chest pains but it turned out to be heartburn. She'd cooked her first ever chilli, worn the wrong glasses to read the recipe, and overdone the cumin. Although I really want to chat, I don't call back. I know I really should tell her about Ashley – a thought giving *me* chest pains, too.

'We slept together,' I blurt to Imogen on the phone, perched precariously on the chaise.

'Who was it with this time, Jude Law in a dinghy?'

'I wish.' I'd previously shared details of my strange erotic dream involving Hugh Jackman in a hammock in one of those trendy camper vans. We'd parked on the side of a track high up in the Swiss mountains. He'd yelled 'yodel leh hee hoo' as he hit his peak. 'Hang on, what, really…' Imogen's voice is steadily rising, '…you mean with Ashley?'

'Yes.'

'Gosh. Wow.' Imogen pauses. 'Let me just turn the oven down – I'm baking some tarte aux pommes – think I need to sit down for this.'

I fill her in on the run of events. 'Sodding hell, I wasn't expecting that one, my lovely,' she says.

'Neither was I!'

'So much for catching up on old times.' Imogen titters.

'I know. I feel bad. The guilt's really getting to me.'

'Well, you shouldn't. The time's obviously right.'

'Maybe … I just wish I didn't feel like this. Before we, you know, did the deed, I thought I could feel Dan's … presence. Then after, it actually felt like he knew. I know it's ridiculous, but it's happened before, moments when I find myself wondering if Dan may have been right, that he hasn't totally … gone … he's still … around … oh, that sounds so silly when it moves from a thought to actual words. Don't send for the shrink, will you?'

'It's OK, I don't think you're bonkers. I understand.'

'I still do that "seeking Dan's approval" thing, wondering what he'd think, whether I'm – I don't know – dishonouring him …'

'You don't need anyone's approval, lovely.'

'You're right. And we had such a great day.'

'That's brilliant.' Imogen pauses. I hear a voice. 'Ben's mum's here.'

'Oh yes, how's it going?'

'Fine. She's so young. I was shocked when I saw her.'

'Of course, she was only sixteen when she had Ben.'

'Yes, but I wasn't expecting her to be so youthful; and glam. The girls love having two nans again. They took to her straight away.'

'And you?'

'She seems really nice. But it all feels a bit strange. Strained. I suppose it will for a while.'

'Of course. It'll take time.'

We say goodbye, then Sunny calls to tell me how much she'd enjoyed *Fame*. She'd been to the matinee as she was unable to join me for the evening performance. As she speaks, I recoil at the thought of her knowing about Ashley; how I'd break it to her – when. 'Eleanor was so good, I just couldn't believe it,' Sunny says. 'What a talented girl.' She pauses. 'Such a shame Dan couldn't see her.' I agree.

Later, I find a message from Sheena on my laptop:

Hi Carrie. The night out was great and Molly's keen to babysit regularly in return for a few driving lessons. We'll see?! Now the bad news – Abigail's been excluded from school for hitting a girl (in the face!) who said her dad was definitely dead and everyone knew it. Although Abi was wrong to react like that, exclusion's so harsh, given what she's been through. I'm shocked because I thought Abi was handling things better than the older two girls. I've spent lots of time talking to her about her feelings. I wonder about getting her professional support? The school's offered to refer us. Children can be so cruel, can't they? I've tried to be honest with the girls, but keep them optimistic as I am. I just KNOW Geoff is still OK. I'm sure I'd feel it if he wasn't. Sheena xxx P.S How did it go with Ashley? Any joy with your job hunting?

There was no let-up for Sheena – and her poor girls.

Could you really feel when someone's dead, I ponder, or was it just the absence?

★★★

Eleanor has very little time at home. She has to be back at school an hour before curtain up. She's a bundle of nervous energy.

'It's kinda sad it's the last show,' she says, breathlessly, searching her bedroom for her spare pair of coloured tights. 'I'm really nervous – there's going to be a photographer tonight.'

I'm in the doorway, quietly observing as she rummages through several piles of clothes, ready to take the blame if the tights can't be located.

'Found them.' Eleanor shoves the tights, and a hairbrush, into her rucksack. 'DO NOT sit at the front.' She scowls. 'Bethany's supposed to be coming with her mum tonight. But she wasn't at school today.'

'I'll look out for them.'

'Hmm. Something's definitely not right with Bethany at home. She got really upset in PSHE yesterday and missed maths. Perhaps her mum's come out as a lezzer.'

'Eleanor! That's an awful thing to say. Anyway, she's married.'

'So? Everyone thinks she looks like one, with her short hair and men's clothes.'

'You can't tell someone's sexuality by how they look. That's stereotyping.'

'Uh.' She raises one side of her top lip. Probably thinks stereotyping's texting with both thumbs.

'Google it,' I say.

By the time I reach the school, my nerves are jangling, too. I can't see Bethany, or her mum in the hall, so I sit what I assume is an acceptable distance, at least ten rows from the stage, fidgeting, shallow breathing and sipping water while I flick through the programme and repeatedly stare at my daughter's name near the top of the cast list.

I think I'm going to faint when the slightly distorted recorded music strikes up and the emerald green curtains – the ones that had framed a million precious moments for generations of parents – jerk slowly open.

Anticipating Eleanor's first entrance, as Serena, the shy actress, I miss several breaths. Then relief hits as the first words leave her mouth in the right order, just about reaching the audience. Her confidence grows with each scene and it's only during a tender moment with Nick, her stage school crush, that she looks self-conscious, arms and head stiff. I think of her first role as an angel at primary school. She's come a long way. And Freya shines, an audience favourite, perfectly typecast as Carmen Diaz, the confident and determined dancer obsessed with fame. Before long I'm totally lost in the action.

The tears that form during the final song – *Bring On Tomorrow* – are still in my eyes as I stand in the corridor giving and receiving 'well dones'. Eleanor appears in a gaggle of excited teenagers, still in their costumes, all squealing, nudging and giggling in shapeless sweatshirts, gaudy trainers and loud leggings, hugs thrown in every direction.

Eleanor's virtually hyperventilating during the drive home. 'Was I really good, or are you just saying it?' she asks for the third time, not waiting for a reply. 'Was my high note out of tune? Did I look silly when I hugged Nick? Freya was great, wasn't she? Did you spot she forgot a line? Mrs Dean had to prompt her. I don't think the audience heard, did they?'

She's a little downcast when I tell her Bethany and her mum weren't in the audience, but soon forgets. There are plans for an after-show party. She can't wait. I tell her, again, how proud I am, that I want to buy her a special present.

Back at home, exhaustion takes over, Eleanor falling quiet before shuffling off to bed.

Then the phone rings. Silence. The rustling sound again, followed by a strange hissing.

'Piss off.' I slam it down. It rings again. 'Who *is* this?'

'That's not a very nice greeting. It's me – Ashley.'

I apologise, explaining about the nuisance calls. 'You need to contact your phone company,' he says. 'I'm sure they can trace the caller, probably block them.'

He'd remembered it was Eleanor's show night and wanted to find out how it had gone. His dress rehearsal for *1984* had been plagued by technical hitches, but there was another one scheduled. 'They've added a few extra dates at another theatre. It's going to be a long run.'

'I'd like to see it. I read it years ago.'

'It's not the best adaptation.' Ashley ignores my less-than-subtle hint.

But then he says he's free Sunday, it would be great to see me, though he'd understand if I'd rather not travel to London again.

I'm still humming *Bring On Tomorrow* in bed.

I can still see the curtains opening, a bright light shining on my daughter – and I can't stop smiling.

CHAPTER 22

I listen to the alien sounds of a city suburb's early wake-up; the grumble of engines, distant shouts, hollow booms and the clatter of metal – bins perhaps – a few determined birds filling gaps in the din.

Sun's streaming through the bottom of the horizontal blind, its cord caught up on one of the slats, pulling it askew and lighting up our lower legs. Seeing the shape of two pairs of feet beneath the quilt quickens my pulse.

I glance at the clock. 5.40 am. I climb out, pull on my skirt. Ashley stirs, eyes still slits that strain to follow me as I gather the rest of my clothes.

He beckons me with outstretched arms. I lean over, then pull away from his sleepy kiss, knowing I won't have the will to leave if I succumb again.

'Shame you have to go so early,' he mumbles.

'I should have left last night. I'm not sure I'll make it to work on time.'

'Never mind. You won't be there much longer.' Ashley grins cheekily, and the thought stays with me.

On the train, I take ages writing an email to Sheena using my new mobile. I ask after Abi. 'Children are so good at hiding how they feel, aren't they?' I'm uneasy about having good news to relay when Sheena continues to have nothing but heartache to contend with. But I don't want to lie; I've always been so truthful to her. I tell her how fabulous *Fame* was, how Eleanor's confidence has had a mighty boost. I confess that I think I'm in love with Ashley again.

Keen not to make it all sound too positive, I mention missing out on interviews for several jobs, that I still haven't heard back from the magazine.

As I snuggle down in a double seat on the train, a text arrives from Ashley: *Hope you get to work OK. Thanks for an amazing day! xxx*

My attempts to snooze are thwarted by recollections of my trip. I decide to put on some make-up, the jolt of the carriage making it hard to keep my fingers steady. We'd had such a great time together. Nothing planned, as ever, the day had found its own rhythm – a walk on the heath, sunbathing on our thin jackets by a heart-shaped pond while we watched crazy, shrieking swimmers diving from a pontoon into the cold, still water. Dipping our toes and giggling like kids. Our feet still wet, we were overtaken by shiny joggers as we climbed to the top of Parliament Hill, looking down on a city washed with gold. A three-course Italian meal, then an early night. I hadn't intended to stay over. I'd told Eleanor I'd be back at home.

A few days before, she'd been in her room, trying on a new strappy top and ultra skinny aqua jeans, when I'd breezed in to tell her my plans. I'd decided it was time for more honesty.

'Looking great,' I'd said.

'Sweet, thanks.' She'd dropped on to the bed.

'Is that your *Fame* party outfit?'

'Probably not.'

I was reluctant to sit by her on the bed – that's what I did when I was trying to be stern – so I fiddled with the curtains. Eleanor strolled over to the mirror.

'You know I told you about meeting Ashley?' I smoothed and regathered the material.

'Yes.'

'Well, we met up last week and I'm going to London to see him this weekend. Is it OK if I ask Freya's mum if you could stay over Sunday as I could be late back?'

I clocked Eleanor's quizzical expression in the reflection. 'I thought he was married.'

'Separated.'

'So is he your boyfriend?'

'I suppose so.' I sucked my cheek.

'Whatever. It's your business. I don't care.'

'Look, Eleanor, no one will ever replace your dad.' I walked over to offer her a hug, but she turned sharply.

'God, heavy.' She stretched the words. 'You're creeping me out.'

I'd walked away.

At the station, I dash to the newsagent's to buy something for breakfast. Passing a row of greetings cards, I see a giant one with a Great Dane pictured on a background of stars, wooing a cat on a ledge above: 'Happy Birthday, Boyfriend'.

I have a boyfriend now.

★★★

234

My late arrival, sparkly top and 'night out' shoes obviously don't go unnoticed by Tash. I'm forced to admit I've come straight from Ashley's. As expected, I get a more intense grilling than the chicken at Nando's.

Mark's also due in late. Tash assumes he has an interview. We're both engrossed in work when he thumps through the door.

Tash is straight in. 'Carrie's still in her evening clothes – that's what you call a long night!' I squirm.

'Disgraceful behavior.' Mark rolls his eyes playfully, pushing back his sleeves.

Tash is called to see Pete, and keen to stretch my legs – keep myself awake – I walk over to Mark's desk. He stops typing. 'An interview this morning, was it?'

'No.' He hesitates, eyes distant. 'I was visiting my sister's grave. Mum wanted me to take her.' He looks apologetic, as if reluctant to mention it. He'd done the same last year; I'd had to prise it out of him.

'Of course, it's the anniversary, isn't it? Sorry, I didn't think.'

'No. Don't be silly. Yes, it's four years today.' His fingers drum on the desk but barely make a sound.

I resist a strong urge to throw my arms around him, to offer some comfort. I walk away.

I'd be lying if I said I wasn't bothered by Mark's revelation. It's stupid, selfish and inappropriate, but along with the sympathy, I feel resentment. Envy even. I want a grave to visit. I wish I could take flowers for Dan, that I had somewhere special, somewhere neutral, that I could go; somewhere to think, and reflect, with a clear sky above and unfamiliar things around. Maybe I'd even talk to him there, tell him how strongly I felt about Ashley, explain that I'd never stop loving him, how difficult it was to move on, but how I felt I should.

I'd never imagined that having a grave would become so important. I hadn't really given it the thought it deserved in the past. I'd never once visited my grandparents' graves. It shamed me to admit it but, until recently, I didn't even know where they were. But it *was* important. It absolutely was. Almost everyone had them – unless loved ones were lost in battle, at sea, or gone missing, never found (God forbid this would be Sheena). Places to remember. Some liked to keep their nearest and dearest close, with ashes in urns on the mantelpiece or the bedside. I'd even read about a man who kept his gran in the glovebox.

Perhaps it was a case of wanting something more when you couldn't have it. Or maybe the various rites, relics and remembrances were somehow essential for the human psyche, a reminder of the permanence of the absence, and our own mortality.

I remember Dan telling me what a fuss the ancient Egyptians and Greeks made, things like mummification, magic spells, grave goods – even sacrifices. All rituals deemed essential if the deceased was to make the arduous journey to the afterlife. No such fuss was needed with cryonics, it seemed – if you'd be popping back for a second stint.

I decide to buy a sandwich to eat on the bench at lunchtime. I'd stared at that seat so often from the office window, watching its various stories unfold. Aside from the regulars, there to read, or eat, in the fresh air – and in peace – I'd watched a tramp fall asleep on it and nearly drown in the family-size bottle of cider he tipped over himself, some yobs completely douse it in paint quicker than you could say 'what aerosols', three talented teenagers line up and perform synchronised peeing on it, and one couple, who'd got to be in their late fifties, virtually having sex on it. 'Bloody hell, look at this!' I'd yelled after spotting the display of lunchtime lust. Tash and Mark had dashed over, by which time the guy, trousers down several inches, had straddled the woman. Mark yelled 'oy oy!' out the window just as a cyclist rounded the corner. They stopped, readjusted their clothing and casually walked off, hands still all over each other.

Yet I'd never once sat there. I can't shake the thoughtful mood that's descended. I want to be on my own.

I half expect to see anorak man still there, but the bench is empty. I soon realise why. It's unbearably hot, trapped in the glare of the midday sun, the surrounding patch of grass scorched brown and balding. It's not the most scenic spot, a wall of uniform evergreen trees screening the road ahead and ugly, dirty grey buildings behind. But it's good to watch people passing; some of them familiar from my window gazing.

A brass plaque in the middle one of three mahogany planks at the back of the bench bears an inscription: 'Dedicated to the memory of Edith Stanwell'. She'd died just over three years ago, aged seventy-eight.

The name seems familiar. I wonder who she was, what she'd done. I think of the antics I'd seen on the bench. Poor Edith, her memory defiled. Maybe she'd had a giggle at it all. Edith sounded like the name of someone with a sense of humour. I picture her, then give her flesh and blood, wavy white hair swept off a furrowed forehead, big glasses, a powerful voice emanating from thin, wrinkled lips; a wheezy laugh. I wonder what sort of funeral she'd had, whether she'd left a husband who'd chosen her favourite hymns and said goodbye as the curtain came across in front of her coffin. I bet her family put flowers on her grave.

Just then, a noise jolts me back into the moment. A skinny, sweat-drenched jogger, with shorts barely covering his bouncing bits, has dropped his water bottle. He scoops it up, keen not to interrupt his rhythm. I wonder what motivates someone to jog on such a hot day. The lure of longevity strikes again.

My sneezy sniffles turn to gentle sobs. I know I have to, but I don't want to go back to the office. I want to follow the runner, go somewhere new. I realise I've rarely seen anyone take that path – a tiny grass track between two buildings – and don't know where it leads. In nearly twenty years I've never walked in that direction, or even wondered.

It finally arrives. The dreaded 'No' to my application for the magazine job. They'd been inundated with applications, admired my writing, but I'd just missed the interview shortlist. My details would be kept on file. That old chestnut.

That night I consume my own weight in mash, then feel so bad I drag the exercise step out of the garage, bouncing up and down through two catch-up episodes of *EastEnders*. I hadn't realised how much I wanted the job.

Imogen channels positive vibes down the phone. 'How many years have you been telling me you're bored at Cullimore's, and I've begged you to do something about it? Now, at bloody long last, you have. That's a big step, my lovely.'

'Yes, and I've been rejected again. I must have sent at least ten articles in to various mags over the years and never been published.'

'Let me know when you've sent a hundred and ten, then I might start to doubt your chances.'

She has a point but I still can't help thinking I'm crazy for entertaining the idea of writing for a national magazine – even a local one. With Imogen's encouraging words whirring in my head, I find another job to apply for, working at a small theatre, a role that includes marketing and publicity duties. It sounds great. I wonder about jobs in London, tempted by one as an editorial assistant for a lifestyle magazine.

Then, not for the first time whilst trawling, I find myself wandering in web land, playing digital detective, trying to search out previous plays that Ashley's been in, theatres where he may have performed, even roles that might suit him. I can't resist it, wondering at my potential to be a cyber stalker in my Acer anorak.

It's great to have Mark's company when Eleanor and I celebrate her *Fame* triumph with a Chinese takeaway. At first, I'm concerned he's still a little 'off' with me, his attention almost exclusively on Eleanor in the kitchen, head turned from me as they talk about pop music and play tracks by The Beatles and other sixties artists she's recently declared 'cool'. It feels like I'm not invited to the concert.

'You're quite good at singing,' Eleanor declares after Mark's fervent burst of *Love Me Do*.

'I was a chorister, you know …' He laughs, looking in my direction at last.

It's later that a possible explanation comes. Mark tells me he's been invited out on a date with Georgia, a businesswoman he interviewed about her latest venture a few weeks ago, over an extended lunch. I remember him coming back all smiles, declaring what a formidable woman she was. And he'd been even more pernickety about the article than usual. They'd subsequently met for a drink. He was playing it cool, but I sensed he was quite keen.

After that, he relaxes, and it's getting on for midnight, my sides sore from laughter and head light from the heavy reds we've consumed, when Mark orders a taxi.

The next day, Sunny brings another dark cloud into my brighter sky.

'They suspect Mick's had a stroke again,' she says on the phone. 'He may have to go into hospital.' She accepts my offer to join her at the care home without hesitation. 'I'd appreciate that.'

Mick's in bed when we arrive. Sunny hovers while the male care worker and a peroxide-haired colleague with tattooed hands fuss over him. Mick looks dazed, eyes too slow to keep up with the movement around him. What resembles a student bedroom – carpet and walls in institutional magnolia and mustard, single beech

240

wardrobe and matching drawers dwarfed by a large TV –
has had the Sunny treatment, a cluster of candles on the
windowsill and several colourful silk cushions at the foot
of the bed.

'The doctor will be back shortly,' the male care worker
says, rushing out to deal with a patient charging up and
down the corridor, chanting loudly.

Within minutes a stick-thin, middle-aged man with
heavily lined cheeks and sunken eyes is telling Sunny, in
a reassuringly soft Welsh voice, that he isn't sure whether
her dad has suffered a stroke; he's stabilised, but it would
be wise to run further tests. We leave the doctor alone with
Mick.

'I'm not sure hospital is absolutely necessary,' Sunny
says, as we overtake a crooked old man with a Zimmer
frame in the corridor. 'I hope he doesn't get left on a drip
all day again, being fed a cocktail of chemicals.'

But things are soon out of her control. An ambulance
has been called, it's been agreed that Sunny will accompany
Mick, and I've been rendered surplus to requirements – a
huge relief. I already know I have to leave. I can't face
seeing the paramedics arrive.

The last time an ambulance was called to a hospital
bed that I was beside, it was for Dan. After doctors had
pronounced him dead. Expired. Terminated. A team of
cryonics volunteers had come to prepare his body, to begin
the procedure they believed could 'save him from oblivion'.
Dan's had been a textbook death apparently. Crucially,
they'd had notice, time to prepare. No post mortem to
delay them. No danger of irreversible cell deterioration.
But the converted emergency vehicle didn't arrive in the

normal way, its bright green and yellow checks blasting past motorists in a blur and turning alarmed, inquisitive heads. It had breezed into the hospital car park as if it was a minibus arriving for an outing to a wildlife park. Four men hopped out wearing sweatshirts, jeans and sensible shoes.

No siren. No superheroes. No battle cries. Just ordinary men, with wives, girlfriends, and regular jobs. Yet with extraordinary hope. One of them tried to talk through the procedures involved in preparing Dan's body for suspension, something about perfusion injections, intravenous fluids and clamps. But I couldn't hear and I wouldn't listen. 'Combitube this … cryoprotectant that … need to massage the heart'. *But his heart's stopped. And mine's broken. And this is making it worse.*

I must be reliving the anguish of that day on my face because I'm stood outside Mick's room, dreamily drinking a mug of coffee, when the care worker comes over to ask if I'm OK.

'Yes, I'm fine. Just had a late night.' I fake a smile.

'He'll be more comfortable in hospital.' He pats my arm. Such a sweet man. He assumes my upset and hurt is for Mick. Maybe it should be.

CHAPTER 23

'Are we nearly there then?' Pete's loitering at my desk, limbs twitching.

'Yes, just finishing the 'facts' panel, then I'll give it a final edit.'

'Good, good.' He continues to hover, staring over my shoulder, breathing audible.

To everyone's great relief, we've won another contract. We're so stretched I've been given several larger articles to write, including a double-pager for Lorex that requires research, and several interviews. Admittedly, it isn't thought-provoking, or glamorous – the latest endoscopy equipment for vets – but I was thrilled when Pete asked if I'd do it.

However, it's deadline day, and the fourth time Pete's crept in – the reflection of his saggy face startling me each time it appears on my screen – and I'm more flustered than flattered. I flash Pete a pained smile.

'OK. Great.' He snaps on his glasses, tweaking his genitals as he strides out.

'I'd finish it a lot quicker if he'd bloody leave me alone,' I snarl. Mark mutters in agreement, Tash stays silent, turning to check Pete's gone before grabbing her mobile.

She's preoccupied, but not with work, coming back from her week in Turkey with a 'real' tan, an extra half a stone and enough anecdotes to fill a large ottoman. She'd got so drunk one night she took a taxi to the wrong hotel, she'd suffered whiplash in a minor car crash with a group of off-duty soldiers, and friends had drawn a willy on her back in sun block after she'd fallen asleep on the beach (she'd proudly shown us its faded remnants). And – her trump card – she'd had sex in the hotel toilets with a waiter she boasted had the biggest doinker she'd ever seen, returning to agonise over her future with Chris.

She's also worrying about her sister, who's decided she can't afford to wait any longer for that elusive reliable boyfriend with potential for her Parenthood Project and managed to conceive with the help of her gay bestie. Even Tash considers it a desperately bad idea.

I stare at the same clumsy sentence for several minutes, willing the words to reshuffle. My confidence is still wobbling from the magazine job blow. And, despite the extra work, we're all jittery. Barbara has let it slip that Mafia Man's a new accountant. Why had Pete got rid of the wide-stripe-suited one with a long chin and halitosis who'd been his trusted money man for years, we all wonder? And why is he still so restless and crotchety?

'You at the bottom of the second page yet?' Mark asks, typing ferociously.

'Not now,' I scold.

'Remember – don't overdo the colons.'

'One more bum comment and I'll have to kill you,' I snap.

Tash giggles, head still hanging over her phone. I've

244

endured endless jokes from Mark about the article. But I'm indulging him – relieved that things appear to be back to normal between us, our friendship seemingly intact. I can't contemplate losing what we had.

'So, what's for lunch today? Eww, rice cakes, gross.' Tash is rummaging through the small pile of food on top of Mark's groaning in-tray. He's ignoring her. They now have daily diet-offs, challenging each other to see who can consume the fewest calories without collapsing over the photocopier.

Later, I ask Mark to give my 800 words a final scan. He's still sat at my desk when I return with drinks. 'Not bad,' he declares. 'Though you could cut down on the 'buts'.'

'Stop! No more puns or this goes over your head.' I hold the steaming mug above him.

Tash is pinning a print schedule on the cork noticeboard. She bundles over, looking puzzled.

'I don't get that one.'

'Butts, you know, with a double 'T',' I explain.

'Oh cringe.' Tash flicks Mark's ear, cuffing him at the same time.

'Hey, this is office abuse,' he says. 'Seriously, the article's great. I've cut a couple of superfluous sentences. And there's one bit I've underlined that needs re-jigging.' Mark taps my shoulder, ambling back to his desk.

'Thanks,' I say, sitting down to do the amends.

I have an intense wave of satisfaction – and, as I've been sat for so long, a feeling that I'd been subjected to the bum-prodding horror I've written so much about – when I finally email the article to Lorex's PR manager at

3.57pm, three minutes before deadline. I have to stay late to finish all the other postponed tasks. Even Mark leaves before me. He's got another date with Georgia.

Before heading home, I ring Ashley, determined to catch him before he sets off for his performance. We had another day together at his flat last weekend as Eleanor was camping on the school field. I spent lots of time staring at his bedroom curtains – we barely set foot outside the door. He'd seemed even more contemplative than usual, saying something that took me by surprise as I lay in his arms. I'd said that I'd love to see his show, how I'd read several great reviews; and how I missed London. 'You could always move back here.' I turned, searching his eyes for meaning, willing him to elaborate. He didn't.

We haven't communicated for several days – he's hard to get hold of – and I'm missing him. I'm keen for him to come to Tetford – to meet Eleanor – on his next free day. A biggie. On the phone, I mention it again. He'll see if he can work something out. I ask after his nephew. He's back at home after a short stint in hospital. But a donor hasn't been found. I feel desperately sad. What an awful thing for a seven-year-old to go through.

Then I ring Imogen to ask about her sex counselling session. We both roar when she recounts how she and Ben had to list five things they liked and disliked about each other.

'It took me back to primary school. I had to do a similar thing after I'd had a fight with my friend Heidi over who'd have the last bit of pink paint to finish our fairy pictures,' Imogen says. 'It was ridiculous. I haven't gone off Ben, I've just gone off bonking!' She isn't convinced the sessions are helping, but she's being referred to a specialist for hormone and various other tests, as her doctor suspects a physical cause.

'That's great news. I'm sure they'll get to the bottom of it,' I say, relieved her recent emotional swings may be due to some simple chemical imbalance that can be easily fixed.

'He mentioned a testosterone patch,' she adds.

'Yikes, Imogen. So you might have a beard and bollocks the next time I see you.'

She shrieks.

★★★

I find Eleanor spread across the corner sofa, simultaneously watching TV, texting and reading *Heat* magazine.

'You're late.' I chuckle. Being chastised by your teenage daughter is still something I can't get used to. 'Kirsten called round. Wants you to call her.'

'Kirsten?'

'Yes. I didn't know who she was at first. Then I remembered she used to be Dad's secretary. She looks different.' Eleanor looks up from the magazine. 'Her car's gross – it's all battered on one side. I've seen it parked in our street a couple of times.'

On the phone, Kirsten says she wants to see me; would I mind going to hers as the children are just back from their nan's house? I'm bemused.

Half an hour later and I'm sat in Kirsten's living room, watching her two girls fight over the electronic till in their pretend shop, while their brother looks on. The smaller boy I'd seen with his mum in the street that day is sprawled across the floor in the corner, colouring in a picture, surrounded by a stash of toys and games. Her baby's already in bed. Pleasantries over, I'm desperate to know why I'm there.

'Right, time for bed, drink up,' Kirsten warns for the third time. No movement. This time, she jumps up, grabs both girls by their wrists, yanking them to their feet.

'OK, OK,' one protests.

'And you,' the eldest says spitefully to her brother, giving him a kick. 'Ow,' he groans, kicking her back.

'Stop it,' the girl snarls. The youngest boy follows them out.

'Right – wash, teeth and pyjamas on. I'll be up later,' Kirsten yells after them through the door.

'Sorry about that.' Kirsten sighs, vibrating her lips noisily. She's barely sat down since I arrived, dashing in and out of the kitchen to fetch bedtime drinks and snacks, scuttling back and forth across the laminate in bare feet to wipe noses, clear toys and put tops on pens. She settles on her aubergine armchair, facing me, tugging repeatedly at her ponytail.

'Well, I didn't want to tell you this, but …' she scratches at a stain on her leggings, '… Dan and I had an affair.'

Shock constricts my breath. I don't believe it. No. 'When?'

'Before I left. It's why he sacked me. He ended it. He chose you.' Kirsten fidgets, a pained look on her make-up-free face, upper teeth nibbling her lower lip.

'But … he,' my voice is hoarse, '… how long?'

'Only a couple of months.' She swallows. 'I think my four-year-old – Jayden – is Dan's child.'

248

There's a crashing sensation in my chest, a rush of agony. I gasp. The whole room's spinning, my thoughts with it. None of them stay still long enough for me to grab hold of. Kirsten ignores a shout of 'Mum' from upstairs.

'Sorry,' she says.

I stand, limbs so light I almost topple. I can feel tears.

'Are you sure? Couldn't it be someone else – your boyfriend?' I try to picture the little boy. He's dark, robust.

'No, I'm pretty sure.'

'Why are you telling me now – not before ... not when Dan—?'

'I didn't want Dan to know. But Jayden's growing up and I think it's right to ...' She rubs her nose. The freckles on her neck and chest are obscured by big, red blotches. 'I'm on my own now. I can't get work—'

'You want money, is that it?' Of course. She's been prompted by recent stories about Dan's donations, his legacy. She wants her due.

'Mum!' Her eldest girl appears in the doorway in floral pyjamas. 'Ethan won't clean his teeth.'

I turn my back to hide my face, swiping at the damp skin under my eyes. 'I must go.'

Kirsten turns too, yanks her ponytail up into its purple scrunchie.

I sniffle my way out of the house, then drive in a trance, trying to drive away a mental image of Kirsten perched on Dan's desk, wearing only a plunge bra, lacy knickers and red heels.

I circle our house in the car, then park up a side street, staring at the dashboard through thick tears. I can't go back yet. I need to get myself together. I ignore a text from Ashley.

Kirsten said Dan sacked her. Yet he'd claimed he encouraged her to leave, it was all amicable. She'd been pretty useless at her job in the end, with so much to contend with in her home life; two toddlers and a baby back then, a boyfriend on drugs.

So Dan *had* cheated. It would explain all the healthy living and fitness madness. I'd always been proud not to be jealous, that I didn't read his emails, track his phone or sniff his shirts like a spaniel, as some wives did. Dan wasn't flirtatious, he was loving and romantic, we still had regular sex, he was still attentive – when he wasn't worshipping at the temple of longevity – so I didn't need to, did I? I'd never seen Kirsten as Dan's type; a threat. How had I been so stupid? Complacent? Conceited? Just because he bought me flowers and didn't throw himself at women. Just because an affair wasn't on a 'to do' list. I wonder what other secrets I may have missed.

I hunch over the steering wheel, heart pounding in my ears, tears silently falling. There's one thought I can't bear: that I couldn't give Dan the boy he wanted, but his mistress had. Worse still, he'd never get to see his son, but it was something I'd have to live with.

At home, I manage to conceal my distress from Eleanor. I hide away in the bath for ages, then busy myself with mindless tasks. I dart around the house as if demented, arriving in rooms with no idea why I've headed there. Imogen's adamant that Kirsten's lying.

'No way. Not Kirsten. Is she the ginger one …' she hesitates '… with four kids by three different fathers?'

'Five kids – she's had a baby quite recently – and, of course, FOUR dads now, so it seems.'

'Stop! No. No way.' Imogen falls quiet. 'Dan wouldn't—'

'It would be an awful thing to make up. Surely no one would … no, it seems we all misjudged Dan, that he burst out of his loyal husband straitjacket, lost all self-control and got his toned leg over his flabby secretary.'

'No. Kirsten knows you can't prove paternity now that Dan's passed away. She's bloody trying it on. She's got no evidence. Did she have a boyfriend at the time?'

'I think so.'

'Then *he* needs to have a DNA test first.' She pauses. 'And any other contenders.'

'The little boy …' I could barely say his name, '… Jayden – has dark hair and dimples, and—'

'Just like about half the toddlers in the population. Come on, really.'

A thought strikes me. 'So it's Kirsten who's been phoning – the silent calls. The hate mail must be from her, too. And the scratch on the car. Eleanor said she'd seen Kirsten's car parked in our street a couple of times.' I wonder if it also explained *CrykeyMoses'* comments on the forum about Dan's 'little problem' and the stud reference.

'What a bitch,' Imogen says. 'I just don't believe it. How did you leave it with her?'

'Her kids were there. I just walked away.'

'You have to get some advice, speak to her again. You can't leave it like this.'

'Yes. I know. I just need time to think.'

CHAPTER 24

It's hard to carry on as normal, but I have to. I'm in a horrid mess for several days, all over the place. There's a loud, incessant hum in my head, a background babble of crowded thoughts, and a tightness in my tummy.

Thinking about what Imogen said about proving paternity when a dad is deceased, I've looked into it. It's possible, it seems, but involves taking DNA from close family members. I can't involve Eleanor – not yet.

I'm beginning to share Imogen's doubts about Kirsten's claims. Dan wouldn't do it. I'd have known. I have absolutely no evidence with which to convict my deceased husband of being a love rat; certainly no justification for the persistent image I have of him covering his naked secretary with Post-its before giving her one in the walk-in stationery cupboard.

At other times, though, it all seems to make perfect sense. Dan was keeping fit for a younger woman, to keep up with a mistress. He'd had his ten-year itch, and given it a good scratch. He wanted to eat his metaphorical cake whilst denying himself the real thing.

I've called Ashley several times, burdening him with my woes. I'm desperate to see him, to hug him, but, sadly, he can't get away.

I crave Mum's support but, while we've talked on the phone, it's hard to have a proper conversation, with so much I'm keeping from her. I still can't bring myself to tell her about Ashley, there's no way I'll tell her about Kirsten, and I don't want to worry her with the menacing mail and calls.

Apart from Ashley and Sheena, Mark's the only other person I've told. He shares Imogen's utter disbelief. He says I need to tackle Kirsten; he hopes I won't give her a penny without proof. I haven't told him I've contemplated writing a huge cheque and asking her to emigrate to New Zealand.

I decide to call Kirsten. She doesn't answer, so I bail out and leave a message, saying I'm 'considering things', I need time, and requesting her discretion as I've not spoken to Eleanor.

For several nights I struggle to sleep, then I oversleep three days in a row, arriving late for work and getting a roasting from Pete.

Then, out of the blue, I get an email inviting me, at short notice, for a first interview for the theatre job in Birmingham. Doing some last-minute preparation, I discover the venue's much larger than I'd envisioned and has recently been rebranded and relaunched as an arts centre, with several studio areas used for a variety of events, workshops and rehearsals.

It's an impressive space – all glass, curves and bold colours – with light bouncing in from every angle and local, modern artwork adorning exposed brick walls. The young manager who interviews me is interested in my background, emphasises that, aside from marketing and publicity, there's plenty of scope for writing, in the form of a newsletter and in-house reviews displayed in the foyer. I come away keen and excited, but uncertain how well I've conveyed myself, with my mind so unfocussed.

Later, I visit Mick. He's not long been discharged from hospital – but there's talk of him returning. He's in bed, looking extremely frail, when Sunny and I arrive, though he manages a strained smile.

'Raaaayyy,' he says, dragging a trembling hand out from under the sheet to meet mine.

I watch Sunny's crinkly plum skirt swish around the room as we chat. She rearranges cushions, tugs the curtains open another few inches to let in more sunlight, swaps a bottle of 'unpleasant', sugary squash for some elderflower cordial, then smothers Mick's dehydrated, cracked lips with a balm she's made with beeswax and almond oil.

I'm sure I can see trepidation in Sunny's eyes, but she bats it away with calm blinks as she strokes the patchy, weatherworn skin on her dad's forearm and curls up a false smile that frames her gappy front teeth. Mick looks shattered – only his lips shining out from the dullness.

Sunny's spell of compelled composure is broken when the regular carer comes in to talk about the doctor's visit.

'I appreciate he feels Mick needs rest, sweetness, but I'm sure he'd benefit from a little walk.'

And the poor man gets a grilling when he brings Mick a fresh jug of water, at Sunny's request.

'More nasty pills. What are these for?' She drops Mick's hand, points an accusing finger at a plastic bottle on his cabinet. I'm embarrassed. Considering Mick's fragile state, it's surely not the time for her to be screwing up her New Age nose at modern medicine. The carer gives a good-natured shrug.

'I'll have to check his notes.'

It turns out to be blood-thinning medication. For the first time, Sunny responds with, what appears to be, a look of resignation, her shoulders dropping several inches.

I'm convinced I can feel the faint breeze of an inaudible sigh of relief in the room when I offer Sunny a lift home. She's tiring. Mick's exhausted.

Next day, I'm a little late for work again.

'No Mark?' I ask Tash, stepping over a collection of tools spread across the office floor and nodding a greeting to a spotty lad in a green polo shirt who's fixing the photocopier.

'He's in later. Pete's not been in yet, you're OK.' Tash stops typing. 'Apparently that accountant's due in again later. It's about time we were told what's going on.'

'I agree.' I sigh. 'It's already unbearably hot in here.'

'I know, babe. We so need air con.'

I tilt the blinds, checking the window's fully open. 'He's there again,' I say. 'The old man. Would you believe it – he's still got that bloody anorak on?'

'On a day like this – what a nutter,' Tash says.

'Actually, hang on, I think he's taken the hood off.'

Tash laughs.

I sit down just in time for the morning inspection. It's the same routine each day. Somewhere between 9 and 9.05, Pete – trailed by Barbara, glasses bouncing between her bosoms – come striding in to greet us. 'Morning, troops,' he'll say, and she'll echo, or 'Aren't we busy bees?'

The pair burst in as expected, both looking perturbed by the obstacles at ground level. Barbara's waving a minifan by her flushed face. Pete's mocking her, frowning at the mess.

The spotty lad takes two hours to fix the photocopier and Pete flits in and out, bald head sweating profusely due to the heat and dread of a big repair bill. Tash turns quiet and then uncharacteristically cranky when, returning from the kitchen with a glass of water to take some painkillers, she trips over a set of screwdrivers, spilling the drink over the twins and down her new ivory prom-style dress.

She's having another one of her 'brain pains', as she calls them. Doctors think they're migraines but Tash self-diagnosed on the internet yesterday and attributes her symptoms to the holiday whiplash injury. 'I knew your loud gob, and that bloody shrill laugh, would get you in the end,' Mark had said, unsympathetically, receiving a two-fingered ear flick.

Later, with our visitor gone and Pete safely tucked away in a meeting, I'm having some crafty computer time when an email drops in from Sheena:

Hi Carrie. I've been worried about you. Have you decided what to do about Kirsten? Keep strong. And take lots of advice. I had to share this with you – there's an article in today's newspaper about a wife who's returned after being missing for THREE years!! It suggested depression may have been a factor. There's a lovely photo of her reunited with her husband and little boy. I cried buckets. I might just email the story to that ignorant reporter writing that 'missing people' story! Seriously, I'm feeling more positive again. Abi seems more settled and the school's monitoring her closely. Maybe Geoff and

I will be in the news next – though I hope it doesn't take that long!!
Always here. Sheena xxx

I realise that Sheena and I are on a see-saw, her downs often coinciding with my ups, and vice versa. I'd love for us to meet in the middle, delighting in the moment when everything around us stops moving, and settles into place.

I try to let her positive vibes wash all over me while I work. Then Tash, feeling better after some fresh air, drags me into the kitchen to tell me about her latest potential Mr Right.

'I'm seeing him this weekend. He's posted some topless photos and he's so ripped, it's ridiculous,' she says, hands held rigid on her traffic-stopping patent yellow belt. 'He's into boats and sailing. I've got a good feeling about this one!'

'I think I've heard that before somewhere. I can't imagine you on the high seas somehow: "Abandon ship, Tash's windswept hair's developed a kink"!'

'Cheeky bitch!'

Back at my desk, I get a text from Ashley. He can come to Tetford on Saturday for a few hours. I'm stoked.

At lunchtime, I'm lured by the bench, still drowning in confused thoughts of Kirsten and Dan, staring at the trees whilst eating a cheese and celery sandwich, when I turn to see a khaki anorak. I've been joined by the little old man I've seen sat here so many times. I recognise the mad, flyaway hair – and the coat, which, to my surprise, he's removing. He drapes it across his thin thighs, smoothing out the material. He's thinner than I imagined, without the big coat, brown jumper baggy at his chest.

'Lovely day again,' he says, beaming.

257

'Yes, it is.'

After a few minutes' silence, I see a girl with a fluffy white dog heading towards the same narrow path I'd seen the runner take a few weeks ago. It prompts another flash of curiosity.

'Do you know where that leads to?'

'To the old canal path, my dear,' the old man says. 'And there's a gate to the back of the churchyard. It used to be a dead end, the canal's been overgrown for years, but they've cleared a section of it.' The dead end joke's clearly unintentional. Only Miss Giggles laughs. 'My Edith's buried there.' I turn to meet a pair of warm, rheumy eyes. 'I visit her grave sometimes. But I prefer to remember her here.' He taps the bench. I'm confused. Then it dawns on me. His Edith must be the woman on the plaque. 'She did so much for the local council they dedicated this bench to her.'

'How lovely,' I say.

'She campaigned to keep these offices here…' he points a shaky finger towards our building, '… not to let them move to that big industrial estate. She loved this town, fought hard to keep it thriving.'

'I work in there,' I say, smiling. 'I remember the campaign well. My boss was so grateful. He's convinced it saved the business.'

No reaction. He's still trapped in his train of thought. 'We were married for forty-five years. I still miss her terribly. She's been gone over four years now; may she rest in peace.' He drops his head. I stand to go, keen to respect the peace he clearly craves. 'I'm Gordon, by the way.'

'I'm Carrie. Nice to meet you.'

★★★

'What's up, Mum?'

I'm sat on the bed. I look up to see Eleanor draped in a towel, hair dripping wet from the shower.

'Why are you crying?'

The letter's in my hands. I can't hide it. I pass it up to her.

She reads it aloud: '*Only The Lord Can Choose Your Afterlife. Let God Decide Our Fate.*'

'What? Who's it from?' Her face is pale, eyes still.

I tell her about the other two notes, the calls, the car. I'm reluctant to worry her unduly, but she has to know. I can't tell her that previously I'd suspected Kirsten was responsible, but now I had doubts. The language, the tone; it just didn't fit.

'What are you going to do?'

'Report it to the police, I guess.'

'Really?' Eleanor rubs her head with the towel. 'I better go and blowdry my hair.' She pauses at the door. 'Don't be upset. Probably just some weirdo.'

'You're right. Thanks.' I smile.

Water has smudged several words on the page. 'God' leaps out in a turquoise hue, the rest of the sentence illegible. I put the letter on my bedside cabinet to dry.

It's anger I feel more than anything. I'm angry with Dan, for all he's left me with. I don't know what to feel about him any more.

And I'm beginning to despise cryonics, despite what I say out loud. It's becoming a burden, one I lack the strength to carry any longer.

CHAPTER 25

Preparing for Ashley's visit is a welcome distraction from recurring thoughts of Kirsten and the menacing mail. I can't wait to see him again, but the excitement of spending time together is mixed with anxiety over how Eleanor will react. I'm desperate for them to like each other.

Eleanor's subdued. I assume that anticipation of her encounter with Ashley's the cause, although the hate mail's clearly making her jumpy. Several times, she's appeared as I answer the phone; lingering, with a quizzical expression, until she knows who's calling.

Yesterday, she'd dashed to collect the post seconds after it dropped through the letterbox, watching as I opened it.

The phone rings after breakfast. It's Imogen; calling to wish me luck. Eleanor hovers in the hallway, listens for a while, then re-inserts her headphones and heads off.

'Introducing your daughter to your new boyfriend feels so wrong – a switcheroo,' I tell Imogen. 'Eleanor will soon be bringing boyfriends home for me to scrutinise and fret over. These past two days, she's had a face on that could turn toffee sour.' But I don't really blame her. I'll be bringing a man she's never met, someone I have history with, into our family home.

'Yes, I guess it will be difficult, and strange, for everyone at first,' Imogen says. 'But it'll soon get better.' I agree.

Ashley's train is delayed, so I distract myself with an email to Sheena, telling her I've read the story about the reunited family online and pray that her happy ending will come sooner. Forget sending the story to that local reporter; she should hand it to her, and give her a slap for being so misinformed and tactless. I have a list of journalists I want to hit. I share my fears about Eleanor meeting Ashley, how I really hope it isn't all too painful for her, and how terrified I am of telling Mum about the relationship. I still care about Mum's opinions, even though I often disagree with them. Our recent chats have been so difficult. I've always been selective about what information I relay to Mum about my private life, for both of our sakes, but the latest edits were pretty radical; and I'm uncomfortable with my deception. Mum knows about the begging letters, but not the others. I don't want to worry her.

The doorbell rings and I snap the laptop shut, rushing down the hall as if I'm the teenager.

'Hey, good to see you.' Ashley hands me a leaflet lodged in the letterbox, then leans in to kiss me, rough whiskers scratching my cheek. 'I was expecting the butler to greet me. Great place.'

'It's his day off,' I say.

He looks different; hair longer, beard much thicker. His face in shadow, the image of him as Hamlet flashes into my mind and my nerves swell. I point upstairs to indicate the coast is clear, then pull Ashley closer for a more prolonged kiss.

Eleanor appears as we chat in the kitchen, wearing her new white top and fully glammed up. But all the make-up in Boots can't conceal her look of unease and mistrust. Ashley's perched on a bar stool, one elbow on the island.

'Hi,' he says, with a gentle grin. 'How you doing?'

'Good, thanks.'

I hold a plate of white chocolate and raspberry cookies in Eleanor's direction but she declines. Ashley lifts up his coffee cup. 'You into this stuff like your mum?'

'No,' she says, sounding terse. She moves closer, eyeing him suspiciously.

'Fizzy stuff? Coke?'

'Yes.'

'She's certainly into that,' I add, hovering nervously.

'I was mad on lemonade when I was your age. Drank bottles of the stuff. Still like it,' Ashley says. He's certainly playing it cool. I wonder what stage direction he's giving himself: (*tries not to show signs of the discomfort he's feeling, to put the surly girl at ease*).

I offer Eleanor a can from the fridge and she grabs it, turning on her heels. 'See you later.'

I shake my head in mock despair. I'm so relieved to have the initial introduction out the way, the adrenalin overload dissipating.

'She's lovely,' Ashley says.

'I warned you she's moody.'

'I don't blame her. She's very grown up for fourteen.'

'She certainly is.'

I don't want to exclude Eleanor, but I know she'll find lunch for three distressing, so I suggest to Ashley that the two of us go to town.

'Or we could have a look at this photography exhibition.' I show him the flyer.

'Britain's Seasides of the South East – sounds good,' he says. 'I spent many summers in Margate. I wonder if the photographer can manage to make it look good. Fair play if he can.'

I chuckle. 'I've never been.'

'Really? We should go some time.'

'Great,' I say, tentatively.

Ashley's in his element at the exhibition, face alight, head cocked in all directions as he stares, at length, at each photograph. At intervals, he stops his wistful gazing to talk to me about the image; the clarity, light, perspective, use of background. There are only a few other viewers and, every now and again, the photographer appears, genie-like, giving us an insight into why and how he took the photo. My wish – which he doesn't grant – is that he'll sod off and leave us in peace. I'm enjoying Ashley's enthusiasm and his eagerness to share it with me. He doesn't seem to mind my ignorance, that I'm a point and shoot woman.

Ashley doesn't mention Kirsten, or the unwelcome mail, and determined not to keep dragging him into it all my problems, spoil our time together, I don't either. He tells me the local newspaper's running an appeal story about his nephew. They believe it might speed up the search for the donor. Doctors are quite hopeful.

Thoughts of that poor little boy accompany me as we stroll home. Seven short years and his body's failing him. The only image of him I have is from the photograph on Ashley's Facebook page, his face painted as a lion. A brave little fighter.

We cut through the park, hand in hand, light rain falling on perfect circular borders packed with pansies, joined only by an elderly couple with a porky pug in a floral mac waddling behind them.

'It's so different to London, so quiet – a nice change,' Ashley says.

My pulse skips at the thought of him moving to Tetford; living together. I squeeze his hand, and, for a moment, yearn for a repeat episode of what happened at his flat the first time; holding hands as we walk the last few streets home, then ravishing each other as soon as the bolt strikes the front door's latch hole behind us. But, of course, we can't.

Back at home, Ashley sits at the kitchen island, flicking through a property supplement, while I order pizza, bemoaning the lack of good local takeaways.

'You get so spoiled for choice in London,' he says.

'True.' I want to say I know he loves London; his life's there. 'I've seen a couple of good jobs in London I'm tempted to go for – assuming I don't get that theatre job,' I add. 'Might be good to get away from here.'

Ashley stays silent, but his head tips slightly; it could be a nod. I'm struggling to read his mixed messages. It may be premature, but I'm desperate to talk about us, what's next, to make plans. We've both proved so adept at skating around it we could give Torvill and Dean a run for their money. A move to London would be a massive upheaval for Eleanor and me, but it may be good for us both. There are fantastic opportunities for young people in the capital. The other night, Ashley had talked about that very thing, London being a young person's city, giving

264

me the impression that he may be tiring of it – that a move to Tetford wasn't out of the question. Earlier, he'd been surprisingly complimentary about the town.

Eleanor joins us for pizza, occupying the chaise while Ashley sits a decent distance from me on the corner sofa. He leans forward, food box perched on a pile of magazines on the edge of the coffee table.

'Pepperoni and chilli beef – fair play.' He slow nods at Eleanor, like it's some big accomplishment. 'You're into the spicy stuff, then?' Eleanor nods back. 'How about curry?'

'It's OK.' She crumples her nose.

'Eleanor's Princess Piri-Piri,' I interrupt. 'If you glazed a sheet of cardboard with it, she'd probably eat it.'

'Funny.' Eleanor shoots me a deadly look. 'Actually, I'm not into it that much now.'

'I wish you'd told me, then – we've got a freezer full of it.' She turns for a glare-off; and wins.

Ashley snaps the tension, asking Eleanor about school, and drama club. He's careful not to grill her too much, also directing questions and comments at me, though my contributions to the conversation are all greeted by sharp scowls from my daughter. Ashley's performing well, I have to applaud him for that. And, to her credit, Eleanor's being reasonably civil. I think she quite likes him. She even looks a tiny bit impressed when Ashley tells her he was one of the brothers in a three-month touring production of *Joseph* but the director turned his microphone down low after the first week because his singing was so rank. It prompts memories of his renditions of Blur songs after a few cans of Stella in the student bar – my room-mate describing it as 'the aural equivalent of running your nipples across a cheese grater'.

Eleanor flits in and out during the rest of the afternoon and early evening, disappearing to watch TV, communicate with friends, and any other excuse she can muster.

When I shout to her that Ashley's leaving she yells 'bye' in a distant, uninterested voice.

We stand by the door, upper bodies stiff, both acutely aware that Eleanor's just a set of stairs away. I long for him to stay, and say so.

'Well, another three weeks of *1984*, then I might be the resting actor again for a while,' Ashley says, patting his fingers on his jeans.

'That's OK, you can rest with me,' I say.

He grins. 'I'll call you tomorrow night.'

'Yes, great,' I say, trying to hide my disappointment over his early departure with a singsong voice.

He leans over, kissing me gently on the lips. Then we both jump at a shadow by the front door. I expect a leaflet to drop through, but there's a strange scraping noise, followed by several taps.

I reluctantly pull away from Ashley and head to the door. He follows. I can't see anyone as I open it, so I flick on the outside light. There are shattered eggs shells on the step and, stepping out, I see a slimy substance down one side of the door and on the porch wall.

'Ugh! Eggs. What a bloody mess,' I say. 'Probably kids playing a prank.'

'Hang on.' Ashley runs down the drive. I wait; anxious. He returns, hunched and breathless. 'I saw a woman running across the road on the right. I'm pretty sure she was carrying an egg box.'

'A woman?'

'Yes, I couldn't catch up. She sped off in a blue car.'

Kirsten, I think, feeling increasingly cross that our farewell's been spoiled. 'Was she plump, with ginger hair; a ponytail?'

'No, she looked slim, short hair; blonde, or it could have been grey.'

Eleanor comes to check out the commotion, then promptly leaves, looking bewildered. Before leaving, Ashley urges that, in the light of recent events, I should report the incident, apologising that he can't stay longer and risk missing his train.

I wonder if Eleanor's been loitering on the landing because she appears at the bottom of the stairs as soon as the door clicks behind Ashley. She's concerned; wonders who did it. She's twitchy. Am I going to report it? I say 'yes', assuring her we're safe, she needn't worry. She watches TV with me for much longer than usual.

'Nice guy, isn't he – Ashley?' I say, trying to sound casual as we head up the hall together, Eleanor to go to her room, me to surreptitiously look out the front window and check everything's locked – again.

'He's OK. I don't like his hair. Or his beard.'

I titter to myself. If that's the worst she can come up with.

CHAPTER 26

A few days after the eggs incident, Mum calls me at work. She wonders why I haven't been in touch. Just been busy, I say, uncomfortable with the extent of my duplicity.

Tash has another one of her 'brain aches' and leaves early. I'm not convinced whiplash is the cause, more likely the late nights and lemon vodkas; and fretting about her sister.

I grab my cardigan from the stand. Mark hops up from his chair, giving my shoulders a gentle shake.

'Right, I'll walk with you to the car.'

'What! You're leaving now? That's three times this month you've left on time. Are you ill?'

'Work to live, not live to work. I've been in since before eight.' He turns his computer off with a decisive snap. 'Besides, I'm off out later.'

'Oh yes? Do spill.'

'I'm taking Georgia to see a Beatles tribute act.'

'A big night then?' I tease, trying overly hard to produce a big smile. He twitches his eyebrows.

Walking to the car park, Mark urges me, again, to report the eggs attack and all the other happenings. It's gone too far, and clearly isn't going to stop.

'You can't put it off any more,' he says.

'I know. I need to make sure it's all logged with the police at least. Ashley said the same. He saw a woman running away, and she didn't fit Kirsten's description. I hate the thought it could be some weird stalker; that there may be worse to come. Eleanor seems really tense.'

'We could go now. I'll come with you, if you want?'

'It's OK, you need to get off, but thanks. Maybe now's the right time to move.'

Mark shrugs his square shoulders, reiterates that I can call him if anything else happens, then wishes me luck for the following day. I've been invited for a second interview for the theatre job.

'It's got to be better than slogging away at Cullimore's,' Mark says, though being stupidly busy's a 'welcome distraction from ex-wife troubles'. Then he tells me Pete's planning to retire next year, his son's going to return from Dubai to take over the business. Pete's been stressing over the finances because he wants to ensure everything will be in order.

'Why didn't you say before?' I ask.

'He swore me to secrecy – wasn't convinced it would work out. It's why he got an outsider in to look at the business. He's going to tell everyone soon, so you need to play dumb. Shouldn't be hard.' I thump him.

My second interview's an improvement on the first, and with a one-in-five chance of getting the job, suddenly it all seems real, and scary – the implications huge.

At home, Eleanor's first question is whether I've reported the incidents to the police.

'Yes,' I say, scuttling down the hall. 'I popped into the station after my interview.'

'What did they say?' She looks incredulous, eyes pulled wide.

I tell her they didn't seem overly concerned, as there were no threats of violence. I have an incident number, and a number to ring if anything else happens, which I assure her is unlikely.

But she seems distracted and, after some probing, persuades me it's because she's really worried about Bethany. She'd been off school all week, was giving everyone conflicting reasons for her absence, and ignoring lots of texts and calls.

'Perhaps you could pop by to see her – I'll take you,' I say, a suggestion that's greeted with Eleanor's best lip curl.

I phone Ashley to tell him about the interview.

'Great – fingers crossed,' he says. I'm disappointed. Part of me hoped he'd admit he didn't really want me to get it, that he'd be unusually assertive, demanding I get a job in London so we could be together sooner.

★★★

I leave for work early, parking at the wrong end of town, despite the marbled clouds and heavy, on-off rain, so I can walk through the churchyard and pass Edith's grave – again. It's become a bit of a habit, since finding it.

The metallic words shine out from a pure white headstone: *In Loving Memory of Edith Stanwell, Beloved Wife of Gordon, Loved and Remembered by Christopher and Paul and Their Families.* On either side stand dappled vases stuffed with wilting spring blooms. I stay for a while.

Tash is already at the office when I arrive. She hops up from her desk and stands, looking stunning in a clingy, capped-sleeve dress, hands held out as if praying to the Lord of Lycra.

'Something's happened!'

'What?' I ask, fluffing up my damp hair. I know it's nothing bad as Tash is grinning strangely.

'I think I've had that cupid thing.'

'Is that a nail treatment?'

'What …' she puzzles, '… oh, cuticles. Funny. Seriously, I think Joel might be the one.'

'Really?'

'Yes, we were sharing a prawn and pepperoni pasta meal last night and I just felt it. Like, I didn't want him to leave. I could hardly sleep, imagining what it would be like if we shared a flat, or lived on one of those luxury boats on the Thames. His friend has one that's so amazing, with a bar and underfloor heating.'

'Gosh. Serious stuff.' I'm bemused by Tash's alarmed look. 'That's good, isn't it?'

'Yes. But, oh my God, it's scary, too.'

'So no more dating websites then?'

'Well, I might just stay registered on a few, just in case.'

I groan. 'Anyway, how was reflexology with the Evil Elf?'

'Oh, Carrie. You know I regret calling Sunny that,' Tash scolds. 'I actually liked it. She put this weird music on, with birds tweeting and water noises and stuff. I nearly fell asleep. She massaged my bunions, too, told me I wore heels too much, then did this head rub. It felt sooo good.'

'Maybe it's the treatment that's got you all loved up. Sunny's messed with your neurons – they're misfiring, making you lose your mind.'

Tash tuts as she makes towards the kitchen. She turns. 'Actually, I haven't had a bad headache since.'

'It was only yesterday, Tash!'

'Good point.'

Only yesterday, I muse as I flick through a marketing report. Dan's birthday. A day I dreaded. I expected Sunny to make a bigger deal of it, like she did last year. Of course, she phoned. And, of course, she mentioned it, though she pretended she was calling to confirm Tash's appointment. 'Fifty-one,' she said, with an elongated sigh. As if I didn't know what age Dan would be. 'Are you doing anything today?' she'd asked. I was tempted to say: 'Yes, paying tribute to your brother by parading through the centre of London flanked by world statesmen and trailed by a military band. Instead I said: 'Nothing much.' Yes – I'd be thinking and hurting. A lot. I didn't need to spell it out.

Last year, Imogen came to stay and took me out for a meal on Dan's birthday again, knowing his absence would be agonising. Sunny looked after Eleanor. The next day, Eleanor told me Auntie had taken her for walk in Crodham Woods – where she and Dan used to make dens as children – then she'd turned off the lights in the living room, lit a candle, and talked about Daddy's flame never going out. 'It creeped me out a bit, Mum,' she said.

This year, there was no fuss or grand gestures. Eleanor was subdued over breakfast. We both were. She spent a long time in her room. I dropped her at the cinema and, later, to Freya's for a sleepover. I successfully filled the day with diversions, finally sitting down with Katie Strutt's magazine column. I was trying to read about how she'd tested out a Shewee device, relieved to join her husband for a crafty wee behind the bushes during a five-hour bike ride, but little switches kept flicking inside me, distracting me, prompting emotions, thoughts and memories. I'd shared so many birthdays with Dan. His fortieth stood out. A trip to Monaco. 'A petrolhead's heaven,' Mark had assured me enthusiastically when I ran the idea past him. I'd been worried about surprising Dan. He didn't do surprises. No time to plan. Yet he'd loved every minute.

In the end, I'd given up reading, given in, and sat on the chaise, just thinking. Reflection was a strange thing, so inclined to editing and distortion; bright colours added to make memories less mundane. 'It's funny how people improve with death; they're always lovelier, cleverer, more popular and successful,' Mark said to me once over a pint. 'When I die, I hope people remember me as that ordinary bloke who was pretty good at writing, quite funny, loved playing rugby but never got beyond county level, and could be a moody bugger at times.' I'd chuckled in agreement.

Kirsten's claim – and all the cryonics repercussions – were rubbing at the rose tints on my retro-specs, blurring and bending my vision of Dan.

'I do often have a headache on a Monday though and I haven't today.' Tash's voice pulls me from my reflections. She's obviously been mulling that one over in the kitchen.

'Did you get drunk last night?' I ask, opening the blinds to see if anyone's sat on the bench, looking out for Gordon.

'No.' She's nibbling a carrot stick.

'That'll be it, then, you daft cow!'

She concedes defeat. I hear a ping and wait for Tash to reach for her phone. She's flicking through a pile of papers, clearly procrastinating.

'That yours, hon.'

I reach into my bag. Ashley has texted from the train: *Don't think this on-board coffee would cut it with you. Piss weak. Missing you. X*

After days of not hearing from him, despite several calls, last night I had: *Big Brother is boring me now. Thinking of you. X*

Mark's late, dashing in at nine, hair still damp, toothpaste dried on his lower lip. Jack's staying while his mum moves them to their new barn conversion in Somerset. Georgia stayed too. He makes it into his chair seconds before Pete arrives for the inspection.

'Morning, troops,' Pete says, with a tip of the head. Barbara follows behind, grinning dutifully, lily of the valley filling the air.

'Morning,' we chorus.

'Carrie, I had the Lorex boss on the phone last night singing your praises again about the articles.' Pete regards me steadily. 'Mark and I have spoken, and given his workload, I want you to take over the magazine writing.'

'Really … oh …' Mark hasn't mentioned it, but he's giving me a goofy grin. 'Of course. Great.' I wind up a big smile. The phone rings. Pete walks away. Tash picks it up.

'OK.' She looks at me. 'For you.' I frown. It's a bit early for client calls. Most respect the 9.30 work watershed.

It's Sunny. Mick's been taken into hospital again.

★★★

I hear the phone as I step through the front door. I hurry to the living room, bag still hanging from my shoulder. It's Mum.

'I hear you're seeing Ashley, then.' My heart dives, throat a knot of tense muscle. Fortunately, she doesn't wait for me to speak. 'Eleanor told us. Your dad skyped her.' My parents skyped – a second seismic shock. 'You kept that quiet.'

My bag drops to the floor. 'Not really,' I say, trying to gather my composure. 'It's all very … casual.'

'I couldn't believe it was THE Ashley at first,' Mum says with palpable venom. 'I thought it must be a different one. But then Eleanor said it was someone you went to primary school with—'

'Yes,' I interrupt, confirming her worst fears.

'Oh Carolina, for goodness sake. After what he did?'

'He had his reasons … you don't know … it's – complicated. Anyway, that was twenty years ago.' I force out an extraordinarily long, deep breath.

Mum asks about his work, his family, falling disturbingly silent when I mention the separation from his wife.

'It doesn't sound like a very practical pairing, him being in London, and still being married, and—'

'Well, we're not planning a wedding or anything. We're just enjoying seeing each other at the moment. Nothing more.'

'Either way, it must be so difficult for poor Eleanor.'

My tongue-biting skills elude me. Non-combat Carrie leaves the living room on her Conflict Dodgem.

'How bloody dare you, Mum! I'll always put Eleanor first. But I've got a right to have a life, to try to find happiness.' I can't stop. 'You haven't got a clue what I've been going through in recent months. This isn't about Eleanor. This is about you not liking Ashley. You never did, and didn't even have the courtesy to hide it. And you bang on about bad manners. Well, I don't care. I don't need your approval any more. If you don't like it then … bloody tough.'

I slam the phone into its cradle and crash on the chaise, the air ringing with my rage. I've just spoken to my mum in a way that no one ever dared, but I feel little shame, and no regret. I want to cry, but want to scream more. I do neither. I stare. I dig deep for some slow breaths and calming mantras, trying to recover from the shock at my eruption.

Heading upstairs to wash my face, I spot something as I pass Eleanor's room – a newly-framed photograph on her desk, of the three of us, taken by a tourist as we rested on a wall during a clifftop walk in Rhodes. Dan's in the middle, looking tanned and gorgeous in a pale pink T-shirt, his strong arms thrown around me and a baby-faced Eleanor, his gold watch turned silver by the sun. We look so happy, eyes shining. We were.

Poor Eleanor's clinging on to the memories, holding them in a sturdy ceramic frame, making a statement – a protest perhaps – in the light of Ashley's entrance into our lives.

I go downstairs, heat up some lazy mash. Sitting on the sofa, I stare at Dan's armchair, wondering if I should move it, maybe sell it. I've never liked it and now it's never used. I decide I can't – or is it shouldn't?

Perhaps Mum's right. Was I being selfish to seek

happiness with Ashley? Stupid to forgive him so readily? Was I being fair to Eleanor?

The phone rings again. I hesitate. It's Kirsten. Can I call round sometime? She'd like to talk some more about possible support for Jayden.

I want to insist that her ex-boyfriend has a DNA test before I get involved – but I can't say it. 'Give me a few days,' I say, cutting the call short.

I cough to clear some mash caught in my throat. A red mist descends and, in a flash, I hurl the bowl at Dan's cushion, watching several clumps cling to the faux suede, while others slowly drop on to the seat of the chair.

I sob uncontrollably. I don't want to cause my daughter more pain. I don't want to care about disappointing my mum. I don't want to be plagued by the past and harassed by some weird stalker, unsure whether my deceased husband had cheated. I don't want to be hesitant about a new job, whether to move, where to go; uncertain about so much.

I want certainty. Damn you, Dan!

CHAPTER 27

Ashley's proving elusive, so I call him before work.

'Hey, I'm on the train, can I call back?'

I hear broken noises – fuzziness – then stifled sounds, distant and indistinct.

'Oh, OK … when?' The sound clarifies; it's a woman's voice in the background, soft but high-pitched.

'Tonight? It's just that—'

'OK. Is someone with you?'

'Yes … Lily, you know … she's on the train with me. She's on her phone.'

'Oh.' I hesitate. 'Is she in the play?'

'Yes.'

Eleanor and I barely speak at breakfast. I don't feel like it. Neither does she – it's the morning of a science test. I stop staring at my cup of Lavazza to read an email from Sheena:

Hi Carrie. Hope things are better with you? Have you told your mum yet? Of course it won't be easy for Eleanor, but you must consider your own happiness too. It's clear how much you love her, she knows that. A friend offered to take Geoff's car for a drive but the battery was flat again. I hate driving it – far too big – but Molly wants to, says my Honda's a granny car! I've booked two driving lessons, but told her she needs a job to help pay for more. Geoff's income is tied up in the firm and I can't access it until he returns. On a course tomorrow. Yawn! Sheena xxx

Eleanor dashes in, grabbing several textbooks from a stack on the table. I follow her down the hallway, opening the door to some angry summer clouds. She plucks out one headphone to say goodbye, accepting a peck on the cheek.

'Good luck with the science exam.' I do a thumbs-up. Her lip curls.

Work's marginally better than a science exam – though I find it testing. Tiredness doesn't help. I'd slept badly, waking up hot and clammy, feeling slightly nauseous for the second morning that week, the dread of an early menopause rearing its head.

I've fallen behind with work, and Tash is up for lots of banter about being an auntie (her sister's scan shows she's further gone than medics had thought) and whether she should move to Brighton as the gay bestie is clearly not fit for fatherhood. She could get in some baby practice. Joel might join her, as it's by the sea.

I sit on the bench at lunchtime, willing the old man to come, though I'm not sure why. He doesn't.

Back home, Sunny calls to say Mick's condition has stabilised. 'I wondered about popping round with some leaflets for Tash on migraine remedies. I've also made a balm.' There it is again – the caring side that makes me feel bad about my intolerance of Sunny. Her dad seriously ill, she's being kind-hearted towards a colleague of mine she hardly knows.

I offer to drive to Sunny's, determined not to hover pathetically by the phone or keep staring at my mobile, waiting for Ashley's call. I wonder whether there's any news on his nephew.

Sunny greets me, looking like a new character from *Sesame Street* in fluffy purple socks and equally hairy purple jumper. I force a snigger into the shape of a smile.

'Hi. Thanks for driving over. Have you got time for a drink?'

'Tea will be great,' I say, following her inside. Sunny's cups of coffee taste like they've been strained through a gymnast's tunic. She summons me to the sofa with a tap on the throw, the loose, frayed sleeves of her jumper hanging over her hands as she passes me several leaflets.

'There's lots of information here for Tash. And ... one moment ...' she fetches a small glass pot from the shelf, '... if she rubs this gently on her temples here, in the little hollows ...' she places an index finger either side of her eyes, making circular movements. '... a few minutes twice a day's fine, or more if the pain's bad.'

'Great,' I say.

'She's having another treatment soon, but this will bring her some more relief meanwhile.'

I can't decide whether it's the right time to mention Ashley. Now that Mum knows. I consider it while Sunny's in the kitchen.

'I'm seeing someone,' I say, heart skipping as she hands me a mug.

'Oh, I wondered if you were.'

'His name's Ashley. We used to go to the same primary school.'

'Does he live in Tetford?' I feel Sunny's still scrutiny.

'No, London. He's an actor – and photographer.'

'Is he the one from the newspaper story?'

'Yes.' I'm surprised she's made the connection.

Sunny walks slowly over to the bookshelf, removes the candle from a terracotta oil burner, then fetches matches to light it. She has her back to me, facing the flame. The silence feels prolonged and painful.

'Has he got a family?'

'No. He's been separated from his wife for a while.'

She turns, hazel eyes narrowed. 'Were you in touch with him before, you know before Dan … passed?'

'Of course not. Why would you think that?' It feels like the anger Mum stirred is loitering inside, ready to rise up and reignite. I put my mug down on the carpet.

'Sorry, it's just you've known him so long … and …' she pauses. 'Are you going to move to London?' Sunny blinks quickly, a flicker of concern perhaps.

'I'm not sure. There's a lot to consider. I've applied for a job in Birmingham. Eleanor loves her school, her friends—'

'Yes, I can see it wouldn't be an easy relationship. Acting's such an unstable profession. And it's such a crucial time for Eleanor, isn't it?' she says, floating towards me. 'I appreciate she's your main concern.'

Fury surges through me. 'Yes, I'll make sure everyone's happy and getting on with their lives and I'll just be miserable and sit around waiting for a miracle to bring my dead husband back. Because that's what it'll take. A BLOODY MIRACLE! You don't believe it any more than I do.'

Sunny stares with a pitying look. She sits.

'You're right, I don't share Dan's faith in cryonics, or his desire for a physical extension to this life. I believe the

281

spirit lives on. But none of us know. He may be right. Besides, it's not about what I believe. Or you. It's about love, and respect.'

'So you think I'm showing disrespect to Dan by trying to find happiness for myself – and our daughter – after two-and-a-half years of hell. And what's love got to do with it?'

'Please stay calm, sweetness. I didn't mean to upset you.' I feel her fingers pressing my hand. 'I'm saying Dan absolutely loved and adored you and deserves ...' she corrected herself, 'deserved—'

'So you think he deserved better, that I wasn't good enough for precious Dan, I didn't love him enough.' I pull my hand away. All I see is a sea of purple fluff and a return of the bright red mist. My breath burns my throat. 'Or as much as you – is that it? I should share his belief in a second go at life, and ... I've tried so bloody hard to be civil to you, to get along for Eleanor's sake, for Dan, but I've had enough. What's your problem with me? I think you're jealous of what we had because you can't find love.'

Sunny snatches a sharp breath, eyes hardening as shock strikes her face. I'm desperate to leave. When other people lose their temper that's what they do – storm out and slam doors, finishing their display of fury with a flourish. I stand, but my foot catches the mug, sending tea flying across the carpet.

'You've no bloody right to judge our relationship, to keep tormenting me with guilt after what I've been through. You think you're on some higher plane, spiritually superior with your fancy potions and ethical ways. But you're not. You're cold-hearted and cruel.'

My cheeks are wet, face contorting. I can't believe the words I've just blurted. Who's the callous one? What's happening – first Mum, now this? Carrie Colwell didn't get really angry, just mild outbursts, and very rarely. She didn't say hurtful things out loud. She kept them inside, fleeing on her Conflict Dodgem, avoiding confrontation, frightened of the repercussions of cross words, terrified of losing control, losing respect, losing friends.

Sunny stays silent, hands clasped. She pulls a tissue from her bag. I wonder if she's crying.

'I don't think I deserved that. I'm – shocked. And you're upsetting yourself.' She hands the tissue to me. I scrape at my cheeks, an angry buzz still coursing through trembling fingers. 'Maybe I *am* jealous of what you and Dan had,' Sunny whispers.

'Well, maybe our marriage wasn't as good as either of us thought.' I don't want to mention Kirsten, but I've lost control. Sunny's eyes narrow. 'Dan's old secretary claims they had an affair; that he's the father of her four-year-old boy.'

'No.' Sunny shakes her head calmly. 'No.' She's almost smiling; a strange reaction, considering what I've told her.

'You see, your brother might not have been so bloody perfect.'

'Please … sit,' Sunny says. I'm stunned by her stillness. Had she already known about Kirsten? 'There's something you should know.' I perch on the sofa, stifling sobs.

'I didn't want to tell you this, but things are being said and I need to.'

'What?' I ask impatiently.

'The fertility thing was a huge burden for Dan. He felt it was all his fault, that he'd failed you somehow. And Eleanor.'

I frown. His fault? 'But the tests—'

'He had a very low sperm count.' She searches out my eyes. 'That first doctor told him, the one Dan got so upset with. Eleanor was a one-in-a-million fluke.' My anger is quashed by bewilderment. It can't be right. Dan hadn't told me. But surely she can't be evil enough to make such a thing up? 'I'm sure that's why he had such a strong desire to keep healthy. He felt there was a chance he could reverse things. I think he was right to try. It's amazing how our bodies can be transformed with a few positive steps. He desperately wanted a second child – with you.'

No. His health obsession was triggered by the desire for longevity, a need to be in control, and vanity; perhaps a fear of death. Maybe to keep fit for a mistress. But not this.

'So he told *you* this, but not his own wife?' I challenge.

Sunny stares through me. 'He thought he could change it, and ...' she seems reluctant to go on, '... feared you might be a little, I don't know, flippant. Turn it into a joke. That you'd dismiss—'

'How could he say that?' I spit the words. 'It's me he should have bloody told.'

'He told me that before his appointment to ... donate ... you'd said, "Don't worry, you'd still love him if he was firing blanks".'

I recoil. It sounds so awful when Sunny says it. It was just a throwaway quip, my attempt to lighten the mood.

'For God's sake, Dan knew I took it seriously, that I'd have supported him, just as it would be the other way

284

around, if I'd been infertile, which I assumed … I can't believe he'd keep this from me.'

Sunny touches my hand with a gentle sigh. 'He was just hurting a great deal. Feeling extremely sensitive. Male pride.'

'So that's why he didn't want me to have further tests. And I thought he'd decided he was happy with our little family of three.'

'He *was* happy. So happy.' Her voice has a reproachful edge. 'He just wanted the best for you all.'

Sunny stands, disappearing into her treatment room. She reappears, rubbing her wrists. I can smell lavender.

Then it strikes me, like a slap round the face awakening the senses. If Sunny's telling the truth, Kirsten is definitely lying.

The deep disappointment over Dan's infertility deception is smothered by relief. He couldn't have fathered a child with another woman – any woman.

Through the tears comes a concealed smile and a thought I shouldn't be having in this moment. Maybe – just maybe – I *could* have another child. With Ashley.

As I sit back, bewildered by my feelings, Sunny tells me about her romance in Spain. Felix was a busker, entertaining people on the terraces of cafes and restaurants. They shared a love of music, meditation, an interest in the spiritual; she'd believed they were soul mates. As she worked all day waitressing and he worked at night, he moved into her flat so they could spend more time together. She loaned him money for a new guitar. Then one day she returned from her shift to find he'd ransacked her home, taking the few things of value she had, including cash and lucky gemstones from her handbag. He left a note saying, '*Sorry, you don't deserve this.*'

Was that why her handbag rarely left her side? Sunny stands up into the sharp silence that follows her revelations. Her eyes are moist. I realise why she doesn't cry. Sunny wraps the serenity shawl impossibly tight around her, putting all her energy into easing the pain and hurt trapped inside, rather than letting it out.

'I'm very sorry if I've upset you with some things I've said. Life's been stressful for me, too. Keeping a spiritual balance hasn't been easy,' Sunny says. 'You see, I *have* been in love – and hurt. I do know something about relationships.

'And Dan was the only man who never let me down.'

With that, her sobs come. Old tears that have been trapped for too long.

★★★

Most of the drive home passes in a blur, my eyes straining to see through tears that obscure the windscreen, head struggling to straighten out thoughts jostling for attention in my fraught mind.

I hate the thought that my husband shared a problem so deeply personal with his sister, not his wife. Dan's sperm count was so low it was highly unlikely he'd ever father another child. A life-changing fact – yet one I never knew.

Who else knew? He thought I'd be insensitive. Flippant. The words he'd written to *CrykeyMoses* on the forum come back and won't leave me: '*Everything's a joke to her.*'

I deeply regret what I said to Sunny – the mean, wild words. And I believe her. It's as if the black voile through which I'd viewed her has been pulled aside. Sunny's not the evil sister-in-law I've cast her as. Far from it. She's been an easy target for my grief, someone to blame. I've been unfair to her.

I know Kirsten's lying, about the child at least. I have to see her.

I hope to hide my emotions from Eleanor that evening, to hold them in; save them for bedtime. But it's impossible. She confronts me the moment I step in the door.

'I only got 35 per cent in the science test.' She spits the words, standing close as I kick off my shoes. 'I have to do a re-test tomorrow.' I can't be sympathetic. Or think in straight lines.

'Maybe you should have worked harder for it,' I say testily.

'I'm just crap at it! It's your fault.' Eleanor stings me with a look of sheer contempt, mouth screwed into a seething mass. 'You should help me. Dad would have.' She storms up the stairs, pausing on the landing. 'I HATE MY LIFE.'

Later, when Eleanor comes down for a glass of water, I'm still at the kitchen table, staring blankly at a magazine, wrapped in my own muddled misery.

'You OK, Mum?' She's giving me a searching stare.

'Things have just got to me.' I sniff into a tissue. 'I'm having one of those days.'

'Maybe you should have some mash, cheer yourself up.' She smiles through a look of concern. Talk about mood swings. Eleanor doesn't know that there isn't enough mashed potato in the kitchen of a care home to console me. She lingers by the table, eyeing me carefully, tears gathering. I sense her remorse.

I stand up, hold out my arms, and she lets me hug her close, crying quietly into my chest.

The latest hate letter's on the table. I'd pulled it out of my bag, looking for tissues. Eleanor looks at it, then at me.

'Mum, I …'

'Yes,' I will her to continue with my eyes. I knew she was about to say something important, her mouth held tight. I wanted it to be about her dad, for her to open up.

'Nothing.'

'I love that photo on your desk, darling,' I say as she walks away. 'Maybe we could frame a few more.' She looks back, half smiles.

Later, I find a message on the answerphone from Ashley asking me to ring back. I don't. I can't bear to hear his voice and not be able to hug him. It's torture.

I wait for Eleanor to go to bed and pour my heart out to Imogen.

CHAPTER 28

'Yes, I lied. I'm sorry.' Kirsten looks directly into my eyes.

I put my handbag next to an upturned beaker and several broken breadsticks on the sofa, between us. If she feels genuine remorse, it's concealed beneath a blank expression.

'You can't just make up something like that, it could ruin lives,' I say.

Kirsten's still in her raincoat. I'd met her in the driveway, after she'd returned from dropping the children at her mum's house, wasting no time telling her why I wanted to see her.

'We only slept together once,' she says glibly. I flinch, breathing restricted by a swell in the chest.

'But, you said you didn't … you'd fibbed— '

'It was the weekend of that London conference. In that posh hotel. Dan was really upset about something. He was stroppy all day. I thought you two were having issues.'

Kirsten fidgets, swiping her nose. 'He got really pissed. I was flirting a lot – he came to my room in the end.' She pauses. 'We shared a bed but he was too drunk to do anything. I let Dan think something had happened. That's why he sacked me.'

'So he thought—'

'Yeah, that he'd cheated on you.'

'Why would you mislead him like that?'

Kirsten grabs a frayed cushion, squeezing it tight to her abdomen. Her face is blotchy.

'I fancied Dan. I was jealous of you two, the things he did – buying flowers and presents, and forever going on about you and Eleanor, and your perfect life.' She tosses the cushion aside. 'My boyfriends have all been bastards. I was with Carl when I got pregnant with Jayden. He was a good dad at first. Then he started going out with his mates all the time. I had to do everything. Then he cheated on me.'

'It doesn't excuse what you've done.' I stand to go. 'It's vindictive and vile—'

'Seeing all the headlines about Dan, how much money he'd paid to get frozen …' she pauses, hands squeezed into fists. 'I can't get a job now 'cause of the kids. It's not fair, how rich people like you can …' She stops.

Compassion crushes some of the anger. I sit, trying to make sense of the surge of sympathy I feel. The tears she's resisting are visible, a shine on her tired, dull eyes.

'Were you really tricked into telling the press about Dan's donation?'

'No. That was a lie, too.'

I pull a cheque from my purse; start writing. 'Here, have this. It'll help until you get work.'

'Shit. Really? Ta.' She takes it, eyes wide with disbelief.

'And you can stop sending those stupid notes, and the calls. Was it you who scratched my car and threw eggs at the door – or got someone else to?'

She looks incredulous, mouth gaping as she shakes her head.

It wasn't her. So who?

★★★

After days of flicking open the blinds and hovering at the window at every opportunity, like an undercover detective, I finally spot the old man on the bench.

'I'm taking an early lunch,' I announce to Mark, dashing past his desk with only one arm in my mac.

I take the back stairs, head across the courtyard. My foot catches a discarded drinks can as I hurry over, sending it flying, noisily, along the concrete path.

'Hi … Gordon,' I say, as he turns to see me approaching.

'Hello, my dear,' he says, with a big smile, strands of wispy hair circling above him in the breeze. He shuffles along the bench. His anorak's unbuttoned over a stripy jumper; steam rising from a plastic cup in his hand. I sit next to him. 'Sorry, I've forgotten your name.'

'Carrie.'

'That's right, I had a second cousin we used to call Carrie – her real name was Carolyn.'

'Mine's Carolina. I can't stand it.'

He looks surprised. 'That's a lovely name.'

After a few more pleasantries and some silences, I can't hold it in.

'I walked through the churchyard the other day. I saw your wife's grave. I hope you don't mind. It's a beautiful headstone.'

Gordon takes a flask from his bag, hand shaking as he pours more coffee.

'I'm afraid to say, I don't tend to the grave like I did. I used to take fresh flowers every week. I prefer thinking of her on this bench. Edith's in here,' he pats his head, then his chest, 'and here.' He stares ahead, hair taking off again in a gust. 'She's weaved into all our lives; mine, our children, grandchildren …' He smiles. 'Have you got family?'

I find myself telling Gordon about Dan. He listens, taking occasional noisy sips. 'I've never heard of that,' he says.

'Nor had I until a few years ago when Dan told me his cryonics plan. He hoped I'd want to do the same when I die.'

'And do you?' Gordon squints into the sun. I don't hesitate.

'No.'

'I've always thought you only get one shot.' He flashes a warm smile.

'But I still feel bad.' I tell him how overwhelming the guilt is at times – especially concerning Ashley – and about the news stories, hate mail and other incidents, how Eleanor's been teased at school and I fret about the effect everything might have on her in the future. I mention the 'nearly cheat' with Kirsten – even divulge Dan's sperm deceit, wincing inwardly as I do so.

All the while I wonder why I'm relaying my life story to a near stranger, lowering my voice as others pass by, and for several minutes when we're joined on the bench by a young man in a red Harrington, a distant beat emanating from huge headphones. But I can't stop. Gordon frowns at some of my revelations, but makes no comment, listening intently.

'You've got to make the most of the here and now,' he says finally. 'Seems to me you're wasting your one shot worrying about things beyond your control. We can't change the past, and predicting the future's a fool's game.'

I nod. His words echo Imogen's, but somehow carry a weight and wisdom that makes them penetrate much deeper.

I fall silent – pensive – watching clouds scroll swiftly above the line of trees ahead, consoled by his sentiments and reluctant to leave. I'm startled when Gordon speaks again.

'Most of us keep secrets, don't we? I lied to my wife for years about being an accountant.'

'Really?' I can't conceal the shock.

'Didn't think I measured up. Edith's family were all high achievers. It was true I worked in an accounts office, but my role was more clerical in the early years. I used to tell my wife I spent some of my wages at the pub with colleagues twice a week, but I was working overtime.

'Nearly ended our marriage when she found out. But I'd done it because I was desperately in love and wasn't going to risk letting her slip through the net. The most attractive, smartest woman I'd ever clapped eyes on. I knew she was the one that first night I saw her in Bridbury Dance Hall with her crazy curls and beautiful smile …' He taps his cup on the side of the bench, emptying the dregs. 'She forgave me – eventually – and years later, I qualified as an accountant.'

'That's … so – such a happy ending.'

He pulls his eyes wide, nodding. 'I was a lucky man.'

Just then a rotund lady with a pale face and stiff perm the colour of my brushed chrome kettle wheels a beige shopping trolley over towards us.

'Must go, the boss has arrived. Hope to see you again, Carrie.' Gordon stands. 'Your husband clearly loved you very much. That's the thing to hang on to.'

He pecks the lady on the cheek, then extends a courteous arm to take the handle of her trolley as they totter off together.

He'd found someone new. I'm so happy for him. And for me.

★★★

After a fitful sleep, and several flushes that creep up through my body by stealth, like an internal intruder, I get up to a grey fuzziness that matches my mood. It's only 5am.

I feel queasy again; exhausted from an endless churn of thoughts. I write an email to Sheena, relaying all the things that have kept my mind awake, how I wonder whether you can ever truly know someone. I still have no idea who's responsible for the horrible notes, and the other malicious pranks. I believed Kirsten's denial. She admitted everything else. I'm hurting over the hotel fiasco; something else Dan kept from me. However, I did feel I understood Sunny better, having witnessed her anguish over her Spanish lover, and seeing her cry for the first time. She'd exposed a vulnerable side. I'd realised the problem between us was as much mine as hers. In a postscript, I apologise to Sheena for being so gloomy. In a further postscript, I try to make amends, telling her about an advert I've seen for a TV documentary she might want to watch on missing people who've returned safe and well.

I shut the laptop and bury my head in my hands. I can't face breakfast. I sit on the sofa staring at the Matisse *Forget-Me-Nots* print on the wall, its vivid colours dulled by dusk. Life's so complicated, my feelings lurching this way and that.

Dan hadn't cheated, but the intention had been there perhaps, albeit fuelled by booze and a devious, desperate younger woman. That night could so easily have ruined what we had, and almost certainly explained why he became so keen to avoid alcohol.

I'm eager to see Ashley, to tell him what I'm going through, to hold him, to sleep with him again. But he's so busy. I have to settle for a call. Telling him about Dan's sperm deceit, that it wasn't me who was infertile, I try to picture the expression on his face, read into his words.

'Poor you. I can't believe what you've been put through. So many lies,' he says.

But he has good news. A donor match has been found for his nephew. Depending on tests and procedures, the transplant will take place tomorrow. I'm overjoyed, yet anxious for the boy and all the family.

'That's the positive power of the media,' I say. I wonder who the donor is. Someone determined to give life to another when their own's over. A thought that leaves a deep impression.

On his only day off, Ashley has to take his car in for more repairs, he's seeing his solicitor and dealing with a few other pressing financial things he doesn't want to bore me with. He sounds a touch downcast – divorce proceedings come to mind. And he has a meeting about a big work project; 'a real corker' he teases, keeping it wrapped in mystery. I wonder why he's being so secretive, if whatever it is will take him away from London and all his twisted ties – bring him closer to me. Birmingham perhaps.

'Tell me more,' I urge.

'All in good time,' he says.

I call Imogen to wish her luck. She's preparing for a three-day break in Paris. I'd suggested it several times, but with a medic adamant that, hormones aside, she's showing signs of exhaustion, Imogen has relented, finally acknowledging she's taken on too much. I offer to have the girls but her sister, in Brittany, is the easier option.

'Let's see if Ben can get his frigid missus to lie back and think of England,' she says facetiously.

'Let's see if you two can enjoy a well-earned rest and perhaps rekindle the passion,' I correct.

After hanging up, I call the doctor to book an appointment. The first one available's in two weeks.

'Are you ill?' Eleanor's at the kitchen door, heavy eyes sweeping me up and down.

'No. Think I've hit the menopause and need some advice.'

'Isn't that when you're old?'

'It can happen early. Grandma was only thirty-nine.'

Eleanor grimaces. Then when I mention having a chat with her this evening – no biggie, just about things in general, and about Ashley – she snaps my head off.

'God, Mum, you've got a boyfriend, what's the big deal? I don't need this stress.' She fling her arms into her blazer, making for the door.

'You may not want to talk, young lady, but we need to,' I say, trailing behind, determined not to relent this time.

'For Christ's sake.' Her nostrils flare. 'I'm so late.' She storms off.

We're going to talk – I'm determined, I tell myself in the hall mirror, surveying the bags under my eyes, checking for thinning skin, hairs, thread veins and other menopausal horrors I've heard about.

My day at work's a slog and I can't wait to get home. As I roll on to the drive, my thoughts are on Kirsten. I've decided not to tell anyone about the cheque, and hope it will help her in some way.

Looking ahead, my stomach appears to float up into my chest, heart hammering against it. The heads of all the flowers I planted in the top borders have been cut off and laid out on the paving in a pattern that resembles a capital 'T', with just a few stray blooms and petals straggled around. I can't believe what I'm seeing; it's beyond bizarre.

Feeling panicky, I run the wheels of the car over the disquieting display, then, realising my mistake, reverse again. I should have taken a photo perhaps, to show the police. It's too late, so I dash to fetch the yard brush from the garage, sweeping the blooms, petals and a few scattered stems into a pile and pushing them into black bags. I grab the hose to shift petals stuck to the wheels of the car.

I'm thankful Eleanor's at Freya's, that she hadn't witnessed any of this, though she'll surely be suspicious seeing the colourful borders stripped to a sea of green.

I change out of my work clothes, returning to dig over the borders with a heavy garden fork and a heavier heart. Whoever did this was a complete crackpot. An act so painstaking and particular. Maybe a hundred flowers, each one beheaded so neatly.

In bed, I lie awake trying to decipher the significance of the letter 'T', though I wonder if the floral arrangement had originally been laid in a different shape. Some of the blooms had clearly been displaced, the culprit disturbed perhaps, or a few flowerheads dispersed by a light breeze. Such an unsettling act, one I just can't fathom.

For the first time, I feel really frightened.

Next morning, after Eleanor's left for school, I'm upstairs searching out the crime case number to contact the police when the phone rings. I dread another silent line. I hope it's Ashley.

Reaching the living room, I hesitate, check the new caller display I've set up. It's Sunny.

'I'm afraid Mick passed away in the night.'

I gasp. 'I'm so sorry. Shall I come over?'

'No, I'm at the hospital. I'll call later.'

'I'm sorry … about some of the things I said the other day.'

'Let's just put that aside now, shall we?' Sunny declines my offer of help. She has lots to sort out. She'll be at the care home most of the day.

I decide work's the best place to be. Tash and Mark are great, drowning me in coffee and sympathy. Barbara hugs me so tightly I'm convinced the chain of her glasses has dug out part of my face. Even Pete's gentle and attentive, twice asking if I'd rather go home. I don't want to miss the meeting.

Pete gathers us all to proudly announce what we already know – his son's taking over the business. He has ambitious plans to expand into the vacant office space next door.

At lunchtime, Tash dashes off to get waxed and I sit on the bench for a while. I still have no appetite – no doubt stress taking its toll. I wonder if Gordon will come, but he doesn't. Maybe he's at home watching *Bargain Hunt* with Mrs Perm or on an outing to some cherished place he hasn't taken her to before.

When I return, Mark follows me into the kitchen with his low-calorie lunch, demanding to talk.

'Let's change the subject, really, I'm fine,' I say, after a chat about all my worries. Mark had no idea about Dan's fertility problem. He's so relieved Kirsten has admitted the truth, makes me promise to call the police about yesterday's incident.

'That's some serious nutter,' he says.

Then he tells me he's moving to Bristol. He's lined up several job interviews on newspapers. He'll be a lot closer to Jack. It happens to be where Georgia lives. Their relationship's going well. I'm happy for him, but surprised; and sad, too.

'I'll miss you,' I say. 'Especially your bad jokes, and bad singing – oh, and flicking your cauliflower ear.'

'You'll find another colleague to abuse.' Mark smiles.

'Seriously. I'll miss you.'

He puts down his tuna wrap, turning to give my shoulder a gentle rub, green eyes narrowed. Then he reaches out, takes both my hands.

'Oh my God!' Tash follows her loud voice into the kitchen and Mark swiftly lets go. 'That woman was a sadist. Nearly pulled my minge off,' she says.

We all roar.

I return home to find Sunny and Eleanor huddled on the sofa. Eleanor's in tears and I guess what's happened, even before Sunny dives in to apologise. She'd wrongly assumed Eleanor already knew her granddad had passed away, that she'd been with me when the bad news was delivered that morning. I can't be cross. It was just unfortunate. But I regret that Eleanor had to find out in such a clumsy way. Sunny never turned up without calling first.

'As I said to Eleanor, Mick wasn't in any pain. He passed peacefully,' Sunny soothes, eyes glazed and sore. She's wearing a long turquoise cardigan, bag resting on her knees, gently stroking one side of Eleanor's hair from root to tip. 'He wouldn't want you to be upset.'

Eleanor rubs at the snot beneath her nose. She looks like a ten-year-old again. She *is* still a child, I think – too young for what life's dealt her. I lean over to give her a kiss. Eleanor lifts herself away from Sunny's clutches, reaching to hug me. I wipe at the wet beneath Eleanor's eyes. I know I'm pushing my luck. She doesn't flinch.

'I've got stuff to do.' Eleanor stands. 'More science.'

'As if the school day isn't long enough, poor thing,' Sunny says. 'Oh, I nearly forgot. I got you this, Elle. I know your other one snapped.' She holds out another friendship bracelet, with delicately twisted turquoise and purple threads. 'And I have two more for your friends.'

'Cool. Thanks, Auntie.' Eleanor cranks up a smile.

Sunny reaches back into her bag. 'And this.' It's the quartz stone from her bookshelf.

'That's your special one, isn't it?'

'Yes. It's been all over the world with me. I want you to have it.'

'You sure? That's awesome.' Eleanor hugs her auntie.

'Thanks, Sunny,' I say, smiling.

After Eleanor leaves the room, it becomes clear there's another reason for Sunny's visit. She pulls a crumpled piece of paper from her bag.

'This note was found in Mick's bedside drawer.' Looking down, her face is lost in a sea of caramel spirals. 'The writing's so shaky. The carer said Mick had been determined to use a pen again. He'd found ink marks all over his sheets.' I sit on the chaise and Sunny stares; a slow blink – then another.

'He may not be my father.' I reel. Her gaze shifts between my stunned face and the note. 'They both had a few affairs, or flings as he put it, in their hippy days. Mum had one with an American man. They both had doubts when I was born, but Mick didn't want to face it, so it wasn't mentioned.'

'No. Surely ...' I can't continue. I want to ask about Dan.

'Dan was definitely Mick's child.' Sunny smiles reassuringly. She must have read my mind.

So Dan may only be her half-brother. Poor Sunny. I can't say it, and neither does she.

'So it's only a 'maybe' then?' I try to sound hopeful.

'I must go.' Sunny stands. 'I need to make calls.'

'I'm so sorry. Did you have any idea?'

'Yes, I always suspected ... actually, I think I knew really.' She swallows. I reach over, rubbing my hand gently on her arm. She lifts her hand to rest on mine. 'There are some things you don't really want confirmed, so you don't ask. Dan was always all a brother could be; and more. And Mick, well, he loved us both dearly.'

So was that why she called him Mick?

And why Dan meant the world.

CHAPTER 29

'I got the job.' It's a shock, saying it out loud.

'That's great, fair play.' Ashley's voice is deeper; fractured. Clearly, he's not been awake long. 'Nice one,' he adds, with a muffled yawn. 'I'm proud of you.'

'I still can't quite believe it,' I say. I'm calling from the car on my way to work, trying hard to concentrate on the road. It's an hour since the theatre manager gave me the news and it still hasn't fully filtered through the part of my brain dealing with hard facts.

'Let's celebrate. How about next Wednesday? I should be able to clear the whole day. Can you get time off? Course you can, you can't be sacked now.'

'True,' I chuckle, indicating left. 'Great. I'll sort something – I can't wait.'

There's a slight twinge of disappointment that he's so pleased for me; he hadn't decided to talk me out of the job at the eleventh hour. But I'm consoled by the news his nephew's op went well, and by the secret project Ashley had previously mentioned, wondering what the implications could be.

'We've put the house on the market,' Ashley says. 'The agent's already had lots of interest and expects a quick sale. That should help sort the finances a bit.'

'Fantastic.' I almost hear the snipping sound of one of his ties being cut. I sense we're moving much closer to a frank discussion about our future.

Mark and Tash are stoked when I burst into the office with my news. Tash claps so frantically a fake nail shoots into her mug and it's a good job her headaches have improved – turns out she needed glasses; and less alcohol – because she lets out an ear-piercing guffaw that could drown out a symphony orchestra. The hysteria draws Barbara, then Pete, into the room prematurely – it's only 8.59! Fortunately, they both accept the commotion's purely prompted by the flying falsey and return to duties. I don't want Pete to know about the job before I'm ready to give official notice.

We celebrate with cream cakes. Now the nausea thing's passed, I have an insatiable appetite. Then Tash turns mushy and maudlin.

'I'm so going to miss you, babe.' She hangs off my arm. 'Pinkie pledge you'll stay in touch. Oh my God, that's both of you going, I can't bear it. Perhaps I *will* go to Brighton next year.'

Mark has already handed in his notice. He flicks a smile at Tash before his eyes rest in line with mine and I'm compelled to look away.

I feel so elated that, driving home, I imagine Ashley's secret to be a leading role in a ground-breaking Shakespeare production set for a huge Midlands and West Country tour that I could go and see a dozen times. I picture us on a rich, burgundy sofa in the cosy living room of a 1930s house with a brick and brass fireplace, chrome wall sconces with milk-glass shades, my satin pencil pleats hung in extra heavy folds at the picture window and the photograph of Ashley as Hamlet lit up on the wall.

I return to an email from Sheena:

Hi Carrie. So sorry to hear about your fallout with Sunny – it sounds like you cleared the air at least. I'm glad Kirsten's admitted lying. Life must be pretty bad for her to do such a vicious thing. I understand your upset at Dan keeping the infertility problem from you, but male pride's a funny thing – I suspect it's more common than you think. The important thing is you know he still loved you, enough to want to be with you forever. I wish I was sure Geoff feels the same about me. I keep wondering if I drove him away. Thanks for the tip-off on that 'Missing' programme. It was quite uplifting. I had six missed calls on my mobile from an 'unknown' number on Friday. I wondered if perhaps it was Geoff on a new phone, but when I called back it was one of those annoying sales calls. Molly loved her driving lessons and I've started Pilates. It's tougher than I thought! Sheena xxx

I call Mum. She's been a little curt with me since our frank exchange – even though we've both apologised – but she sounds genuinely pleased about the job and is far more talkative again. Her voice still turns sharp at any mention of Ashley, but I appreciate that she's trying.

Then I contact the police about the flowers incident. The officer taking notes is astounded.

'Well, that's a new one on us,' he declares, sounding almost amused, following up with a few half-hearted questions.

Later, I take Eleanor for a Chinese meal to celebrate my job, and the end of term. While we tuck into spring roll starters, I talk about how there are changes going on in our lives, but I won't do anything she isn't happy with. Some things would never change – I love her to bits and her dad can never be replaced, or forgotten. She looks uncomfortable at times, desperate for me to stop – throwing her eyes heavenwards and sighing – but I ignore the peaks on her cringe-ometer, pushing on with my lecture.

'I know, Mum. Jeez,' she says finally.

I wait a while, then tell her the police are sending an officer to speak to me in person about the flowers. She chews her mouthful slowly, then sits bolt upright.

'Bethany's mum did it,' she says decisively. 'And all the other stuff – the notes and that.' I put down my fork with a clang.

Eleanor blurts it all out, how Bethany's mum had always made her feel a little unwelcome at their house; how it had got worse recently. A few months ago, in the car after their trip to the cinema, she'd actually yelled at Eleanor for being on her mobile too much. 'It's why I haven't been there – although it's boring anyway as they haven't got a computer and Beth's barely allowed to watch TV or anything.'

Then Eleanor admits that during one of their fallouts, when Bethany had said her mum thought cryonics was immoral, she'd lost her temper.

'I told Bethany you said her mum was a bit of a fruitcake.' I tut. 'Well, you did!'

'Yes, I probably did, but I shouldn't have done, and you certainly shouldn't have repeated it outside our house. But none of this proves—'

'I haven't finished. In our RE lesson, when we were talking about abortion, Bethany said she was against it, that we should "Let God Decide Our Fate".' My pulse quickens at those words, the ones in the note. 'And I've heard her mum say it before.'

'But still—'

'So I asked Bethany a couple of weeks ago, and she said it *was* her mum. She's really lost the plot. Won't see a doctor. Apparently, Bethany's dad hasn't been living with them for ages. Last time I went there, she told me he was away on business, but she was lying. He wants a divorce, but her mum won't.' Eleanor takes a loud breath. 'Bethany's been so upset about it all, and she's staying with her dad at the moment because her mum's being so weird. Thinks it's depression, or like a breakdown or something.'

I hold my hand to my forehead. Words fail me.

'Are you going to tell the police?' Eleanor nibbles her lip. 'Please, don't make a major fuss, Mum.'

'I don't know. I can't ignore it.'

Although we change the subject, try to enjoy the rest of the evening, Eleanor picks at her chow mein, and we both pass on pudding.

Back at home, I make Eleanor promise she won't communicate with Bethany about the issue until I've decided what to do.

Imogen's back from Paris, and can't believe it when I bombard her with all my news. 'Bloody hell, I've been missing the English soaps but you've given me a few episodes,' she says. She's concerned about my intention to confront Bethany's mum. I should leave it to the police.

But Imogen squeals with delight when I tell her about the job. It sounds like one of her girls has found a bucket of sweets in an unlocked cupboard.

307

'Wowzer, wowzer. That's brilliant.' Her bubbles pop down the phone line. 'Aw, I'm so happy for you, my lovely. You're due a bit of good news. You'll love it, I'm sure.' Another squeal.

'I hope so. I must admit that now it's sinking in, I'm getting scared.'

'Oh no you don't,' she rebukes. 'Have you told Ashley?'

'Yes.'

'Maybe he'll move now. There are lots of great rep theatre groups in Birmingham. I did some graphics for a few.' I told her he was selling the house, and about his mystery mission. 'Maybe he's going to ask if he can move in.'

'I wondered the same,' I say.

'Are you ready for that so soon?'

'I think so. You can't take things too slowly when you're over the hill like us.'

'True. And one of you needs to be brave and ask the question, you can't be Mr and Mrs Evasive forever.'

'Anyway, how did your break go – did the Parisian Palace live up to its name?'

'Oh God, it was gorgeous, and the food was bloody heavenly. I've bought back a bouillabaisse recipe to die for – that's fish stew to you …' Imogen chuckles, '… and we've promised ourselves an annual stay.'

'You should make it more regular than that, and have that longer break you promised me you would. I'd love to have the girls.'

'We'll see.' Imogen pauses. 'Anyway, I've decided to say 'no' to that new graphics contract and I'm reducing my hours on two others.'

'That's brilliant. Make sure you do.'

'By the way, we looked for the Hotel de Calanthe, but someone told us it had been converted into a luxury spa.'

'Oh, really.' It was where Dan and I stayed on our honeymoon. I change the subject. 'So things were OK with you and Ben?'

'Yes, still a way to go, I think, but we had a lovely time, away from work and the girls—'

'And ...'

'And, yes, we had a bit of rumpy, helped by a bottle of Moët and some orgasmic almond truffles.'

'Oh, that's fantastic! Well done, lady.'

'And I'm having the testosterone patch on Tuesday. So when I phone next, you might mistake me for Barry White.'

We both roar. I just know her nose is wrinkling.

★★★

That night, my turbulent thoughts drag me back to our honeymoon hotel ...

PARIS, AUGUST 1998

... 'Bonjour, beautiful. OK, what's it to be, a bus tour after breakfast or the Louvre after lunch?' Dan rolls over to greet me with a sleep-creased face.

'Definitely the Louvre then, gives us a few more hours of – you know...' I say, with a cheeky smile, stroking my toes across the silk sheet.

After two bottles of Hotel de Calanthe's best bubbly last night, we'd made slightly clumsy, alcohol-blurred love, several times, until a nagging soreness down below and

309

Dan's laboured breathing signalled it was time to sleep. We'd done the same the night before, and the one before that. We're on our honeymoon, in Paris – capital of romance and carnal capers – determined to relish every minute. We were only staying four nights. It's all we could afford.

'And what about this evening, darling – a posh meal perhaps, as it's our last night?'

'Why don't we wait and see? Be spontaneous.'

'We can't waste our last day.' Dan rests his tousled hair against the carved wooden headboard.

'Having saucy sex with your new wife isn't wasting the day.' I reach up, digging my nails into his broad shoulders. 'Come on.'

Room service arrives just as we're finishing our honeymoon ritual. Dan grabs the white robe he'd thrown on the floor last night, greets the softly-spoken French waiter with a flushed face.

'Heer iz yor brekfuzt, zir,' the round-shouldered man announces, placing the trays on the mahogany table, gaze averted, before scuttling out.

Dan lifts the two silver-domed lids; one in each hand. As he stands, straight-backed, dark features highlighted by the white robe, I imagine him as a Roman emperor holding the trophies of a battle triumph aloft. I suspect Dan would prefer to be envisaged as a sharp-suited businessman holding up six-figured cheques from his latest acquisitions, but it's *my* fantasy. Even with bed hair and a crumpled face, he looks ludicrously handsome. I melt.

'Deux croissants et scrambled eggz, madame.' Dan rests a tray on the ivory bed cover draped over my knees and climbs in.

'I still can't believe we're actually married.'

'Four days of wedded bliss.' His wide smile accentuates his deep dimples. I have another 'father of the bride' flashback.

'I still can't get over how drunk my dad was on Saturday. He was hilarious. Although Mum clearly didn't think so! How many times did he bore people with the story of how he'd told that local newspaper reporter interviewing them for their silver wedding anniversary that the secret to a successful marriage was "wanting the same things"?'

Dan smirks, scooping out his soft-boiled egg. 'Yes, it's the first time you've seen your dad drunk in public and the first time I've seen my dad not drunk!'

'So, if my parents want the same things, why do they bicker all the bloody time!' A scary thought strikes. 'I hope we don't end up arguing like them.'

Dan lands an eggy peck on my cheek. 'Course we won't.' He switches to his serious face. 'So – what do *you* want?'

'Some ketchup would be good. This scrambled egg's on the dry side!'

He shakes his head. 'We're in France, you know ketchup is contraband. But seriously …' he shuffles, '… do you still want children?'

Woah, a bit heavy for a honeymoon breakfast conversation. We've talked about it before, but only casually and after a fair few drinks. I have to reply, he looks so earnest.

'Yeah. One day.'

'How many?'

'I don't know. Three maybe.'

'Really? Sounds expensive. Names?'

'Betty, Bob, and Bertha.'

He rolls his eyes. 'I really like the name Lara.'

'Oh no! We had a Lara in our class at primary – a right bitch. Stole my favourite ink pen and swore blind her mum had bought her exactly the same one.' I allow myself a moment to bristle. It still irked me fourteen years on. 'I quite like Azaria.'

'Is that a name or a make of car?' Dan's proud of his joke, eyes flashing.

'Funny bugger. Course it's a name.' I give him a playful kick under the cover. 'She'll have blonde hair, blue eyes, a large boot and power steering.'

Dan laughs, although I sense his mild annoyance at my flippancy. Clearly, he really *does* want a serious conversation during breakfast on the final morning of our honeymoon.

'I like the name Eleanor, too,' he says.

'Yes, that's pretty.'

'Any other ambitions?'

'I like the idea of being a published writer.' Dan stares and I move on swiftly. 'I don't know – to earn lots of money, have luxury holidays, shop all the time, that sort of thing.'

'Well, we won't be able to do that on our wages just yet.' Dan stares ahead thoughtfully. 'Wouldn't it be good to have our own business?'

'I guess. If it means no more taking orders from po-faced Pete.'

'I think we should do it. With our combined skills, we'd be great. We could take a few existing clients with us – charm them!'

I leave Dan with his thoughts, no doubt planning the finer

details of his exit strategy. As I devour a croissant, my mind wanders. 'I'd love a villa somewhere hot. With a big pool.'

'Sounds like a plan. Shame to earn all that dosh and not have somewhere to relax. Italy?'

'Perfect. Sun, spaghetti – and loads of hot sex.'

'We could have a vineyard – as you seem to be developing a taste for wine. We could bottle it, have our names on the label.'

'Do they have many vineyards in Italy?'

'Are you serious?' Dan raises an eyebrow. 'You've drunk Italian wine, haven't you?'

'Maybe. I don't look at the labels!'

'You've just had another of your blonde moments. Miss Silly Socks.' Dan hits me with one of his best mocking smiles, then kisses my cheek.

'We can't all be bloody mastermind,' I say playfully, pushing my plate aside. 'Anyway only Dad's allowed to call me that. And it's Mrs now, not Miss.'

'I'd like an Aston Martin. With leather seats,' Dan declares, pulling me into his shoulder and stroking my hair. 'Any pets?'

'I'd love a golden retriever. I've always wanted a dog, but Mum thinks all animals are unhygienic. You should have seen her face when I once asked for a chinchilla.'

Dan places his hand on mine, fiddles with my beaded wedding band. 'Anything else on our wish list?'

I smack my lips. 'How about croissants for breakfast every day?'…

I wake up feeling queasy and thinking of croissants. I can't recall having them for breakfast more than twice since our

313

honeymoon. And what happened to our other plans? We had the big house and the holidays. Dan had his sports car – and the business. There was no vineyard.

No villa in the Med. No dog; or chinchilla.

We only had one child.

Looking back, I'd been so eager to please.

But I wasn't sure they were *our* plans. And life, it seemed, had a wicked way of scuppering even the best-laid ones.

CHAPTER 30

I ring the doorbell for the third time, cradling the bundle of paper to my chest. I know she's in there – I'd glimpsed a figure through the leaded window, sidling from the front room. A dog's barking.

The door opens.

'Hi. Eleanor thought Bethany might want these notes – on some of the work she's missed.' I hold out the papers with a faltering smile. Ruth's reluctant to meet my gaze, small eyes darting beneath owlish glasses that swamp her face, deep brackets around a mouth held firm. Her velvety grey hair's close-cropped in a boyish style but is messy, overgrown. She pushes it to one side, out of her eyes, but still fails to look at me.

'Can I come in?'

She hesitates; I can tell she wants to say 'no', an unfriendly frown forming, chin tucked into the collar of a shapeless shirt. She turns and walks away, heading down the hall and through a door at the end, which she slams behind her.

Left alone by the open front door, I'm unsure what to do. I glance around the little square of sixties terraces to see if anyone's watching; wondering.

Then she returns. 'OK,' she says, with a slow nod, no explanation, or trace of a smile.

I follow her into a small back room that feels empty, a touch eerie. There's a strange, earthy smell. A pair of heavy green curtains are half-drawn, a shadeless lamp on one of two mahogany side tables with spider legs providing most of the light in the gloomy space. On the other table's a phone face down. My eyes linger on the black handset, recollections of all the mystery calls heightening my anxiety.

I sit, tentatively, on a small green sofa covered in fair dog hair. Ruth perches on a pine chair a little distance away. Her tiny feet are tucked into a pair of badly worn black desert sandals, one foot scuffing lightly across the textured tan carpet. The barking grows louder, and more frantic, accompanied by a scratching sound. Ruth looks irritated, making a sound like a growl as her head flicks towards the noise, coming from behind the door I assume leads to the kitchen.

I'm about to speak when she hops up, leaves the room, returning with the dog – a large, lively thing with curly hair on its ears. It jumps on to the sofa next to me, climbing on to my lap and circling wildly. Ruth lunges at the dog, yanking its collar.

'Get off,' she yells, her voice so loud that both the dog and I cower. 'He has to see you – then he'll stop barking,' she adds, eyes sliding quickly across my face several times. I can smell a faint feminine fragrance.

She leaves the room again, impatiently pulling the dog with her. I look around. There's a pile of books by the chair, mostly in shades of brown – torn strips of paper poking out from between pages – and a tiny, old portable TV with a huge aerial on the floor in the corner.

The barking stops. I lean forwards, craning and squinting at the photos on a low, floating shelf above the fireplace, several of baby Bethany and a more recent one of their family of three – taken in a restaurant. Bethany's dad, a theology lecturer I recall, is wearing a badge saying 'The Big 50'.

I expected more religious paraphernalia, but there's only a small wooden cross mounted on the wall. It dawns on me then – the flowers on the drive had been arranged in the shape of a cross.

'I'm cooking,' Ruth snaps, re-entering. 'These things catch fire so easily.'

She sits, a flash of sunlight catching her through the gap in the curtains. Her face looks drawn; sallow, winter skin marked by unfriendly creases.

'What do you want?' Her eyes move slowly from my legs, up my T-shirt, pausing at my beaded necklace before landing in line with mine for the first time. I reach into my bag, pull out the notes.

'I know it's you who sent these.' I unfold one. 'You damaged my car, and the plants, and threw the eggs, didn't you?' She stares; a defiant look. 'But I think I owe you an apology.' She looks doubtful, wary. 'I understand Eleanor told Bethany something I'd said about you that was hurtful, and wrong. But the things you've done to me …' I shake my head firmly.

She rubs her hands together, making a dry, grating noise.

'You think I'm mad. So do they. Your husband. He's the mad one.' I wait. 'Cryonics is wrong,' she says, voice hard. 'Only the Lord will bring a person back – at the

Resurrection.' She looks at the notes, then stares at me with a sober intensity. 'God has appointed death; Romans, Chapter five.'

'It was my husband's wish and—'

'And yours.' She stands, turning her back.

'No. It's not my wish.'

'You're lying.' She swings round, eyes spookily wide. 'And the money's disgusting. People are starving.' She dashes out again. I hear several loud clatters.

'You've made it burn dry,' she says sternly, walking back in. She hovers by the chair, beginning to twitch slightly. 'Your husband's evil.' I'm angry, but concerned by her agitated state. My heart pounds.

'He's not,' I say firmly, steadying my breath, trying to sound calm. 'You clearly need help. What you've been doing – it's not right.'

She leans over, tears the notes from my hand and pushes me back against the sofa. Her mouth's close, a sour smell emanating from dry, parted lips.

'His soul will go to hell. HELL.' I'm pitched into sudden dread. Her hand's quite firm on my throat. I can feel the hot breath behind her words.

'Stop! No.' I try to pull her fingers away, but her grip tightens. I lash out, striking her outstretched arm with my fist. She lets go, and I push her away. She looks startled, body stiff, as it suddenly dawns on her what she's done.

I stand to go, hand rubbing my sore neck. I'm petrified, want to run, blood rampaging in my head. But I have to tell her.

'He was a good man,' I say. She sits, a little calmer, still gripping the notes, fidgeting from side to side, head bowed. 'Forgiveness,' she mutters. 'Forgiveness. Sorry.' I walk towards the door, grabbing the handle for support.

'Maybe cryonics *is* wrong; certainly for some people. Maybe I would have preferred my husband to have a Christian burial.' My voice is shaky, throat tight and sore. 'In hindsight, if I could change his decision, I probably would. It's caused me a lot of pain. And Eleanor, too.' She looks at me and I stare back, determined to make her listen. 'But that wasn't his intention. Like I said, he was a good man, a BLOODY good man.' She flinches at my words, shifting position in the chair.

'It was *his* choice, his will.' I raise my voice, tears forming, pulse erratic. 'And YOU don't make the judgement. It has nothing to do with you, or anyone else. Most keep their cryonics wishes a secret because of narrow-minded people and their ignorant reactions. Dan showed great courage.' She stands, hands flinching by her sides.

'Get out!' she yells, head quivering.

The scrape of a key follows her shout. I see a tall figure the other side of the door. I stand back.

'What's going on?' It's Ruth's husband. He looks at me, then at Ruth, his long forehead creased with concern. 'Are you OK?'

'I came to talk to Ruth about what she's been doing.' I search for words, try to snatch breaths. 'She's been expressing her disapproval over my husband's decision to be—'

'I know about the notes – Bethany mentioned it,' he cuts in. 'I'm so sorry. She's been causing a lot of problems.' His eyes are veined and sore under drooping lids.

'It's not just the notes. She's been calling, and …' I stop. He looks so distressed.

'Sorry. She's really unwell, but won't see a doctor.' He puts down his satchel.

'What's it got to do with you?' Ruth snarls. 'You want a divorce, to break the vows. In Sickness …' she accentuates each word, '… And In Health.'

'Shut up, not now, in front … I'm calling the doctor.'

'No!' Ruth shouts, pacing by the phone.

He asks me what else she'd done. Bethany had been reluctant to go into detail. I tell him. He glares at Ruth.

'That's awful. She's been harassing my sister, too, and several other people have been disturbed by her behaviour. I'll pay for any damage and—'

'Don't talk about me as if I'm not here.' Ruth strides into the kitchen, slams the door.

'It has to stop, or I'll have no choice but to involve the police again,' I say, apologetically. He nods with a pained look, fingers splayed across a widow's peak.

'She's had mental health issues before, but nothing we couldn't cope with, nothing like …' the end of his sentence is drowned by banging in the kitchen.

'It's such a shame. Do you know what's caused … why she—?'

'I think it all started after she lost her job.' He walks over to yank open the curtains. 'She'd been at the opticians for ten years, since Bethany started school. They had to let one of the receptionists go. I think Ruth may have upset a few customers – she can be a bit terse – although she was extremely efficient.' He pulls a hand across the sheen on his forehead. 'She didn't tell us for ages, still left the house

320

the same time each morning. I think she's worried about money, though she still insists on giving regular payments to our church and a ridiculous number of charities.'

'I hope she can be persuaded to see someone,' I say. 'Bethany's welcome to stay with us any time.'

'Thanks.' He walks me politely to the front door.

'And if I can do anything else to help.' It occurs to me that Sunny may be able to help in some way. Perhaps Ruth would talk to her at least. I decide not to say anything until I've spoken to Sunny.

I step out into a brightness and sense of release that's overwhelming.

'*Earth to earth, ashes to ashes, dust to dust; in the sure and certain hope of the Resurrection to eternal life.*'

The vicar's sombre monotone voice cuts through the respectful silence as huddles of grey mourners gather in the corner of a packed graveyard. The smell of dew hangs in the air and the sky's bruised with morning cloud. I shiver, the intermittent sun not a match for a chilly breeze.

Eleanor collapses into my shoulder, hair wet with tears, as we watch Mick's coffin being lowered into the damp ground, next to his beloved Mary. I know she's not just grieving for her granddad. She's thinking of her dad. Maybe she's wondering, as I am, why she couldn't have said goodbye this way.

Mick's gone to meet his maker, or hang out in hippy heaven with the flower-power and pot fairies, or whatever

321

he believes awaits him. And we've all waved him off on his way. I kiss Eleanor's head.

'I know, darling, I know,' I whisper as her body heaves.

Sunny brushes away her own tears, flashing her niece a soothing smile as she strokes her shoulder. She's wearing a floaty blue dress and sober navy jacket with a patterned scarf in muted colours.

For a moment, my wet eyes are drawn to a mossy headstone to my right, inscribing their own words into the grey granite: '*In Loving Memory of Edith Stanwell. Beloved Wife of Gordon*'. In the past few days I've thought about Gordon a lot – the stranger who knows so much about me, whose words had truly spoken to me.

I blink hard and Dan's name appears, in gleaming, silver lettering. '*Dan Colwell. R.I.P*' R-*stop*. I-*stop*. P. *Full stop*. Dan had put an ellipsis by his life, but my eyes are struggling to see it any more.

Later, in the car, Eleanor falls into a brooding silence and I'm left to my musings, new grief tugging at old wounds.

'Do you wish Dad had been buried?' Eleanor turns to me. I'm stunned. I stare at the road ahead.

'Yes.' I have to be honest. 'Or cremated.'

'So do I. I think Dad was a bit selfish. It's horrible for us, knowing his body is … he's still … kind of, around … but sort of … not …'

'I know. But we all have a right to choose – it's what your dad wanted.'

'Do you want to be buried, Mum?' I pause to brake in a line of traffic, turning for a moment to meet Eleanor's earnest eyes.

322

'Yes.'

'Me, too.' I reach to touch her leg, smile a little. I can't believe that, at last, Eleanor's expressing how she really feels, and in such a calm, collected way. All her outpourings in the early days after Dan's death were drowned in grief, anger and a zillion other emotions she couldn't comprehend. Then the protective barrier went up, and I'd failed in all my attempts to break through her robust defence. I suspect Eleanor had read the cryonics leaflets and lingered on websites when I wasn't around. Maybe she'd even chatted on forums with other children in her position. But I know this moment's crucial; the breakthrough had to come.

'I'm glad you're happier. I don't mind you having a boyfriend.'

I turn. 'Thanks, darling.'

'What's for tea tonight?' I suppress a snigger at Eleanor's blatant signal that she wants to change the subject.

'A run around the table and a kick of the cat,' I say – another stupid saying to credit Dad with.

'GOD, MUM!'

CHAPTER 31

I feel awful asking Pete for time off a week after officially handing in my notice – and so soon after Mark had done the same. Poor Pete. At least Tash is staying. She's ruled out Brighton as her sister's becoming 'high mental maintenance' and she doesn't think she could stand living too close. She and Joel have decided to start flat-hunting.

I wonder if it's really bad form to see Ashley the day after the funeral, but it's been too long and his life's so hectic, I don't know when the next opportunity will arise. Time spent apart feels like it used to when we were students, the absence agonising at times. The difference was that, back then, I could talk to my room-mate about my non-stop, guilt-free yearning for him to rip my knickers off until she begged me to stop or threatened to take my head off with her hockey stick. Now I have to hold it in.

'Do you have to go?' Ashley sighs, pulling me into his arms. He's leaning against his car, an old blue Polo with a huge dent in the door and two missing hubcaps.

''Fraid so.' I try to sound resolute.

We've just been snogging like a couple of teenagers in a dark corner at the school disco, and my lips are still tingling. So are other parts of my body, but we're in Sainsbury's car park, surrounded by frazzled mums and petulant toddlers, so any serious contact below the neckline's out of the question.

Ashley didn't make it to Tetford. His car had broken down on the way so we were left with a couple of snatched hours, time for a drink and a walk hand-in-hand around a few housing estates on the outskirts of a dingy town. He was so sorry to have spoiled our plans. I'd offered him a loan towards a new car. He'd agreed to consider it.

'I really should take my leave, sire.' I pull away, glance at my watch. 'Shit, Eleanor's back from her drama workshop at six and hasn't taken a key, so I really must sling my hook.'

'Fair play – you just covered five hundred years' evolution of the English language right there.' Ashley smiles. 'I'm so sorry, again. I'll make it up to you, sort out some free time really soon.'

'You couldn't help it. That bloody car. I mean it about that loan.'

He nods. 'Thanks.'

He kisses me tenderly on the neck and I yearn for more time together, for full-on seduction. I suspect Ashley feels the same, judging by his loose, wandering hands. I have a moment of intense weakness, kissing his bristly lips once more. I can't stop myself. I pull back.

'OK, come back with me, ring your director and tell him you're being held hostage in Sainsbury's and can't make it to tonight's performance.'

'I wish.' He traps me with glittering eyes, we kiss again and I clench my muscles, trying to push the physical desire down towards my suede wedges, to trap it there.

Ashley holds me at arm's length, staring at me intensely, fairer strands in his hair lit up by the sun.

'I wish it didn't have to be like this.' My heart rate gathers pace. I'm desperate for him to go on. He obliges. 'I wish I had a normal job, that we could be together more.' I almost choke on an adrenalin rush. 'Saying that, I might have to get one soon. I've heard nothing on the roles I've been up for.'

'I want that too – to be together,' I say.

Ashley's phone rings in his pocket. He pulls it partially out, neck held awkwardly to view it. 'Just a friend,' he says dismissively, sliding it back in. It rings again.

'A persistent one,' I say, urging him to answer with my eyes.

'It's Lily.' He looks at the screen as I lean over, then opens the car door, throwing the phone on to the passenger seat.

'Are you sure she's just a friend?' I say, with an anxious smile, pretending to tease.

'Yes.' He rubs his hands down his trousers, looks offended.

'So – that project you mentioned. Heard anything?'

'Nope.' He sniffs. 'So I'm guessing it's not good news.'

Then he does it. He bids me 'adieu' as we part. And I don't bat back a witty reply.

Eleanor's on the doorstep when I pull into the drive. She's indignant, hands on hips.

'I've been here ages, I texted, like, about five times.'

'I was driving. Sorry, the traffic was bad. And I have to be at the doctor's …' I look at my watch, '… ten minutes ago.'

Later, I'm mashing several pounds of spuds – in a complete daze and in desperate need of comfort food – when Eleanor brings my mobile, telling me I've missed two calls and must be deaf. Both are Ashley's number. I wonder why he'd ring so soon after seeing me, hoping it isn't bad news about his nephew – though he'd told me earlier what fantastic progress he was making, amazing the medics. I call.

'Now does my project gather to a head.' Ashley's really hamming it up. 'The hour's now come; the very minute bids thee open thine ear.'

'What? Have you been mixing lemonades again?' I'm confused.

'I've got the project,' he says. 'I'll be doing the photography, and some of the research, for a book and exhibition based on the history of London theatres. It should keep me busy – and fed – for months, maybe a year.'

I should be pleased for him. Yet my heart dives with despair. I have an enormous acting challenge – to sound happy when I'm really, really not.

'Oh wow. So that's what the mysterious biggie was. That's incredible.'

I don't think I pull it off. It's not quite the news I was wishing for.

★★★

'Thanks for coming over. I just had to see you before I leave,' Sunny says, releasing my hands.

We've been stood by her front door for ages, Sunny prolonging the goodbye. She scoops Eleanor into another tight hug.

Sunny's departure announcement – she was flying to the States later tonight; her taxi due any minute – was sudden, though not entirely unexpected.

Apart from when she'd popped round to tell me Ruth had finally seen a doctor, that a stay in a hospital unit looked likely if they could get her to agree to it, Sunny had kept a low profile since Mick's death. We soon discovered why.

She'd been searching for the man her mum had the affair with, using information Mick left in his letter. And, not only had she found him, but he'd happily agreed to a paternity test that confirmed he was her dad. He was a Green Party activist living in Arcata, California and Sunny was flying out to see him and her two half-sisters and half-brother.

'How long will you be gone?' Eleanor asks, hands still held tight in Sunny's.

'Just for a few weeks for now, sweetness,' she assures, the bottom of her Madonna gap visible between slightly parted lips. 'I haven't really thought beyond that.'

I think we all know that once Sunny's back on a plane, her absence could end up being much, much longer. Maybe that's why she'd given Eleanor the agate. Had she known then that it could be a special leaving gift?

It's a time of great upheaval for Sunny, but she's clearly excited at the prospect of meeting her new family. She's less serene, eyes alight, movements more animated.

I'm bemused when she asks Eleanor to double-check the upstairs windows are closed. Then Sunny tells me. She didn't want to say in front of Eleanor, but she's checked with the company in Arizona, where Dan's body's being

328

stored, and established that it's permissible for relatives to visit. Would I mind?

'Of course not – if that's what you want to do.' I try to wipe a visual of that stark, sanitised space from my mind.

'Only if you're sure. Are you?' Sunny stares, eyes moist.

'Absolutely.'

'I didn't get a chance to say goodbye to him. I need to.'

'I know,' I say, with a half smile. 'I understand.' And I really did. 'And thanks again for helping out with Ruth – I really appreciate it.' I pat her arm gently. 'And at such a difficult time. Her daughter says Ruth really responded to you.'

'That's so good to hear. I hope she gets the support she clearly needs.'

'Goodbye. Take care.'

Tash is wide-eyed when I deliver the news about Sunny the next day. 'She's not hanging about, is she? Well, I don't think I need any more reflexology – the specs have done the trick.' She chuckles. She's already bought two pairs of designer glasses to colour co-ordinate with her outfits, and contacts for 'special nights out and shagging'.

I don't want to let Pete down with Lorex, so despite everything, I knuckle down to some writing. It's Mark's last day at the office – he's planning a well-earned break before heading off to Bristol. I only have two more weeks.

Although I've brooded a bit about Ashley's job, I've accepted it. I'm proud of his achievement. He's worked so hard, made so many sacrifices. Our lives haven't been simplified as I'd hoped, far from it, but the obstacles aren't insurmountable.

I'm nervous stepping into Pete's office before we leave for Mark's farewell drink. He's speechless for a moment when I hand the cheque across his desk.

'I can't take this.' He looks down at the piece of paper, then back at me, one hand fiddling with his tie. 'You can't give me – the business – this amount. It's a wonderful gesture, but it's too much—'

'It's not from me. It's from Dan,' I interrupt. 'This business gave him the start he needed. It meant so much. Your son was a good friend.'

'It's too generous.' His hand's shaking, face blank as if stuck for the right expression.

'It's great that your son has plans to expand. He needs investment – Dan would have wanted to help.'

Pete spends the next five minutes trying to talk me out of it. He still looks dazed, but small smiles break out now and then. He finally relents.

At the pub, Mark enjoys telling us all how little he has planned for his two weeks off.

'I'll think of you all when I climb out of bed at lunchtime,' he says, raising his pint with glee. He's going to rent a flat near Bristol, then he and Georgia will look for a place together and everyone will be invited to the house-warming.

He has some great leaving gifts – a new briefcase from me, a few silly things Tash and I bought, including a cauliflower-shaped stress ball, and, after a short speech, Pete proudly presents him with a posh silver pen, pointing out that it's one of the pressurised, 'space' ones and can even write upside down.

'Great for when I'm legless then,' Mark says, holding up one of the pub menus to scribble on.

'Or during sex,' Tash says with a shriek. Pete squirms, but Barbara's on her second gin and tonic and giggles like a schoolgirl.

After Pete and Barbara leave, and while Tash heads to the ladies, Mark gives me a present that renders me speechless. Somehow he's found a copy of my favourite joke book, the one Eleanor ruined and has been out of print for years.

'You can think of me when you read the really bad ones,' he says. Then he pulls another gift from his case – a Marge Simpson air freshener to put in my new office.

'Perfect. Thanks.' I giggle.

I'm prepared for a teary goodbye, but Mark decides to share a taxi with Tash, who's extremely tipsy, lolling in the back seat and exchanging jokes with the driver that snap the tension.

'Bye,' I say, giving Mark a big hug before he climbs into the front seat. 'Let's make sure we keep in touch.'

'Absolutely.'

'Eleanor would like another sixties night soon – without the singing,' I say. Mark flashes a huge smile that soaks his eyes.

I get home to another lovely surprise. Imogen has sent an exquisite, embossed leather journal, with a message on the inside page: '*Congratulations on your new job. Bonne Chance, My Lovely*'. And, tucked in the back, I find a note saying she has a gift for Eleanor, too, but will be hand-delivering it when they come to Tetford in September.

YES! Imogen's coming to stay – for two bloody weeks. I'm so thrilled. I've never needed to see her more.

I call Ashley three times that evening. Finally, he answers. It's nearly midnight. He's sorry he's been difficult to get hold of, he's had a hell of a few days and, to top it, the house sale's fallen through. But he can catch an early train to Tetford in the morning. He could do with escaping. I bristle a little. I want to say 'no', he can't just spring it on me, expect me to drop everything.

'Eleanor will be here, but, yes; OK, great,' I say instead.

I hardly sleep and get up early but Ashley misses his train, so our time together's cut short again, and plans for lunch at a rosette restaurant become afternoon tea in a new café in Tetford High Street.

I've prepared for a serious talk about our future – I have no choice now – to tell him things can't go on in a meandering, non-committal way with us. But while I select words and rearrange sentences in my head as we munch our way through carefully cut sandwiches, dainty drizzle cakes and multi-coloured macaroons all arranged on a silver-stemmed stand, I lose my nerve. The time isn't right. Ashley looks exhausted and nerves are suppressing my appetite, something that doesn't go unnoticed.

'Come on, keep up. You're at least three cakes behind,' he jokes, dropping more crumbs from a heavily-iced French Fancy down the gap at the neck of his linen shirt.

Passing through the park, a jazz quartet's playing on the recently refurbished bandstand; four accomplished musicians – average age seventy, we guess – framed by decorative cast iron columns and ornate balustrading.

A large audience has gathered, so we settle in a couple of vacant deckchairs, soaking up the music, along with a bit of intermittent sunshine that takes the edge off the damp breeze, and my weariness. At one point, Ashley dozes off and I startle him by leaning across to jolt his chair. An elderly lady sitting the other side of him chuckles as he shoots me a well-honed mock glare.

Back at home and Ashley stifles several yawns as we walk through the front door.

'Sorry, I'm so tired. I think those cakes are sending me into a sugar coma.'

Eleanor gives us a ten-second greeting, then disappears back upstairs.

'Well, not long before you'll get some proper time off,' I say, settling next to him on the sofa. I can't wait. I have lots of plans, which include introducing him to Imogen.

'Actually, that might not work out. They want me to start the project earlier.'

'Oh no,' I exclaim, failing to hide my dismay.

'Bloody nuisance, I know,' Ashley says, 'but what can I do?' He wraps his arm around me, trying to pull me close, but my shoulders resist.

'What's up?' He turns and I shake my head, taking time to calm the swell of frustration and get a grip of the words flying around in my inner ear. 'Look, I'm disappointed too, but—'

'There's always something, though. I just want to know where we're going, to have some idea about what you want because you don't make …' I falter, flustered; searching for the right words.

'Hang on. You're surely not blaming me.' Ashley shuffles forwards. 'I want to see more of you, make firm plans – course I do.'

'Really? It doesn't seem that way at times, that's all. You can be …' I stall, panicking that the conversation isn't going as planned, '… remote; hard to get hold of at times.'

He frowns. 'Look, I have other commitments, and being an actor isn't office hours, as you know. We've been through this – I didn't expect to have to explain again—'

'Of course, I know that, but there's all the other complications, and we never talk properly about the future. Us.' I feel cross; defiant. I find his eyes. 'I was hoping you might talk me out of the job, try to persuade me to move to London.' I wince at my words. They sound crazy spoken out loud, seem to echo around the room, gathering momentum and magnitude. Yet I felt I deserved the romantic gesture, after what Ashley did to me last time.

Ashley looks irritated, squeezes a cushion. 'I wouldn't ask that of you. I didn't want to get in the way of your career.'

'Is it really about *my* career?' I scoff. 'Some evidence, some show of commitment would have been nice – after what you did …' I stop. I've said more than I intended to, let the past bully its way into the present. He tugs on his beard, lips pursed.

'Look, this isn't going to work if you're going to be like this. Life's not like it was when we were students.'

'Don't you think I know that?' I shake my head in disbelief. 'But you don't make it any easier. It's as if you're avoiding things – just like you did back then.'

Ashley throws the cushion aside; leaps to his feet. 'Well maybe I can make it a bit simpler for you then.' He heads for the door.

'That's your speciality isn't it – walking away?' I'm dismayed as soon as the sentence leaves my lips. I shouldn't have said it – I'd kept those words locked securely inside – but I'm so angry, I've unleashed the most painful barb I can think of.

He stands in the doorway, head moving slowly from side to side. I see several emotions fast forward across his face, stopping at what looks more like disappointment than indignation.

Then he leaves.

★★★

I lie in bed, a damp Mr Fluff pressed to my face, fur feeling coarse against my wet skin. He hasn't called. I can't call him. Maybe in the morning. Another wretched, groggy morning. But what can I say? I've said enough – more than enough.

I lift the letter from the pillow by my side. I read: '*To My Leading Lady.*'

I'd had a second chance to be Ashley's leading lady, but this time it's me who's ruined it. If only I could rewrite the horrible scene that unfolded earlier, edit the dialogue, modify the sentiments, add back in the control and air of calm to my character that I'd planned.

Despite the dark, I leave the curtains open in hope.

CHAPTER 32

'I can't wait to see you. You must stay here.'

'Great. I'm just stoked you're taking the job, lovely,' Imogen gushes down the phone. 'I thought for a while there that you were going to back out. I'd have worn my highest stilettos over to England and kicked your arse.'

I switch the subject, updating her on how dire things were with Ashley, how I'd done with the weeping – my tear ducts on a drought alert – but was still livid with myself for messing things up and being such an idiot; so needy. We'd spoken, briefly, on the phone, both apologised, but nothing had really been resolved and I'd not heard from him for three days.

'I think we're well and truly over.'

'I'm not so sure. I think you can still work it out.'

'No, I've blown it, just as …' I have to stop myself saying too much. I need to talk to her face-to-face.

We move on. I'm glad to hear things are still improving with Ben. Imogen thinks the testosterone's helping.

'And I haven't sprouted a tash yet, although I keep craving the remote and picking fluff out my belly,' she says. We roar.

Bethany's staying with us for a few days to give her dad a break, and Freya's keen to show off her new two-tone hair when she joins us for a Chinese takeaway that evening. She breezes in, swishing her locks around, wide grin sewn on her face. The three girls are breathless with chat, whispering and giggling into their sweet and sour every time their mobiles ping.

I find myself tipping away a half-empty bottle of wine left in the fridge – or is it half full? I rinse it over and over. No one likes the taste when it's been opened for more than a week, I assure myself. No one.

I feel exhausted, energy depleted to a level that leaves no option but the chaise. I make a coffee, stretch out in my bleached leggings, propping the laptop on the table, a sensible – yet uncomfortable – reach away. I check my phone, but, of course, there's nothing from Ashley. I find an email from Sheena:

Hi Carrie. I just had to tell you. I KNOW GEOFF IS DEAD. It was Molly's 18th birthday yesterday. For years, he's been desperate to give her the antique ring passed down to his mum by his gran and great-gran before her. He decided to keep it a secret and wait until she turned 18 – it's in a box in his bedside cabinet. We'd often talked about what a special moment it would be. If he didn't come back for that, then I know he must be gone forever. I'm sorry you've had to hear this, but I hope you'll understand why I've told you. I had to tell someone. I won't say anything to the girls, I want to keep their hopes up as long as they need or want it. In a way, it's a bit of a relief. At least now I know. Sadly, it's another five years before the authorities will declare him dead in absentia …

I can't read on. It feels like someone's punched my chest wearing a steel glove. I hope Sheena is wrong. But she sounds so sure.

Five years is such a long time. I contemplate how different our lives will be then. Eleanor will be nineteen, an adult, making her own way. I've never really allowed myself to look that far ahead before.

But now I have to.

I go to sip my coffee, but Sheena's words swim in the liquid: '*I know Geoff's dead*', '*I know he's dead*'.

'Dan's dead too,' I say out loud. *I know Dan's dead*. Even Sunny's saying goodbye. And I have to.

From nowhere, my mind conjures up an image of Pippa, my best friend from primary school, and a day I'd made myself forget. We were only about seven or eight and had gone to her nan's house for sweets. Pippa was a 'little devil', according to my mum, a bad influence. 'Your nan's not here. She's popped next door,' Pippa's granddad had said. 'There's been a passing'. We were both shocked when we breezed into the neighbour's house to find a big oak coffin in the middle of the living room. We couldn't stop looking at it, and the smell in the air was so vile, I could still conjure it up in my nostrils. I'd always found Pippa's nan so scary, with her cap of dirty grey hair and loose skin hanging from her cheeks. She explained that her friend's husband had died and she was minding the house while the lady visited the priest.

The family were Catholics and it was a wake, she'd said. I didn't understand and remembered wondering why someone in a coffin would be 'awake'. For some reason, Pippa's nan left the room and that's when we did it. We dared each other with our wide eyes. We lifted the lid, both gasping as we saw the old man lying there, dressed in full military uniform – shiny war medals perfectly pinned on his chest. Maybe he *was* 'awake', I'd thought. He looked alive. I don't know what I'd expected a dead person to look like – diseased and mangled; some blood perhaps – but not like that. I half-expected him to sit up and speak. It totally spooked us both. It's one of those things you do that you immediately, and wholeheartedly, wish you hadn't. I think I had some of the daring knocked out of me that day.

Pippa had dropped the lid at the sound of her nan's footsteps. Then we'd giggled until our sides hurt, although we both knew that neither of us really found it funny. 'It's no time for laughter is it, girls?' Pippa's nan had said sternly, black eyes glaring. No, it wasn't. We both knew it. The clothes had done it, and the perfectly neat hair. They'd made him look alive.

With Dan it was different. I'd slipped off his gold wedding ring while he lay in the hospital bed, the curtain drawn around him so other patients didn't have to see a corpse while they slurped their thin soup. But there was no life in that finger; nor in his legs, his arms, his face … not anywhere, not a sign. He didn't even smell like Dan. He'd gone. Gone.

Yes, I KNEW now that Dan was dead. And forever. Cryonics couldn't save him – of course it couldn't. I'd always known it, really. Now I had the confidence to state it; had 'the courage of my convictions' as Dad would say. And if I was wrong, if he got the second go at life he craved, I wouldn't be here. Like Gordon, I'll have moved on, taken a different path; leaving the guilt behind now.

I'm jolted back by a ping – as if someone's added the 'lightbulb moment' sound to my epiphany.

Another ping.

I take my phone from my handbag. It's from Ashley: *Hi.*

I text back: *Hi.*

Another text arrives: *No – Hi. Aren't you gonna let me in?*
I'm confused, still dazed, still with Sheena, and Pippa, and
…

I climb off the chaise and make my way, tentatively, to
the front door. Surely not. I open it slowly.

'Hi.' Ashley's standing there, white shirt bright against
a sepia sky, grin stretched wide. 'I thought I'd come to see
you in my new motor,' he points to a pale blue hatchback,
'surprise you. Maybe I could stay …' he holds up the Gola
bag, '… or I could stay at a B&B, or in the car, it's got
amazing recliners …'

'God, yes, I mean … come in.' I cringe inwardly as
I catch a glimpse of my horrendous leggings. 'You've
certainly surprised me. Eleanor's got friends here.' Three
inquisitive heads appear over the bannister.

'Who is it, Mum?'

'Ashley,' I say.

'Oh hi.' It's Eleanor's voice. 'Hi,' Freya and Bethany
chirp.

Ashley goes ahead of me into the living room, while
I fetch a beer from the kitchen. He's acting like our row
never happened. I stand at the fridge for a few seconds,
trying to gather my composure and recover from the
shock, let the galloping giddiness pass. I wonder if this is
just the friendly first scene – the verbal post-mortem of
our row yet to come.

I walk into the living room to another surprise, the
sight of Ashley sat in Dan's chair, cradling the lumbar
cushion on his lap.

My mind corrects itself: no, not Dan's chair any more!

340

The chair Dan bought. The chair I was planning to move to the spare room, where he loved to do his work and exercise. I could think of him there sometimes, like Gordon on his beloved wife's bench. But not in the living room. Not the room for living in.

'I've got a day off tomorrow, the only one for a while – thought I could take you out,' Ashley says. 'I hope you haven't got any better plans?'

'No, I mean yes … to going out,' I say, clumsily. He opens his bag, pulls out a bottle of bubbly.

'Thought we could celebrate our future.' I flash an uncertain smile. 'And here …' He holds up two tickets. 'Would be great if you and Eleanor could come to the project's launch night. We're knocking up a one-act play.'

'Sound great. Thanks.' I perch on the chaise, heart clattering.

'I hope I'm showing you …' he pauses, '… proving how I feel.' I smile.

Then he tells me that now things are more sorted in his life, he wants us to be together more.

'We can make it work. It might not be ideal, but I'm not going away or giving up.' He taps his fingers resolutely on his trouser pockets.

I don't know what to say. I'm not going to move to London, make the sacrifice. Not this time. But he's come today, on impulse, unannounced, despite my harsh words, and being with him, however, whenever, could be so right, especially now I'm …

He stands, slips his thumbs from his pockets, pulling me to him. He kisses me gently on the forehead.

'I love you.'

'I love you too,' I say, gasping inwardly, butterflies going hyper, '… but …'

'What?' He stares, shoulders dropping. I move his hand to my stomach.

'I'm pregnant … we're … pregnant.'

'Woah … my God … wow.' He smiles, head darting, eyes huge. He looks at my face, then down at my middle. 'Really? … I mean … that's really … great … fantastic. When, I mean, how long?'

'The due date's March.'

'Are you sure? Course you are.' He hugs me briefly. 'I'm shocked – pleased though, stoked. It's just … wow …' he stands back, touching my stomach again, '… I can't take it in.' He meets my eyes. 'What about you – how do you feel?'

'Same as you, I guess. It's a big shock.'

'What about the job?'

'I'm not sure now. It certainly complicates things.'

'Yes.' He bites his lip. 'We can make this work,' he says resolutely, holding both my hands and staring deep into my eyes. He steps back. 'We *can* make it work. Where there's a will …'

I see my eleven-year-old Joseph standing there, declaring that there's no room at all the inns, but one innkeeper's kindly offered us a stable.

Stood in the middle of our creaky school stage, he'd delivered that sentence with such confidence. And, as I'd braced myself to throw my big line out into the sea of smiling mums and dads in the audience, all eager to hear what Mary had to say, he'd tipped me a reassuring nod of his gorgeous head that made all the stage fright rise out of my C&A robe and float off into the starry sky.

'Thank you, innkeeper, for being so kind and letting us stay in your stable,' I'd said.

There had to be a way, now that Dan was dead.

CHAPTER 33

There's a small gap in the flimsy green curtain; one end caught on the over-bed table, giving me a restricted view of the woman in the bed opposite if I crane my neck. She's pale with bruised lids and short, feathery fair hair that blends into her face from a distance.

She looks up from her magazine, shoots me a pained smile. I smile back. Minutes before I couldn't have done it. All I could think of was the blood, the fear of what it signified, what I could be losing. All just one ward away from where I lost Dan on that longest, darkest day.

I want to pull back the curtain, put faces to the chaotic, layered voices and countless pairs of feet padding up and down the ward. Imogen appears through the gap, lidded latte in hand.

'So what did the doctor say, lovely?' She sits on the bed, thigh tight against my knee, anxious, but beaming her bolstering rays at me.

'Everything seems OK.' I release a sigh of relief as the words leave me; along with tears that stay in my eye sockets, blurring my view. 'I just need to take care, rest up here for a week or so.'

'That's fabulous news – oh, thank God.' Imogen's eyes close momentarily as she leans over to embrace me. 'And make sure you do what the doctor says.'

'Says you!' I say, adjusting a starched pillow behind my neck.

She pulls two supersized blueberry muffins from a carrier bag, placing them next to an empty medicine cup on the table. 'I just knew we'd be celebrating. Shall I open these curtains so you can see what's going on?'

'Thanks.'

Imogen yanks them around the rectangular track. Heads turn to see me being unveiled – a new me, not the petrified, snivelling wreck the doctor's just examined. Imogen views me too, her face straight and scrutinising.

'Why don't you ring him again?'

I nod tentatively. 'I will later.'

I slowly ease my hand from the soft cotton blanket, hoping Finley's wrapped in a sleep so deep he won't sense the warmth and scent of his mum drifting away.

I can't resist peering over the side of the cot, eyes lingering on all the perfect dips, folds and crinkles of my beautiful baby boy. He's on his side, eyes puffy and shut firm after an exhausting morning, hair damp and patchy next to a tiny ear that curls at the top.

I glance at Bezziwotnot, the one-eared teddy bear on his cot bumper and pictured, in denim dungarees, hanging from a tree swing on the pale blue wall behind. A blissful smile spreads across my cheeks. I creep to the window, flick the blinds, then tiptoe out; taking a huge snort of the sweet, medicinal air.

A voice yells from the kitchen as my steps hit the laminate hallway.

'Coffee's on its way, love – go put your feet up. I'm just doing the shelf.'

'Thanks,' I say.

'So just to clarify – you did want it put up straight?'

I laugh. 'Preferably, yes.'

In the living room, I stand on a spiky rubber dinosaur, sidestepping all the other hurdles on the oatmeal carpet – the baby mat and animal mobile with the wonky monkey, the lullaby rocking seat, an upturned yellow dumper truck and several unpacked removal boxes marked '*Fragile*'.

It still feels strange – the new scents and surroundings. The intimate cosiness of a 1920s house with small, boxy rooms, imperfect flooring and fittings and walls that are marked and scuffed. It's six weeks since we moved in, but it feels so much shorter, a whirlwind of visitors, unpacking, DIY stores and nappies. And lots of noise – wonderful family sounds that filled rooms, spiralled through walls and floors and made it home. I've felt permanently dizzy, swaying from exhaustion to elation, mostly feeling both at the same time.

I flick a firm hand down the crushed taffeta curtains, one of several new pairs, not yet hanging perfectly in the wide window, which overlooks the street. Renault Megane Street we call it; every other house has one.

'So, which biscuits do you fancy?'

I turn to see Mark in the doorway, looking dishevelled, fringe fluffy and lopsided, a pencil behind one ear and a packet in each hand.

It still startles me when he appears in rooms. A figure so familiar but cast in so many different lights now; intense rays that repeatedly reveal new and wonderful things.

'The nutty ones, please,' I say. Mark places the biscuits next to his collection of chewy mints on the coffee table, then stands behind me, hands resting in the heavily cushioned curve of my waist. He turns, kisses me on the lips with a loud 'mwah' sound.

'Did the little fella go down OK?' He smooths the hair from my forehead.

'Yes, spark out,' I say, holding crossed fingers between us.

Mark beams. 'Wow. All credit to Jack and Eleanor for keeping him amused. Jack's convinced a five-month-old appreciates his dinosaur stories.' He kisses me again, then releases me. He walks towards the door. 'Do you think Finley's first word will be stegosaurus?'

I chuckle. I hadn't thought about his first word, still millions of precious moments away.

I sit on the chaise, next to Mark's grey sofa. I look at the clock: 3.15. Finley's afternoon naps are usually short, but Jack's staying over and has worn him out with non-stop stimulation since breakfast, racing cars around and over him, flicking the animals wildly on the mobile hanging above his play mat, reading stories and giving him his precious dinosaur figures to play with – though most headed straight for Finley's mouth.

I pull a packing box towards me, catching sight of Dan's photo on the sideboard. Mark insisted we put it in a prominent place.

I open the flaps of the box to find Sunny's postcards tucked in the top. And the letter; with the photographs. I study an image of Sunny stood between her half-siblings. She's the shortest, but the resemblance is striking. All of them slight, delicate featured; similar thin noses. There's a sense of belonging in Sunny's smile, an arm draped around her from each side.

It was a brave letter she'd sent from America. She was glad she'd said goodbye to Dan. She hoped I didn't mind her mentioning it – she suspected I'd already seen images – but the cryonics storage facility struck her as such a sterile place. Soulless.

I didn't mind. Soulless was the perfect description. Not a place for souls.

I no longer saw the cryonics as a burden. Maybe Dan had been selfish, but he had convictions. And now, at last, I had mine. He'd left me a challenge – forcing me to formulate my own thoughts about mortality, not to dodge them through fear and idleness.

Yes, Dan had been a little controlling at times. He liked to sit in the driving seat – but someone had to. I'd been lazy; and weak. He was a good person. I'd loved him, and he'd loved me.

I was so pleased that Pete's son had secured more investment in Cullimore's and was insisting on a permanent dedication to Dan in recognition of his donation – a plaque in the new office extension. I'd been invited to the official opening. I was amazed, and thrilled, to see Gordon there too. Turns out Pete had forged a connection with his late wife after all her campaigning.

Mark's singing rattles me out of my foggy brain. I love to hear the constant whirr and whine of his digital radio around the house, his resonant baritone cutting through now and then.

After a slow start, things had moved quite quickly between us, I reflect, pulling bubble wrap from a red handkerchief vase, unable to resist popping a few of the tiny air pouches. But I have no doubts. Not any more.

Ashley had assured me we could make it work, and for a while I wanted to believe it. But in the weeks after he'd turned up making declarations of love he'd kept his distance. He was rarely in when I called, always quick with an excuse. He made it to the first baby scan. Not the second. And when I had the miscarriage scare, two weeks of rest in hospital, he was unable to get away.

It was then, lying in that starchy bed all day long, the baby now declared safe inside me, empty hours stretching ahead, time to think in straight, uninterrupted lines, that I knew I could be brave. I realised I was in love with the idea of Ashley; as Joseph, Hamlet and all the other characters I'd imagined him to be. I'd looked at him through a soft focus lens that obscured the details I didn't want to see.

I didn't set out to reap some kind of revenge, to sleep with Ashley, build his hopes, make declarations and then walk away, as he'd done to me. I desperately wanted it to work with my Joseph and our beloved infant, to play the part of the actor's wife, sharing in all the bright lights and first nights.

I'd shared several dramatic scenes with Ashley in the past, and I needed to know why his stage exit had been so abrupt and mysterious. Now that I did, I could no longer see a role for me. Besides, I wasn't sure who the enigmatic

Ashley really was. His was a double life in reality. It was the same in our student days. I only spent one weekend at his drama college, rarely visited his house. He shared my life, lingering in all my scenes, but I wasn't really written into many of his. And I remained unsure about Lily's latest part, wondering if she might be waiting patiently in the wings for her moment of glory.

Ashley is Finley's father and will always have a part in our lives, I think, unpacking ornaments and lining them up on the floor next to me. He adores his boy, has seen far more of him than I'd expected – though he still looks scared when he nurses Finley, like he's an unfamiliar prop. Once he can crawl, Finley will be stopping over with his dad in London occasionally. I dread it. I ache for my baby during the shortest absences.

So things are a little complicated, with Jack staying every weekend and Mark's ex-wife Sue being awkward about it all. But then things don't always go to plan, as Dan discovered.

And I couldn't be happier. I've always wanted a house full of family and now it is, and I relish all the mayhem that goes with it. Mark and I have the same approach – we muddle through with as much mirth as we can muster; and a little Merlot.

'One strong coffee, love.' Mark walks in with a mug. 'I need to drill more holes if you really insist on that shelf being straight, but I don't want to wake Finley.'

'He'll sleep through anything once he's gone. You'll need a better excuse than that.'

'Damn! I need more screws then. I'll have to nip to the shop.'

'Again? That's the third time. So you *did* need a list,' I tease. 'The kids need chocolate while you're at it.'

'The kids?'

'OK – and me. I've got the card.' I reach into my purse. 'Here.'

'I don't think you can pay with that currency,' Mark says. I look down.

'Oops.' It's my donor card. 'I meant to keep that elsewhere.'

'I'm really proud of you.' Mark hugs me.

'Thanks.'

I've always felt silly using my squeamishness as an excuse not to be an organ donor. So much has happened in recent months to prompt my change of perspective – the controversy surrounding Dan obviously; and especially Ashley's nephew. I realise I can't close my eyes to the future, but have to plan ahead, face what may come.

Mark turns to go. 'Is Jack still pestering Eleanor upstairs?'

'I assume so. Don't worry, she loves having a little brother to boss around. Finley's boring apparently; just screams, sleeps and poos. She's never going to have a baby.'

Mark raises his eyebrows as he retreats. 'She'll change her mind.'

I think of Imogen's question to me about Mark. 'When, and what changed your mind?' My answer was – in hospital. He'd visited nearly every day, despite the distance, sitting by my bedside and cheering me up with his silliness. I couldn't have got through it without Mark. One evening we completed four crosswords, one with made-up clues and crude answers, and he was late back for a dinner party Georgia had spent days preparing. Another time, he'd forgotten arrangements to join her and a few colleagues at the pub. She was livid. In the end, she made him choose. And he chose me.

Looking back, I think I'd known how I really felt the first time Mark told me he was seeing Georgia. But I'd still believed things were impossible for us. Dan was the cement in the huge wall standing between Mark and me. Gordon had given me a hammer, Kirsten, Ruth, Sunny – and Ashley – had all given me the impetus, and it took a lot of knocking down; but it had finally tumbled.

The day after I'd come out of hospital, Mark came to see me. We ended up cuddling, talking and laughing until the early hours. He told me he'd always adored me, it had killed him to suppress his feelings all those years, how his ex-wife had shattered his confidence.

We shared a bed and made love; a gentle, in the moment, act, with no guilt, no remorse, no imagination running wild. He was so tender, so giving, so aware of the life inside.

Within weeks we were talking about the practicalities of being together, Mark was visiting regularly with Jack, armed with baby magazines – and liquorice sticks and lemon-scented Glades to satisfy my cravings – and staying over sometimes.

And when he talked about finding a way to work things out, that he'd love to be a second dad to Ashley's baby, I really believed him. I knew there would be compromises, but Mark wasn't asking me to give anything up. The realisation hit me, as we ate croissants in bed one morning.

Mark wanted me to fulfil my dreams. He wanted Eleanor to be settled. And he wanted me to love air freshener and make bad jokes.

Mark has quit the newspaper job in Bristol to freelance from our new home in Gloucestershire so he can help look after Finley. The move means he's closer to Jack. He's secured several contracts, including regular work for Cullimore's.

I have a fifty-minute trip to the theatre four days a week. It's tiring on a few hours sleep, but I love it. And I've had an article on cryonics published in a woman's magazine. Spurred on by my experiences, particularly what happened with Ruth, I contacted the magazine about writing a first-hand account, my attempt to put to rest some of the ignorance and sensationalism. I had a great response, lots of supportive messages – one from a vicar who's signed up – and the odd nasty one I zapped with the delete button.

Eleanor kicked up a bit of a fuss about moving at first but she still sees a lot of her friends and really likes her new school – and a boy who lives up the road.

Mum had several flushes when I told her I was pregnant with Ashley's baby and several more when she saw things unfolding with Mark. Of course, she won't tell anyone about Finley's father, not for a while at least. But she seems to accept it. She stunned me the other day when she visited.

'I just want you to be happy – and I can see you are,' she said, cooing over Finley. Hormones still crazy, I burst out blubbing and we ended up in an unusually tight embrace. We look at life from different angles, but it seems we've both got better at moving our heads to appreciate each other's viewing positions. But then Mum was right about Ashley. And I think that's a little bit of compensation.

I pull my feet up on to the chaise, stretching out. I must doze off, because I jump at the sound of the door.

'Done.' Mark bursts in, collapsing on the sofa next to me. 'That's one up, I'll do the other next year.'

'Come here, my DIY hero.' I pull him close.

Eleanor walks in. 'Where's the dog?' Her face crumples in disgust as she spots us cuddling. 'Uggh. Get a room.'

'We have …' I point up and around, totting it up, '… about seven of them.'

Larry, our crazy golden retriever puppy, scampers in, his bony body a blur as he heads to the corner of the room behind several boxes, rear pushed into the air. Jack hurtles in next, green eyes casting about. He spots the wagging tail.

'He escaped. I found him in your room,' Jack says, breathless and excited.

'Uh-oh, who's been up to no good again?' Mark races over. 'He's got a ball of wool or something.' The dog's shaking his head wildly, making playful growling noises.

Jack grabs the dog's favourite toy. 'Bone, bone,' he says, in a high voice, trailing the dog to entice him to drop it. I see a mass of copper threads hanging over Larry's jowls as he dashes past, relishing the game of chase.

'It's Mr Fluff,' I say.

Mark lunges, rugby-tackles the dog, cupping one hand over his upper jaw and pulling with the other. 'Drop, you little bugger.'

'Nice one, Dad.' Jack gives a cheesy thumbs-up, his spiky-haired head tilted.

'I think your cuddly toy's well and truly wrecked.' Mark hands it to me with a concerned look.

'You could have one of mine – I've got loads,' Jack offers. I reach out and squeeze him into a big hug. 'Thanks, Jack. That would be great.'

'Naughty dog.' I shake my head at Larry, smile, then pop Mr Fluff into the bin.

Acknowledgements

I'd like to thank Marge Clouts for her wisdom and motivation at the start of this journey, Henrietta Smethurst-McIntyre for her editorial input and being an enthusiastic champion of this book, and Hilary Johnson for her copy-editing, advice and encouragement.

Thanks also to Megan Pelta Lennox for the cover design, to Karen, Clare, members of Cotswold Creative Writing and friends and readers who have given feedback at various stages of writing and to Tim Gibson, from Cryonics UK, for being so open, honest and helpful during my research and for allowing me to attend the group's training weekend.

Huge gratitude to my parents and Alex for their love and support, Frank for being there all the way, and especially to Andy for his patience and putting up with me, my pens and my Post-its during the creation of this.

ANDREA DARBY

is a prize-winning journalist and has worked as a
writer and sub-editor for a variety of newspapers and
magazines. Her articles have been published in regional
and national titles, including Prima, Best, Take a Break
and Cotswold Life. When she isn't writing, Andrea
teaches piano from her home in Gloucestershire.
The Husband Who Refused to Die is her first novel.

www.andreadarby.co.uk

@andreadarby27